THE PALLISERS

Anthony Trollope

The Pallisers

Abridged and introduced by
MICHAEL HARDWICK

Coward, McCann & Geoghegan, Inc.

NEW YORK

Contents

INTRODUCTION

UNLIKE his Barchester novels, which grew into a series by chance, Anthony Trollope's Palliser stories were intended from the start to follow the destinies of Plantagenet Palliser, politician and heir to the great Duke of Omnium, and his beautiful, extrovert young wife, Lady Glencora. This is not to say that Trollope had the whole sequence planned; but he was aware, when he presented his readers in 1863 with *Can You Forgive Her?*, that he was beginning a multi-volumed reflection of 'the faults and frailties and vices,—as also the virtues, the graces, and the strength of our highest classes'.

In fact, the stories are by no means merely about the Pallisers themselves, who frequently retire from the scene for very long periods while the conflicts of other characters are being worked out. Yet, one is ever conscious of their background presence—of 'Planty Pall's' continuing labour at his duties and of Glencora's influence as the very leader of London society. This is as Trollope intended. He believed that characters in a story should be permitted to live as their real-life counterparts would, not in a perpetual state of involvement in critical situations, but for most of their time as lookers-on and limited participants in the affairs of others. It was also his dictum that fictional beings should be seen to age naturally, and to undergo the character-changes which the processes of ageing, maturing, succeeding and suffering should be expected to produce. He achieved this to a large extent by removing people from sight from time to time, so that, as in real life, one sees the changes in them more readily when they return.

To help attain this effect he spread the writing of the Palliser novels over thirteen years—1863–1876—doing a vast amount of other work in between writing each one. He was able to write in his *Autobiography* that the string of characters he had created in this sequence represented the best work of his life: 'Plantagenet Palliser stands more firmly on the ground than any other personage I have created.' But he mistakenly added that he doubted that anyone would ever wish to read the books consecutively, or would even know that they should be so read.

In extent the six novels consume more than a million-and-a-half words. Victorian novel-readers—or, at any rate, their principal librarian, Mr Mudie—demanded monumental works in two, three or four volumes of several hundred pages each. The result was a great deal of over-writing; not necessarily deliberate, but instinctive and habitual. In one of the long digressions in that most readable *Autobiography* Trollope is actually condemning novelists who digress from their themes; yet he was always doing it, either to pass on his personal reflections about real-life institutions and behaviour, or to chat confidentially with his reader about the motivation behind a character's actions. This practice added greatly to the wordage of his works, and, to present-day tastes, to the difficulty of ploughing through them. He was also much given to repetition, saying the same thing about the same character or event three or four different ways in consecutive sentences, and recapitulating happenings and situations from chapter to chapter.

It has been my task to 'boil down' this huge body of work into this single volume, which is about one-tenth of the length of the sixteen volumes that make up the original, without finishing up with something that is a travesty of Trollope. He himself, when told by a publisher that one of his three-volume works was too long for its theme, but could be published if cut by one-third, angrily retorted that such a task was a literary impossibility. It was, to him; and it has always been so to the majority of authors, who cannot be objective enough about their own work to see how easily it might be pruned without loss of effect, and even improved. Yet for many years now abridgment has been an accepted thing. Every dramatization

8

of a work, for stage, television or radio, is an abridgment, in that it selects the essentials of a story and its characters and manages without the rest. The abridged version for straight reading has been a staple of radio broadcasting almost since it began, and has brought classic and modern literature to millions of people who would never have tackled the originals. Very often, an acquaintance with a work and an author gained in this way has sent people to the originals and to the discovery of delight and inspiration which would otherwise have been missed. It is not, as some purists charge, that people are too lazy to read nowadays. There is a restlessness about our natures that reacts against the mere sight of those masses of print in which the Victorians revelled. Palates need tempting, and I hold that there is a valid case for the 'classics' to be revived in a form that will be acceptable to today's taste —that is, abridged. Those people who oppose abridgment can still indulge themselves in the originals; but those were written by Victorians for Victorians, and unless they are to remain neglected by the majority of today's reading public they need bold editing.

The editor's task carries with it a lot of responsibility, unless, as one has witnessed in the case of some condensed versions, he and his publisher are irresponsible types. He must retain the chief elements of the story, the principal characters, and those minor ones with significant influence upon events. He must not lose the atmosphere of the period, nor distort the author's views. Above all, he must keep faith with the author, and maintain the spirit in which he created his tale and its people and reflected the attitudes and prejudices of his own and their times.

Anthony Trollope is easy to cut—at first: I simply jettisoned three out of every four repetitions, all the expendable digressions, and certain sub-plots and unimportant set-piece scenes. But so vast was the original wordage that I was still left with several hundred-thousand words too many, and a more detailed, difficult editing had to be undertaken; a word-by-word search for anything that did not have something essential or useful to say. For example, a thousand words or more could be cut simply by expunging 'he said' or 'said she'

9

when it is perfectly clear who is addressing whom; and the Victorian device of ,— in punctuation can be expressed much better by , or ; thus saving one letter-space several times per page—and how such savings add up!

Just occasionally, making a cut necessitated dropping a vital sentence surrounded by a hundred or a thousand redundant words. In such a case I have allowed myself to invent a line, or to transpose a sentence or a paragraph, in order to retain the piece of information without disjointing the flow of narrative. Apart from this, and the modernization of the punctuation, and the very occasional substitution of a more illuminating word for an archaism, everything in this book is by Anthony Trollope.

MICHAEL HARDWICK

THE PALLISERS

Can You Forgive Her?

CHAPTER ONE

OLD Lady Macleod was a good woman, though subject to two most serious drawbacks. She was a Calvinistic Sabbatarian in religion, and a devout believer in the high rank of her noble relatives. She could almost worship a youthful marquis, though he lived a life that would disgrace a heathen among heathens; and she could condemn crowds of commonplace men and women to eternal torments because they listened to profane music in a park on Sunday. Yet she was a good woman. She strove to love her neighbours, and lived in trust of a better world.

Alice Vavasor, who was her cousin, had been brought up by Lady Macleod; but at nineteen she had made an arrangement with her widowed father that they two would keep house together in London; and so they had lived for the last five years. But their lives had been quite apart. For a short time John Vavasor had striven to dine at home and even to remain at home through the evening; but the work had been too hard for him and he had said that his health would fail him under the effects of so great a change made so late in life. Now they did little more than see each other daily. They did not even breakfast together, and after three o'clock Mr Vavasor was never to be found in his own house.

Alice Vavasor was twenty-four. Her hair was brown, but very dark. Her eyes, too, were dark, and her complexion, though not quite that of a brunette, was far away from being fair. Taking her for all in all, she was a handsome young woman, but there was nothing girlish in her manners. Her demeanour was as staid, and her voice as self-possessed as though she had been ten years married. She was, in fact, already engaged.

Their house in Queen Anne Street was not a pleasant house. It was squeezed in between two large mansions which seemed to crush it. The stairs were narrow; the dining-room was dark. All this would have been as nothing if the drawing-room had been pretty, as it is the bounden duty of drawing-rooms to be. But her father had chosen green paper, a green carpet, green curtains, and green damask chairs. There was a green damask sofa, and two green arm-chairs at the two sides of the fireplace. Alice would greatly have liked to banish the green sofa, to have re-papered the wall, and to have hung up curtains with a dash of pink through them.

It was now June 186–; and that month Lady Macleod was in the habit of spending among her noble relatives in London. She hired a little parlour and bedroom in Saint James's, going about at nights to gatherings of fashionable people of which she in her heart disapproved, and telling herself that she made this journey to the modern Babylon for the good of Alice Vavasor.

'Well, Aunt,' said Alice, as the old lady walked into the drawing-room one morning at eleven o'clock.

'Would you mind shutting the window, my dear?' said Lady Macleod, seating herself stiffly on one of the small ugly green chairs. She could still boast, at seventy-six, that she never leaned back.

For half an hour she expatiated on the advantages which would accrue to Alice as a married woman from an acquaintance with her noble relatives. Then, at last, they came to another subject: a Swiss tour which Alice was about to make.

'And when do you go, Alice?'

'Early in July. It will be very hot, but Kate must be back by the middle of August.' Kate Vavasor was Alice's first cousin.

'Oh! Kate is to go with you?'

'I could not go alone, or with no one but George.'

'Of course you could not go alone with George,' said Lady Macleod, very grimly. Now George Vavasor was Kate's brother, and first cousin to Alice. He was heir to the old squire

14

down in Westmorland, with whom Kate lived, their father being dead.

'That is exactly what I say,' answered Alice. 'But he is going as an escort to me and Kate, as we don't like the rôle of unprotected females.'

'And has your father been told that he is going?'

'Of course he has.'

'And does . . .' Lady Macleod hesitated a little before she went on. 'And does Mr Grey know that he is going?'

Alice's engagement, she had sometimes told herself, was very respectable, and had as often told herself that it lacked other attractions which it should have possessed. She was not quite pleased with herself in having come to love John Grey. She was sometimes almost angry with herself that she had permitted her heart to be thus easily taken from her. Mr Grey was a man of high character, of good though moderate means; he was well educated, of good birth, a gentleman, and a man of talent. No one could deny that the marriage would be highly respectable, and her father had been more than satisfied.

'I might tell you simply that he does,' said Alice at last, 'seeing that I wrote to him yesterday; but I feel that you want to know whether Mr Grey will approve. Of course I have not heard yet; but it would make no change in my plans.'

'What! the disapproval of the man you are going to marry make no change in your plans?'

'He has no right to claim my obedience on any subject,' said Alice; and Aunt Macleod jumped at the vehemence of the words. 'His advice he may give me, but I am quite sure he will not ask for obedience.'

'And if he advises you you will slight his advice?'

'I should be careful to let him know how much I was offended by any such counsel from him. It would show a littleness on his part, and a suspicion of which I cannot suppose him to be capable.'

'I think you are very wrong indeed. Two years ago you had—had . . .'

'Had what, Aunt? If you mean to say that two years ago I was engaged to my cousin George you are mistaken. I told

15

him that under certain conditions I would become engaged to him. But no engagement was ever made. Mr Grey knows the history of the whole thing.'

'Alice, you are the promised wife of a very worthy man. George Vavasor has the name of being very wild.'

'The worthy man and the wild man must fight it out between them. If I were going away with George by himself there might be something in what you say.'

'That would be monstrous.'

'Monstrous or not, it isn't what I'm about to do. Kate and I are going to have an outing, and as we should be poor travellers alone George has promised to go with his sister. Papa never thought of making any objection.'

'I can only say again,' said Lady Macleod, 'that I think Mr Grey will have very great cause for displeasure.'

Mr Grey's answer to Alice's letter was dated from Nethercoats, a small country-house in Cambridgeshire which belonged to him, at which he intended they should live after their marriage.

Dearest Alice,

I am glad you have settled your foreign affairs. I quite agree that you and Kate would have been uncomfortable alone. I don't quite know whether your cousin George is the best possible knight you might have chosen. I should consider myself to be infinitely preferable, had my going been upon the cards. Luckily, however, neither you nor Kate are without wills of your own, and perhaps you may be able to reduce Mr Vavasor to obedience.

The garden is going on very well. Your commands have been obeyed in all things, and Morrison always says 'The mistress didn't mean this', or 'The mistress did intend that'. God bless the mistress is what I now say, and send her home, to her own home, to her flowers, and her fruit, and her house, and her husband, as soon as may be, with no more of these delays which are to me so grievous, and which seem to me to be so unnecessary.

Yours ever and always,

J.G.

'I didn't give commands,' Alice said to herself. 'He asked me how I liked the things, and of course I was obliged to seem to care, even if I didn't care.'

He spoke of their engagement as though they were already married; that his house was even now her home. She had no wish to go back from her pledged word. She loved him much, and admired him even more than she loved him. He was noble, generous, clever, good—so good as to be almost perfect. Would that he had some faults! Would that he had!

But she had once loved her cousin, and was tormented by a feeling that she had had a more full delight in that love than in this other. Yet he had been untrue to her. She had parted from him with an oath to herself that no promised contrition on his part should ever bring them again together. But she had pardoned him as a man, though never as a lover, and had bade him welcome again as a cousin. Now, as she told herself that in truth she loved the man to whom her troth was plighted, she almost thought more of that other man from whom she had torn herself asunder.

And then John Grey came up to town, to say good-bye to his betrothed.

'Well, Alice,' he said. 'Is there any reason why you'd rather not have this thing settled? Do you fear coming to me as my wife?'

'No. I love you too entirely for that.'

'My darling!' And now he passed his arm round her waist as they stood near the empty fireplace. 'Then why should you not wish to come to me?'

'A person may wish for a thing altogether, and yet not wish for it instantly.'

'Instantly! This is still June. Will you say the middle of September?'

'John,' she said, 'do not press me about this till I return.'

'But then you will say the time is short.'

'I cannot answer you now.'

He did not press her further then, but kissed her and bade her farewell.

.   .   .   .   .   .

17

George Vavasor had lived in London since he was twenty, and now he was a year or two over thirty. He was the heir to his grandfather's estate; but that estate was small. When George first came to London he had been placed in the office of a parliamentary land agent, to whom he had made himself so useful that he had before him the prospects of a lucrative partnership. All was going on swimmingly, when one day he knocked down the parliamentary agent with a blow between the eyes, and then there was an end of that. He was wont to say that he regretted nothing. At any rate the deed was looked upon with approving eyes by many men of good standing, and within six weeks he had become a partner in a firm of wine merchants.

In this employment he was supposed to be doing very well. At the end of five years Vavasor left the house, not having knocked anyone down on this occasion, and taking with him a very nice sum of money. It was during the two last of these five years that he had had his love passages with his cousin. He had, however, behaved very badly to Alice, and the match had been broken off.

He had also during the last two years quarrelled with his grandfather. He had wished to raise a sum of money on the Vavasor estate, which, as it was unentailed, he could only do with his grandfather's concurrence. The old gentleman would not hear of it. They had never seen each other since. 'He shall have the estate for his life,' the squire said to his son John. 'I don't think I have a right to leave it away from him. It never has been left away from the heir. But I'll tie it up so that he shan't cut a tree on it.'

George Vavasor was now a stockbroker. After his breach with Alice he had gone back greatly in the estimation of men. He had lived in open defiance of decency. He had spent much money and had apparently made none, and had been, as all his friends declared, on the high road to ruin.

One side of his face had been dreadfully scarred by a cicatrice, which in healing had left a dark indented line down from his left eye to his lower jaw. On some occasions, when he was angry or disappointed, he would so contort his face that the scar would, as it were, stretch itself out, revealing all its horrors, and his countenance would become all scar. But in other respects George's face might have been thought handsome by many women. His hair was black, and was parted in the front. His forehead, though low, was broad. His eyes were dark and bright, and his eyebrows were very full, and perfectly black. At those periods of his anger, all his face which was not scar was eye and eyebrow. He wore a thick black moustache, which covered his mouth, but no whiskers. People said that he was so proud of his wound that he would not grow a hair to cover it.

When he was hardly more than a boy, before he had come up to London, he had been living in a house which his father then occupied. At the time his father was absent, and he and his sister only were in the house with the maidservants. His sister had a few jewels in her room, and an exaggerated report of them having come to the ears of certain burglars, a window was opened and a stout individual crept upstairs in his stocking-feet, and was already at Kate Vavasor's door when, dressed only in his nightshirt, wholly unarmed, George Vavasor flew at the fellow's throat. Two hours elapsed before the horror-stricken women of the house could bring men to the place. George's face had been ripped open from the eye downwards, with some house-breaking instrument. But the man was dead. George had wrenched the instrument from him and had driven the steel through his windpipe.

During the first weeks of the holiday in Switzerland no word was said which would have displeased Mr Grey; but at last, when the time for their return was drawing nigh, and that feeling of melancholy was coming on them which always pervades the last hours of any period that has been pleasant, then words became softer than they had been, and references were made to old days.

The three were sitting at Basle one evening in the balcony of the big hotel which overlooks the Rhine. Coffee was before them on a little table, and George's cigar, as usual, was in his mouth.

'It's nearly all over,' said he, after they had remained silent for some minutes.

'And I do think it has been a success,' said Kate. 'Always

excepting about the money. I'm ruined for ever.'

'I'll make your money all straight,' said George.

'Indeed you'll do nothing of the kind,' said Kate. 'I'm ruined, but you are ruineder. But what signifies? It is such a great thing ever to have had six weeks' happiness. What do you say, Alice?'

'I think we've done it very well. I have enjoyed myself thoroughly.'

'And now you've got to go home to John Grey and Cambridgeshire! It's no wonder you should be melancholy.' That was the thought in Kate's mind, but she did not speak it out. Instead, she got up, saying, 'I'm going upstairs to begin the final packing. '

'I'll come with you, dear.'

'No, don't. I'll be down again very soon. Then we'll take one turn on the bridge and go to bed.'

Alice and George were left together sitting in the balcony. The Rhine was running by with that delicious sound of rapidly moving waters which is so delicious to the ear at all times. Alice felt that the air kissed her, that the river sang for her its sweetest song, that the moon shone for her with its softest light, that light which lends the poetry of half-developed beauty to everything that it touches. Why should she leave it?

'When are you to be married, Alice?' said George at last.

'It is not fixed.'

'But about when, I mean? This summer? This winter? In ten years' time?'

'Before the expiration of the ten years, I suppose.'

'But you like the prospect of it?'

'Of course I like it, or I shouldn't have accepted it.'

'That does not follow. But I have no right to cross-question you. If I ever had such right on the score of cousinship, I have lost it on the score of . . . But we won't mind that, will we, Alice?'

'Will we what?'

'Recur to the old days.'

'Why should we recur to them? They are passed, and as we are again friends and dear cousins the sting of them is gone.'

'Since we have been out together, we have been dear friends, is it not so?'

'And shall we not always be dear friends?'

'How can I really be your friend when you are the mistress of that man's house in Cambridgeshire?'

'George!'

'I mean nothing disrespectful. Let me say that gentleman's house.'

'That he certainly is.'

'But how can I be your friend when you are his wife? I may still call you cousin Alice, and pat your children on the head if I chance to see them; and shall stop in the streets and shake hands with him if I meet him; but as for friendship, that will be over when you and I shall have parted next Thursday evening at London Bridge.'

'Do you mean that you won't come to Queen Anne Street any more?'

'Yes, that is what I do mean. But I have one word to say.'

'George, do not say it. Let me go upstairs. Let me go to Kate.'

'Certainly you shall go to Kate, if you refuse to hear me. But after all that has passed between us, after these six weeks of intimate companionship, I think you ought to listen to me. Between you and me there can be no necessity for falsehood. I perfectly understood your breaking away from me; but I did not understand you when you accepted Mr Grey. Knowing you as I thought I did, I could not understand your loving such a man as him. It was as though one who had lived on brandy should take himself suddenly to a milk diet, and enjoy the change. A milk diet is no doubt the best. But men who have lived on brandy can't make those changes very suddenly. They perish in the attempt.'

What her cousin was now telling her was a repetition of words which she had spoken to herself hundreds of times during the last two months. Had she not, in truth, rioted upon brandy, till the innocence of milk was unfitted for her?

'I have learned this since we have been again together, Alice; and finding you to be the same woman I had once loved, the safety that I anticipated has not fallen to my lot. That's all. Here's Kate, and now we'll go for our walk.'

Alice had written to John Grey occasionally from Switzerland. Her letters had referred almost exclusively to the tour. Alice had never written much of love in her love-letters, and Grey was well enough contented. It was not in the heart of the man to doubt her love. Her first two letters had been very pleasant; but after that there had seemed to have crept over her a melancholy which she unconsciously transferred to her words, and which he could not but taste in them. During the three or four last days of the journey home she had not written. But she did write on the day after her arrival, having then received from Mr Grey a letter, in which he told her how very much she would add to his happiness if she would now agree that their marriage should not be postponed beyond the end of October.

Dearest John,

We reached home yesterday tired enough, as we came through from Paris without stopping.

I got your letter directly I came in last night, and I suppose I had better dash at it at once, and tell you that I cannot let you hope that we should be married this year.

Marriage is a great change in life—much greater to me than to you, who will remain in your old house, will keep your old pursuits, will still be your own master, and will change in nothing—except that you will have a companion who probably may not be all that you expect. I shall see nothing that I have been accustomed to see, and must abandon all the ways of life that I have hitherto adopted. I must tune myself to the change that I have to make.

You must not ask me again till the winter shall have passed away. If the delay is so contrary to your own plans, you are free to tell me so, and to say that our engagement shall be over.

Dear John, let me hear that this letter does not make you unhappy.

> Most affectionately yours,
> Alice Vavasor.

At Nethercoats the post was brought in at breakfast-time, and Mr Grey was sitting with his tea and eggs before him when he read Alice's letter. He read it twice, and then referred to one or two others which he had received from Switzerland, reading them also very carefully. By that day's post he wrote a short note to her.

Dearest Alice, I have resolved to go to London at once. I will be with you in the evening at eight, the day after tomorrow.

Yours, J.G.

The two days passed by. As the minute hand on the drawing-room clock came round to the full hour her heart was beating with a violence she could not repress. When the knock at the door was at last heard she trembled.

As he walked across the room Alice felt that he was a man of whom a wife might be very proud. He was tall and very handsome, with brown hair, bright blue eyes, and a mouth like a god. It was his beauty that made Alice afraid of him. 'My dearest,' he said, and before she knew how to stop herself or him, he had taken her in his arms and kissed her.

He did not immediately begin about the letter, but placed her upon the sofa, seating himself by her side, and looked into her face with loving eyes, not as though to scrutinize what might be amiss there, but as though determined to enjoy to the full his privilege as a lover. There was no reproach at any rate in his countenance.

'So your Swiss journey went off pleasantly?'

'Very pleasantly.'

'And Kate has now left you?'

'Yes; she is with her aunt, at the seaside.'

'And your cousin George?'

'I never know much of George's movements. I have not seen him since I came back. But John, you have come up to London in this sudden way to speak to me about my letter to you. Is it not so?'

'Certainly.'

'I have thought much, since, of what I wrote, and I feel sure that we had better . . .'

'Stop a moment, love. Do not speak hurriedly. Shall I tell you what I learned from your letter? I learned that something had been said or done during your journey, or perhaps only something thought, that had made you melancholy and filled your mind for a while with those regrets for the past which we are all apt to feel. Alice, I know that you love me. Tell me that I may again plead my cause for an early marriage.'

'I cannot do so,' she said. And the tone of her voice was different to any that he had heard before from her. 'I feel quite sure that I should not make you happy as your wife; and I think I am right to ask your forgiveness, and to beg that our engagement may be over.'

'No, Alice, no; never with my consent. Nothing but your marriage with someone else would convince me.'

'I cannot convince you in that way.'

'You will convince me in no other. I will not ask your reasons, or even listen to them, because I do not believe that they will long have effect even on yourself.'

There was something in the imperturbed security of his manner which almost made her angry with him. It seemed as though he assumed so great a superiority that he felt himself able to treat any resolve of hers as the petulance of a child.

'Perhaps,' he said, 'I had better not come tomorrow.'

'It is better not.'

'I advise you not to tell your father of this. But if you do tell him, let me know that you have done so.'

'Why?'

'Because in such case I also must see him. God bless you, dearest, dearest Alice!' Then he went, and she sat there on the sofa without moving, till she heard her father's feet as he came up the stairs.

'What, Alice, not in bed yet?'

'Not yet, Papa.'

'Is anything the matter, Alice?'

'No, Papa, nothing is the matter.'

'Mr Grey has not made himself disagreeable, has he?'

'Not in the least. He never does anything wrong.'

24

'So that is it. He is just a shade too good. Well, I have always thought that myself. But it's a fault on the right side.'

'If there be any fault, it is not with him. But I am yawning and tired, and I will go to bed. Good night, Papa.'

Before she went to bed she wrote a letter to her cousin Kate.

On the following morning she did tell her father. 'What!' said he, putting down his tea-cup. 'Not marry John Grey!'

'No, Papa. By degrees I have learned to feel that I should not make him happy as his wife.'

'It's damned nonsense,' said Mr Vavasor. Such an expression as this showed that he was very deeply moved.

'We are not suited to each other.'

'But what's the matter with him? He's a gentleman, and with good means, and with all that knowledge and reading you profess to like. Look here, Alice; I am not going to interfere. But I do hope there is nothing again between you and your cousin.'

'There is nothing, Papa.'

'Well, you are your own mistress, and your fortune is in your own keeping. I can't make you marry John Grey. I think you very foolish, and if he comes to me I shall tell him so. You are going down to Cheltenham, are you?'

'Yes, I have promised Lady Macleod.'

'Very well.' Then he took up his newspaper, thereby showing that he had nothing further to say on the matter, and Alice left him alone.

CHAPTER TWO

BURGO FITZGERALD was a young man born in the purple of the English aristocracy. He was related to half the dukes in the kingdom, and had three countesses for his aunts. When he came of age he was master of a sufficient fortune to make it quite out of the question that he should be asked to earn his bread; though that, and other windfalls that had come to him, had long since been spent. He was now thirty, and known to be much worse than penniless; but still he lived on in the same circles, still slept softly and drank of the best, and went about with his valet and his groom and his horses, and fared sumptuously every day, setting tradesmen at defiance, and laughing to scorn all the rules which regulate the lives of other men.

About eighteen months ago he had almost succeeded in making himself one of the richest men in England. There had been then a great heiress on whom the properties of half-a-dozen ancient families had concentrated; and Burgo, who in spite of his iniquities still kept his position in the drawing-rooms of the great, had almost succeeded in obtaining the hand and the wealth of the Lady Glencora M'Cluskie. But sundry mighty magnates, driven almost to despair at the prospect of such a sacrifice, had sagaciously put their heads together, and the result had been that the Lady Glencora had heard reason. She had listened, with many haughty tossings indeed of her proud little head, with many throbbings of her passionate young heart; but in the end she saw Burgo for the last time, and told him that she was the promised bride of Plantagenet Palliser, nephew and heir of the Duke of Omnium.

He had borne it like a man. She had married Mr Palliser at St George's Square, and on the morning of the marriage he had hung about his club door in Pall Mall, listening to the bells. And then he went about, living with the same recklessness as ever. He was one of those young men with dark hair and blue eyes, who wear no beard, and are certainly among the handsomest of all God's creatures. But he lived without conscience, without purpose.

The Lady Glencora who had loved him, and would have married him had not those sagacious heads prevented it, was a cousin of Alice Vavasor's. Burgo had had money dealings with George Vavasor, and knew him intimately. From the time of the marriage Alice had heard no more of Lady Glencora. She had been married late in the preceding season and had gone away with Mr Palliser. They had not returned to England till the time had come for the magnificent Christmas festivities of Mr Palliser's uncle, the Duke. On this occasion Gatherum Castle, the vast palace which the Duke had built at a cost of nearly a quarter of a million, was opened as it had never been opened before; for the Duke's heir had married to the Duke's liking, and the Duke was a man who could do such things handsomely when he was well pleased. Then there had been a succession of bridal gaieties which had continued themselves even past the time at which Mr Palliser was due at Westminster; and Mr Palliser was a legislator who served his country with the utmost assiduity. So the London season commenced, progressed, and was consumed; and still Alice heard nothing more of her friend and cousin Lady Glencora, until, one morning, about three days after Mr Grey's visit, there came a letter from her.

Matching Priory,
Thursday.

Dear Cousin,

I have just come home from Scotland, where they have been telling me something of your little troubles. I had little troubles once too. Will you come to us here for a few weeks? My husband is very quiet and works very hard at politics; but I think you will like him. Do come! There will be a good many people here, so that you will not find it dull.

Yours affectionately,
G. Palliser.

P.S. I know what will be in your mind. You will say, why did not she come to me in London? She knew the way to Queen Anne Street well enough. Believe me, I had much to do and think of in London. Mr Palliser says I am to give you his love—as being a cousin—and say that you must come!

That allusion to her little troubles jarred upon Alice's feelings; yet she accepted the invitation.

On the day before Alice was to go to Matching Priory, she found on her table a note from her cousin George. 'I hear you are going down to the Pallisers tomorrow, and as I shall be glad to say one word to you before you go will you let me see you this evening?' She completed her arrangements for her journey and then awaited him in the drawing-room.

'I'm so glad you're going to Matching Priory,' were his first words.

'How did you learn that I was going?'

'From a friend of mine—Burgo Fitzgerald.'

'From Mr Fitzgerald?' said Alice, in profound astonishment. 'How could Mr Fitzgerald have heard of it?'

'That's more than I know, Alice. Not directly from Lady Glencora, I should say.'

'That would be impossible.'

'Yes; no doubt. I think she keeps up her intimacy with Burgo's sister, and perhaps it got round to him in that way. But I am so glad you are going. Mind you cement a close intimacy with Mr Palliser.'

'With Mr Palliser?'

'He will be the new Chancellor of the Exchequer without a doubt.'

'Will he indeed? But why should I make a bosom friend of the Chancellor of the Exchequer. I don't want any public money.'

'But I do, my girl. Don't you see?'

'No, I don't.'

'I propose to stand again at this next election.'

'I'm sure I hope you will be returned.'

'If I do, of course it will be my game to support the ministry; or rather the new ministry, for of course there will be changes. I must spare no chance. It would be something to me that Mr Palliser should become the friend of any dear friend of mine—especially of a dear friend bearing the same name.'

'I'm afraid, George, you'll find me a bad hand at making any such friendship.'

'They say he is led immensely by his wife, and that she is very clever. But I do hope, Alice, that I shall have all your

28

sympathy in any political career that I may make, and all your assistance also.'

'My sympathy I think I can promise you. My assistance, I fear, would be worthless.'

'By no means worthless; not if I see you take that place in the world which I hope to see you fill. Do you think women nowadays have no bearing upon the politics of the times? Almost as much as men have.'

George left her without saying a word about her marriage prospects past or future.

.   .   .   .   .

Alice reached the Matching Road Station about three o'clock in the afternoon. A servant in livery, touching his hat to her, inquired if she were Miss Vavasor. Then her dressing-bag and shawls and cloaks were taken from her, and she was conveyed through the station by the station-master on one side of her, the footman on the other, and by the railway porter behind. She perceived that she had become possessed of great privileges by belonging even for a time to Matching Priory.

On the broad drive before the little station, she saw a light stylish open carriage, with two beautiful smart horses, in which was sitting a lady enveloped in furs. Another servant was holding the horses of the carriage and the cart.

'Dear Alice, I'm so glad you've come,' said a voice from the furs. 'Look here, dear; your maid can go in the dog-cart with your things. Are you very cold?'

'Oh! Lady Glencora, I am so sorry that I've brought you out on such a morning,' said Alice, getting in.

'What nonsense! If it had snowed all the morning I should have come just the same. I drive out almost every day when I'm down here. I like driving better than anything, I think. Mr Palliser doesn't like ladies to hunt, and of course he doesn't hunt himself. I almost fancy I should like to drive four-in-hand, only I know I should be afraid.'

'It would look very terrible,' said Alice.

'Yes, wouldn't it? Sometimes I wish there were no such

things as looks. I don't mean anything improper, you know; only one does get so hampered, right and left. Baker, you must put Dandy in the bar; he pulls so, going home, that I can't hold him in the check. They're called Dandy and Flirt,' continued Lady Glencora to Alice. 'Ain't they a beautiful match? The Duke gave them to me and named them himself. Did you ever see the Duke?'

'Never,' said Alice.

'He won't be here before Christmas, but you shall be introduced some day in London. He's an excellent creature and I'm a great pet of his. He's one of those people who never talk. I'm one of those who like talking, as you'll find out. I think it runs in families; and the Pallisers are non-talkers. That doesn't mean that they are not speakers. Mr Palliser has plenty to say in the House, and they declare that he's one of the few public men who've got lungs enough to make a financial statement without breaking down.'

Alice was aware that she had as yet hardly spoken herself, so she asked, 'Is there a town at Matching?'

'Oh, a little bit of a place. It was a borough once, and belonged to the Duke; but they put it out at the Reform Bill. They had some kind of bargain; he was to keep either Silverbridge or Matching, but not both. The Duke chose Silverbridge, or rather his father did. He was sitting for Matching himself when the Reform Bill passed. Then his father died, and he hasn't lived there much since. It's a great deal nicer place than Gatherum Castle, only not half so grand. I hate grandeur; don't you?'

'I never tried much of it, as you have.'

'Come now, there's no one in the world less grand than I am. I'll take you under my shield. Mr Grey shan't be named to you, except that I shall expect you to tell me all about it; and you must tell me all about that dangerous cousin, too, of whom they were saying such terrible things down in Scotland. I had heard of him before.'

Alice remained silent. 'This is the beginning of the park,' said Lady Glencora. 'And that is Matching oak, under which Cœur de Lion or Edward the Third, I forget which, was met by Sir Guy de Palisere as he came from the war, or from

30

hunting, or something of that kind. It was the king, you know, who had been fighting, or whatever it was, and Sir Guy entertained him when he was very tired. Old Sir Guy luckily pulled out his brandy-flask and the king immediately gave him all the lands of Matching—only there was a priory then and a lot of monks, and I don't quite understand how that was. But I know one of the younger brothers always used to be abbot and sit in the House of Lords.'

'I suppose that's the way most of the old families got their estates.'

'Either so, or by robbery. But since that they have always called some of the Pallisers Plantagenet. My husband's name is Plantagenet. The Duke is called George Plantagenet, and the king was his godfather. The queen is my godmother, I believe, but I don't know that I'm much the better for it. Oh, Alice, it's a dreadful thing not to have a child when so much depends on it!'

'But you're such a short time married yet.'

'Ah, well; I can see it in his eyes when he asks me questions; but I don't think he'd say an unkind word, not if his own position depended on it. Ah, well; this is Matching.'

As they drove up through the park Lady Glencora pointed out first the church and then the ruins, through the midst of which the road ran, and then they were at once before the front door. The modern house was large and very pretty, with two long fronts. It was built with gabled roofs, four of which formed the side from which the windows of the drawing-rooms opened out upon a lawn which separated the house from the old ruins, and which indeed surrounded the ruins, and went inside them, forming the present flooring of the old chapel, and the old refectory, and the old cloisters. Much of the cloisters indeed was standing, and there the stone pavement remained; but the square of the cloisters was all turfed, and in the middle of it stood a large modern stone vase, out of the broad basin of which hung flowering creepers and green tendrils.

As Lady Glencora drove up to the door, a gentleman came forth to meet them. 'There's Mr Palliser,' said she; 'that shows that you are an honoured guest. Plantagenet, here is

Miss Vavasor, perished. Alice, my husband.' Then Mr Palliser helped her out of the carriage.

'I hope you've not found it very cold,' said he. 'The winter has come upon us quite suddenly.'

He was a tall thin man, apparently not more than thirty years of age, looking in all respects like a gentleman, but with nothing in his appearance that was remarkable. It was a face that you might see and forget. But Mr Palliser was a man who had never thought of assisting his position in the world by his outward appearance. Not to be looked at, but to be read about in the newspapers, was his ambition.

'Are the people all out?' his wife asked him.

'The men have not come in from shooting—at least I think not—and some of the ladies are driving, I suppose. But I haven't seen anybody since you went.'

'Of course you haven't. He never has time, Alice, to see anyone. But we'll go upstairs, dear. I told them to let us have tea in my dressing-room before you had taken off your things.' So saying she skipped upstairs and Alice followed her. 'Here's my dressing-room, and here's your room all but opposite. You look out into the park. It's pretty, isn't it? But come into my dressing-room, and see the ruins out of the window.'

Alice followed Lady Glencora across the passage into what she called her dressing-room, and there found herself surrounded by an infinitude of feminine luxuries. The prettiest of tables were there; the easiest of chairs; the most costly of cabinets; the quaintest of old china ornaments. It was bright with the gayest colours, having nymphs painted on the ceiling and little Cupids on the doors. 'Isn't it pretty?' she said, turning quickly on Alice.

'Very pretty.'

'Now Mr Palliser cares for nothing being pretty; not even his wife.'

'You wouldn't say that if you meant it.'

'Sometimes when I look at myself, when I simply am myself, with no making up, I think I'm the ugliest young woman the sun ever shone on. And in ten years' time I shall be the ugliest old woman. Only think, my hair is beginning to get grey, and I'm not twenty-one yet. But there's one comfort; he doesn't care about beauty. How old are you?'

'Over five-and-twenty,' said Alice.

'Nonsense; then I oughtn't to have asked you. I am so sorry.'

'Why should you think I should be ashamed of my age?'

'Somehow, people are; and five-and-twenty seems so old to me. It would be nothing if you were married; only, you see, you won't get married.'

'Perhaps I may yet.'

'Of course you will. You'll have to give way. You'll find that they'll get the better of you. Your father will storm at you, and Lady Macleod will preach at you.'

'I'm not a bit afraid of Lady Macleod.'

'I know what it is, my dear. We talked with such horror of the French people giving their daughters in marriage, just as they might sell a house or a field, but we do exactly the same thing ourselves. But never mind; I didn't mean to talk about that—not yet at any rate. Well, now, my dear, I must go down. The Duchess of St Bungay is here, and Mr Palliser will be angry if I don't do pretty to her. The Duke is to be the new President of the Council, or I believe he is President now. I try to remember it all, but it is so hard when one doesn't really care two pence how it goes. I'll call for you when I go down to dinner. We dine at eight.'

Alice decided that she would stay in her own room till dinner-time, and was taken there by Lady Glencora. When she sat down alone she felt that if it were possible for her to fly away, back to the dullness of Queen Anne Street, she would do so immediately. What business had she to come to such a house as this? Lady Glencora was very kind to her, but frightened her even by her kindness. Moreover, she was aware that Lady Glencora could not devote herself especially to any such guest as she was. Lady Glencora must of course look after her duchesses, and do pretty, as she called it, to her husband's important political alliances.

The two hours seemed to her very long, as though she were passing her time in absolute seclusion at Matching. Of course she did not dare to go downstairs. But at last Lady Glencora came for her, and took her arm to lead her to the drawing-room. Alice saw that she was magnificently dressed.

33

'Oh dear!' Lady Glencora said, as they went downstairs, 'what fun it would be to be sitting somewhere in Asia, eating a chicken with one's fingers, and lighting a big fire outside one's tent to keep off the lions and tigers. Fancy your being on one side of the fire and the lions and tigers on the other, grinning at you through the flames!' Then she strove to look like a lion, and grinned at herself in the glass.

'That sort of grin wouldn't frighten me,' said Alice.

'I dare say not. Oh, here they are, and I mustn't make any more faces Duchess, do come to the fire. I hope you've got warm again. This is my cousin, Miss Vavasor.'

Then the gentlemen came in one after another, and other ladies, till about thirty people were assembled. Mr Palliser came up and spoke another word to Alice in a kind voice. 'My wife has been thinking so much of your coming. I hope we shall be able to amuse you.' Alice, who had already begun to feel desolate, was grateful, and made up her mind that she would try to like Mr Palliser.

Alice found that she got on very well during dinner. But she was conscious of a certain inferiority to Lady Glencora which almost made her unhappy. As regarded the Duke of St Bungay, she had no such feeling. He was old enough to be her father, and was a Cabinet Minister; therefore he was entitled to her reverence. But she could not help accepting the other people round her as being indeed superior to herself.

The evening passed pleasantly. Eventually the ladies went upstairs on their way to bed. 'I'll come into your room just for one minute,' Lady Glencora said. She got into a little chair by the fireside. 'I must tell you something. Sit down opposite me and look at the fire while I look at you.'

'Is it anything terrible?'

'It's nothing wrong.'

Alice felt sure that the thing to be told would have some reference to Mr Fitzgerald, and so it proved to be.

'I told you in my letter that I didn't come to you in London last year because I had so many things on hand. Of course that was a fib.'

'Everybody makes excuses of that kind,' said Alice.

'I was longing to come to you every day. But I feared I

could not come without speaking of *him*—and I had determined never to speak of him again.' This she said in that peculiar low voice which she assumed at times.

'Then why do it now, Lady Glencora?'

'I won't be called Lady Glencora. Call me Cora. I'll tell you why I do it now. Because I cannot help it. Besides, I've met him. I've been in the same room with him, and have spoken to him. What's the good of any such resolution now?'

'You have met him?'

'Yes; Mr Palliser knew all about it. When he talked of taking me to someone's house I whispered to him that I thought Burgo would be there.'

'Well?'

'He said it didn't signify, and that I had better learn to bear it. Bear it, indeed! Oh, Alice, I do so want to go right, and it is so hard!'

Alice began to feel now that she had been enticed to Matching Priory because her cousin wanted a friend. She got up from her chair, and kneeling down at the other's feet put up her face and kissed her.

'I knew you would be good to me,' said Lady Glencora. 'And you may say whatever you like. But I could not bear that you should not know the real reason why I neither came to you nor sent for you after we went to London.' She smiled and returned the kiss Alice had given her. 'I declare it's ever so much past twelve. Good night, now, dear. I wonder whether he's come up. He seldom gives over work till after one, and sometimes goes on till three. It's the only thing he likes, I believe. God bless you! I've such a deal more to say to you; and, Alice, you must tell me something about yourself, too, won't you, dear?' Then without waiting for an answer Lady Glencora went, leaving Alice in a maze of bewilderment. She could hardly believe that all she had heard, and all she had done, had happened since she left Queen Anne Street that morning.

.　　　.　　　.　　　.　　　.

Mr Palliser was one of those politicians in possessing whom England has perhaps more reason to be proud than of any other of her resources, and who, as a body, give to her that exquisite combination of conservatism and progress which is her present strength and best security for the future. He could afford to learn to be a statesman, and had the industry wanted for such training. He was born in the purple, noble himself, and heir to the highest rank as well as one of the greatest fortunes of the country, already very rich, surrounded by all the temptations of luxury and pleasure; and yet he devoted himself to work with the grinding energy of a young penniless barrister labouring for a penniless wife, and did so without any motive more selfish than that of being counted in the roll of the public servants of England. He was not a brilliant man, and understood well that such was the case. He was now listened to in the House, as the phrase goes; but he was listened to as a laborious man, who was in earnest in what he did, who got up his facts with accuracy, and who, dull though he be, was worthy of confidence. He rather prided himself on being dull, and on conquering in spite of his dullness. He never allowed himself a joke in his speeches, nor attempted even the smallest flourish of rhetoric. He was very careful in his language, labouring night and day to learn to express himself with accuracy, with no needless repetition of words.

If he was dull as a statesman he was more dull in private life, and such a woman as his wife inevitably found some difficulty in making his society the source of her happiness. Their marriage, in a point of view regarding business, had been a complete success. The story of Burgo Fitzgerald was told to him, and he supposed that most girls had some such story to tell. He thought little about it and by no means understood Lady Glencora when she said to him, with all the impressiveness which she could throw into the words, 'You must know that I have really loved him.' 'You must love me now,' he had replied with a smile; and then, as regarded his mind, the thing was over. And since his marriage he had thought that things matrimonial had gone well with him, and with her too. He had hoped that before this he might have heard that she would give him a child. But the days were young yet and the care had not become a sorrow.

36

She might have learned to forget her early love, or to look back upon it with a soft melancholy hardly amounting to regret, had her new lord been more tender in his ways with her. She wanted the little daily assurance of her supremacy in the man's feelings, the constant touch of love, half accidental, half contrived, the passing glance of the eye telling perhaps of some little joke understood only between them two rather than of love, the softness of an occasional kiss given here and there when chance might bring them together, some half-pretended interest in her little doings. But Mr Palliser understood none of these things; and therefore the image of Burgo Fitzgerald in all his beauty was ever before her eyes.

At the end of ten days Alice Vavasor found herself quite comfortable at Matching Priory. She had now promised to remain there till the second week of December, at which time she was to go to Vavasor Hall, there to meet her father and Kate. The Pallisers were to pass their Christmas with the Duke of Omnium in Barsetshire.

Lady Glencora was now in the habit of having Alice with her in her dressing-room every evening, and they would sit till the small hours. Mr Palliser always burnt the midnight oil and came to bed with the owls. They would often talk of him and his prospects till Alice had perhaps inspired his wife with more of interest in him and them than she had before felt. And Alice had managed generally to drive her friend away from topics which were dangerous—allusions to her childlessness, and hints that Burgo Fitzgerald was still in her thoughts. And sometimes, of course, they had spoken of Alice's own prospects, till she got into a way of telling her cousin freely all that she felt. On such occasions Lady Glencora would always tell her that she had been right—if she did not love the man.

'But I did love him,' said Alice.

As soon as the words were out of her mouth she knew that they should not have been spoken. It was exactly what Glencora had done. She had loved a man and had separated herself from him and had married another, all within a month or two. Lady Glencora first became red as fire over her whole face and shoulders, and Alice afterwards did the same as she looked up, as though searching in her cousin's eyes for pardon.

'It is an unmaidenly thing to do, certainly,' said Lady Glencora very slowly, and in her lowest voice. 'But one may be driven. One may be so driven that all gentleness of womanhood is driven out of one.'

'Glencora!'

'Oh, Alice, if you know how I hate myself! He can't love me. How is it possible?'

'Mr Palliser does love you.'

'It is impossible. I have never said a word to him that could make him love me. I have never done a thing for him that can make him love me. The mother of his child he might have loved, because of that. We were told to marry each other and did it. When could he have learned to love me? But Alice, he requires no loving, either to take it or to give it. I wish it were so with me. I am so grateful that you love me! Someone's love I must have found—or I could not have remained here.'

.   .   .   .   .

On the night before Christmas Eve George Vavasor sat alone in his room thinking of the days in which he had wished to assist his friend Burgo Fitzgerald with reference to Lady Glencora; or rather he began to think of Alice's behaviour then, and of Alice's words. Alice had steadfastly refused to give any aid. But she had been very earnest in declaring that it was Glencora's duty to stand by her promise to Burgo. 'He is a desperate spendthrift,' Kate Vavasor had said to her. 'Then let her teach him to be otherwise,' Alice had answered. 'If a woman won't venture her fortune for the man she loves, her love is not worth having.'

All this George Vavasor remembered now; and as he remembered it he asked himself whether the woman that had once loved him would venture her fortune for him still.

Though his sister had pressed him on the subject with all the vehemence that she could use, he had hardly hitherto made up his mind that he really desired to marry Alice. He was almost inclined to think that marriage was an old-fashioned custom, not adapted to his advanced intelligence. If he loved any woman he loved his cousin Alice. But that idea of tying himself down to a household was in itself distasteful to him. 'It is a thing terrible to think of,' he once said to a friend, 'that a man should give permission to a priest to tie him to another human being like a Siamese twin, so that all power of separate and solitary action should be taken from him for ever! But, nevertheless, as he thought of Alice Vavasor on this occasion, he began to feel that if a Siamese twin were necessary for him, she of all others was the woman to whom he would wish to be so bound.

And if he did it at all, he must do it now. He sat down at a writing-desk. 'I needn't send it when it's written,' he said to himself, 'and the chances are that I won't.' Then he took his paper, and wrote.

Dear Alice,

When you told me that I might no longer hope to make you my wife, I had no word of remonstrance that I could utter. You acted as any woman would act. Then came the episode of Mr Grey; and bitter as have been my feelings whilst that engagement lasted, I never made any attempt to come between you. But once again, I ask you to be my wife. We are both older than when we loved before. You know my mode of life, and what are my hopes and my chances of success. It may be that I shall encounter ruin where I look for reputation and a career of honour. But whatever may be the chances I shall go on as long as any means of carrying on the fight are at my disposal. If you were my wife tomorrow I should expect to use your money, if it were needed, in struggling to obtain a seat in Parliament. I will hardly stoop to tell you that I do not ask you to be my wife for the sake of this aid; but if you were to become my wife I should expect all your co-operation.

Alice—dearest Alice, will you be my wife? Since the time in which I might sit with my arm round your waist I have sat with it round no other waist. Since your lips were mine no other lips have been dear to me. Since you were my counsellor I have had no other counsellor, unless it be poor

39

Kate, whose wish that we may at length be married is second in earnestness only to my own.

Dear Alice, will you be my wife?

Yours, in any event, most affectionately,

George Vavasor.

The next morning was the morning of Christmas Eve. At about nine o'clock a boy came into his room who was accustomed to call for orders for the day. 'Jem,' he said to the boy, 'there's half a crown lying there on the looking-glass. Is it a head or a tail?' Jem scrutinized the coin, and declared that the uppermost surface showed a tail. 'Then take that letter and post it,' said George Vavasor. It reached Vavasor Hall and was delivered to Alice on the Christmas morning. Before the end of the week the answer came.

My dear George,

Could I have my own way, I should make no answer to your letter at present, but leave it for the next six months. This will be little flattering to you, but it is less flattering to myself. We have been like children who have quarrelled over our game of play, till now, at the close of our little day of pleasure, we acknowledge that we have looked for delights where no delights were to be found.

Kate, who is here, talks to me of passionate love. There is no such passion left to me; nor, as I think, to you either. We could not stand up together as man and wife with any hope of a happy marriage unless we had both agreed that such happiness might be had without passionate love.

You will see from all this that I do not refuse your offer. I have for you a warm affection, which enables me to take a livelier interest in your career than in any other matters. Of course, if I become your wife that interest will be still closer and dearer.

I have suffered much from the past conflicts of my life, and there has been very much with which I must reproach myself. I must beg you to allow me some time for a cure. A perfect cure I may never expect, but I think that in twelve months from this time I may so far have recovered my usual spirit and ease of mind as to enable me to devote myself to your happiness. Dear George, if you will accept me under such circumstances, I will be your wife, and will endeavour to do my duty by you faithfully.

Even now, as your cousin, I take a lively interest in your hopes of entering Parliament. I understand what you have said about my fortune, and I perfectly appreciate your truth and frankness. My money may be absolutely necessary to you within this year, and whatever you want for your political purposes shall be forthcoming at your slightest wish.

Your affectionate cousin,

Alice Vavasor.

George Vavasor when he had read the letter threw it carelessly from him on to the breakfast table, and began to munch his toast. 'Very well,' said he; 'so be it.' Then he took up his newspaper. But before the day was over he had made many plans as to the benefit which might accrue to him from the offer which she had made of her money. And before night he had written to her deprecating the delay of twelve months, thanking her heartily for her confidence, and assuring her that if the nature of his coming contest at Chelsea should make it necessary, he would use her offer as frankly as it had been made.

Alice Vavasor returned to London with her father, leaving Kate at Vavasor Hall with her grandfather. The journey was not a pleasant one. Mr Vavasor had been told of Alice's decision, and knew that it was his duty to do something with the view of preventing the marriage; but he did not know what that something should be, and he did know that, whatever it might be, the doing of it would be thoroughly disagreeable. When they started from Vavasor he had as yet hardly spoken to her a word on the subject. 'I cannot congratulate you,' he had simply said. 'I hope the time may come, Papa, when you will,' Alice had answered; and that had been all.

To tell the truth, Alice was frightened at what she had done, and almost repented of it already. 'If I can do him good why should I not marry him?' In that feeling had been the chief argument which had induced her to return such an answer as she had sent to her cousin. He had been ever dear to her from her earliest years. She believed in his intellect, even if she could not believe in his conduct. Kate, her friend, longed for this thing. As for that dream of love, it meant nothing; and as for those arguments of prudence, that cold calculation about her money, which all people seemed to expect from her, she would throw it to the winds.

On the day after their return to Queen Anne Street the servant announced her cousin George. She felt the blood rush violently to her heart. But he was there in the room with her before she had had a moment allowed to her for thought.

'Alice,' said he, coming up to her with his extended hand. 'Dearest Alice!'

She gave him her hand, and immediately endeavoured to resume it, but he held it clenched within his own, and she felt that she was his prisoner.

'Alice, I am a man once again. It is only now that I can tell you what I have suffered during these last few years. Will you not let me thank you for what you have done for me?'

'I have done nothing for you, George. Nothing at all.' Then she got her hand away from him, and retreated back to a sofa where she seated herself. 'That you may do much for yourself is my greatest hope. If I can help you, I will do so most heartily.'

'Of course you will help me. I am full of plans, all of which you must share with me. But now, at this moment, my one great plan is that in which you have already consented to be my partner. Tell me that it will make you happy to call me your husband.'

That word husband was painful to Alice's ear. She shrunk from it with palpable bodily suffering.

'You have come to me too quickly, George,' she said.

There was something in her look as she spoke, and in the tone of her voice that was very sad. It struck him forcibly. Her money had been his chief object when he offered to renew his engagement with her, but, nevertheless, he desired something more than money: the triumph of having John Grey sent altogether adrift, in order that his old love might be recovered. As he would by no means have consented to pro-

42

ceed with the arrangement without the benefit of his cousin's money, so also did he feel unwilling to dispense with some expression of her love for him, which would be to him triumphant.

'Alice,' he said, 'your greeting to me is hardly all that I had hoped.'

'Indeed, George, I am sorry that you should be disappointed; but you would not have me affect a lightness of spirit I do not feel?'

'If you wish,' said he, very slowly—'if you wish to retract your letter to me, you now have my leave to do so.'

What an opportunity was this of escape! But she had not the courage to accept it. 'I do not wish to retract my letter,' said she, speaking as slowly as he had spoken; 'but I wish to be left awhile.'

'And is that all you can say to me, Alice?'

'What would you have me say?'

'I would hear one word of love from you; is that unreasonable? It might have been that I was over-bold in pressing my suit upon you again; but as you accepted it, have I not a right to expect that you should show me that you have been happy in accepting it?'

And now she feared that there would come some demand for an outward demonstration of love, such as he might have a right to make. She would make for him any sacrifice, but this sacrifice was not possible.

'And you have not a word to say to me?' he asked. She looked up at him, and saw that the cicatrice on his face was becoming ominous; his eyes were bent upon her with all their forbidding brilliance, and he was assuming that look of angry audacity which so often cowed those with whom he was brought in contact.

'You wish me then to go from you?'

'Do not be angry with me, George!'

'Angry! By heaven, I am angry. I think you owed it me to give me some warmer welcome. Is it to be thus with us always for the next accursed year?'

'If you speak to me like that, and look at me like that, how can I answer you?'

'I want no answer. I wanted you to put your hand in mine, to kiss me, and to tell me that you are once more my own. Alice, think better of it; kiss me, and let me feel my arm once more round your waist.'

She shuddered, and he saw that she shuddered. With all his desire for her money, his instant need of it, he turned upon his heel, and left the room without another word. She heard the door slam as he left the house. And this was the man from whom, within the last few days, she had accepted an offer of marriage.

George, when he left the house, walked hurriedly towards the house of his parliamentary attorney, Mr Scruby. As he had left Queen Anne Street he had thought of nothing but that shudder which Alice had been unable to repress. He had been feeding on his anger, telling himself at one moment that he would let her and her money go from him, and making inward threats in the next that the time should come in which he would punish her for this ill-usage. But there was the necessity of resolving what he would say to Mr Scruby. The election would not take place till the summer, but there were preliminary expenses which needed ready money. Mr Scruby wanted the present payment of some five hundred pounds, and a well-grounded assurance that he would be put in full funds by the beginning of next June. Other candidates, with money in their pockets, might find their way into Mr Scruby's offices. As George Vavasor crossed Regent Street he applied his mind to business. Should he prepare himself to give orders that Kate's little property should be sold out? But as he reached Mr Scruby's door he had decided it was preferable that he should use his wife's fortune, and explain to Mr Scruby that he would be justified in doing so by the fact that his own heritage would be settled on her at her marriage. Her behaviour to him this very morning had made the affair more difficult and unpleasant than it would have been had she smiled on him; but even as it was, he managed to assure himself that he was doing her no wrong, and with this self-assurance he entered Mr Scruby's office.

'Yes, yes, a family arrangement,' said Mr Scruby, as he congratulated him on his proposed marriage. Mr Scruby did not care a straw from what source the necessary funds might be drawn.

·   ·   ·   ·   ·

Alice did not, as she had intended, write to Mr Grey quite at once. But the letter must be written, and it was duly done. When John Grey received it he was sitting at breakfast in his study at Nethercoats. As soon as the envelope touched his hand he became aware that it was from Alice. He read it twice over, and the work was one of intense agony. He had ever disliked and feared George Vavasor for his influence upon Alice. He had also feared the influence of her cousin Kate. There was less hope now than before, but there might still be hope; hope for her, even though there might be none for him. George Vavasor was known to be needy, reckless, and on the brink of ruin. Such a marriage to Alice Vavasor would be altogether ruinous. Whatever might be Grey's own ultimate fate he would still seek to save her from that. Her cousin, doubtless, wanted her money. Might it not be possible that he would be satisfied with her money, and that thus the woman might be saved?

Grey thought it improbable that Alice would find herself able to give herself in marriage to her cousin so soon after her breach with him; but as to this he had no assurance, and he determined to have the facts from her own lips, if she would see him. So he wrote to her, naming a day on which he would call upon her early in the morning; and having received from her no prohibition he was in Queen Anne Street at the hour appointed.

He had conceived a scheme: he himself would buy off George Vavasor. If Vavasor was such a man as people represented him, such a purchase might be possible. But then, before this was attempted, he must be quite sure that he knew his man, and he must satisfy himself also that in doing so he would not, in truth, add to Alice's misery.

He gently opened the door for himself. Then, before he even looked at her, he closed it again. It was this perfect command of himself at all seasons which had in part made Alice afraid of him, and drove her to believe that they were not fitted for each other. She, when he thus turned for a moment from her, and then walked slowly towards her, stood with both her hands leaning on the centre table of the room, and with her eyes fixed upon its surface.

'Alice,' he said, walking up to her very slowly. And then, as slowly she looked up at him, he asked for her hand. 'You may give it me,' he said, 'as to an old friend.' She put her hand in his hand, and then, withdrawing it, felt that she must never trust herself to do so again.

'Alice,' he continued, 'there is a question or two which I think you will answer. Has a day been fixed for this marriage?'

'No,' she replied hurriedly; and he knew at once by her voice that she already dreaded this new wedlock.

'Can you tell me why you have again accepted your cousin's offer?'

'Because—but you would never understand me, and there can be no reason why I should dare to hope that you should ever think well of me again.'

'Alice, nothing has yet been done which need to a certainty separate you and me. I love you now as well as ever, and should things change with you I cannot tell you with how much joy and eagerness I should take you back to my bosom. My heart is yours now as it has been since I knew you.'

Then he again just touched her hand, and left her before she had been able to answer a word.

In the afternoon her father came to her. Mr Grey, when he left Queen Anne Street, had gone to his lawyer, and from thence had made his way to Mr Vavasor. Mr Vavasor had returned with Grey to the lawyer's chambers. He had been startled at the precision with which all the circumstances of his daughter's position had been explained to a mild-eyed old gentleman, with a bald head, who carried on his business in a narrow street behind Doctors' Commons Mr Tombe was his name. Mr Tombe had evinced no surprise, no dismay, and certainly no mock delicacy, when the whole affair was under discussion. George Vavasor was to get present moneys, but, if it could be so arranged, from John Grey rather than from Alice; and then George Vavasor was to be made to sur-

46

render his bride. John Vavasor sat by in silence as the arrangement was being made. 'I wish you to understand from the lady's father,' Grey said to the lawyer, 'that the marriage would be regarded by him with as much dismay as by myself.'

'Certainly,' Mr Vavasor had agreed.

'And you see, Mr Tombe,' Grey went on, 'we only wish to try the man. If he is worthy of her, he can take her.'

'You merely wish to open her eyes, Mr Grey,' said the mild-eyed lawyer.

'I wish that he should have what money he wants, and then we shall find what it is he really wishes.'

'Yes; we shall know our man,' said the lawyer. 'He shall have the money, Mr Grey,' and so the interview had been ended.

Mr Vavasor, when he entered the drawing-room, addressed his daughter in a cheery voice. 'What, all in the dark?'

'Yes, Papa. I did not expect you.'

'No, I suppose not. I came here because I want to say a few words to you about business.'

'What business, Papa?'

'Well, my love, if I understood you rightly, your cousin George wants some money.'

'I think he will want some before the time for the election comes.'

'He has not asked you for it yet?'

'No; he has merely said that should he be in need he would take me at my word.'

'I wish to know what to do when the demand is made. I am not going to oppose you now; your money is your own, and you have a right to do with it as you please. But would you gratify me in one thing?'

'What is it, Papa?'

'When he does apply, let the amount be raised through me?'

'How through you?'

'Come to me; I mean, so that I may see the lawyer, and have the arrangements made.' Then he explained to her that in dealing with large sums of money it could not be right that she should do so without his knowledge, even though the property was her own. 'I will promise you that I will not oppose

47

your wishes,' he said. Then Alice undertook that when such case should arise the money should be raised through his means.

· · · · ·

When George Vavasor left the office of Mr Scruby, the parliamentary lawyer, he was well aware that the job to be undertaken was a very disagreeable one. He did not like the task of borrowing his cousin Alice's money. How was he to make his first step towards getting his hand into his cousin's purse? He resolved at last that Kate should do the work for him. He could talk to Kate as he could not talk to Alice; and then, between the women, those hard money necessities would be softened down. With this view he went down to Westmorland, to a small wayside inn at Shap among the fells, which had been known to him of old, and begged his sister to come over to him as early as she might find it possible.

Vavasor Hall was about five miles from Shap, and it was not altogether an easy task for Kate to get over to the village without informing her grandfather that the visit was to be made, and what was its purport.

'To Shap! What on earth can take you to Shap?'

'I want to see someone there.'

'Whom can you want to see at Shap?'

Then it occurred to Kate on the spur of the moment that she might as well tell her grandfather the fact. 'My brother has come down,' she said; 'and is at the inn there. I had not intended to tell you, as I did not wish to mention his name till you had consented to receive him here.'

'And he expects to come here now, does he?' said the squire.

'Oh, no, sir. He has come down simply to see me—about business, I believe.'

'Business! I suppose he wants to get your money from you?'

'I think it is with reference to his marriage.'

'Look here, Kate; if ever you lend him your money I will never speak to him again under any circumstance. The property will become his for his life when I die, unless I change

48

my will. If he gets your money from you, I will change it.'

What unlucky chance had it been which had put this idea into the old squire's head on this especial morning? Kate had resolved that she would entreat her brother to make use of her little fortune. She would have given up every shilling of her own money without a moment's hesitation, or any feeling that her brother would be wrong to accept it. But she could not endure to think that he should take the money off the girl whom he was engaged to marry.

'Grandpapa knows that you are here, George,' said Kate, when their first greeting was over.

'The deuce he does!'

'I could not get the jaunting car to come in without letting him know why I wanted it.'

'What did he say about my coming?'

'He didn't say much.'

'He made no offer as to my going there?'

'No.'

'I should not have gone if he had. I don't know that I ever shall go. To be there to do any good, so as to make him alter his will and leave me in the position which I have a right to expect would take more time than the whole property is worth. And he would endeavour to tie me down in some way I could not stand—perhaps ask me to give up my notion for going into Parliament. But I'll tell you what I do want, Kate. I want some money.'

'Whatever I have can be yours tomorrow,' said Kate, in a hesitating voice.

'No, I shall not take your money. All that you have would only just suffice for my present wants, and I should not choose to make you a beggar.'

'What is it you wish then?'

'When Alice and I are married, of course there will be a settlement made on her, and as we are both the grandchildren of the old squire I shall propose that the Vavasor property shall be hers for life in the event of her outliving me. And if this be done there can be no harm in my forestalling some of her property, which would of course become mine when we are married.'

'But the squire might leave the property to whom he pleases.'

'We know very well that he won't leave it out of the family. In fact, he would only be too glad to consent to such an agreement, because he would thereby rob me of all power in the matter.'

'But that could not be done till you are married.'

'Look here, Kate, don't you make difficulties.' And now, as he looked at her, the cicatrice on his face seemed to open and yawn at her. 'If you mean to say that you won't help me I will go back to London.'

'I would do anything in my power to help you—that was not wrong.'

'Will you write to Alice—or better still, go to her, and explain that I want the money? It will come much better from you than me. Explain that I must pay in advance the expenses of this contest.'

'George,' she said, slowly. 'I do not think you ought to take Alice's money.'

'My dear Kate, Alice has offered it. I would rather that you should tell her how much I want, and that I want it now, than that I should do so. That is all.'

Kate was quite awake to the fact that her brother was ashamed of the thing he was about to do.

'Do you think Alice will refuse to lend it me?'

'I am sure she would not, but I think that you ought not to take it. There seems to me to be something sacred about property that belongs to the girl you are going to marry.'

'If there is anything on earth I hate,' said George, walking about the room, 'it is romance. If you keep it for reading in your bedroom, it's all very well for those who like it, but when it comes to be mixed up with one's business it plays the devil. Alice and I are to be man and wife. All our interests, and all our money, and our station in life, whatever it may be, are to be joint property. And yet she is the last person in the world to whom I ought to go for money to improve her prospects as well as my own! That's what you call delicacy. I call it infernal nonsense.'

Kate was hesitating when there came a knock at the door, and a little crumpled note was brought up to her. A boy had just come with it from Vavasor Hall, and Kate, as soon as she saw her name on the outside, knew that it was from her grandfather. It read: 'If George wishes to come to the Hall, let him come. If he chooses to tell me that he regrets his conduct to me, I will see him.'

'I'll do nothing of the kind,' George said. 'What good should I get by going to the old man's house?'

'Every good,' said Kate. 'If you don't go now you never can do so.'

'Never till it's my own,' said George.

'If you show him that you are determined to be at variance with him, it never will be your own; unless, indeed, it should some day come to you as part of Alice's fortune. Think of it, George; you would not like to receive everything from her.'

He walked about the room, muttering maledictions between his teeth and balancing his pride against his profit.

'I'll tell you what I'll do,' he said. 'I'll go to Vavasor and put up with the old squire's insolence, if you'll make this application for me to Alice.'

She hesitated again, feeling that she would almost do anything to achieve a reconciliation between her grandfather and her brother. Then, with a sore conscience, with a full knowledge that she was undertaking to do wrong, she promised that she would apply to Alice for her money. Thereupon, George graciously consented to proceed to his bedroom, and put together his clothes with a view to his visit to the Hall.

The old squire was standing at the hall steps when the jaunting car drove up. He put out his hand to help Kate down, keeping his eye all the time on George's face.

'So you've come back,' the squire said to him.

'Yes, sir. I've come back, like the prodigal son in the parable.'

'The prodigal son was contrite. I hope you are so.'

'Pretty well for that, sir. I'm sorry there has been any quarrel, and all that, you know.'

'Go in,' said the squire, very angrily. 'To expect anything

gracious from you would be to expect pearls from swine. Go in.'

George went in, shrugging his shoulders as his eyes met his sister's.

CHAPTER THREE

DURING the time George Vavasor remained beneath his grandfather's roof he was not happy himself, nor did he contribute to the happiness of anyone else. Kate did all in her power to induce her brother to be, at any rate, kind in his manner towards his grandfather, but it was in vain. The squire would not be the first to be gracious; and George quite as obstinate as the old man, would take no steps in that direction. Poor Kate entreated each of them to begin, but her entreaties were of no avail. 'He is an ill-mannered cub,' the old man said, 'and I was a fool to let him into the house. Don't mention his name to me again.'

With a sorrowful heart, and with fingers that could hardly form the needful letters, Kate wrote to her cousin. It was a stiff, uncomfortable letter, telling its own tale of grief and shame. Alice understood very plainly all the circumstances under which it was written, but she sent back word to Kate at once, undertaking that the money should be forthcoming; and she wrote again before the end of January, saying that the sum named had been paid to George's credit at his own bankers.

George returned to town at the end of those four days, and found that the thousand pounds was duly placed to his credit. This money had, of course, come from Mr Tombe, who duly debited Mr Grey with the amount. Alice, in accordance with her promise, had told her father that the money was needed, and her father had procured it without a word of remonstrance. 'Surely I must sign some paper,' Alice had said. But she had been contented when her father told her that the lawyers would manage all that.

It was nearly the end of February when George Vavasor made his first payment to Mr Scruby on behalf of the coming election.

'You haven't heard the news,' said Scruby.

'What news?' said George.

'The Marquis is as nearly off the hooks as a man can be.' Mr Scruby showed clearly by his face and voice that this was supposed to be of very great importance; but Vavasor did not at first seem to be as much interested in the fate of 'the Marquis' as Scruby had intended.

'I'm very sorry for him,' said George. 'Who is the Marquis?'

'It's the Marquis of Bunratty; and if he drops, our young Member here will go into the Upper House.'

'What, before the end of the Session?'

'To be sure,' said Scruby. 'The writ would be out immediately. Travers's people have heard of it before us, and they're ready to be up with their posters directly the breath is out of the Marquis's body. We must go to work immediately.'

'It will only be for part of a Session.' said George.

'Just so,' said Mr Scruby.

'And then there'll be the cost of another election.'

'That's true,' said Mr Scruby; 'but in such cases we do manage to make it come a little cheaper. If you lick Travers now, it may be that you'll have a walk-over for the next.'

Vavasor was inclined to doubt the extent of his luck. He would be called upon to spend certainly not less than three thousand pounds of his cousin's money on the chance of being able to sit in Parliament for a few months. He might, to be sure, allow the remainder of this Session to run, and stand, as he had intended, at the general election; but he knew that if he now allowed a Liberal to win the seat the holder of the seat would be almost sure of subsequent success. He must either fight now, or give up the fight altogether; and he was a man who did not love to abandon any contest in which he had been engaged. He found himself compelled to say that he would stand; and Scruby undertook to give orders at once.

53

As he walked from the attorney's office to his club George Vavasor thought that everything was going wrong with him. His grandfather, who was eighty years of age, appeared to have no symptoms of dying, whereas this Marquis, who was not yet much over fifty, was rushing headlong out of the world, simply because he was the one man whose continued life at the present moment would be serviceable to George Vavasor. As he thought of his grandfather he almost broke his umbrella against the pavement. What right could an ignorant old fool like that have to live for ever, keeping the possession of a property which he could not use, and ruining those who were to come after him? If at this moment that wretched place down in Westmorland could become his he might yet ride triumphantly over his difficulties, and refrain from sullying his hands with more of his cousin's money till she should become his wife.

Even that thousand pounds had not passed through his hands without giving him much bitter suffering. He had taught himself to look at it lightly whilst it was yet unaccomplished; but he could not think of it lightly now. In these days he did not go near Queen Anne Street, trying to persuade himself that he stayed away because of Alice's coldness to him. But, in truth, he was afraid of seeing her without speaking of her money, and afraid to see her if he were to speak of it.

'You have seen the *Globe*?' someone said to him as he entered his club.

'I have seen nothing.'

'Bunratty died in Ireland this morning. I suppose you'll be up for the Chelsea Districts?'

.   .   .   .   .

Parliament opened that year on the twelfth of February, and Mr Palliser was one of the first Members to take his seat. It had been generally asserted through the country that the Chancellor of the Exchequer had differed with his friend and chief, the Prime Minister, as to the expediency of repealing certain taxes, and was prepared to launch himself into opposition

54

with his small bodyguard of followers, with all his energy and with all his venom. But when the House of Commons met that gentleman took his seat on the Treasury Bench. Mr Palliser, who had by no means given a general support to the Ministry in the last Session, took his seat on the same side of the House indeed, but low down.

The House was all agog, as was the crowded gallery. Would the Chancellor of the Exchequer get up and declare his purposes? There came on a general debate about money matters, in which the purse-bearer did say a few words, but he said nothing as to the great question at issue. At last up got Mr Palliser, towards the close of the evening, and occupied a full hour in explaining what taxes the Government might remit with safety, and what they might not. The Members went out gradually during this oration; but the newspapers declared next morning that his speech had been the speech of the night, and that the perspicuity of Mr Palliser pointed him out as the coming man.

He returned home to his house in Park Lane quite triumphant, and found Lady Glencora sitting alone. She had arrived in town that day. She had expressed herself unwilling to remain at Matching without him; but, in truth, she had another reason. While she was there a letter had reached her from Burgo Fitzgerald, and had contained a direct proposal that she should go off with him. 'I am at Matching,' the letter said, 'at the Inn; but I do not dare to show myself. If I am wrong in thinking that you love me, I would not for worlds insult you by my presence; but if you love me still, I ask you to throw aside from you that fictitious marriage, and give yourself to the man whom, if you love him, you should regard as your husband.'

She told no one of the letter, but she read it over and over again in the solitude of her room. She determined not to undergo the danger of remaining at Matching while Burgo Fitzgerald should be in the vicinity. She could not analyse her own wishes. She declared to herself that she loved this man with all her heart. She protested that the fault would not be hers, but theirs who had forced her to marry the man she did not love. She assured herself that her husband had no affection for her, and that their marriage was in every respect prejudicial to him. She recurred over and over again in her thoughts to her childlessness, and to his extreme desire for an heir. But yet she fled to London. She sent no answer to the letter. She longed to see Alice, to whom alone, since her marriage, had she ever spoken of her love, and intended to tell her the whole tale of that letter.

Mr Palliser, on that night of his return from the House, had not seen her since her arrival in London, and, of course, he took her by the hand and kissed her. But it was the embrace of a brother rather than of a lover or a husband. Lady Glencora, with her full woman's nature, understood this thoroughly. 'I hope you are well?' she said.

'Oh, yes; quite well. And you? A little fatigued with your journey, I suppose?'

'No, not much.'

'Well, we have had a pretty important debate. Don't you want to know how it has gone?'

'If it has concerned you particularly.'

'Concerned me! It has concerned me certainly.'

'They haven't appointed you yet, have they?'

'No; they don't appoint people during debates in the House of Commons. But I fear I shall never make you a politician.'

'I'm almost afraid you never will. I don't understand why you should work so very hard; but, as you like it, I'm as anxious as anybody can be that you should triumph.'

'Yes, I do like it,' he said. 'A man must like something, and I don't know what there is to like better. Some people can eat and drink all day; and some people can care about a horse. I can do neither.'

And there were others, Lady Glencora thought, who could love to lie in the sun, and could look up into the eyes of women, and seek their happiness there. She was sure that she knew one such. But she said nothing of this.

He endeavoured to give her a lecture on the working of the British Constitution, and the manner in which British politics evolved themselves. Lady Glencora yawned, and strove ineffectually to hide her yawn in her handkerchief.

'I see you don't care a bit about it,' said he.

'Don't be angry, Plantagenet. I do care about it, but I am so ignorant that I can't understand it all at once. I am rather tired, and I think I'll go to bed now. Shall you be late?'

'I shall be rather late. I've a lot of letters to write tonight, as I must be at work all tomorrow. By-the-by, Mr Bott is coming to dine here. There will be no one else.'

'Mr Bott!' said Lady Glencora. He was the Member for St Helens, a self-professed Radical who liked to live with aristocrats, and who was well known to be striving hard to get his finger into the public pie.

'Have you any objection?'

'Oh, no. Would you like to dine alone with him?'

'Why should I dine alone with him? Why shouldn't you eat your dinner with us? Mrs Marsham is in town, and I dare say she'll come to you if you ask her.'

But this was too much for Lady Glencora. Mrs Marsham would be worse than Mr Bott. Mr Bott would be engaged with Mr Palliser during the greater part of the evening. 'I thought,' said she, 'of asking my cousin, Alice Vavasor, to spend the evening with me.'

'Miss Vavasor?'

'I hope you have nothing to say against my cousin? She is my only near relative that I really care for. The only woman, I mean.'

'No, I don't mean to say anything against her. I would sooner you would ask Mrs Marsham tomorrow.'

'As there will be no other ladies here tomorrow evening, Plantagenet, and as I have not yet seen Alice since I have been in town, I wish you would let me have my way in this.'

'Very well. Of course you will do as you please. I am sorry that you have refused the first favour I have asked you this year.' Then he left the room, and she went away to bed.

But Lady Glencora was not brought to repentance by her husband's last words. She wrote a line to Alice before she went to bed, begging her cousin to come to her early on the following day, so that they might go out together, and then afterwards dine in company with Mr Bott.

Then she sat herself down to think—to think especially

about the cruelty of husbands. What could be so unendurable as this total want of sympathy, as this deadness in life, which her present lot entailed upon her? She thought of the beauty of Burgo's eyes, of the softness of his touch, of the loving, almost worshipping, tones of his voice. The British Constitution indeed! Had she married Burgo they would have been in sunny Italy, and he would have told her some other tale than that as they sat together under the pale moonlight. She might have sat in marble balconies, while the vines clustered over her head, and he would have been at her knee, hardly speaking to her, but making his presence felt by the halo of its divinity. He would have called upon her for no hard replies. With him near her she would have enjoyed the soft air, and would have sat happy, without trouble, lapped in the delight of loving.

'Have you written to your cousin?' her husband asked her the next morning. His voice clearly showed that his anger was either over or suppressed.

'Yes; I have asked her to come and drive, and then to stay for dinner.'

'Very well,' said Mr Palliser, mildly. 'As that is settled, perhaps you would have no objection to ask Mrs Marsham also?'

'Won't she probably be engaged?'

'I think not,' said Mr Palliser. And then he added, being ashamed of the tinge of falsehood of which he would otherwise have been guilty, 'I know she is not engaged.'

'She expects to come, then?' said Lady Glencora.

'I have not asked her, if you mean that, Glencora. Had I done so, I should have said so.'

'I will write to her, if you please,' said the wife, who felt that she could hardly refuse any longer.

'Do, my dear.' So Lady Glencora did write to Mrs Marsham, who promised to come, as did also Alice Vavasor.

The greeting between the cousins was very affectionate. They sat so long over the fire in the drawing-room that at last they agreed that the driving should be abandoned. Lady Glencora's hand was at length on Burgo Fitzgerald's letter, and it would have been out in the next moment, and thrown upon Alice's lap, had not the servant opened the door and announced Mrs Marsham.

Mrs Marsham was one of those women ambitious of power and not very scrupulous as to the manner in which they obtain it. She was not above any artifice by which she might ingratiate herself with those whom it suited her purpose to conciliate. She thought evil rather than good. She had been the bosom friend of Mr Palliser's mother, and she took a special interest in Mr Palliser's welfare. When he married, she heard the story of the loves of Burgo and Lady Glencora. She made up her mind that the young lady would want watching, and she was of opinion that no one would be so well able to watch Lady Glencora as herself. Mr Palliser would have rejected any such suggestion, and Mrs Marsham knew that he would do so, but she had let a word or two drop hinting that Lady Glencora was very young; that Lady Glencora's manners were charming in their childlike simplicity; but hinting also that precaution was, for that reason, the more necessary. She might do silly things, and not know how to live a life becoming the wife of a Chancellor of the Exchequer. Therefore Mr Palliser submitted Glencora—and, to a certain extent, himself—into the hands of Mrs Marsham.

Lady Glencora might be very ignorant about the British Constitution, and very ignorant also as to the real elements of right and wrong in a woman's conduct, but she was no fool. When a woman knows that she is guarded by a watch-dog, she is bound to deceive it, if it be possible, and is usually not ill-disposed to deceive also its owner. Lady Glencora was heartily resolved that if she was to be kept in the proper line at all, she would not be so kept by Mrs Marsham.

Alice rose and accepted Mrs Marsham's salutation quite as coldly as it had been given. Mrs Marsham had made up her mind that Alice was not the sort of friend that Lady Glencora should have about her. Alice recognized and accepted the feud.

'I thought I might find you at home,' said Mrs Marsham, 'as I know you are lazy about going out in the cold.' She was a little woman, with sharp small eyes, with a permanent colour in her face, and two short, crisp, grey curls at each side of her face; always well dressed, always in good health, and, as Lady Glencora believed, altogether incapable of fatigue.

'One ought to go out of the house every day,' said Mrs Marsham.

'I hate all those rules.'

'My dear Glencora, one must live by rules in this life. You might as well say that you hated sitting down to dinner.'

'So I do, very often; almost always when there's company.'

'You'll get over that feeling after another season in town,' said Mrs Marsham.

'I don't think I shall. Mr Bott is coming to dine here to-night.'

There was no mistaking the meaning of this. Now, Mrs Marsham had accepted the right hand of fellowship from Mr Bott, not because she especially liked him, but in compliance with the apparent necessities of Mr Palliser's position.

'Mr Bott is a Member of Parliament, and a very service-able friend of Mr Palliser's,' said Mrs Marsham.

'All the same; we do not like Mr Bott—do we, Alice?'

'I certainly do not like him,' said Alice.

'It can be but of small matter to you, Miss Vavasor,' said Mrs Marsham, 'as you will not probably have to see much of him.'

'Of the very smallest moment,' said Alice. 'Glencora, I think I'll leave you alone with Mrs Marsham.'

But Lady Glencora would not let her go. 'Nonsense, Alice,' she said. 'If you and I can't fight our little battles against Mr Bott and Mrs Marsham without running away, it is odd.'

'I hope, Glencora, you do not count me as your enemy?' said Mrs Marsham, drawing herself up.

'But I shall, certainly, if you attack Alice, the best friend I have in the world.'

'I did not mean to offend Miss Vavasor,' said Mrs Marsham, looking at her very grimly. After that she took herself off, saying that she would be back to dinner.

Lady Glencora felt no further inclination to show Burgo's

letter to Alice on that occasion. They sat over the drawing-room fire, talking chiefly of Alice's affairs, till it was time for them to dress. But Alice, though she spoke much of Mr Grey, said no word as to her engagement with George Vavasor. How could she speak of it, inasmuch as she had almost resolved that that engagement also should be broken?

Alice, when she came down to the drawing-room, after dinner, found Mr Bott there alone. 'I did not expect the pleasure of meeting Miss Vavasor today,' he said, offering his hand. She gave him her hand, and then sat down, merely muttering some word of reply. Then Mr Palliser entered the room along with Mrs Marsham.

The two gentlemen shook hands, and then Mr Palliser turned to Alice. She perceived at once by his face that she was unwelcome, and wished herself away from his house. It might be all very well for Lady Glencora to fight with Mrs Marsham, and with her husband, too, in regard to the Marsham persecution, but there could be no reason why she should do so. He just asked her how she was, then turned away and began talking to Mrs Marsham. Alice felt the blood mount into her face and regretted greatly that she had ever come among these people.

During dinner-time Alice said very little, nor was there given to her opportunity of saying much. She occupied one side of the table by herself, away from the fire, where she felt cold and desolate in the gloom of the large half-lighted room. Mr Palliser occupied himself with Mrs Marsham, who talked politics to him; and Mr Bott never lost a moment in his endeavours to say some civil word to Lady Glencora. Lady Glencora gave him no encouragement; but she hardly dared to snub him openly in her husband's presence. Twenty times during dinner she said some little word to Alice, attempting to give some relief. But it was of no avail. She felt that the halls of the Pallisers were too cold for her, and that the sooner she escaped from their gloom and hard discourtesy the better for her.

The gentlemen did not return to the drawing-room that evening, having work to do in arranging the great financial calculations of the nation; at an early hour Alice was taken

61

home in Lady Glencora's brougham, leaving her cousin still in the hands of Mrs Marsham.

.   .   .   .   .

The election came on in the Chelsea Districts, and the whole of the south-western part of the metropolis was covered with posters bearing George Vavasor's name. 'Vote for Vavasor and the River Bank.' It was Mr Scruby who invented the legend. There was a question in those days as to embanking the river, and Mr Scruby recommended the coming Member to pledge himself that he would have the work carried on. 'You must have a subject,' pleaded Mr Scruby. 'No young Member can do anything without a subject. And it should be local. Such a subject as that, if it's well worked, may save you thousands of pounds at future elections.'

'It won't save me anything at this one, I take it.'

'But it may secure the seat, Mr Vavasor, and afterwards make you the most popular metropolitan Member in the House; that is, with your own constituency. Only look at the money that would be spent in the districts if that were done! It would come to millions, sir!'

'But it never will be done.'

'What matters that?' Mr Scruby explained the nature of a good parliamentary subject: 'Get the figures by heart, and then, as nobody else will do so, nobody can put you down. Of course it won't be done. But you can always promise it at the hustings, and can always demand it in the House.'

Vavasor allowed Mr Scruby to manage the matter for him, and 'Vavasor and the River Bank' was carried about by an army of men with iron shoulder-straps, and huge pasteboard placards six feet high on the top of them. With much labour he actually did get up the subject of the River Bank. He was able even to work himself into an apparent heat when he was told that the thing was out of the question; and soon found that he had disciples who really believed in him. He spoke vehemently, and promised the men of Chelsea, Pimlico, and Brompton that the path of London westwards had hardly commenced as yet. There should be palaces there for the rich, because the rich spend their riches; but no rich man's palace should interfere with the poor man's right to the River Bank. Three millions and a half should be spent on the noble street to be constructed, the grandest pathway that the world should ever yet have seen; three millions and a half to be drawn from —from anywhere except from Chelsea; from the bloated money-bags of the City Corporation, Vavasor once ventured to declare, amidst the encouraging shouts of the men of Chelsea. Mr Scruby was forced to own that his pupil worked the subject well. 'Upon my word, that was uncommon good,' he said, almost patting Vavasor on the back after a speech in which he had vehemently asserted that his ambition to represent the Chelsea Districts had come of his long-fixed idea that the glory of future London would be brought about by the embankment of the river at Chelsea.

But armies of men carrying big boards, and placards in which the letters are three feet long, cost money. Those few modest hundreds which Mr Scruby had already received before the work began had been paid on the supposition that the election would not take place till September. Mr Scruby made an early request that a further sum of fifteen hundred pounds should be placed in his hands.

The thing had come so suddenly upon George Vavasor that there was not time for him to carry on his further operations through his sister. He himself wrote to Alice. He wanted two thousand pounds instantly, and felt little scruple in asking her for it. Then he said a word or two as to his prolonged absence from Queen Anne Street. He had not been there because he had felt that she would for a while prefer to be left free from such interviews. But should he be triumphant in his present contest, he should go to her to share his triumph with her; or, should he fail, he should go to her to console him in his failure.

Within three days he had heard from her, saying that the money would be at once placed to his credit. She sent him also her candid good wishes for success in his enterprise, but beyond this her letter said nothing. There was no word of love, no expression of a desire to see him. Vavasor, as he perceived all this, felt a triumph in the possession of her money. She was ill-using him by her coldness, and there was comfort in revenge. 'It serves her right,' he said to himself. 'She should have married me at once when she said she would do so, and then it would have been my own.'

When Mr Tombe had communicated with John Grey on the matter of this increased demand Grey had telegraphed back that Vavasor's demand for money, if made through Mr John Vavasor, was to be honoured to the extent of five thousand pounds. Mr Tombe raised his eyebrows, and reflected that some men were very foolish. But the money was paid to George Vavasor's account.

At the close of the poll Vavasor's name stood at the head by a considerable majority. 'And you've done it very cheap, Mr Vavasor,' said Scruby, 'considering that the seat is metropolitan. Another twelve hundred will cover everything—say thirteen at the outside. And when you have fought the battle once again you'll have paid your footing and the fellows will let you in almost for nothing after that.'

A further sum of thirteen hundred pounds was wanted at once, and then the whole thing was to be repeated over again in three months' time! This was not consolatory. But, nevertheless, there was a triumph in the thing itself which George Vavasor was man enough to enjoy. It would be something to have sat in the House of Commons, though it should only have been for half a Session. As he went on for the first time, under the guardianship of Mr Bott, he felt great pride. Mr Bott had the new Member in hand, not because there had been any old friendship between them, but Mr Bott was on the look-out for followers, and Vavasor was on the look-out for a party. A man gets no great thanks for attaching himself to existing power. He might have enrolled himself among the general supporters of the Government without attracting much attention. He would in such a case have been at the bottom of a long list. But Mr Palliser was a rising man, round whom, almost without wish of his own, a party was forming itself. If he came into power, then they who had acknowledged the new light before its brightness had been declared might expect their reward.

64

Vavasor, as he passed through the lobby to the door of the House, leaning on Mr Bott's arm, was silent. He was going to sit among the first men of his nation, and to take his chance of making himself one of them.

'Of course you have heard a debate?' said Mr Bott.

'Yes,' answered Vavasor.

'Let me give you one bit of advice, my dear fellow—don't think of speaking this Session. A Member can do no good at that work till he has learned something of the forms of the House. The forms of the House are everything; upon my word they are.'

Vavasor, as he walked up the House to the Clerk's table and took the oath and then walked down again, felt himself to be almost taken aback by the little notice which was accorded to him. It was not that he had expected to create a sensation, but the thing which he was doing was so great to him that the indifference of those around him was a surprise. After he had taken his seat, a few men came up by degrees and shook hands with him; but it seemed, as they did so, merely because they were passing that way. He was anxious not to sit next to Mr Bott, but that gentleman stuck to him pertinaciously. So he found himself sitting behind Mr Palliser, a little to the right, while Mr Bott occupied the ear of the rising man.

The Chancellor of the Exchequer was on his legs, and Mr Palliser was watching him as a cat watches a mouse. The speaker was full of figures, and as every new budget of them fell from him, Mr Bott, with audible whispers, poured into the ear of his chief certain calculations of his own, most of which went to prove that the financier in office was altogether wrong. Vavasor thought that he could see that Mr Palliser was receiving more of his assistance than was palatable to him. He would listen, if he did listen, without making any sign that he heard, and would occasionally shake his head with symptoms of impatience. But Mr Bott was a man not to be repressed. When Mr Palliser shook his head he became more assiduous than ever, and when Mr Palliser slightly moved himself to the left, he boldly followed him.

No general debate arose on the subject which the Minister

had in hand, and when he sat down Mr Palliser would not get up, though Mr Bott counselled him to do so. The matter was over for the night, and the time had arrived for Lord Middlesex on certain matters of church reform; but, alas, for him and for his feelings, before his energy had got itself into full swing the Members were swarming away through the doors like a flock of sheep. Mr Palliser got up and went, and was followed at once by Mr Bott, who succeeded in getting hold of his arm in the lobby.

Vavasor was able to walk home by himself. He told himself over and over again that he had done a great thing in obtaining that which he now possessed, and he endeavoured to teach himself that the price he was paying for it was not too dear. But already there had come upon him something of that feeling which deprives every prize that is gained of half its value. There had been nothing of brilliance in the debate, and the Members had loomed no larger than ordinary men at ordinary clubs. The great men with whose names the papers are filled had sat silent, gloomy, and apparently idle. As soon as a fair opportunity was given them they escaped out of the House, as boys might escape from school. Vavasor had spent everything that he had to become a Member of that House, and now he could not but ask himself whether the thing purchased was worth the purchase-money.

But his courage was high. Though he was gloomy, and almost sad, on the morrow he would go to Queen Anne Street, and would demand sympathy there from her who had professed to sympathize with him so strongly in his political desires.

When Alice heard of her cousin's success, and understood that he was actually Member of Parliament for the Chelsea Districts, she resolved that she would be triumphant. She had sacrificed nearly everything to her desire for his success in public life, and now that he had achieved the first great step towards that success it would have been madness on her .part to decline her share in the ovation. If she could not rejoice in that, what source of joy would then be left for her? She strove, therefore, to be triumphant on his behalf, but she knew that she was striving ineffectually.

66

She sat down to write him a word or two of congratulation, but she found the task more difficult then she had expected and she gave it up. But she wrote to Kate, and contrived to put some note of triumph into her letter. Kate had written to her at length, filling her sheet with a loud paean of sincere rejoicing. 'I am proud,' she said, in her letter to Alice. 'No other thing that he could have done would have made me so proud of him. When I think that he has forced his way into Parliament without any great friend, with nothing to back him but his own wit'—she had, in truth, forgotten Alice's money as she wrote—'that he has achieved his triumph in the metropolis, among the most wealthy and most fastidious of the richest city in the world, I do feel proud of my brother. And, Alice, I hope that you are proud of your lover.'

'He is not my lover,' Alice said to herself. 'He knows that he is not. He understands it, though she may not. And if not your lover, Alice Vavasor, what is he then to you? And what are you to him, if not his love?' She was beginning to understand that she had put herself in the way of utter destruction; that she had walked to the brink of a precipice, and that she must now topple over it.

On the same afternoon she saw her father for a moment or two. 'So George has got himself returned,' he said, raising his eyebrows.

'Yes. I'm sure you must be glad, Papa.'

'Upon my word I'm not. He has bought a seat for three months; and with whose money?'

'Don't let us always speak of money, Papa.'

'They have let him in for his money because there are only a few months left before the general election. Two thousand pounds he has had, I believe?'

'And if as much more is wanted for the next election he shall have it.'

'Very well, my dear. I shall not complain though he should spend all your money, if you do not marry him at last.' In answer to this, Alice said nothing. On that point her father's wishes were fast growing to be identical with her own.

Then he left her, and it seemed to Alice that he had been very cruel. If he had spoken to her differently might she not even now have confessed everything to him? But herein Alice accused him wrongfully. He could not let her know that all that was done was with the view of driving her into John Grey's arms.

The next morning George went to her. Alice perceived that the gash on his face was nearly closed. The mark of existing anger was not there. He had come to her intending to be gentle, if it might be possible, as though he wished to try once again if the rôle of lover might be within his reach.

Alice was the first to speak. 'George, I am so glad that you have succeeded! I wish you joy with my whole heart.'

'Thanks, dearest. But before I say another word, let me acknowledge my debt. Unless you had aided me with your money I could not have succeeded.'

'Oh, George! Pray don't speak of that!'

'Let me rather speak of it at once, and have done.' He smiled and looked pleasant, as he used to do in those Swiss days.

'Well, then, speak and have done.'

'I need hardly say that I could not have stood for this last election without it; and I must try to make you understand that it is quite upon the cards that I may be forced to ask for another loan when the autumn comes.'

'You shall have it, George.'

'Thanks, Alice. And now I will tell you what I propose. You know that I have been reconciled—with a sort of reconciliation—to my grandfather? Well, when the next affair is over, I propose to tell him exactly how you and I then stand.'

'Do not go into that now, George. I want you to feel the full joy of your success, and you will do so more thoroughly if you will banish all these money troubles from your mind for a while.'

'They shall, at any rate, be banished while I am with you,' said he. 'There; let them go!' And he lifted up his right hand, and blew at the tips of his fingers.

It was a pretty bit of acting when he blew away his cares. But Alice saw through it, and he knew that she did so. The whole thing was uncomfortable to him. He must extract from her some show of sympathy, some spark of affection, true or pretended, in order that he might be enabled to speak of the

68

future without open embarrassment. How could even he take her money from her, unless he might presume that he stood with her upon some ground that belonged mutually to them both?

'I have already taken my seat,' said he.

'I saw that in the newspapers. My acquaintance among Members of Parliament is very small, but I see that you were introduced, as they call it, by one of the few men I do know. Is Mr Bott a friend of yours?'

'He is a vulgar ass,' said George. 'But he will get on in Parliament to a certain extent. His ambition, I take it, does not go beyond a desire to be parliamentary flunkey to a big man.'

'And yours?'

'Oh, there are some things, Alice, that a man does not tell to anyone. The schoolboy, when he sits down to make his rhymes, dares not say that he hopes to rival Milton; but he nurses such a hope. The preacher, when he preaches his sermon, does not whisper, even to his wife, his belief that thousands may perhaps be turned to repentance by the strength of his words; but he thinks that the thousand converts are possible.'

'And you, though you will not say so, intend to make your thousand converts in politics.'

'I like to hear you laugh at me—I do indeed. It does me good to hear your voice again with some touch of satire in it. It brings back the old days, the days to which I hope we may soon revert without pain. Shall it not be so, dearest?'

Her playful manner at once deserted her. 'I do not know,' she said, gloomily.

For a few minutes he sat silent fingering some article belonging to her which was lying on the table. It was a small steel paper-knife, of which the handle was cast and gilt; a thing of which the price may have been five shillings.

'Who gave you this paper-cutter?' he said, suddenly.

'It was given me by Mr Grey.'

He let it drop on to the table with a noise, and then pushed it from him, so that it fell on the other side, near to where she sat.

'George,' she said, as she stooped and picked it up, 'your violence is unreasonable; pray do not repeat it.'

'I did not mean it,' he said, 'and I beg your pardon. I was simply unfortunate in the article I selected. And who gave you this?' In saying which he took up a little ivory foot-rule that was folded up so as to bring it within the compass of three inches.

'It so happens that no one gave me that; I bought it at a stupid bazaar.'

'Then this will do. You shall give it me as a present, on the renewal of our love.'

'It is too poor a thing to give,' said she, speaking still more gloomily than she had done before.

'By no means; nothing is too poor if given in that way. Anything will do; a ribbon, a glove, a broken sixpence. Will you give me something that I may take, and, taking it, may know that your heart is given with it?'

'Take the rule, if you please,' she said.

'And about the heart?' he asked.

'I would so much rather talk about politics, George,' said she.

The cicatrice began to make itself very visible in his face, and the debonair manner was fast vanishing.

'Look here, Alice,' he said. 'I find it very hard to understand you. When you first loved me I understood that well enough. And when you quarrelled with me, judging somewhat harshly of my offences, I understood that also. When I heard that you had accepted the offer made to you by that gentleman in Cambridgeshire I understood it, and accused myself, not you, in that I had driven you to so fatal a remedy. And I understood it well when I heard that this cure had been too much for you. I meant no insult to the man when I upset his little toy just now. And Alice, I understood it also when you again consented to be my wife. I may have been vain to think so, but I believed that the old love had come back upon you, and again warmed your heart. But now your present behaviour makes all the rest a riddle. When last I was here I asked you for a kiss. If you are to be my wife you can have no shame in granting me such a request. What am I to think of such a promise if you deny me all customary signs of your affection?'

Still she said nothing. He had in his hand the little rule which she had told him that he might take, but he held it as though in doubt what he would do with it. 'Well, Alice, am I to hear anything from you?'

'Not now, George; you are angry, and I will not speak to you in your anger.'

'Have I not cause to be angry? Do you not know that you are treating me badly?'

'I know that my head aches, and that I am very wretched. I wish you would leave me.'

'There, then, is your gift,' said he, and he threw the rule over on to the sofa behind her. 'And there is the trumpery trinket which I had hoped you would have worn for my sake.' Whereupon something which he had taken from his waistcoat-pocket was thrown violently into the fender, beneath the fire-grate. He then walked with quick steps to the door; but when his hand was on the handle he turned. 'Alice,' he said, 'when I am gone, try to think honestly of your conduct to me.' Then he went, and she remained still, till she heard the front door close behind him.

Her first movement was made in search of the trinket. It was not that she had any desire for the jewel, or any curiosity even to see it. But she had a feminine reluctance that any-thing of value should be destroyed without a purpose. So she took the shovel, and poked among the ashes, and found the ring which her cousin had thrown there. It was a valuable ring, bearing a ruby on it between two small diamonds; but one of the side stones had been knocked out by the violence with which the ring had been flung. She searched even for this, scorching her face and eyes, but in vain. Then she made up her mind that the diamond should be lost for ever, and that it should go out among the cinders into the huge dust-heaps of the metropolis. Better that, though it was distasteful to her feminine economy, than the other alternative of setting the servants to search, and thereby telling them something of what had been done.

When her search was over, she placed the ring on the man-telpiece; but she knew that it would not do to leave it there, so she folded it up carefully in a new sheet of note-paper, and put it in the drawer of her desk. After that she sat herself down at the table to think what she would do; but her head was, in truth, racked with pain, and she could bring her thoughts to no conclusion.

CHAPTER FOUR

EARLY in April Lady Monk gave a grand party in London. Lady Monk's town house in Gloucester Square was a large mansion, and Lady Monk's parties in London were known to be very great affairs. It was generally acknowledged to be the proper thing to go to Lady Monk's parties. When she was first told that Mr Bott wanted to come she positively declined to have him. When it was afterwards intimated to her that Mr Palliser wished it, and that Mr Palliser probably would not come himself unless his wishes were gratified, she gave way. She was especially anxious that Lady Glencora should come to her gathering, and she knew that Lady Glencora could not be had without Mr Palliser.

It was very much desired by her that Lady Glencora should be there. 'Burgo,' said she to her nephew, who was staying with her, 'you see that she is not afraid of coming.'

'I suppose she doesn't think much about it,' said Burgo.

'If that's what you really believe, you'd better give it up. Nothing on earth would justify such a step on your part except a thorough conviction that she is attached to you.'

'I'd do it tomorrow if it depended on me. No one can say that I'm afraid of anybody or of anything. I've got no money,' said Burgo.

Lady Glencora's property was worth not less than fifty thousand a year. He was a young man ambitious of obtaining that almost incredible amount of wealth, and who once had nearly reached it, by means of her love.

'I've got no money for you, Burgo. I have not five pounds belonging to me.'

'You have jewels, Aunt. Could you not raise it for me? I would redeem them with the very first money I got.'

Lady Monk rose in a passion, but before the interview was over she had promised that she would endeavour to do something. Such love as she had to give she gave to Burgo, and she promised him money though she knew that she must raise it by some villainous falsehood to her husband.

On the same morning Lady Glencora went to Queen Anne Street with the purpose of inducing Alice to go to Lady Monk's party; but Alice would not accede to the proposition. 'I don't know her,' she said.

'My dear,' said Lady Glencora, 'half the people there won't know her.'

'But they know her set, or know her friends. I certainly shall not go. I can't conceive why you should wish it.'

'Mr Fitzgerald will be there,' said Lady Glencora, altering her voice altogether.

'That may be a reason for your staying away,' said Alice, slowly, 'but hardly a reason for my going with you.'

Lady Glencora would not condescend to tell her friend in so many words that she wanted her protection, though she wished it to be understood.

'Do you know, Alice, though they all say that Plantagenet is one of the wisest men in London, I sometimes think that he is one of the greatest fools. I told him that we had better not go to that woman's house. He simply said that he wished that I should do so. "There can be no reason why my wife should not go to Lady Monk's house as well as to any other," he said. He insists that I shall go, but he sends my duenna with me. Dear Mrs Marsham is to be there!'

'She'll do you no harm, I suppose?'

'I'm not so sure of that, Alice. I can fancy a woman being driven to do wrong simply by a desire to show her policeman that she can be too many for him.'

'Glencora, you make me so wretched when you talk like that.'

'Will you go with me, then, so that I may have a policeman of my own choosing?'

Alice hesitated a moment. 'It is against the whole tenor of my life's way,' she said. 'And, Glencora, I am not happy myself. I am not fit for parties. I sometimes think I shall never never trust you again.'

'Oh, very well,' said Lady Glencora. 'I suppose I shall get through it. If he asks me to dance I shall stand up with him, just as though I had never seen him before.' Then she remembered the letter in her pocket, remembered that at this moment she bore about with her a written proposition from this man to go off with him and leave her husband's house. 'You'll come to me the morning after,' said Lady Glencora, as she went. This Alice promised to do; and then she was left alone.

There had been another word or two between Burgo Fitzgerald and his aunt before the evening of Lady Monk's party came. She was prepared with two hundred pounds for him. 'Burgo,' she said, 'if I find that you deceive me now I will never trust you again.'

'All right,' said Burgo, as he barely counted the money before he thrust it into his breast-pocket.

On the morning of the party a few very uncomfortable words passed between Mr Palliser and his wife.

'Your cousin is not going, then?' said he.

'Alice is not going.'

'Then you can give Mrs Marsham a seat in your carriage?'

'Impossible, Plantagenet. I thought I had told you that I had promised my cousin Jane.'

'But you can take three.'

'You must know, Plantagenet, that it is impossible for three women dressed to go out in one carriage. I am sure you wouldn't like to see me afterwards if I had been one of them.'

'You need not have said anything to Lady Jane when Miss Vavasor refused. I had asked you before that.'

'And I had told you that I liked going with young women, and not with old ones.'

'Then, I suppose, the carriage must go for Mrs Marsham after it has taken you?'

74

'It shall go before. Jane will not be in a hurry, and I am sure I shall not.'

'She will think you very uncivil, that is all. I told her that she could go with you when I heard that Miss Vavasor was not to be there.'

'Then if it's only what she thinks I don't care two straws about it. She may have the carriage to herself if she likes, but she shan't have me in it. I don't like her, and I won't pretend to like her. My belief is that she follows me about to tell you if she thinks I do wrong.'

'Glencora!'

'And that odious baboon with the red bristles does the same thing; only he goes to her because he doesn't dare to go to you.'

Plantagenet Palliser was struck wild with dismay. He understood that it was Mr Bott whom his wife intended to describe; but that she should have spoken of any man as a baboon with red bristles was terrible to his mind! He was beginning to think that he hardly knew how to manage his wife.

When the evening came the carriage went first for Mrs Marsham, and having deposited her at Lady Monk's, went back to Park Lane for Lady Glencora. It was past eleven before Lady Glencora arrived, and Burgo Fitzgerald had begun to think that his evil stars intended that he should never see her again. He had settled in his mind no accurate plan of campaign. He had attempted to make some such plan, but concluded at last that he had better leave it to the course of events. He had written to her, making his proposition in bold terms, and he felt that if she were utterly decided against him her refusal would have been made known to him in some way. From ten o'clock to past eleven he stood about on the staircase of his aunt's house, waiting for the name which he almost feared to hear. Men spoke to him, and women also, but he hardly answered. 'Don't look so dreadfully preoccupied,' his aunt said to him in a whisper. But he shook his head at her, almost savagely, and went down into the dining-room. He took a large beer-glass full of champagne and soon after that another. The drink did not flush his cheeks or make his fore-

75

head red, or bring out the sweat-drops on his brow; but it added a peculiar brightness to his blue eyes. It was by the light of his eyes that men knew when Burgo had been drinking.

At last, while he was still in the supper-room, he heard Lady Glencora's name announced. He had already seen Mr Palliser come in and make his way upstairs some quarter of an hour before; but he had known that the husband was to be there. When the long-expected name reached his ears his heart seemed to jump within him. She was just above him as he got out into the hall. He looked up and moved his hand to her in salutation. She looked down at him, and the expression of her face altered visibly as her glance met his. She barely bowed to him—with her eyes rather than with her head—but there was, at any rate, no anger in her countenance. As she made her slow way up the stairs she felt that his eyes were on her, and where the stairs turned she could not restrain herself from one other glance. As her eyes fell on his again, his mouth opened, and she fancied that she could hear the faint sigh that he uttered. It was a glorious mouth, such as the old sculptors gave to their marble gods! And Burgo, if it was so that he had not heart enough to love truly, could look as though he loved. It was not in him deceit, or acting. At this moment Burgo Fitzgerald looked as though it were possible that he might die of love.

Just within the dancing-room Lady Glencora found her husband, standing in a corner, looking as though he were making calculations. 'I'm going away,' said he. 'I only just came because I said I would. Shall you be late?'

'Oh no; I suppose not.'

'Shall you dance?'

'Perhaps once, just to show that I'm not an old woman.'

'Don't heat yourself. Good-bye.' Then he went, and in the crush of the doorway he passed Burgo Fitzgerald, whose eye was intently fixed upon his wife. He looked at Burgo, and some thought of that young man's former hopes flashed across his mind—some remembrance, too, of a caution that had been whispered to him; but for no moment did a suspicion come to him that he ought to stop and watch by his wife.

Burgo made his way first into the front room and then into

the larger room where the dancing was in progress, and there he saw Lady Glencora. She looked at him softly and kindly, and though she uttered no word her countenance seemed to show that the meeting was not unpleasant to her.

'Will you waltz?' said Burgo, asking it exactly as he might have done had they been in the habit of dancing with each other every other night for the last three months.

Burgo waltzed excellently, and before her marriage Lady Glencora had been passionately fond of dancing. She seemed to give herself up to it now as though old days had come back to her. Lady Monk, creeping to the door between her den and the dancing-room, looked in on them, and then crept back again. Mrs Marsham and Mr Bott standing together just inside the other door, near to the staircase, looked on also—in horror.

'He shouldn't have gone away and left her,' said Mr Bott, almost hoarsely.

'But who could have thought it?' said Mrs Marsham. 'I'm sure I didn't.'

'I suppose you'd better tell him?' said Mr Bott.

The waltzers went on till they were stopped by want of breath. 'I am so much out of practice,' said Lady Glencora. 'I didn't think—I should have been able—to dance at all.'

'You'll take another turn?' said he.

'Presently,' said she, beginning to have some thought in her mind as to whether Mrs Marsham was watching her. Then there was a little pause, after which he spoke in an altered voice.

'Does it put you in mind of old days?' said he.

The words at once dissipated her dream. The facts all rushed upon her in an instant.

'You must not talk of that,' she said, very softly.

'May I not?' And now his tongue was unloosed, so that he began to speak quickly. 'And why not? They were happy days—so happy! Were not you happy when you thought . . .? Ah, dear! I suppose it is best not even to think of them?'

'Much the best.'

'Only it is impossible. I wish I knew the inside of your heart, Cora, so that I could see what it is that you really wish.'

In the old days he had always called her Cora, and now the name came upon her ears as a thing of custom, causing no surprise.

'You should not have come to me at all,' she said.

'And why not? Who has a better right to come to you? Who has ever loved you as I have done? Cora, did you get my letter?'

'Come and dance,' she said; 'I see a pair of eyes looking at us.' The pair of eyes which Lady Glencora saw were in the possession of Mr Bott, who was standing alone, leaning against the side of the doorway, every now and then raising his heels from the ground so that he might look down upon the sinners as from a vantage ground. Mrs Marsham had left him and had gone away in Lady Glencora's own carriage to Park Lane, in order that she might find Mr Palliser there.

But there were others besides Mr Bott who looked on and wondered. The Duchess of St Bungay shook her head sorrowing, for the Duchess was good at heart. Lady Monk also saw, and a frown gathered on her brow. 'The fool!' she said to herself. She knew that Burgo would not help his success by drawing down the eyes of all her guests upon his attempt. In the meantime Mr Bott stood there, mounting still higher on his toes, straightening his back against the wall.

'Did you get my letter?' Burgo said again, as soon as a moment's pause gave him breath to speak. She did not answer him. 'Let us go out upon the stairs,' he said. 'I must speak to you.'

'I wish I had not come here,' she said.

'Because you have seen me? That is not kind of you.'

They were now making their way slowly down the stairs, in the crowd, towards the supper-room.

'I'll get you some champagne with water in it,' said Burgo. 'I know that is what you like.'

They had now got into the room, and had escaped Mr Bott's eyes for the moment. 'Mr Fitzgerald'—and now her words had become a whisper in his ear—'do what I ask you. For the sake of the old days of which you spoke, the dear old days which can never come again . . .'

'By God they can!' said he. 'They can and they shall.'

78

'Never. But you can still do me a kindness. Go away, and leave me. You are doing me an injury while you remain with me. We are watched.' Mr Bott had now again got his eyes on them, round the supper-room door.

'Who is watching us?' said Burgo. 'And what does it matter? Come with me, abroad, and you shall yet be my wife. Come with me—tonight.'

'Mr Fitzgerald,' she said, 'I asked you to go and leave me. If you do not do so I must leave you. It will be much more difficult.'

'I will not go,' he said, leaning before her with utter indifference as to the eyes of any that might see them.

Looking up again towards the doorway, in fear of Mr Bott's eyes, she saw the face of Mr Palliser as he entered the room. Mr Bott had also seen him, and had tried to clutch him by the arm; but Mr Palliser had shaken him off, apparently with indifference. Lady Glencora, when she saw her husband, immediately recovered her courage. She would not cower before him, or show herself ashamed of what she had done. For the matter of that, if he pressed her on the subject, she could bring herself to tell him that she loved Burgo Fitzgerald much more easily than she could whisper such a word to Burgo himself. Mr Bott's eyes were odious to her as they watched her; but her husband's glance she could meet without quailing before it. 'Here is Mr Palliser,' said she, speaking again in her ordinary clear-toned voice.

Mr Palliser made his way as best he could through the crowd up to his wife. There was neither anger nor dismay in his face, nor was there any untoward hurry in his movement. Burgo stood aside as he came up, and Lady Glencora was the first to speak. 'I thought you were gone home hours ago,' she said.

'I did go home,' he answered, 'but I thought I might as well come back for you.'

'What a model of a husband! Well, I am ready. Mr Fitzgerald, I left a scarf in your aunt's room, a little black and yellow scarf. Would you mind getting it for me?'

'I will fetch it,' said Mr Palliser.

'If you will allow me . . .' said Burgo.

79

'I will do it,' said Mr Palliser; and away he went, making his slow progress up through the crowd, leaving Mr Bott still watching at the door.

There was a touch of chivalry in his leaving them again together which so far conquered her. He might have bade her leave the scarf and come at once. She had seen, moreover, that he had not spoken to Mr Bott, and was thankful to him also for that. Burgo seemed to have become aware that his chance for that time was over. 'I will say good night,' he said. 'Good night, Mr Fitzgerald,' she answered, giving him her hand. He pressed it for a moment, and then turned and went. When Mr Palliser came back he was no more to be seen.

Lady Glencora was at the dining-room door when her husband returned, standing close to Mr Bott. Mr Bott had spoken to her, but she made no reply. He spoke again, but her face remained as immovable as though she had been deaf. 'And what shall we do about Mrs Marsham?' she said, quite out loud, as soon as she put her hand on her husband's arm. 'I had forgotten her.'

'Mrs Marsham has gone home,' he replied.

'Have you seen her?'

'Yes.'

'When did you see her?'

'She came to Park Lane.'

These questions were asked and answered as he was putting her into the carriage.

'I suppose she went,' continued Lady Glencora, 'to tell you that I was dancing with Mr Fitzgerald. Was that it?'

'I think, Glencora, we had better not discuss it now.'

'I don't mean to discuss it now, or ever. If you did not wish me to see Mr Fitzgerald you should not have sent me to Lady Monk's. But, Plantagenet, I hope you will forgive me if I say that no consideration shall induce me to receive again as a guest, in my own house, either Mrs Marsham or Mr Bott.'

Mr Palliser absolutely declined to say anything on the subject on that occasion, and the evening of Lady Monk's party in this way came to an end.

.   .   .   .   .

George Vavasor was not in a very happy mood when he left Queen Anne Street, after having flung his gift ring under the grate. Alice was engaged to be his wife, and had as yet said nothing to show that she meditated any breach of that engagement, but she had treated him in a way which made him long to throw her promise in her teeth. He was in Parliament, but Parliament would be dissolved within three months. Having sacrificed so much for his position, should he let it all fall from him now? That wretched old man in Westmorland, who seemed gifted almost with immortality—why could he not die and surrender his paltry acres to one who could use them?

But he soon found himself talking to Mr Scruby as though there were no doubts as to the forthcoming funds for the next elections. In their discussion Mr Scruby injudiciously mentioned the name of Mr Tombe. No precise caution had been given to him, but he had become aware that the matter was being managed through an agency that was not recognized by his client, and he should have held his tongue. When George heard the name mentioned in connection with his own money matters he remembered that Mr Tombe was John Grey's lawyer. As soon as he could escape out into the street he set off for Mr Tombe's chambers.

Mr Tombe was at his desk. He rose as Vavasor entered, and bowed his head very meekly as he asked his visitor to sit down. 'Mr Vavasor; oh, yes.' He had heard the name. Yes, he was in the habit of acting for his very old friend Mr John Grey. There could not be a nicer gentleman than Mr John Grey. At every new sentence Mr Tombe caught his poor asthmatic breath, and bowed his meek old head, and wheezed apologetically, and seemed to ask pardon of his visitor for not knowing intuitively what was the nature of that visitor's business. But he was a sly old fox, and was considering all this time how much he should tell Mr Vavasor, and how much conceal. He would tell as little as he could; but he decided during his last wheeze that he could not lie in the matter with any chance of benefiting his client.

'Can you tell me, Mr Tombe,' said George, 'whether you or Mr Grey have anything to do with the payment of certain sums to my credit?'

'May I ask you why you put the question to me, Mr Vavasor?'

'I don't think you may.'

'Well, upon my word, you've taken me a little by surprise. Let me see. Pinkle—Pinkle!' Pinkle was a clerk who sat in an inner room. 'Pinkle, didn't we pay some money a few weeks since to the credit of Mr George Vavasor?'

'Did we, sir?' Pinkle had caught something of the fox nature himself.

'I think we did. Just look, Pinkle; and, Pinkle, see the date, and let me know all about it. It's fine bright weather for this time of year, Mr Vavasor; but these easterly winds!—ugh—ugh—ugh!'

Vavasor found himself sitting for an apparently interminable number of minutes in Mr Tombe's dingy chamber, and was coughed at, and wheezed at, till he began to be tired of his position.

'I'm sorry to give your clerk so much trouble,' he said in an angry voice. 'Surely you know whether Mr Grey has commissioned you to pay money for me?'

'We have so many things to do, Mr Vavasor; and so many clients. But I think there was something done. I do, indeed.'

'Perhaps it will be better that I should go to him, as you do not seem inclined to give me any information,' said George Then he took up his hat, and hardly bowing to Mr Tombe left the chambers. He knew Grey's London address, but whether he would be there, or at Nethercoats, he could not know. As it chanced, Grey was not only in London at that time, but was at home when Vavasor arrived at his lodgings.

'Will you take a chair, Mr Vavasor?' he said.

'No,' said Vavasor; 'I will stand up.' And he stood up, holding his hat behind his back with his left hand, with his right leg forward, and the thumb of his right hand in his waistcoat-pocket. He looked full into Grey's face, and Grey looked full into his; and as he looked the great cicatrice seemed to open itself and to become purple with fresh bloodstains.

'I have come here from Mr Tombe's office in the City,' said Vavasor, 'to ask you of what nature has been the interference which you have taken in my money matters.'

This was a question which Mr Grey could not answer very quickly. In the first place it was altogether unexpected; in the next place he did not know what Mr Tombe had told.

'When you have answered that,' George continued, 'I shall have other questions to ask you.'

'But, Mr Vavasor, has it occurred to you that I may not be disposed to answer?'

'If there has been such interference on your part I have a right to demand that you should explain to me its nature.'

'There has been such interference, Mr Vavasor, if you choose to call it so. Money, to the extent of two thousand pounds, I think, has by my directions been paid to your credit by Mr Tombe. I hardly know how to explain all the circumstances under which this has been done.'

'I dare say not; but, nevertheless, you must explain them.'

Grey was a man tranquil in temperament, very little prone to quarrelling, but he was a man whose courage was quite as high as that of his opponent. It was clear enough that Vavasor intended to bully him, and he made up his mind at once that if the quarrel were forced upon him it should find him ready to take his own part. 'My difficulty in explaining it comes from consideration for you,' he said. 'It was by agreement with your uncle that I commissioned Mr Tombe to raise for you the money you were desirous of borrowing from your cousin.'

'But what had you to do with it? Why should he come to you of all men to raise money on his daughter's behalf?'

'It was I who suggested to your uncle that this arrangement should be made. I did not wish to see Miss Vavasor's fortune squandered.'

'And what was her fortune to you, sir? Are you aware that she is engaged to me as my wife? I now find you meddling with her money matters, so as to get a hold upon her fortune.'

'I have no hold upon her fortune.'

'You do not advance two thousand pounds without knowing that you have security. She has rejected you; and in order that you may be revenged, or that you may have some further hold upon her, you have contrived this rascally pettifogging way of obtaining power over her income. The money shall be

83

repaid at once, with any interest that can be due; and if I find you interfering again I will expose you.'

'Mr Vavasor,' said Grey in a low tone of voice, but with something in his eye which would have told any bystander that he was much in earnest, 'you have used words which I cannot allow to pass. You must recall them.'

'What were the words? I said that you were a pettifogging rascal. I now repeat them.' As he spoke he put on his hat, so as to leave both his hands ready for action if action should be required.

Grey was much the larger man and much the stronger. The first thing he did was to open the door, and as he did so he became conscious that his mouth was full of blood from a sharp blow upon his face. Vavasor had struck him with his fist, and had cut his lip against his teeth. Then there came a scramble. Vavasor struck him repeatedly, but Grey was unconscious of the blows. He had but one object now in his mind, and that was kicking his assailant down the stairs. He forced him back through the door on to the landing, succeeded in pushing him down the first flight of steps, and had the satisfaction of seeing him sprawling on the landing-place.

Vavasor, when he raised himself, prepared to make another rush at the room, but before he could do so a man from below, hearing the noise, appeared. 'Mr Jones,' said Grey, speaking from above, 'if that gentleman does not leave the house, I must get you to search for a policeman.'

George Vavasor had no alternative but to relinquish the fight. He walked himself off, and went home to his lodgings in Cecil Street, that he might smooth his feathers after the late encounter before he went down to Westminster to take his seat in the House of Commons. He had not been hurt, but he had been worsted. He might probably have got over the annoyance of this feeling had he not been overwhelmed by a consciousness that everything was going badly with him. He was already beginning to hate his seat in Parliament. What good had it done for him, or was it likely to do for him? Two thousand pounds of his own money, and two thousand more of Alice's money—or Grey's—he had already spent to make his way into that assembly. He must spend, at any rate, two thousand more if he intended that his career should be prolonged beyond a three months' sitting; and how was he to get this further sum after what had taken place today?

He would get it. That was his resolve. As long as Alice had a pound over which he could obtain mastery by any act or violence within his compass he would get it; even though it should come through the hands of John Grey and Mr Tombe; even though in doing so he might destroy his cousin Alice and ruin his sister Kate. He had gone too far to stick at any scruples.

That wretched old man in Westmorland! If he would but die!

In fact, the old man was dying, attended by Kate Vavasor. Early one morning she crept silently into her grandfather's room, as was her habit; but he was apparently sleeping. The old servant told her that the squire had been awake at four, and at five, and at six. Then he had seemed to go to sleep. Four or five times in the course of the morning Kate went into the room, but her grandfather did not notice her. At last she feared he might already have passed away, and she put her hand upon his shoulder, and down his arm. He then gently touched her hand with his, showing her plainly that he was not only alive, but conscious. She then offered him the thin porridge which he was wont to take, and his medicine. She offered him some wine too, but he would take nothing.

At twelve o'clock a letter was brought to her. She saw that it was from Alice, and opening it found that it was very long. At that moment she could not read it, but she saw words in it that made her wish to know its contents as quickly as possible. But she could not leave her grandfather then. At two o'clock the doctor came to him, and remained there till the dusk of the evening had commenced. At eight o'clock the old man was dead.

Poor Kate's condition at the old Hall on that night was very sad. The old man who had just passed away upstairs was fully due to go. He had lived his span all out, and had himself known that to die was the one thing left for him to do. But death close to one is always sad as it is solemn.

It was late at night, near eleven, before Kate took out her

letter and read it. It had been written with great struggles, and with many tears, and made Kate almost forget that her grandfather was lying dead in the room above her.

Queen Anne Street, April, 186–.

Dearest Kate,

I hardly know how to write to you—what I have to tell, and yet I must tell it. The fact that your brother has quarrelled with me cannot be concealed from you, and I must not leave him to tell you of the manner of it. He came to me yesterday in great anger. He asked me how it had come to pass that I had sent him the money which he had asked of me through the hands of Mr Grey. Of course I had not done this. I had spoken of the matter to no one but Papa, and he had managed it for me. George disbelieved me, and said that I had conspired to lower him before the world.

I told him then that I should never become his wife. He swore, with a great oath, that if I went back a second time from my word to him he would leave me no peace—that he would deal me some fearful punishment. Oh, Kate, I cannot tell you what he looked like. He had then come quite close to me, as though he were going to strike me. Then he sat down and began to talk about money. I forget what he said at first, but I know that I assured him that he might take what he wanted so long as enough was left to prevent my being absolutely a burden on Papa.

He then desired me to write a letter to him which he might show to our lawyer, in order that money might be raised to pay back what Mr Grey had advanced, and give him what he now required. I think he said it was to be five thousand pounds. When he asked this I was unable to move. Then he swore at me again, demanding that I should write the letter. He came and sat by me, and took hold of my arms. He put his mouth close to my ear, and said words which were terrible, though I did not understand them. He was threatening me if I did not obey him. Before he left me, I found my voice to tell him that he should certainly have the money which he required. And so he shall. But I hope I may never be made to see my cousin again.

It is very possible that you will not believe all I say. Of course your heart will prompt you to accuse me rather than him; but I cannot keep all this back from you. He has treated me as I should have thought no man could have treated a woman. As regards money, I did all that I could do to show that I trusted him thoroughly, and my confidence has only led to suspicion. I do not know whether he understands that everything must be over between us; but, if not, I must ask you to tell him so. Nothing shall induce me to see him.

Yours always affectionately,
Alice Vavasor.

Kate found herself walking the room with quick, impetuous steps, hot with indignation. Not for a moment did she think of defending her brother. One o'clock, and two o'clock, still found her in the dark sombre parlour, every now and then pacing the floor of the room. The fire had gone out. Cold as she was, she wrote a letter. It was very short: 'Dear Alice, today I received your letter, and today our poor old grandfather died. Tell my uncle John of his father's death. You will understand that I cannot write much now about that other matter; but I must tell you, even at such a moment as this, that there shall be no quarrel between you and me. I have telegraphed to George, and I suppose he will come down. Uncle John will of course come or not as he thinks fitting.' And then she added a line below. 'My own Alice—If you will let me, you shall be my sister, and be the nearest to me and the dearest.'

Alice, when she received this, went immediately to her father and handed him Kate's letter. 'Of course I shall go down,' he said. 'What does she mean by saying that there shall be no quarrel between you and her?'

Alice said, 'I think I ought to tell you that everything is over between me and George.'

'Have you quarrelled with him too?'

'I cannot explain it to you in a hurry like this. Papa, you

may understand something of the shame I feel, and you should not question me now.'

'And John Grey?'

'There is nothing different in regard to him.'

'I'll be shot if I can understand you. George, you know, has had two thousand pounds of your money—of yours or somebody else's. Well, we can't talk about it now, as I must be off. Thinking as I do of George, I'm glad of it, that's all.'

Two days went by, and the hour of the funeral came. There was the doctor and the late squire's attorney, Mr Gogram, and the uncle and the nephew, to follow the corpse, the nephew taking upon himself ostentatiously the foremost place, as though he could thereby help to maintain his pretensions as heir. The funeral was very plain, and not a word was spoken by George Vavasor during the journey back. John Vavasor asked a few questions of the doctor as to the last weeks of his father's life; and it was incidentally mentioned, both by the doctor and by the attorney, that the old squire's intellect had remained unimpaired up to the last moment that he had been seen by either of them. When they returned to the Hall they all went to the dining-room, and drank each a glass of sherry. George took two or three glasses. The doctor then withdrew, and drove himself back to Penrith.

Mr Gogram pulled a document out of his pocket. John Vavasor stood behind one of the chairs and leaned upon it, looking across the roof, up at the ceiling. George stood on the rug before the fire, with his hands in the pockets of his trousers, and his coat tails over his arms.

Mr Gogram opened the document.

The will began by expressing the testator's desire that his property might descend in his own family, and that the house might be held and inhabited by someone bearing the name of Vavasor. He then declared that he felt himself obliged to pass over his natural heir, believing that the property would not be safe in his hands. He devised it to George's eldest son, should George ever marry and have a son, as soon as he might reach the age of twenty-five. In the meantime the property should remain in the hands of John Vavasor for his use and benefit, with a lien on it of five hundred a year to be paid annually to his grand-daughter Kate. In the event of George having no son, the property was to go to the eldest son of Kate, or failing that to the eldest son of his other grand-daughter who might take the name of Vavasor. All his personal property he left to his son, John Vavasor.

'It is as I supposed,' said George. His voice was very unpleasant, and so was the fire of his eyes and the ghastly rage of his scarred face. 'Where is his other will—the one he made before that?'

'If I remember rightly we executed two before this.'

'And where are they?'

'It is not my business to know, Mr Vavasor. I believe that I saw him destroy one, but I have no absolute knowledge. As to the other, I can say nothing.'

'And what do you mean to do?' said George, turning to his uncle.

'Do? I shall carry out the will. I have no alternative.'

George stood for a few moments thinking. Might it not be possible that by means of Alice and Kate together—by marrying the former—perhaps he might still obtain possession of the property? But that which he wanted was the command of the property at once, the power of raising money upon it instantly. The will had been so framed as to make that impossible in any way. Kate's share in it had not been left to her unconditionally, but was to be received even by her through the hands of her uncle John. Such a will shut him out from all his hopes. 'It is a piece of damned roguery,' he said.

'What do you mean by that, sir?' said Gogram.

'I mean exactly what I say. Who was in the room when that thing was written?'

'I was here with your grandfather.'

'And no one else?'

'No one else. The presence of anyone else at such a time would be very unusual.'

'Then I regard the document simply as waste paper.' George Vavasor left the room, and slammed the door after him.

'I never was insulted in such a way before,' said the attorney.

'He is a disappointed and I fear a ruined man,' said John Vavasor. 'I do not think you need regard what he says.'

The attorney went, having suggested to Mr Vavasor that he should instruct his attorney in London to take steps in reference to the proving of the will. 'It's as good a will as ever was made,' said Mr Gogram. 'If he can set that aside, I'll give up making wills altogether.'

George when he left the room went immediately across to the parlour in which his sister was sitting. 'Kate,' said he, 'put on your hat and come and walk with me. That business is over.' Kate's hat and shawl were in the room, and they were out of the house together within a minute.

'Which way shall we go?' said Kate. 'Up across the Fell,' said George; 'the day is fine, and I want to get away from my uncle for a time.'

They had reached the top of the beacon hill, and were out upon the Fell, before George began his story. Kate was half beside herself with curiosity, but still she was afraid to ask. 'Well,' said George, when they paused a moment as they stepped over a plank that crossed the boundary ditch of the wood: 'don't you want to know what that dear old man has done for you?' Then he looked into her face very steadfastly. 'But perhaps you know already.' He had come out determined not to quarrel with his sister. He had resolved that his best hope for the present required that he should keep himself on good terms with her, at any rate till he had settled what line of conduct he would pursue. But he was so sore with anger and disappointment, and that continued, unappeased wrath in which he now indulged against all the world, that he could not refrain himself from bitter words.

'I know nothing of it,' said Kate.

'I am beginning to doubt,' said he, 'whether a man can be safe in trusting anyone. My grandfather has done his best to rob me of the property altogether. He has made you his heir.'

'Me?'

'Yes, you.'

'Then, George, I shall do that which I once told him I should do in the event of his making such a will; I told him I should restore the estate to you, and upon that he swore that he would not leave it to me. I will sign anything necessary to make over my right in the property to you.'

'You can make over nothing,' he said. 'The old robber has been too cunning for that; he has left it all in the hands of my uncle John. Damn him. Damn them both.'

'George! George! He is dead now.'

'What of that? I wish he had been dead ten years ago, or twenty. Do you suppose I am to forgive him because he is dead? I'll heap his grave with curses.'

'You can only punish the living that way.'

'And I will punish them. My uncle John shall have such a life of it for the next year or two that he shall bitterly regret the hour he stepped between me and my rights.'

'I do not believe that he has done so.'

'Not done so! Do you pretend to think that that make-believe will was concocted without his knowledge?'

'I'm sure he knew nothing of it.'

'Look here, Kate; I do believe that you at any rate have no mind to assist in this robbery. That it is a robbery you can't have any doubt. I said he had left the estate to you. That is not what he has done. He has left the estate to my uncle John.'

'Why tell me, then, what was untrue?'

'Are you disappointed?'

'Of course I am; uncle John won't give it you. George, I don't understand you; I don't, indeed.'

'The estate is left in the hands of John Vavasor; but he has left you five hundred a year out of it till somebody is twenty-five years old who is not yet born, and probably never will be born. The will itself shows the old fool to have been mad.'

'He was no more mad than you are, George. If anybody asks me if his mind was gone, or his intellect was deranged, I cannot say that there was anything of the kind.'

'You will not?'

'Certainly not. It would be untrue.'

'Then you are determined to throw me over and claim the property for yourself. You had better take care, Kate.'

They were now upon the Fell side, more than three miles away from the Hall; and Kate, as she looked round, saw that they were all alone. Not a cottage, not a sign of humanity.

'Kate,' said he, 'you have made many promises to me, and I have believed them. You can now keep them all, by simply saying what you know to be the truth—that that old man was a drivelling idiot when he made this will. Think before you answer me, for, by God, if I cannot have justice among you, I will have revenge.' And he put his hand upon her breast up near to her throat.

'Take your hand down, George,' said she. 'I'm not such a fool that you can frighten me in that way.'

'Answer me!' he said, and shook her.

'I have answered you. I will say nothing of the kind that you want me to say. My grandfather, up to the latest moment that I saw him, knew what he was about. He was not an idiot. You will not make me change what I say by looking at me like that, nor get it by shaking me. You don't know me, George, if you think you can frighten me like a child.'

'Oh,' said he, when she had done, 'that's your idea of honesty. The very idea of the money being your own has been too much for you. I wonder whether you and my uncle had contrived it all between you beforehand?'

'You will not dare to ask him, because he is a man,' said Kate.

'You will see what I dare do. Say that you will do as I desire you, or I will be the death of you.'

'Do you mean you will murder me?'

'Murder you! Why not? Do you suppose I shall stick at anything? Why should I not murder you—you and Alice, too, seeing how you have betrayed me?'

'Poor Alice!'

'Poor Alice, indeed! Damned hypocrite! There's a pair of you; cursed, whining, false, intriguing hypocrites. There; go down and tell your uncle that I threatened to murder you. Tell the judge so, when you're brought into court to swear me out of my property. You false liar!' Then he pushed her from him with great violence, so that she fell heavily on the stony ground.

He did not stop to help her up, or even to look at her as she lay, but walked away across the heath. He went away northwards across the wild Fell. Kate, having risen up and seated herself on a small cairn of stones, watched him as he descended the slope of the hill till he was out of sight. He did not run, but he seemed to move rapidly, and he never once turned round to look at her. As he passed from out of her sight it seemed to her as though he were rushing straight into some hell from which there could be no escape.

When he had been gone some ten minutes, she rose to her feet, finding that the movement pained her greatly and that her right arm was powerless. She put up her left hand and became aware that the bone of her arm was broken below the elbow. She started off to walk down home, holding her right arm steadily against her body with her left hand. When she got into the wood the path was very dark. The heavens were overcast with clouds, and a few drops began to fall. Then the rain fell faster and faster, and before she had gone a quarter of a mile down the beacon hill the clouds had opened themselves and the shower had become a storm of water. Suffering as she was she stood for a few moments under a large tree. Then it occurred to her that she might possibly meet him again before she reached the house; and she began for the first time to fear him. Would he come out from the trees and really kill her? She made a little attempt to run, but running was impracticable from the pain the movement caused her. Then she walked on through the hard rain, steadily holding her arm against her side, but still looking every moment through the trees on the side from which George might be expected to reach her. But no one came near her on her way homewards. He had gone away altogether, across the fells. The Fury was driving him on, and he himself was not aware whither he was driven.

It was just five when Kate reached the front door of the Hall. This she opened with her left hand, and turning at once into the dining-room found her uncle standing before the fire.

'You are wet, Kate,' said John Vavasor. 'Where is George?'

Kate seated herself in her chair. 'I don't quite know where

he is,' she said. 'My arm, my arm!' Then she slipped down and had fainted.

John Vavasor stood confounded, wishing himself back in Queen Anne Street.

CHAPTER FIVE

LADY GLENCORA had played her part very well after Lady Monk's party. She had declined to be frightened by her husband; had been the first to mention Burgo's name, and had done so with no tremor in her voice. While she was in the carriage with her husband she felt some triumph in her own strength; and as she wished him good night on the staircase, and slowly walked up to her room, without having once lowered her eyes before his, something of this consciousness of triumph still supported her. But when she was alone all her triumph departed from her.

She bade her maid go while she was still sitting in her dressing-gown; and when the girl was gone she got close over the fire, sitting with her slippers on the fender, with her elbows on her knees, and her face resting on her hands. In this position she remained for an hour, with her eyes fixed on the altering shapes of the hot coals; and then, when the coals were no longer red, and the shapes altered themselves no more, she crept into bed.

Exactly at half-past eleven the following morning she entered the little breakfast parlour. Mr Palliser was sitting with the morning paper in his hand. He rose when she entered, and just touched her with his lips.

'Have you any headache this morning?' he asked.

'Oh, no,' she said. Then he spoke some word to her about the fineness of the weather, told her some scraps of news, and soon returned to the absorbing interest of a possible break-up in the Cabinet, as to which the rumours were, he said, so rife through the country as to have destroyed all feeling of security in the existing Government. If such rupture were to take place, it must be in his favour. He felt himself at this moment to be full of politics, to be near the object of his ambition, to have affairs upon his hands which required all his attention. Was it absolutely incumbent on him to refer again to the incidents of last night? He was deferring the evil moment. She had no newspaper, and made no endeavour to deceive herself.

'Plantagenet,' she said, 'you told me last night that you had something to say about Lady Monk's party.'

He put down the newspaper slowly, and turned towards her. 'Yes, my dear. After what happened I believe I must say something.'

'If you think anything, pray say it,' said Glencora. She settled herself in her chair with an air of mockery which her husband did not love to see.

'Do you know why Mrs Marsham came here from Lady Monk's last night?' he began.

'Of course I do. She came to tell you that I was waltzing with Burgo Fitzgerald. You might as well ask me whether I knew Mr Bott was standing at all the doors, glaring at me.'

'I don't know anything about Mr Bott.'

'I know something about him though,' she said.

'I am speaking now of Mrs Marsham.'

'You should speak of them both together as they hunt in couples.'

'Mrs Marsham came here, not simply to tell me that you were waltzing with Mr Fitzgerald.'

'And it was not simply to see me waltzing that Mr Bott stood in the doorways.'

'Glencora, will you oblige me by not speaking of Mr Bott?'

'I wish you would oblige me by not speaking of Mrs Marsham.'

'Mrs Marsham came here because she saw that everyone in the room was regarding you with wonder. She saw that you were not only dancing with Mr Fitzgerald, but that you were dancing with him—what shall I say?'

'Upon my word I can't tell you.'

'Recklessly.'

'Oh! What was I reckless of?'

'Reckless of what people might say; reckless of what I might feel about it; reckless of your own position. I think she was right to come to me.'

'What's the good of having spies, if they don't run and tell as soon as they see anything—reckless.'

'Glencora, you are determined to make me angry. I have employed no spies. If it were ever to come to that it would be all over with me.'

There was something of feeling in his voice as he said this —something that almost approached to passion which touched his wife's heart. She knew that she had in truth done that of which he had never suspected her. She had listened to words of love from her former lover. She had received and now carried about with her a letter from this man, in which he asked her to elope with him. She had by no means resolved that she would not do this thing.

'I know that I have never made you happy,' she said.

He saw that her whole manner and demeanour were changed. 'I do not understand what you mean,' he said. 'You have not made me unhappy.'

But now her heart was loosed and she spoke out, at first slowly, but after a while with strong passion. 'No, Plantagenet; I shall never make you happy. You have never loved me, nor I you. We have never loved each other for a single moment. I have been wrong to talk to you about spies; I was wrong to go to Lady Monk's; I have been wrong in everything that I have done; but never so wrong as when I let them persuade me to be your wife.'

'Glencora!'

'Let me speak now, Plantagenet. It is better that I should tell you everything; and I will. I do love Burgo Fitzgerald. I do! I do! I do! When I went to Lady Monk's last night I had almost made up my mind that I must tell him so, and that I must go away with him. But when he came to speak to me . . .'

'He has asked you to go with him, then?'

'Would it not have been best for you? Plantagenet, I do

not love you as women love their husbands when they do love them. But, before God, my first wish is to free you from the misfortune that I have brought on you.' She started up from her chair and took him by the coat.

'What matters it whether I throw myself away by going with such a one as him, so that you might marry again, and have a child?'

Softly, slowly, very gradually, as though he were afraid of what he was doing, he put his arm round her waist. 'You are wrong in one thing,' he said. 'I do love you.'

She shook her head, touching his breast with her hair as she did so.

'I do love you,' he repeated. 'If you mean that I am not apt at telling you so, it is true. My mind is running on other things. But I do love you. If you cannot love me, it is a great misfortune to us both. As for that other thing, of our having, as yet, no child'—and in saying this he pressed her somewhat closer with his arm—'you allow yourself to think too much of it; much more of it than I do.'

'I know what your thoughts are, Plantagenet.'

'I would rather have you for my wife, childless, if you will try to love me, than any other woman, though another might give me an heir. Will you try to love me?'

She was silent. At this moment, after the confession that she had made, she could not bring herself to say that she would even try.

'I think, dear,' he said, still holding her by her waist, 'that we had better leave England for a while. I will give up politics for this season. Should you like to go to Switzerland for the summer, and then on to Italy when the weather is cold enough?' Still she was silent. 'Perhaps your friend, Miss Vavasor, would go with us?'

He was killing her by his goodness. She could not speak to him yet; but now, as he mentioned Alice's name, she gently put up her hand and rested it on the back of his.

At that moment there came a knock at the door, a sharp knock, which was quickly repeated.

'Come in,' said Mr Palliser, dropping his arm from his wife's waist, and standing away from her.

97

It was the butler who had knocked, showing that the knock was of importance.

'If you please, sir, the Duke of St Bungay is here.'

'The Duke of St Bungay!'

'Yes, sir, his Grace is in the library.'

'Tell his grace I will be with him in two minutes.' Then the butler retired, and Mr Palliser was again alone with his wife.

'I must go now, my dear,' he said; 'and perhaps I shall not see you again till the evening.'

'Don't let me put you out in any way,' she answered. 'You must not think more of Italy. He has come to tell you that you are wanted in the Cabinet.'

He turned very red. 'It may be so,' he answered, 'but though I am wanted, I need not go. But I must not keep the Duke waiting. Good-bye.' And he turned to the door.

She followed him and took hold of him as he went, so that he was forced to turn to her once again. She managed to get hold of both his hands, and pressed them closely, looking up into his face with her eyes laden with tears. He smiled at her gently, returned the pressure of the hands, and then left her, without kissing her.

As soon as she was alone she took that letter from her pocket, and tearing it into very small fragments, without reading it, threw the pieces on the fire.

Mr Palliser had not time for much thought before he found himself closeted with the Duke. 'Duke,' he said, 'I'm afraid I have kept you waiting.'

'And I suppose you guess why I'm come?' said the Duke. 'He has resigned at last. I am here to ask you to take his place.' The Duke had been the first to declare that Plantagenet Palliser was the coming Chancellor of the Exchequer; and it had been long known that the Duke did not sit comfortably in the same Cabinet with the gentleman who had now resigned.

'I am afraid I must decline the offer you bring me,' said Mr Palliser.

'Decline it!'

'I fear I must.'

'Nonsense, Palliser. You must have got some false notion

into your head. There can be no possible reason why you should not join us.'

'I have promised to take my wife abroad.'

'Then you have made a promise which it behoves you to break. I am sure Lady Glencora will see it in that light.'

'If you will allow me, Duke. My wife has told me that, this morning, which makes me feel that absence from England is requisite for her present comfort. I was with her when you came and had just promised her that she should go.'

'But, Palliser, think of it. A man in your position has public duties. He owes his services to his country.'

'When a man has given his word, it cannot be right that he should go back from that.'

'A man may be absolved from a promise. Lady Glencora . . .'

'My wife would, of course, absolve me. It is not that. Her happiness demands it, and it is partly my fault that it is so. I cannot explain to you more fully why it is that I must give up the great object for which I have striven with all my strength.'

'Oh, no!' said the Duke. 'If you are sure that it is imperative . . .'

'It is imperative.'

'I could give you twenty-four hours, you know.' Mr. Palliser did not answer at once, and the Duke thought that he saw some sign of hesitation. 'I suppose it would not be possible that I should speak to Lady Glencora?'

'It could be of no avail, Duke. She would only declare that she would remain in London; but it would not be the less my duty to take her abroad.'

'Well, of course, I can't say. You are throwing away from you the finest political position that the world can offer to the ambition of any man. That a man under thirty should be thought fit to be Chancellor of the Exchequer, and should refuse it, because he wants to take his wife abroad! Palliser, if she were dying, you should remain under such an emergency as this. She might go, but you should remain.'

Mr Palliser remained silent for a moment or two, then

99

rose and walked towards the window. 'There are things worse than death,' he said, when his back was turned.

.   .   .   .   .

One morning, early in May, a servant in grand livery got out of a cab at the door in Queen Anne Street and sent up a note for Miss Vavasor. The message was from Lady Glencora. 'Do come—instantly if you can. I have so much to tell you, and so much to ask of you.'

Alice found her friend in the small breakfast-room upstairs, sitting close by the window. They had not met since the evening of Lady Monk's party, nor had Lady Glencora seen Alice in the mourning which she now wore for her grandfather. 'Oh, dear, what a change it makes in you,' she said. 'I never thought of your being in black.'

'I don't know what it is you want, but shan't I do in mourning as well as I would in colours?'

'You'll do in anything, dear. But do take your bonnet off, for I shall be hours in doing it. I don't know how to begin.'

'Hours in telling me!'

'Yes; and in getting your consent to what I want you to do. I'm to be taken abroad immediately, and you are to be one of the party.'

'I!'

'My husband is to take us.'

'But Mr Palliser can't leave London at this time of the year?'

'It's all settled. We are to be off next Tuesday night, if you can make yourself ready.'

'Why is Mr Palliser going abroad in the middle of Parliament in this way?'

'Alice, you must swear that you won't repeat what I'm going to tell you now. They have asked him to be Chancellor of the Exchequer, and he has refused. Think of that.'

'But why?'

'Because of me—of me, and my folly, and wickedness, and abominations. Because he has been fool enough to plague himself with a wife—he who of all men ought to have kept himself free from such troubles. Oh, he has been so good! If you could know how he has longed for this office; how he has worked for it day and night, wearing his eyes out with figures when everybody else has been asleep, shutting himself up with such creatures as Mr Bott when other men have been shooting and hunting and flirting and spending their money. This has been his excitement—what racing and gambling are to other men. At last, the place was there, ready for him, and they offered it to him. They begged him to take it, almost on their knees. The Duke of St Bungay was here all one morning about it; but Mr Palliser sent him away, and refused the place.'

'But why?'

'I keep on telling you—because of me.' Then Lady Glencora told her the story of Lady Monk's ball, and of all that had eventuated from it. 'And for my sake you will go with us?' she concluded. 'He understands himself that I am not fit to have no companion but him. Now there is a spirit of wisdom about you that will do for him, and a spirit of folly that will suit me. I can manage to put myself on a par with a girl who has played such a wild game with her lovers as you have done.'

Alice had undertaken to go down to Westmorland and comfort Kate in the affliction of her broken arm. 'And I must go,' she said, remembering how necessary it was that she should plead her own cause with George Vavasor's sister. But it was at last decided that the Pallisers should postpone their journey for four or five days, and that Alice should go with them immediately upon her return from Vavasor Hall.

Mr Palliser took his wife down to Matching Priory, having obtained leave to be absent from the House for the remainder of the Session, and remained with her there till within two days of their departure. That week down at Matching, as she afterwards told Alice, was very terrible. He never spoke a word to rebuke her. He treated her with a respect that was perfect, and with more outward signs of affection than had ever been customary with him. He went with his wife hither and thither, allowing himself to be driven about behind Dandy and Flirt. He himself proposed these little excursions. They were tedious to him, but doubly tedious to his wife, who now found it more difficult than ever to talk to him. She struggled to talk, and he struggled to talk, but the very struggles themselves made the thing impossible. He sat with her in the mornings, and he sat with her in the evenings; he breakfasted with her, lunched with her, and dined with her. He went to bed early, having no figures which now claimed his attention. And so the week at last wore itself away. 'I saw him yawning sometimes,' Lady Glencora said afterwards, 'as though he would fall in pieces.'

.   .   .   .   .

They stayed in Paris for a week, and then went to Lucerne by Basle, and put up at the big hotel with the balcony over the Rhine, which Alice remembered so well. On the first evening of her arrival she found herself again looking down upon the river, as though it might have been from the same spot which she had occupied together with George and Kate. Here, on this very spot, was brought to her a letter from her cousin, Kate. 'George has lost his election,' the letter began. For one moment Alice thought of her money. For one moment, something like regret for the futility of the effort she had made came upon her. But it passed away at once. 'It was worth our while to try it,' she said to herself, and then went on with her letter.

Mr Palliser was seated in the same balcony, almost buried in newspapers which conveyed intelligence as to the general elections then in progress. Lady Glencora was standing on the other side of him, and she also had received letters. 'Sophy tells me that you are returned for Silverbridge,' she said at last.

'Who? I! Yes, I'm returned,' said Mr Palliser, with something like disdain in his voice as to the possibility of anybody having stood with a chance of success against him in his own family borough. 'I'm sorry to see, Miss Vavasor, that your cousin has not been so fortunate.'

'So I find,' said Alice. 'It will be a great misfortune to him.'

On the day after that Mr Palliser and his party went on to

Lucerne. Mr Palliser did not much enjoy this part of his tour abroad. When he first reached Lucerne there was no one there with whom he could associate pleasantly. He did not care for scenery. He had none of that passion for mountains and lakes which would have compensated many another man for the loss of all that Mr Palliser was losing. His mind was ever at home in the House of Commons, or in that august assembly which men call the Cabinet, of the meetings of which he read from week to week.

Lady Glencora herself had a love for the mountains and lakes, but it was a love of that kind which requires to be stimulated by society, and which is keenest among cold chickens, picnic-pies, and the flying of champagne corks. When they first entered Switzerland she was very enthusiastic, and declared her intention of climbing up all the mountains, and going through all the passes. But by the time they were settled at Lucerne she had voted the mountains to be bores, and had almost learned to hate the lake.

Mr Palliser had put the ladies into their carriage, and was standing between the front door of the hotel and the lake on a certain day, doubting whether he would walk up the hill or turn into the town, when he was accosted by an English gentleman, who, raising his hat, said that he believed that he spoke to Mr Palliser.

'My name is John Grey,' said the stranger.

Mr Palliser put out his hand. After the interchange of a very few words the two men started off for a walk together.

When Mr Palliser, on his return, was seen by Alice and Lady Glencora, he was alone. They dined together and nothing was said. Together they sauntered out in the evening, and together came in and drank their tea; but still nothing was said. At last, Alice and her cousin took their candles from Mr Palliser's hands and left the sitting-room for the night.

'Alice,' said Lady Glencora, as soon as they were in the passage together. 'I have been dying for this time to come. Let us go into your room at once. Who do you think is here, at Lucerne, at this very moment?'

'Who is it, Glencora?' Alice asked, very calmly.

'Mr John Grey has come.' Then Lady Glencora paused for

a moment, waiting that Alice might say something. But Alice said nothing. 'Well?' said Lady Glencora. 'Well?'

'Well?' said Alice.

'Have you nothing to say? Is it the same to you as though Mr Smith had come?'

'No; not exactly the same. I am quite alive to the importance of Mr Grey's arrival, and shall probably lie awake all night thinking about it; but I don't feel that I have much to say about it. His being here will do no good to anyone.'

'No good! Look here, Alice. If you do not altogether make it up with him before tomorrow evening I shall believe you to be utterly heartless. Had I been you I should have been in his arms before this. I'll go now, and leave you to lie awake, as you say you will.' Then she left the room, but returned in a moment to ask another question. 'What is Plantagenet to say to him about seeing you tomorrow? Of course he has asked permission to call.'

'He may come if he pleases. You don't think I have quarrelled with him, or would refuse to see him!'

'And may we ask him to dine with us?'

'Oh, yes.'

'And make up a picnic, and all the rest of it. In fact, he is to be regarded as only an ordinary person. Well—good night. I don't understand you, that's all.'

But Mr Grey did not wait till dinner-time to see Alice. Early in the morning his card was brought up, and Lady Glencora, as soon as she saw the name, immediately ran away.

'You need not go,' said Alice.

'Indeed I shall go,' said her ladyship. 'I know what's proper on these occasions, if you don't.'

So she went, whisking herself along the passages with a little run; and Mr Grey, as he was shown into her ladyship's usual sitting-room, saw the skirt of her ladyship's dress as she whisked herself off towards her husband.

He took Alice's hand, and held it, pressing it warmly. She hardly knew with what words first to address him.

'I am very glad to see you—as an old friend,' she said; 'but I hope . . .'

'You hope what?'

'I hope you have had some better cause for travelling than a desire to see me?'

'No, dearest; no. I have come on purpose to see you; and had Mr Palliser taken you off to Asia or Africa, I think I should have felt myself compelled to follow him. You know why I follow you?'

'I am not fit to be your wife.'

'I am the best judge of that, Alice. You have to make up your mind whether I am fit to be your husband.'

'You would be disgraced if you were to take me, after all that has passed—after what I have done. What would other men say of you when they knew the story?'

'I don't very much care what men say of me.'

'But I care, Mr Grey; and though you may forgive me, I cannot forgive myself. I have done that which makes me feel that I have no right to marry anyone.' These words she said, jerking out the different sentences almost in convulsions; and when she had come to the end of them, the tears were streaming down her cheeks. 'I have thought about it, and I will not. I will not. After what has passed, I know that it will be better, more seemly, that I should remain as I am.'

Soon after that she left him; not, however, till she had told him that she would meet him again at dinner, and had begged him to treat her simply as a friend. 'In spite of everything, I hope that we may always be dear friends,' she said.

'I hope we may,' he answered; 'the very dearest.'

In the afternoon he again encountered Mr Palliser, and having thought over the matter since his interview with Alice he resolved to tell his whole story to his new acquaintance, not in order that he might ask for counsel from him, for in this matter he wanted no man's advice, but that he might get some assistance. So the two men walked off together.

So great had been the desolation of Mr Palliser's life since his banishment from London that he almost felt tempted in return to tell the story of his troubles to this absolute stranger. But he bethought himself of the blood of the Pallisers, and refrained. There are comforts which royalty may never enjoy, and luxuries in which such men as Plantagenet Palliser may not permit themselves to indulge.

The little dinner-party that evening was pleasant enough, and nothing more was said about love. Lady Glencora talked nonsense to Mr Grey, and Mr Palliser contradicted all the nonsense which his wife talked. It was tacitly admitted among them that Mr Grey was to be allowed to come among them as a friend, and Lady Glencora managed to say one word to him aside, in which she promised to give him her most cordial co-operation.

.　　　.　　　.　　　.　　　.

Before resolving to travel to Lucerne Mr Grey had undergone another quarrel with George Vavasor. It has been already said that George Vavasor lost his election for the Chelsea Districts, after all the money which he had spent. There he was, ex-Member of Parliament, with five hundred pounds left in his pocket, and little or nothing else that he could call his own. What was he to do with himself?

At his lodgings in Cecil Street he endeavoured to consider calmly his position in the world. He had lost his inheritance. He had abandoned one profession after another. He had estranged from himself every friend that he had ever possessed. He had driven from him with violence the devotion even of his sister. He had robbed the girl whom he intended to marry of her money, and had so insulted her that no feeling of amity between them was any longer possible.

From the moment in which he had first become convinced that the election would go against him he had resolved that he would be calm amidst his ruin. Sometimes he assumed a little smile, as though he were laughing at his own position. There came to him a moment in which he laughed out very audibly, rising up from his chair and walking about the room, holding a large paper-knife in his hand. Then he threw the knife away from him, and thrusting his hands into his trousers-pockets, laughed again. He stood still in the centre of the room, and the laughter was very plainly visible on his face, had there been anybody there to see it.

But suddenly there was a change upon his face, as he stood

there all alone, and his eyes became fierce, and the cicatrice that marred his countenance grew to be red and ghastly, and he clenched his fists as he still held them within his pockets. A bottle of brandy stood near him. He half filled a tumbler, and then, dashing some water on it, swallowed it greedily.

He went to a desk and took out a revolving pistol. He looked at it, and tried the lock, and snapped it without caps, to see that the barrel went round fairly. Then he poured out more brandy-and-water. After that he took up some papers, referring to steam packets, which were lying on his table. They showed how one vessel went on one day to New York, and another on another day would take out a load of emigrants for New Zealand and Australia.

He remained up half the night destroying papers. All the pigeon-holes of his desk were emptied out and their contents thrown into the flames. At first he looked at the papers before he burned them; but the trouble of doing so soon tired him and he condemned them all, without examination. Then he selected a considerable amount of his clothes, and packed up two portmanteaus. When that was done he took from his desk a bag of sovereigns and divided them among the two portmanteaus.

He was up early the next morning, and had some coffee brought to him, and as he drank it he had an interview with his landlady. He was going, he said; going that very day. He would pay her then what he owed her and what would be due for her lodgings under a week's notice. The woman stared, and curtseyed, and took her money. Vavasor, though he had lately been much pressed for money, had never been so foolish as to owe debts where he lived. 'There will be some things left about, Mrs Bunsby,' he said. 'I will get you to keep them till I call or send.'

When he was left alone he put on a rough morning coat, placed the pistol carefully in his pocket, and sallied forth to the house where John Grey lodged.

Vavasor rang the bell, and as soon as the servant came he went quickly into the house. The girl said that Mr Grey was at home, but suggested that she had better announce the gentleman. But Vavasor was already halfway up the stairs, and before the girl had reached the first landing-place he had entered Mr Grey's room and closed the door behind him.

Grey was sitting near the open window. He rose from his chair quickly. 'Mr Vavasor,' he said, 'I hardly expected to see you in my lodgings again!'

'I dare say not,' said Vavasor; 'but, nevertheless, here I am.' He kept his right hand in the pocket which held the pistol.

'May I ask why you have come?' said Grey.

'I intend to tell you, in your own hearing, as I am in the habit of doing occasionally behind your back, that you are a blackguard—to spit in your face, and defy you.'

'Nothing that you can say to me, Mr Vavasor, will have any effect upon me; except that you can, of course, annoy me.'

'And I mean to annoy you, too, before I have done with you. Will you fight me?'

'Fight a duel with you? Certainly not.'

'You are a coward, and a liar, and a blackguard. I have given you the option of behaving like a gentleman, and you have refused it. Now, look here. I have come here with arms, and I do not intend to leave this room without using them, unless you will promise to give me the meeting I have proposed.' And he took the pistol out of his pocket.

'Do you mean you are going to murder me?' Grey asked. His visitor was standing immediately between him and the door. Grey was by no means a timid man. He did not think, even now, that this disappointed, ruined man had come there with any intention of killing him. But he knew that a pistol in the hands of an angry man is dangerous.

He thought of rushing across the room at his adversary, calculating that a shot fired at him as he did so might miss him, and that he would then have a fair chance of disarming the madman. He made, instead, towards the bell, trusting that Vavasor would not fire. He heard the click of the pistol's hammer as it fell, and was aware that his eyes were dazzled, though he was unconscious of seeing any flame. He felt something in the air, but he did not know whether the shot had struck him or had missed him. His hand was out for the bell-handle, and he had pulled it before he was sure that he was unhurt.

'Damnation!' exclaimed the murderer. But he did not pull the trigger again. There were five other chambers for him, each making itself ready by the discharge of the other. But he had paused, forgetting, in his excitement, the use of his weapon, and before he had bethought himself that the man was still in his power he heard the sound of the bell. 'Damnation!' he exclaimed. Then he turned round, left the room, hurried down the stairs, and made his way out into the street.

Grey turned round to look for the bullet or its mark. He soon found the little hole in the window-shutter, and probing it with the point of his pencil came upon the morsel of lead which might now just as readily have been within his own brain. Then he made some calculation, and found, from the height of the hole, that the shot must have passed close beneath his ear.

Would he put the police at once upon the track of the murderer, who was, as he remembered too well, the first cousin of the woman whom he still desired to make his wife? That he was called upon by duty to do something he felt almost assured. The man who had been allowed to make such an attempt once with impunity might probably make it again.

At eleven o'clock he went to Scotland Yard and told some high officer all the circumstances. Towards evening a policeman in plain clothes paid a visit to Vavasor's lodgings in Cecil Street. But Vavasor lodged there no longer. At that moment he was leaning over the side of an American steamer which had just got up steam and weighed her anchor in the Mersey. Of course, it was soon known that he had gone to America, but it was not thought worth while to take any further steps towards arresting him.

To Kate, down in Westmorland, no tidings came of her brother. Mr Grey himself told the story to no one, till he told it to Mr Palliser at Lucerne.

They continued to live at Lucerne for a fortnight after Grey's arrival. Though he was not unfrequently alone with Alice he did not plead his suit in direct words. He understood that she must be taught to forgive herself. Thus they all went on together at Lucerne, passing quiet, idle days, with some pretence of reading, with a considerable amount of letter-writing, with boat excursions and pony excursions, till the pony excursions came to a sudden end by means of a violent edict. Lady Glencora had whispered into her husband's ear that she thought it probable—she wasn't sure—she didn't know. And then she burst out into tears on his bosom as he sat by her on her bedside.

When he left her he did not quite remember where he was, or what he was doing. The one thing in the world which he had lacked; the one joy which he had wanted so much, and which is so common among men, was coming to him also. In a few minutes it was to him as though each hand already rested on the fair head of a little male Palliser, of whom one should rule in the halls at Gatherum, and the other be eloquent among the Commons of England.

He then remembered that he had promised to send Alice up to his wife. She was alone in the breakfast-room. She perceived at once that some matter was astir. 'Alice,' he said, 'would you mind going up to Glencora's room? She wishes to speak to you.' He had never called her Alice before, and as soon as the word was spoken he remembered himself and blushed.

'She isn't ill, I hope?' said Alice.

'No; she isn't ill. At least I think she had better not get up quite yet. Don't let her excite herself, if you can help it.'

'I'll go to her at once,' said Alice, rising.

'I'm so much obliged to you. But, if you please, do be as calm with her as you can. She is so easily excited, you know. Of course, if there's anything she fancies, we'll take care to get it for her; but she must be kept quiet.'

When Alice entered the room, her friend was up and in her dressing-gown, lying on a sofa. 'Oh, Alice, I'm so glad you've come,' said Lady Glencora. Then Alice knelt beside her, and asked her if she were ill.

'He hasn't told you? But of course he wouldn't. But, Alice, how did he look? Did you observe anything about him? Was he pleased?'

'I did observe something, and I think he was pleased. He

called me Alice and seemed quite unlike himself. But what is it?'

'Oh, Alice, can't you guess?' Then suddenly Alice did guess the secret, and whispered her guess into Lady Glencora's ear. 'I suppose it is so,' said Lady Glencora. 'I know what they'll do. They'll kill me by fussing over me. If I could go about my work like a washerwoman I should be all right.'

'We shall all have to go home, I suppose?' said Alice.

'He says so; but he seems to think that I oughtn't to travel above a mile and a half a day. When I talked of going down the Rhine in one of the steamers, I thought he would have gone into a fit. I know he'll make a goose of himself; and he'll make geese of us, which is worse.'

When the first consternation arising from the news had somewhat subsided, and when tidings had been duly sent to the Duke, and a gratified answer from his Grace had come, arrangements were made for the return of the party to England. There was great trouble about the mode of their return.

'Oh, what nonsense,' said Glencora. 'Let us get into an express train, and go right through to London.' Mr Palliser looked at her with a countenance full of rebuke and sorrow. He was always so looking at her now. 'If you mean, Plantagenet, that we are to be dragged all across the Continent in that horrible carriage, and be a thousand days on the road, I for one won't submit to it.' 'I wish I had never told him a word about it,' she said afterwards to Alice. 'He would never have found it out himself till this thing was all over.'

Mr Palliser did at last consent to take the joint opinion of a Swiss doctor and an English one. They suggested the railway; and it was agreed, at last, that they should return by that means; but they were to make various halts on the way, stopping at each halting-place for a day. The first was Basle, and from Basle they were to go on to Baden.

These arrangements did not include Mr Grey. 'I suppose we shall see you in England before long?' said Mr Palliser. 'Come to us at Matching. We shall be most happy to have you.' He had become very fond of Mr Grey, and on this occasion, as he had done on some others, pressed him warmly to make an attempt at Parliament. 'It isn't nearly so difficult as you think,' said he, when Grey declared that he would not know where to look for a seat. 'You might easily find some quiet little borough. I'll put you in the way of it.'

But the sole object which Mr Grey had now in view was a renewal of his engagement with Alice, and he felt that he must obtain an answer before they left Lucerne. If she still persisted in refusing to give him her hand, it would not be consistent with his dignity as a man to continue his immediate pursuit of her any longer. He asked her, as he left her one evening, whether she would walk with him on the following morning? That morning would be the morning of her last day at Lucerne, and as she assented she knew well what was to come.

'Where are you going?' said Lady Glencora, when she came in with her hat on, soon after breakfast.

'I am going to walk—with Mr Grey.'

'By appointment?'

'Yes, by appointment.'

'Of course he is now going to say the very thing that he has come all this way for the purpose of saying. He has been wonderfully slow about it; but then you are slower. If you don't make it up with him now I really shall think you are very wicked. I know you want to be his wife, and I know he wants to be your husband, and the only thing that keeps you apart is your obstinacy, just because you have said you wouldn't have him.'

Directly upon that he came in. Alice at once got up to start with him. 'So you and Alice are going to make your adieux,' said Lady Glencora.

'It must be done sooner or later,' said Mr Grey; and then they went off.

'Alice,' he said at length, 'this has been a bad year to me, and I do not think that it has been a happy one for you.'

'Indeed, no.'

'Let us forget it, or rather, let us treat it as though it were forgotten. Twelve months ago you were mine. No man was ever better contented with his bargain. Let us go back to it, and the last twelve months shall be as though they had never been.'

'That cannot be, Mr Grey.'

'Why cannot it be?'

'Because I cannot forgive myself what I have done, and because you ought not to forgive me.'

'But I do. I think you have been foolish, misguided. I never believed that you would marry your cousin. Alice, you should scold me for my vanity, for I have believed all through that you loved me, and me only. Come to me, dear, and tell me that it is so, and the past shall be only as a dream.'

'I shall never cease to reproach myself. I have done that which no woman can do and honour herself afterwards. I have been—a jilt. There are things which, if a woman does them, should never be forgotten; which she should never permit herself to forget.'

'And am I to be punished, then, because of your fault? Is that your sense of justice? Alice, if you tell me that you do not love me I will believe you, and will trouble you no more. I know that you will say nothing to me that is false. Through it all you have spoken no word of falsehood. If you love me, after what has passed, I have a right to demand your hand. I do demand it. If you love me, Alice, I tell you that you dare not refuse me. If you do so, you will fail hereafter to reconcile it to your conscience before God.'

She knew now that she must yield to him, that his power over her was omnipotent. He stood over her, waiting for her answer. Then gradually he put his arm round her waist. She put up her hand to impede his, but his hand, like his character and his words, was full of power. It would not be impeded. 'Alice,' he said, as he pressed her close with his arm, 'the battle is over now, and I have won it.'

'You win everything—always,' she said, whispering to him.

'In winning you I have won everything.' Then he pressed his lips to hers.

Alice insisted on his returning to their inn alone, urging that she wanted to 'think about it all', but, in truth, fearing that she might not be able to carry herself well, if she were to walk down with her lover. To this he made no objection, and met Mr Palliser in the hall. Mr Palliser was already inspecting the arrangement of certain large trunks which had been brought downstairs, and was preparing for their departure. As he could not be Chancellor of the Exchequer, and as, by the nature of his disposition, some employment was necessary to him, he was looking to the cording of the boxes. 'Good morning! good morning!' he said to Grey. 'I am going up to the station to see after a carriage for tomorrow. Perhaps you'll come with me. Sometimes, you know, the springs of the carriages are so very rough.' Then, in a very few words, Mr Grey told him what had been his own morning's work. Mr Palliser congratulated him very cordially, and then, running upstairs for his gloves or his stick, or, more probably, that he might give his wife one other caution as to her care of herself, he told her also that Alice had yielded at last. 'Of course she has,' said Lady Glencora.

'I really didn't think she would,' said he.

'That's because you don't understand things of that sort,' said his wife. Then the caution was repeated, the mother of the future duke was kissed, and Mr Palliser went off on his mission about the carriage, its cushions, and its springs. In the course of their walk Mr Palliser suggested that, as things were settled so pleasantly, Mr Grey might as well return with them to England, and Mr Grey assented.

Alice remained alone for nearly an hour before returning to the hotel.

'Vanquished at last!' said Lady Glencora, as Alice entered the room.

'Yes, vanquished; if you like to call it so,' said Alice. 'I feel I ought to stand before him always as a penitent, in a white sheet.'

'He will like it better, I dare say, if you will sit upon his knee. Some penitents do, you know.'

They sat together the whole morning, and by degrees Alice began to enjoy her happiness. As she did so her friend enjoyed it with her. 'I'll tell you what, Alice; you shall come and be married at Matching, in August, or perhaps September. That's the only way I can be present.'

On the following morning they all started together, a first-class compartment having been taken for the Palliser family, and a second-class compartment for the Palliser servants. Mr

Palliser, as he slowly handed his wife in, was a triumphant man; as was also Mr Grey, as he handed in his lady-love. Both gentlemen had been very fortunate while at Lucerne. Mr Palliser had come abroad with a feeling that all the world had been cut from under his feet. He certainly had his reward, now in his triumphant return. And he had in his pocket a letter which he had that morning received from the Duke of St Bungay, marked private and confidential, in which he was told that Lord Brock and Mr Finespun were totally at variance about French policy. No one knew what would be the consequence of this disagreement. Here might be another chance, if only Mr Palliser could give up his winter in Italy! Mr Palliser, as he took his place opposite his wife, was very triumphant. He was Chancellor of the Exchequer from that moment, and in a short time would be on his legs in the House proposing for his country's use his scheme of finance, with the assured support of at least one newly elected Member, Mr John Grey, who had come to him at last and accepted his offer of the Palliser family borough of Silverbridge.

And Mr Grey was triumphant, as he placed himself gently in his seat opposite to Alice. He was quiet and subdued in his joy, but not the less was he triumphant. He had never given her up for a day, and now the event proved that he had been right.

They stopped a night at Basle, and again she stood upon the balcony. He was close to her as she stood there. 'You are thinking of something, Alice,' he said. 'What is it?'

'It was here,' she said—'here, on this very balcony, that I first rebelled against you, and now you have brought me here that I should confess and submit on the same spot. I do confess. How am I to thank you for forgiving me?'

He put his arm round her and kissed her.

Phineas Finn

CHAPTER ONE

Dr Malachi Finn had obtained a wide reputation as a country practitioner in the west of Ireland. He had five daughters and one son, Phineas, and no provision in the way of marriage or profession had been made for any of them. It was his son's wish that he might go to the English Bar. The doctor paid the usual fee and allowed his son one hundred and fifty pounds per annum for three years.

In London, Phineas belonged to the Reform Club and went into very good society. He was intimate with Barrington Erle, who had been private secretary to the great Whig Prime Minister who was now out. He had dined three or four times with that great Whig nobleman, the Earl of Brentford. At the end of the three years Phineas was called to the Bar. This came at the moment of a dissolution of Parliament; and it had just been suggested to Phineas that he should stand for the Irish borough of Loughshane. An Irish candidate was wanted, and a Roman Catholic. Then 'the party' required that the candidate should be a safe man who would support 'the party', not a cantankerous, red-hot semi-Fenian, with views of his own about tenant-right and the Irish Church. 'But I have views of my own,' said Phineas. 'Of course you have,' said Erle. 'But your views and ours are the same. You mightn't have such an opening again in your life.'

But could a man sit in Parliament upon a hundred and fifty pounds a year? He had heard of penniless men who had got into Parliament and who had gone to the dogs before they were thirty. Yet he also knew of others whose fortunes had been made by happy audacity when they were young.

'I shall take you at your word,' Phineas said. He went to
Ireland, walked over the course at Loughshane, and was duly
elected Member of Parliament for the borough. The Finn family could not restrain their triumphings at Killaloe. The doctor had his misgivings, but undertook to allow Phineas two
hundred and fifty pounds a year as long as the Session should
last.

There was a widow lady living at Killaloe who was named
Mrs Flood Jones, and she had one daughter, Mary. Mary
was a little girl about twenty years of age, and as pretty as
ever she could be. She was one of those girls, so common in
Ireland, whom men, with tastes that way given, feel inclined
to take up and devour on the spur of the moment.

'I shall be off tomorrow morning by the early train,' said
Phineas to her. 'I shall have to take my seat on Friday.'

'When shall we hear of your saying something?'

'Never probably. Not one in ten who go into Parliament
ever do say anything.'

'But you will; won't you? I do so hope you will distinguish
yourself. Mind you come back. But I don't suppose you ever
will. You will be going somewhere to see Lady Laura Standish when you are not wanted in Parliament.'

'Lady Laura Standish!'

'With your prospects, you should go as much as possible
among people of that sort. Is Lady Laura very pretty?'

'She's about six feet high. She has thick lumpy red hair.
She has large hands and feet, and she straggles.'

'Why, Phineas, you are making her out to be an ogress,
and yet I know you admire her.'

'So I do, because she possesses such an appearance of
power.'

'Are you in love with her, Phineas?'

'No. I daresay I shall marry some day, but if I was not
fool enough to have what men call a high ambition I might
venture to be in love now. Mary, one kiss before we part.'

'No, Phineas, no!' But the kiss had been taken and given
before she had even answered him. 'Oh, Phineas, you
shouldn't!'

'Why? And, Mary, I will have one morsel of your hair.'

'Indeed you shall not!' But the ringlet was cut before she was ready with her resistance. There was nothing further; and Mary went away with her veil down, weeping silent tears which no one saw.

Phineas admired Lady Laura very much, and she was worthy of admiration. It was probably the greatest pride of his life that she was his friend. Barrington Erle was her cousin; and Phineas was not without a suspicion that his selection for Loughshane may have been in some degree owing to Lady Laura's influence with Erle.

Lady Laura Standish was the daughter of the widowed Earl of Brentford. Phineas had declared at Killaloe that she was six feet high. She was in fact about five feet seven. There was something of nobility in her gait, and she seemed thus to be taller. Her hair was in truth red, of a deep thorough redness. Her face was very fair, though it lacked softness. As to that accusation of straggling, she never straggled when she stood or walked; but she would lean forward, when sitting, as a man does, and would put her hand over her face, and pass her fingers through her hair, after the fashion of men; and she seemed to despise that soft quiescence of her sex in which are found so many charms. Phineas Finn had been untrue to his appreciation of the lady when he had described her in disparaging terms to Mary Flood Jones.

And now he was back in London and calling at her family home in Portman Square on a Sunday morning.

'I am so very glad that you have been successful, Mr Finn,' she said. 'I think it is a man's duty to make his way into the House if he ever means to be anybody. Of course it is not every man who can get there by the time he is five-and-twenty. Let me see, can you dine here on Wednesday?'

'I shall be delighted.'

'Mr Kennedy dines here—you know Mr Kennedy, of Loughlinter.'

At that moment the door of the room was opened and a man entered with quick steps, and then retreated, slamming the door after him. He was a man with thick short red hair, and an abundance of very red beard. And his face was red, and, as it seemed to Phineas, his very eyes. There was something in the countenance approaching to ferocity.

There was a pause, and then Lady Laura spoke. 'It was my brother Chiltern. I do not think you have ever met him.'

Lord Chiltern, the Earl's son and heir, lived at the house; but he was a man of whom Lady Laura's set did not often speak, and Phineas had never seen him at the house before. He was a young nobleman of whom various accounts were given by various people; but the account most readily accepted in London attributed to him a great intimacy with affairs of Newmarket, and a partiality for convivial pleasures.

Almost immediately other persons came in, and Phineas took his leave. Lady Laura Standish had rejoiced in his triumph. He had often told himself that he was not in love with her; but why should he not now tell himself that he was? She could not have taken him by the hand so warmly, and looked into his face so keenly, had she not felt for him something stronger than common friendship.

But if he resolved that he would ask Lady Laura Standish to be his wife, in what manner might he propose to her that they should live? He could hardly ask her to share the allowance made to him by his father. Lady Laura was related to almost everybody who was anybody among the high Whigs. She was second cousin to Mr Mildmay, who for years had been the leader of the Whigs. The Mildmay people and the Brentford people had all some sort of connection with the Palliser people, of whom the heir and coming chief, Plantagenet Palliser, would certainly be Chancellor of the Exchequer in the next Government. As an introduction into official life nothing could be more conducive to chances of success than a matrimonial alliance with Lady Laura. Not that he would have thought of such a thing on that account! No; he thought of it because he loved her. He swore to that half a dozen times, for his own satisfaction.

When Phineas entered Lady Laura's drawing-room on the Wednesday before dinner he found the other guests discussing the forthcoming division of the House of Commons which it was confidently expected would bring about a defeat for Mr Mildmay's Conservative administration. There were Lady

Laura and Mrs Bonteen. The latter was the wife of a gentleman who had been a junior Lord of the Admiralty in the late government, and who lived in the expectation of filling higher office in a new government. There were also Mr Bonteen himself, Mr Kennedy, Barrington Erle and Lord Brentford.

'How many do you say our majority will be, Mr Finn?' said Lady Laura.

'Seventeen, I suppose,' said Phineas.

'I'll bet four pounds to two it's over nineteen,' said Mr Bonteen, as he passed into dinner.

'I never bet,' said Kennedy.

Phineas had observed that Mr Kennedy had been standing very near to Lady Laura in the drawing-room. He would probably have been moody and unhappy throughout the whole dinner had not Lady Laura called him to a chair at her left hand. It was very generous of her; and the more so as Mr Kennedy had prepared to seat himself in that very place. As it was, Phineas and Mr Kennedy were neighbours, but Phineas had the place of honour.

Phineas went up into the drawing-room for a few minutes after dinner, and again found Mr Kennedy standing close to Lady Laura. Mr Kennedy was an unmarried man, with an immense fortune, a magnificent place, a seat in Parliament, and was not perhaps above forty years of age. Though he was a plain, unattractive man, he was a gentleman in his demeanour. Phineas was six feet high, and very handsome, with bright blue eyes, and brown wavy hair, and light silken beard. He felt that Mr Kennedy ought to be despised by such a one as Lady Laura Standish because his looks were not good. Phineas Finn began to feel himself to be an injured man. Then Lady Laura walked away from Mr Kennedy to Phineas.

'After the division come and tell me what are your impressions, and what you think of Mr Daubeny's speech.'

'Certainly I will.'

'I have asked Mr Kennedy to come. I want to hear what different people say.'

'Do you expect to hear much of an opinion from Mr Kennedy?'

'Yes, I do. He has sound opinions.'

'The truth is I do not know him,' said he, trying to correct his blunder.

'I hope that you may some day. He is one of those men who are both useful and estimable.'

'I do not know that I can use him,' said Phineas; 'but if you wish it I will endeavour to esteem him.'

'I wish you to do both in due time. I think it probable that in the early autumn there will be a great gathering of the real Whig Liberals at Loughlinter, so I should be sorry that you should not be there.'

Then Phineas went away. The Earl had been courteous, but had been in no way specially kind to him. And then Mr Kennedy! As to going to Loughlinter, he would not do such a thing.

.   .   .   .   .

It was three o'clock on the Thursday night before Mr Daubeny's speech was finished. Mr Daubeny showed himself to be a gladiator thoroughly well trained for the arena. His arrows were poisoned, and his lance was barbed. Mr Mildmay heard him without once raising his hat from his brow. Mr Mildmay was an impassive man who rarely spoke of his own feelings, and no doubt sat with his hat low down over his eyes in order that no man might judge of them.

Then came the division. The Liberals had 333 votes to 314 for the Conservatives, and therefore counted a majority of 19.

The following afternoon Phineas called on Lady Laura, and at once saw Mr Kennedy.

'I hope you are satisfied, Mr Finn,' said Lady Laura.

'Well, yes. The question is whether we might not have had a majority of twenty-one.'

'Mr Mildmay might, at the Queen's request, make another attempt.'

'With a majority of nineteen against him!' said Phineas. 'Surely Mr Mildmay is not the only man in the country. There is the Duke of St Bungay, and there is Mr Gresham, and there is Mr Monk.'

'I should hardly think the Duke would venture,' said Mr Kennedy.

'Mr Kennedy must, of course, be right,' said Phineas. 'But the Duke has held his own in both Houses successfully, and he is both honest and popular.'

'I don't find it quite so easy to make up my mind as you do,' said Mr Kennedy. Then the objectionable man took his leave.

'Mr Finn,' said Lady Laura, smiling, 'you were uncourteous to Mr Kennedy.'

'I didn't intend to be uncourteous.'

'I know how clever you are, but I see that you are a little impetuous. I wonder whether you will be angry if I take upon myself the task of mentor.'

'You shall be if you will only be kind enough to say what you really think.'

'You must be a little more careful to be civil to persons to whom you may not take any particular fancy. Now Mr Kennedy is a man who may be very useful to you. Why do you not like him, Mr Finn?'

Phineas paused for a moment before he answered her. 'Do you like him?'

'Yes—I think I may say that I do like him.'

'No more than that?'

'Wait a moment, you impetuous Irish boy.' Phineas liked being called an impetuous Irish boy, and there came a smile upon his face, and he was very handsome. 'I had been telling Mr Kennedy how much I thought of you—as a good Liberal,' she said.

'And I came in and spoilt it all.'

'If you are to be my political pupil you must be obedient. The next time you meet Mr Kennedy, ask him his opinion instead of telling him your own. He has been in Parliament twelve years. At this moment the red-haired, red-bearded man whom Phineas had seen before entered the room. He hesitated a moment, as though he were going to retreat again.

'Oswald,' she said, 'let me introduce you to Mr Finn. Mr Finn, I do not think you have ever met my brother, Lord Chiltern.' The two young men bowed.

'Here is Mr Finn come to tell us who are all the possible new Prime Ministers. He is uncivil enough not to have named Papa.'

'I know nothing whatever about politics,' said Lord Chiltern.

'I wish you did,' said his sister, 'with all my heart.'

'I never did, and I never shall. It's the meanest trade going I think. I don't know whether you are in Parliament, Mr Finn.'

'Yes; but do not mind me.'

'I beg your pardon. Of course there are honest men there, and no doubt you are one of them. I'll never go into the House, as you call it. But, I'll tell you what; I shall be very happy if you'll dine with me tomorrow at Moroni's. They've the best Château Yquem in London.'

'Do,' said Lady Laura. 'Oblige me.' He said that he should be most happy to dine with Lord Chiltern.

'That's right; 7.30 sharp.' Then the servant announced more visitors, and Lord Chiltern escaped out of the room. In twenty or thirty minutes there was a gathering of Liberal political notabilities in Lady Laura's drawing-room. There was a great piece of news: Mr Mildmay would not be Prime Minister. He was to be with the Queen at Windsor on the morrow, and from this and other circumstances it was surmised that Mr Mildmay would decline the task.

While this was going on Lady Laura took Phineas apart for a moment. 'I am so much obliged to you,' she said. 'I can't explain it all now, but I do so want you to know my brother. You may be of the greatest service to him. He is not half so bad as people say he is. I am so very anxious to try to put him on his legs, and I find it so difficult to get any connecting link with him. Papa will not speak with him, because of money. I wonder whether you would go abroad with him in the autumn? But I have no right to think of such a thing, have I? Good-bye. I shall see you perhaps on Sunday if you are in town.'

Phineas walked down to Westminster with his mind very full of Lady Laura. That she could not love Mr Kennedy he thought he was quite sure. As to Lord Chiltern, Phineas would

126

do whatever might be in his power. All that he really knew of Lord Chiltern was that he had gambled and that he had drunk.

.   .   .   .   .

The political portion of London was in a ferment for the next few days. The Government was at last formed, however, and Mr Mildmay was Prime Minister. Mr Gresham was at the Foreign Office; Mr Monk was at the Board of Trade; the Duke of St Bungay was President of the Council; the Earl of Brentford was Privy Seal; and Mr Palliser was Chancellor of the Exchequer. Barrington Erle made a step up in the world, and went to the Admiralty as Secretary; and Mr Bonteen was sent again to the Admiralty. The appointment which disgusted Phineas was the offer of an office—not in the Cabinet, indeed—to Mr Kennedy. Mr Kennedy refused, and this somewhat lessened Finn's disgust, but the offer itself made him unhappy.

The dinner at Moroni's had been eaten, and Phineas had given an account of it to Lord Chiltern's sister.

'I want him to know some men who think of something besides horses,' said Lady Laura. 'He is very well educated, you know, and would certainly have taken honours if he had not quarrelled with the people at Christ Church.'

'Did he take a degree?'

'No; they sent him down because he was drunk.'

Phineas consoled her, and swore that if in any way he could befriend her brother he would do so. Then he took his leave.

There was staying with Lady Laura in Portman Square a dear friend of hers, by name Violet Effingham. Violet Effingham was an orphan, an heiress, and a beauty; with a terrible aunt, Lady Baldock, who was supposed to be the dragon who had Violet in charge. But as Miss Effingham was of age, and mistress of her own fortune, Lady Baldock was, in truth, not omnipotent. The dragon, at any rate, was not now staying in Portman Square. Violet Effingham was small, with light crispy hair, and soft grey eyes, which never looked at you long, yet nearly killed you by the power of their sweetness.

127

Violet Effingham was sitting with Lady Laura, and they were discussing matters of high import to the interests of both of them.

'I do not ask you to accept him,' said Lady Laura. She was referring to her brother, Lord Chiltern.

'That is lucky,' said the other, 'as he has never asked me.'

'You know that he loves you. He has told me that if you will accept him he will do anything that you and I may ask him.'

'I do not love him,' said Violet. 'I am not near to loving any man. I like, perhaps, half a dozen. But as for wanting to marry one for love, and have him all to myself, and that sort of thing—I don't know what it means.'

'But you intend to be married some day.'

'Certainly I do. And I don't intend to wait very much longer. I am heartily tired of Lady Baldock.'

'Oswald may have an equal chance then among the other favourites?' said Lady Laura.

'There are no favourites. Why do you press me about your brother in this way?'

'Because I am so anxious. Because it would save him. And because his father would be reconciled to him tomorrow if he heard that you and he were engaged.'

'Laura, my dear, it seems to me that all your reasons are reasons why he should marry me, not why I should marry him. As for saving him, I don't know that I have any special mission for saving young men. Now, Lord Chiltern does not bear the best reputation in this world. I like a roué myself; and a prig who sits all night in the House and talks about nothing but church-rates and suffrage is to me intolerable. I prefer men who are improper. If I were a man myself I should go in for everything I ought to leave alone. But you see I must take care of myself. I know that I must not dare to marry the sort of man that I like.'

'The truth is, Violet, there is risk with every man, unless you will be contented with the prig you described. Of course there would be risk with my brother. He has been a gambler. But he has given it up in part, and would entirely at your instance.'

'And they say other things of him, Laura.'

'It is true. He has had paroxysms of evil life which have well-nigh ruined him.'

'Is he not in debt?'

'He is—but not deeply. Mind, I know all his circumstances, and I give you my word that every shilling should be paid. He has told me everything. His father could not leave an acre away from him if he would, and would not if he could.'

'It might be that he would do fearful things to me.'

'I believe that if he were married tomorrow his vices would fall from him like old clothes.'

'The men in the city would call this double-dangerous, I think,' said Violet. Then the door was opened, and the man of whom they were speaking entered the room.

'I am so glad to see you, Miss Effingham,' he said. 'I came in thinking that I might find you.'

'Here I am, as large as life,' she said, giving him her hand. She could not help looking first at his eye and then at his hand, because the idea of a drunkard's eye and a drunkard's hand had been brought before her mind. Lord Chiltern's hand was like the hand of any other man, but there was something in his eye that looked as though he would not hesitate to wring his wife's neck round, if ever he should be brought to do so.

'If I did not come and see you here, I suppose I should never see you,' said he, seating himself. 'I do not often go to parties, and when I do you are not likely to be there.'

'My aunt, Lady Baldock, is going to have an evening next week.'

'The servants would be ordered to put me out of the house.' He passed his hand over his face. 'Do you remember my taking you away right through Saulsby Wood once on the old pony, and not bringing you back till tea-time, and Miss Blink going and telling my father?'

'Do I remember it? I think it was the happiest day in my life. His pockets were crammed full of gingerbread, and we had three bottles of lemonade slung on to the pony's saddle-bows. I thought it was a pity that we should ever come back.'

'It was a pity,' said Lord Chiltern.

'You took off my shoes and dried them for me at a wood-man's cottage. I am obliged to put up with my maid's doing those things now. And Miss Blink the mild is changed for Lady Baldock the martinet. And so you see everything is changed as well as my name.'

'Everything is not changed,' said Lord Chiltern. 'I am not changed. I then loved you better than any being in the world —better even than Laura there—and so do I love you now infinitely the best of all. Laura knows it. There is no secret to be kept in the matter among us three.'

'Lord Chiltern,' she replied, 'I did not think when I was going back so joyfully to our old childish days that you would turn the tables on me in this way. As an old friend I have always regarded you, and I hope that I may always do so.' Then she got up and left the room.

'Why were you so sudden with her—so abrupt, so loud?' said his sister.

'It would make no difference. She does not care for me.'

'It makes all the difference in the world. You must begin again.'

'I have begun and ended.'

'That is nonsense. Do something now to make her fear you no longer. Speak to her softly. Tell her of the sort of life which you would live with her. Tell her that all is changed.'

'Am I to tell her a lie?' said Lord Chiltern. Then he left her.

. . . . .

The parliamentary Session went on very calmly after the initial excitement. It was now the middle of July, and Phineas Finn had not yet addressed the House. He had meditated doing so, composing speeches walking round the Park on his way down to the House; only to find on hearing those subjects discussed that he really knew little or nothing about them. Lady Laura recommended patience, and expressed her opinion that a young Member would be better to sit in silence at least for one Session.

To the forms and technicalities of parliamentary business

he did give close attention, and was unremitting in his attendance, telling himself that he was going through his education—that he was learning to be a working Member, and perhaps to be a statesman.

He was supported in all his difficulties by the kindness of Lady Laura Standish, and in Portman Square he had been introduced to Miss Effingham, and had found Miss Effingham to be—very nice. Miss Effingham had quite taken to him, and he had danced with her at two or three parties.

During the summer he had often met Mr Kennedy, and on one occasion Phineas had accepted an invitation to dinner with Mr Kennedy. Nevertheless he disliked Mr Kennedy, and felt quite sure that Mr Kennedy disliked him. He was therefore surprised when he received the following note:

Albany, Z 3, July 17, 186–

My dear Mr Finn,

I shall have some friends at Loughlinter next month, and should be very glad if you will join us. I will name the 16th August. I don't know whether you shoot, but there are grouse and deer.

Yours truly,
Robert Kennedy.

'Of course you will go,' said Lady Laura.

'And why?'

'We are going,' said Lady Laura, 'and I shall be disappointed if you do not go too. Mr Gresham and Mr Monk will be there, and I believe they have never stayed together in the same house before. I have no doubt there are a dozen men on your side of the House who would give their eyes to be there.'

Of course he did agree to go. 'I am so glad,' said Lady Laura, 'because I can now ask you to run down to us at Saulsby for a couple of days on your way to Loughlinter. But remember, Mr Finn, we have got no grouse at Saulsby.' Phineas declared that he did not care a straw for grouse.

Phineas found that the house was full at Saulsby. There were three or four there on their way on to Loughlinter, like himself—Mr Bonteen, and Mr Palliser, the Chancellor of the Exchequer, and his wife; and there was Violet Effingham, who, however, was not going to Loughlinter.

At Saulsby Phineas did not see much of his hostess, but she said a soft word of apology to him. 'I am so busy with all these people that I hardly know what I am doing. But we shall be able to find a quiet minute or two at Loughlinter.'

On that one day there was a riding party made up. Phineas found himself delightfully established by the side of Violet Effingham.

'Do you see that cottage there?' said she as they rode through a vast wood.

'What a pretty cottage it is!'

'Twelve years ago I took off my shoes and stockings and had them dried in that cottage, and when I got back to the house I was put to bed for having been out all day in the wood.'

'Were you wandering about alone?'

'Oswald Standish was with me. We were children then. Do you know him?'

'Lord Chiltern; yes, I know him.'

'And you like him?'

'Very much.'

'I used to like him so much when he was a boy. Lord Chiltern is quite changed, is he not?'

'Changed—in what way?'

'They used to say that he was—unsteady.'

'I think he is changed. But Chiltern is at heart a Bohemian. He hates the decencies of life.'

'I suppose he does,' said Violet. 'If he were married that would all be cured—don't you think so?'

'I cannot fancy him with a wife,' said Phineas. 'There is a savagery about him which would make him an uncomfortable companion for a woman.'

'But he would love his wife?'

'Yes, as he does his horses. And he would treat her well, as he does his horses. But he expects every horse he has to do anything that any horse can do; and he would expect the same of his wife.'

Miss Effingham rode on in silence, and then she said but one word more about Lord Chiltern. 'He was so good to me in that cottage.'

CHAPTER TWO

LOUGHLINTER seemed to Phineas to be a much finer place than Saulsby. It stood on a gentle slope with greensward falling from the front entrance down to a mountain lake. And on the other side of the Lough there rose a mighty mountain to the skies, Ben Linter. All round there ran the woods of Linter, stretching for miles through crags and bogs and mountain lands. And the Linter, rushing down into the Lough, ran so near to the house that the pleasant noise of its cataracts could be heard from the hall door. The whole territory belonged to Mr Kennedy.

The rooms at Loughlinter were splendid, but there was a certain stiffness in the movement of things, and in the manner of some of those present. Phineas at once missed the grace and prettiness and cheery audacity of Violet Effingham. At Loughlinter they were met for business. When he entered the drawing-room before dinner on the first evening, Mr Monk and Mr Palliser, and Mr Kennedy and Mr Gresham, with sundry others, were standing in a wide group before the fireplace, and among them were Lady Glencora Palliser and Lady Laura and Mrs Bonteen. As he approached them it seemed as though a sort of opening was made for himself; but he could see that the movement came from Lady Laura. Yet by the end of a week Phineas found himself on terms of friendly intercourse with all the political magnates, especially with Mr Monk.

Mr Monk was in the Cabinet, and of all the members of

the Cabinet was the most advanced Liberal. Phineas liked to be the chosen receptacle of Mr Monk's confidence.

He had seen little of Mr Kennedy, but he had found himself very frequently with Lady Laura. And he had received a letter from Lord Chiltern.

Dear Finn,
Are you going to Paris with me?

Yours, C.

Before he answered it he made up his mind to tell Lady Laura the truth. He could not go to Paris because he had no money. 'It seems to be a shocking admission to make,' he added.

'I like you all the better for making it. I am very sorry, for Oswald's sake. It's so hard to find any companion for him whom he would like and whom we should think altogether . . . You know what I mean, Mr Finn.'

'I daresay, Lady Laura, you can hardly conceive how very poor a man I am.'

'A ten-pound note at the present moment I should look upon as great riches,' she answered. This was the first time she had ever spoken to him of her own position as regards money. The more he saw of Lady Laura the more he feared that it was impossible that she should become his wife. He had never made love to her. She seemed to be a woman for whom all the ordinary stages of love-making were quite unsuitable. Of course he could declare his love and ask her to be his wife on any occasion on which he might find himself to be alone with her. And on the last morning he made up his mind that he would do so before the day was over.

There had been some half promise on Lady Laura's part that she would walk with him that afternoon up the Linter and come down upon the lake. At five o'clock he was under the portico before the front door, and there he found Lady Laura waiting for him. She had on her hat and gloves, and her parasol was in her hand. He thought that he had never seen her look so young, so pretty, and so fit to receive a lover's vows. They went up the path by the brook till they found themselves out upon the open mountain at the top. 'After all that climbing,' he said, 'will you not sit down for a moment? I have something that I desire to say to you, and to say it here.'

'I will,' she said; 'but I believe I may guess what it is you wish to say, and also have something to tell you, and will say it while I am yet standing. This morning I accepted an offer of marriage from Mr Kennedy.'

.   .   .   .   .

On the next morning, six or seven men were going away, and there was an early breakfast. Mr Kennedy took Phineas aside. 'Laura has told me that she has acquainted you with my good fortune.'

'And I congratulate you,' said Phineas. 'You are indeed a lucky fellow.'

'I feel myself to be so,' said Mr Kennedy. 'Such a wife was all that was wanting to me.'

Phineas, as he was being carried away to the railway station, could not keep himself from speculating as to how much Kennedy knew of what had taken place on that mountainside above the Linter. He felt quite sure that Mr Kennedy knew nothing.

Of course he was as wretched as a man can be. But, nevertheless, he had his consolations. He had not been despised by the woman to whom he had told his love. And then, in all other respects, his visit to Loughlinter had been pre-eminently successful. Mr Monk had become his friend, and had encouraged him. Lord Brentford had become intimate with him. He was on pleasant terms with Mr Palliser and Mr Gresham. As to his friendship with Mr Kennedy there could be no reason why he should not be a friend for his wife's sake.

He went over to Ireland, and came down upon them at Killaloe like a god out of the heavens. Mary Flood Jones was in a great tremor when first she met the hero of Loughshane. She had been somewhat disappointed because the newspapers had not been full of the speeches he had made in Parliament. But she had never expressed the slightest doubt of his capacity or of his judgment.

When she met him she remembered all the circumstances of their last interview. Could it be that he wore that ringlet near his heart? Since she had seen Phineas she had refused an offer of marriage, and told herself that she would never be false to Phineas Finn.

'Are you glad to see me, Mary?'

'Very glad.'

'If you knew, Mary, how often I think about you.' Mary was very happy at hearing such words. She knew that Phineas in his position could not marry at once; but she would wait for him for ever, if he would only ask her.

'Mary, you are a fool to think of that man,' Mrs Flood Jones said to her daughter. 'He is beginning to give himself airs.' Mary made no answer.

At last came the time which called him again to London and the glories of London life—to lobbies, and the clubs, and the gossip of men in office, and the chance of promotion for himself.

'Good-bye, Mary,' he said, with his sweetest smile. But on this occasion there was no kiss, and no culling of locks. 'I know he cannot help it,' said Mary to herself. 'It is his position. But whether it be for good or evil, I will be true to him.' Then, when he was gone, she cried heartily.

.   .   .   .   .

Immediately on his return to town Phineas found himself summoned to a political meeting at Mr Mildmay's house in St James's Square. 'We're going to begin in earnest this time,' Barrington Erle said to him.

'I am glad of that,' said Phineas. 'I suppose we are to have a Reform Bill.'

'That is a matter of course.'

'And I suppose we are not to touch the question of a secret or an open ballot.'

'That's the difficulty,' said Barrington Erle. 'But of course we shan't touch it as long as Mr Mildmay is First Minister of the Crown. He will never consent to the open ballot.'

'Nor would Gresham, or Palliser,' said Phineas. 'And Monk is opposed to the ballot.'

'Ah, that's the question. I don't know how far Monk would be steady.'

'Whatever he says, he'll stick to.'

'He is your leader, then?' asked Barrington.

'Mr Mildmay leads our side; and if anybody leads me, he does. But I have great faith in Mr Monk.'

Mr Mildmay made a long speech. Mr Turnbull, the great Radical of the day—the man who was supposed to represent what many called the Manchester school of politics—asked half a dozen questions. In answer to these Mr Gresham made a short speech. Then Mr Mildmay made another speech, and then all was over. The gist of the whole thing was that there should be a Reform Bill, very generous in its enlargement of the franchise, but no open ballot. Mr Turnbull expressed his doubt whether this would be satisfactory to the country.

The following day Phineas went to call on Lady Laura, who was by now married and living in Grosvenor Place. He hardly knew how to address her, and felt awkward. She evidently expected him to speak, and for a few seconds sat waiting for what he might say.

'Who was there at the marriage?' he managed at length.

'Oswald was not there. Papa said that he might come if he pleased. Oswald stipulated that he should be received as a son. Then my father spoke the hardest word that ever fell from his mouth.'

'And where is Chiltern now?' said Phineas.

'At my father's in Portman Square, until the country frosts are over. He generally stays down in Northamptonshire, at some inn where he is quite alone. He hunts five or six days a week there, and reads at night. I wish you would go and see him.'

'If I can I will. Why doesn't your brother marry?' said Phineas. 'If he were to marry well, that would bring your father round.'

'He is violently in love, and the girl he loves has refused him twice.'

'Is it with Miss Effingham?' asked Phineas, guessing the truth at once.

'Yes, with Violet Effingham; my father's pet, his favourite, whom he loves next to myself; whom he would really welcome as a daughter. He would gladly make her mistress of his house, and of Saulsby. Everything would then go smoothly.'

'But she does not like Lord Chiltern?'

'I believe she loves him in her heart; but she is afraid of him. With all her seeming frolic, Violet Effingham is very wise.'

Phineas, though not conscious of jealousy, was annoyed at the revelation. He did not like Lord Chiltern quite as well as he had done before. He himself had simply admired Miss Effingham, and had taken pleasure in her society; but he did not like to hear of another man wanting to marry her. It did not as yet occur to him that the love of such a girl as Violet would be a great treasure—to himself.

At about three o'clock he went up to Portman Square to look for Lord Chiltern. As he was passing through the hall he met Lord Brentford himself. He was thus driven to speak, and felt himself called upon to explain why he was there. 'I am come to see Lord Chiltern,' he said.

'You will find him upstairs, I suppose,' said the Earl. He spoke as though he resented the fact that anyone should come to his house to call upon his son; and turned his back quickly upon Phineas. But he thought better of it before he reached the front door, and turned again. 'If you see Lord Chiltern will you tell him that I should be glad to see him before he leaves London?'

Phineas found his friend standing in the middle of the room, without coat and waistcoat, with a pair of dumb-bells in his hands. 'When there's no hunting I'm driven to this kind of thing,' said Lord Chiltern. 'I've no occupation for my days whatever, and no place to take myself. I should disgrace any decent club if I went there.'

Then Phineas gave him the message from his father. 'I know what he wants very well,' said Lord Chiltern. 'Laura has been interfering and doing no good. You know Violet Effingham?'

'Yes; I know her.'

'They want her to marry me.'

'And you do not wish to marry her?'

'I would take her tomorrow, if she would have me. But what is the use of my liking her? They have painted me so black that no decent girl would think of marrying me.'

'Your father can't be angry with you if you do your best to comply with his wishes.'

'I don't care a straw whether he be angry or not. He allows me eight hundred a year, and he knows that if he stopped it I could not help myself. He can't leave an acre away from me, and yet he won't join me in raising money for the sake of paying Laura her fortune.'

'Lady Laura can hardly want money now.'

'That detestable pig whom she has chosen to marry, and whom I hate with all my heart, is richer than ever Croesus was; but nevertheless Laura ought to have her own money. She shall have it some day.'

'I would see Lord Brentford, if I were you.'

'I will think about it.' And on the next morning Lord Chiltern strode by appointment into his father's room.

'Oswald,' said the father, 'I have sent for you because I think it may be as well to speak to you on some business. I feel very unhappy about your sister's fortune.'

'So do I—very unhappy. We can raise the money between us, and pay her tomorrow, if you please it.'

'I will join with you in raising the money for your sister on one condition. Laura has told me often that you are attached to Violet Effingham.'

'But Violet Effingham, my lord, is unhappily not attached to me.'

'Laura tells me that she believes that Violet would consent. I have so great faith in Violet Effingham that I would receive her acceptance of your hand as the only proof which would be convincing to me of amendment in your mode of life. If she were to do so, I would join with you in raising money to pay your sister, would make some further sacrifice with reference to an income for you and your wife, and—would make you both welcome to Saulsby—if you chose to come.'

'But I have asked her, and she has refused me. I don't even know where to find her to ask her again.'

'Miss Effingham is staying with your sister in Grosvenor Place. I saw her yesterday.'

'Very well, my lord. Then I will do the best I can. Laura will tell you of the result.'

He went back to his room, and looked out of his window. The streets were in a mess of slush. White snow was becoming black mud, and the violence of frost was giving way to the horrors of thaw. All would be soft and comparatively pleasant in Northamptonshire on the following morning, and if everything went right he would go down by the hunting train and be at his inn, the Willingford Bull, by ten. In the meantime he would go and do his work. He had a cab called, and within half an hour he was at the door of his sister's house in Grosvenor Place. The ordinary greetings took place, and Miss Effingham made some remark about the frost. 'But it seems to be going,' she said, 'and I suppose that you will soon be at work again?'

'Yes; I shall hunt tomorrow,' said Lord Chiltern.

'And the next day, and the next, and the next,' said Violet, ''till about the middle of April; and then your period of misery will begin!'

'Exactly,' said Lord Chiltern. 'I have nothing but hunting that I can call an occupation.'

'Why don't you make one?' said his sister.

'I mean to do so, if it be possible. Laura, would you mind leaving me and Miss Effingham alone for a few minutes?'

Lady Laura got up, and so also did Miss Effingham. 'For what purpose?' said the latter.

'At any rate I wish it, and I will not harm you.' Then Lady Laura went.

'It was not that I feared you would harm me, Lord Chiltern,' said Violet.

'No; I know it was not. But what I say is always said awkwardly. Look here, Violet, my father is unreasonable. He has ever believed evil of me, and has believed it often when all

140

the world knew that he was wrong. I care little for being reconciled to a father who has been so cruel to me.'

'He loves me dearly, and is my friend. I would rather that
you should not speak against him to me.'

'You will understand, at least, that I am asking nothing
from you because he wishes it. Laura probably has told you
that you may make things straight by becoming my wife.'

'She has.'

'It is an argument to which you should not listen for a
moment. There would be very little made straight by such a
marriage, if it were not that I loved you. Violet, that is my
plea, and my only one. I love you so well that I do believe
that if you took me I should return to the old ways, and become as other men are, and be in time as respectable, as stupid
—perhaps as ill-natured as old Lady Baldock herself.'

'My poor aunt!'

'You know she says worse things of me than that. Now,
dearest, you have heard all that I have to say to you. I have
no other argument to use.'

'How am I to answer you?' she said.

'With your love, if you can give it to me. Do you remember
how you swore once that you would love me for ever and
always?'

'You should not remind me of that. I was a child then—
a naughty child,' she added, smiling; 'and was put to bed
for what I did on that day.'

'Be a child still.'

'Ah, if we but could! Lord Chiltern, I am sorry that I
cannot give you the love for which you ask.'

'Is it myself personally, or what you have heard of me,
that is so hateful to you?'

'Nothing is hateful to me. But there are many things which
a woman is bound to consider before she allows herself to
become a wife.'

'Allow herself! Then it is a matter entirely of calculation.'

'I suppose there should be some thought in it, Lord Chiltern.'

He walked once or twice across the room and then he
stopped closely opposite to her.

141

'I shall never try again,' he said.

'It will be better so,' she replied.

'Just tell Laura, will you, that it is all over; and she may as well tell my father. Good-bye.'

She then tendered her hand to him, but he did not take it, probably did not see it, and at once left the room and the house. He walked through the slush and dirt to a haunt of his in the neighbourhood of Covent Garden, and there he remained through the whole afternoon and evening. A certain Captain Clutterbuck dined with him. He told nothing to Captain Clutterbuck of his sorrow, but Captain Clutterbuck could see that he was unhappy.

'Let's have another bottle of "cham",' said Captain Clutterbuck, when their dinner was nearly over. ' "Cham" is the only thing to screw one up when one is down a peg.'

'You can have what you like,' said Lord Chiltern; 'but I shall have brandy-and-water.'

Lord Chiltern went down to Peterborough next day by the hunting train, and rode his horse Bonebreaker so well in that famous run from Sutton springs to Gidding that after the run young Piles offered him three hundred pounds for the animal.

'You couldn't ride him if you'd got him,' said Lord Chiltern.

'Oh, couldn't I!' said Piles. But Mr Piles did not continue the conversation, contenting himself that that red devil Chiltern was as drunk as a lord.

CHAPTER THREE

PHINEAS left London by a night mail train on Easter Sunday, and found himself at the Willingford Bull about half an hour after midnight. Lord Chiltern was up and waiting for him and supper was on the table. The Willingford Bull was an English inn of the old stamp, which had, in these years of railway travelling, ceased to have a road business, but it had acquired a new trade as a dépôt for hunters and hunting men. The house was generally filled from the beginning of November till the middle of April. Then it became a desert in the summer, and no guests were seen there, till the pink coats flocked down again into the shires.

'How many days do you mean to give us?' said Lord Chiltern, as he helped his friend to a devilled leg of a turkey.

'I must go back on Wednesday.'

'That means Wednesday night. I'll tell you what we'll do. We've the Cottesmore tomorrow. We'll get into Tailby's country on Tuesday, and Fitzwilliam will be only twelve miles off on Wednesday.'

They sat up half the night smoking and talking, and Phineas learned more about Lord Chiltern then than ever he had learned before. There was brandy and water before them, but neither of them drank. Lord Chiltern had a pint of beer by his side from which he sipped occasionally. 'I've taken to beer,' he said. 'When a man hunts six days a week he can afford to drink beer. I'm on an allowance, three pints a day.'

'And you drink nothing else?'

'Nothing when I'm alone. I never cared for drink. I do like excitement, and have been less careful than I ought to have been as to what it has come from. I could give up drink tomorrow if it were worth my while. I never do gamble now, because I've got no money; but I own I like it better than anything in the world. There is life in it. How does Laura get on with her husband?'

'Very happily, I should say.'

'I don't believe it. Her temper is too much like mine to allow her to be happy with such a log of wood as Robert Kennedy. It is such men as he who drive me out of the pale of decent life. If that is decency, I'd sooner be indecent. She'll never be able to stand it. Is Violet Effingham still in Grosvenor Place?'

'No; she's with Lady Baldock.'

'That old grandmother of evil has come to town, has she?

Poor Violet! When we were young together we used to have such fun about that old woman. You know Violet Effingham, of course. Don't you think her very charming?' said Lord Chiltern.

'Exceedingly charming.'

'I have asked that girl to marry me three times, and I shall never ask her again. There is a point beyond which a man shouldn't go. I've loved her all my life—since I used to buy cakes for her. But I shall never ask her again.'

'I would if I were you,' said Phineas, hardly knowing what it might be best for him to say.

'No; I never will. Of course she'll marry, and that soon. Then I shall make a fool of myself. When I hear that she is engaged I shall go and quarrel with the man. All the world will turn against me, and I shall be called a wild beast. Though I have no property in her at all, no right to her, it is as though she were the most private thing in the world to me. I should be half mad, and in my madness I could not master the idea that I was being robbed. But, of course, I cannot make her marry me. Light another cigar, old fellow.'

They had a fair day's sport with the Cottesmore; and Phineas went through his day's work with credit. He had been riding since he was a child and had an Irishman's natural aptitude for jumping. 'It wasn't fast, you know,' said Chiltern, 'and I don't call that a stiff country. You shall ride Bonebreaker tomorrow at Somerby, and you'll find that better fun.'

'Bonebreaker? Haven't I heard you say he rushes like mischief?'

'By George! you want a horse to rush in that country. When you have to go right through four or five feet of stiff green wood, like a bullet through a target, you want a little force, or you're apt to be left up a tree.'

'And what do you ride?'

'A brute I never put my leg on yet. He was sent down out of Lincolnshire, because they couldn't get anybody to ride him there. These are the sort of horses I like.'

Again they dined alone, and Lord Chiltern explained that he rarely associated with the men of the hunts in which he rode. 'There is a set of fellows down here who are poison to me, and there is another set, and I am poison to them. Every-body is very civil, as you see, but I have no associates. And gradually I am getting to have a reputation as though I were the devil himself. I think I shall come out next year dressed entirely in black.'

The next day they started early. Phineas was rather afraid of Bonebreaker, and looked forward to the probability of an accident. 'Just let him have his own way at everything,' said Lord Chiltern, 'and if you'll only sit on his back, he'll carry you through as safe as a church.' As he spoke an old hound opened true and sharp—and an old hound whom all the pack believed—and in a moment there was no doubt that the fox had been found.

The very moment Bonebreaker heard the old hound's note he stretched out his head, and put his mouth upon the bit, and began to tremble in every muscle. Lord Chiltern, with the horse out of Lincolnshire, went away across the brow of the hill and selected, as his point of exit into the next field, a stiff rail which, had there been an accident, must have put a very wide margin of ground between the rider and his horse. 'Go hard at your fences, and then you'll fall clear,' he had said to Phineas. Phineas took the fence a little lower down, Bonebreaker sailed over it, and he soon found himself by his friend's side.

He began to find that Bonebreaker knew pretty well what he was about. He seemed to have a passion for smashing through big, high-grown ox-fences, and by degrees his rider came to feel that if there was nothing worse coming, the fun was not bad.

They had now crossed a road and had got into closer coun-try. The fields were not so big, and the fences were not so high. Phineas got a moment to look about him and saw Lord Chiltern riding without his cap. He was very red in the face, and his eyes seemed to glare, and he was tugging at his horse with all his might. But the animal seemed still to go with perfect command of strength, and Phineas saw someone, a farmer, as he thought, speak to Lord Chiltern as they rode close together; but Chiltern only shook his head and pulled at his horse.

145

There were brooks in those parts. Bonebreaker had gone gallantly over two, and now there came a third in the way. Phineas had long given up the idea of having a will of his own. He looked round, and there was Chiltern close to him, still fighting with his horse. He thought that Chiltern nodded to him, as much as to tell him to go on. The brook, when he came to it, seemed to be a huge black hole, yawning beneath him. The banks were quite steep, and just where he was to take off there was an ugly stump. It was too late to think of anything. He stuck his knees against his saddle—and in a moment was on the other side. Phineas, as soon as he was safe, looked back, and there was Lord Chiltern's horse in the very act of his spring, higher up the rivulet, where it was even broader. The animal rushed at the brook, and in a moment the horse and horseman were lost to sight. Phineas arrested his horse and came back to his friend.

He found that Lord Chiltern was wedged in between the horse and the bank. He was very pale, and seemed to be quite helpless where he lay. The horse did not move, and never did move again.

'I told you so,' said the farmer, coming and looking down from the bank. 'I told you, but you wouldn't be said.' Between them both they extricated Lord Chiltern and got him on to the bank.

'That un's a dead un,' said the farmer, pointing to the horse.

'So much the better,' said his lordship. 'Give us a drop of sherry, Finn.'

He had broken his collar-bone and three of his ribs. They got a farmer's trap and took him to the Willingford Bull before he would have his bones set. Phineas remained with him for a couple of days, and became very fond of his patient.

'That was a good run though, wasn't it?' said Lord Chiltern as Phineas took his leave. 'And, by George, Phineas, you rode Bonebreaker well. I don't know how it is, but you Irish fellows always ride.'

Phineas's first work on reaching London was to see Lord Chiltern's friends and tell them of the accident.

'Of course he will kill himself some day,' said the Earl, with a tear, however, in each eye.

'I hope not, my lord. He is a magnificent horseman; but accidents will happen.'

'I should fear that he would be so liable to inflammation.'

'The doctor says there is none. He has been taking an enormous deal of exercise,' said Phineas, 'and drinking no wine. I rather think, my lord, you are a little mistaken about his habits. I don't fancy he ever drinks unless he is provoked to do it.'

'Provoked! Could anything provoke you to make a brute of yourself? But I am glad he is in no danger. If you hear of him, let me know how he goes on.'

Lady Laura was full of concern. 'I wanted to go down to him,' she said, 'but Mr Kennedy advises me not to go. He says my duty does not require it, unless Oswald be in danger. Don't you know, Mr Finn, how hard it is for a wife not to take advice when it is so given?' This she said, within six months of her marriage, to the man who had been her husband's rival!

Thursday was Lady Baldock's night, and Phineas went from Grosvenor Place to Berkeley Square. There he saw Violet, and found that she had heard of the accident.

'I am so glad to see you, Mr Finn,' she said. 'Do tell me; you think there is no danger?'

'None whatever. His hunting is done for this year, and he will be very desolate. I shall go down again in a few days and try to bring him up to town.'

'Do—do. If he is laid up in his father's house his father must see him.'

On the Sunday afternoon Phineas went to Lord Brentford's in Portman Square, intending to say a word or two about Lord Chiltern, and having a hope also that he might find Lady Laura Kennedy with her father. He had come to understand that Lady Laura was not to be visited at her own house on Sundays, but that she rebelled in heart against this Sabbath tyranny and would escape from it when possible. She had now come to talk to her father about her brother, and had brought Violet Effingham with her.

147

'The local surgeon says that he had better not be moved for a month,' said Phineas.

'I wish I were with him,' said Lady Laura.

'That is, of course, out of the question,' said the Earl. 'They know him at that inn, and it really seems to me best that he should stay there. I do not think he would be so much at his ease here.' They all perceived that as soon as he had learned that there was no real danger as to his son's life he was determined that this accident should not work him up to any show of tenderness.

Phineas went down to the House, and was present when the debate was resumed. Mr Turnbull had declared that he would vote against the second reading of Mr Mildmay's bill, because he could consent to no Reform Bill which did not include the open ballot as one of its measures. One or two of Mr Turnbull's followers declared that they also would vote against the bill. Then Mr Palliser got up and addressed the House for an hour, struggling hard to bring back the real subject, and to make the House understand that whether the ballot were good or bad, Members had no right at the present moment to consider anything but the expediency or inexpediency of so much Reform as Mr Mildmay presented to them in the present bill.

Phineas was determined to speak for the first time, if he could catch the Speaker's eye. He felt his blood beating hard at his heart. He started up wildly when Mr Palliser had completed his speech; but the Speaker's eye had travelled to the other side of the House and there was a Tory of the old school upon his legs, who spoke with a ponderous, unimpressive voice for some twenty minutes, pleading against any Reform, with all the old arguments. Phineas did not hear a word he said; did not attempt to hear. At last the Member for East Barset sat down, and Phineas heard himself called upon to address the House. There he was with a crowded House, bound to be his auditors as long as he should think fit to address them, and reporters by tens and twenties in the gallery ready and eager to let the country know what the young Member for Loughshane would say in his maiden speech.

Phineas Finn had sundry gifts, a powerful and pleasant

voice, which he had learned to modulate, a handsome presence, and a certain natural mixture of modesty and self-reliance, which would certainly protect him from the faults of arrogance and pomposity. But he had not that gift of slow blood which would have placed all his own resources within his own reach. He began with the expression of an opinion that every true reformer ought to accept Mr Mildmay's bill, even if it were accepted only as an instalment—but before he had got through these sentences he became painfully conscious that he was repeating his own words.

He had certain arguments at his fingers' ends—and he forgot even these. He found that he was going on with one platitude after another. He pressed on, fearing that words would fail him altogether if he paused; but he spoke much too fast, knocking his words together so that no reporter could properly catch them. But he had nothing to say for the bill except what hundreds had said before, and hundreds would say again.

When he sat down he was cheered as a new Member is usually cheered. At last, at about two, the debate was adjourned, and then as he was slowly leaving the House Mr Monk took him by the arm.

'Are you going to walk?' said Mr Monk.

'Yes,' said Phineas.

'Then we may go together as far as Pall Mall. Come along.' Mr Monk did not speak again till they were out in Palace Yard. 'It was not much amiss,' he said; 'but you'll do better than that yet.'

'Mr Monk,' said Phineas. 'I have made an ass of myself.'

'Ah! I thought you had some such feeling as that. You may be sure, Finn, that I do not care to flatter you. Your speech, which was certainly nothing great, was about on a par with other maiden speeches in the House of Commons. You have done yourself neither good nor harm. My advice to you is never to avoid speaking on any subject that interests you, but never to speak for above three minutes till you find yourself as much at home on your legs as you are when sitting. But do not suppose that you have made an ass of yourself—that is, in any special degree. Now, good night.'

Lady Laura Kennedy heard two accounts of her friend's speech. Her husband had been in his place, and Lord Brentford had been seated in the peers' gallery.

'And you think it was a failure?' Lady Laura said to her husband.

'It certainly was not a success. There was a good deal of it you could hardly hear.'

After that she got the morning newspapers. The speech was given six lines, and at the end there was an intimation that the young orator had better speak more slowly.

Later in the day Lady Laura saw her father, and Miss Effingham was with her at the time. Lady Laura instantly began to ask him about Phineas.

'The less said the better,' was the Earl's reply. 'Mildmay will lose his bill. There does not seem to be a doubt about that.'

'And what will you all do?'

'We must go to the country, I suppose. They say there are no less than twenty-seven men on our side of the House who will either vote with Turnbull against us, or will decline to vote at all.'

'And will Mr Finn lose his seat?' asked Violet Effingham.

'Most probably.'

'You must find him a seat somewhere in England,' said Violet.

'That might be difficult,' said the Earl, who then left the room.

Then Lady Laura said, 'If there be a dissolution I hope Oswald will stand for Loughton.' Loughton was a borough close to Saulsby, in which Lord Brentford was supposed to have considerable influence.

'Would not that be just the place for Mr Finn?' said Violet.

Then Lady Laura became very serious. 'Oswald would of course have a better right to it than anybody else.'

'But would Lord Chiltern go into Parliament? I have heard him declare that he would not.'

'If we could get Papa to ask him I think he would change his mind,' said Lady Laura.

Violet said, 'It would be a thousand pities that Mr Finn should be turned out into the cold.'

'I for one, should be very sorry.'

'So should I. I shall think it a great shame if they turn him out.'

'Violet,' said Lady Laura; 'I believe you are in love with Mr Finn.'

'Why shouldn't I be in love with him, if I like?'

'He has not got a penny.'

'But I have, my dear.'

'And I doubt whether you have any reason for supposing that he is in love with you.'

'That would be my affair.'

'Then you are in love with him?'

'I am not in love with him. If he were to marry my dearest friend in the world, I should tell him to kiss me and be my brother.'

'What you say is very odd.'

'Why odd?'

'Simply because my sentiments are the same.'

'I once thought, Laura, that you did love him; that you meant to be his wife.'

'So I did, nearly . . .' said Lady Laura; 'very nearly. You told me just now that you had money, and could therefore do as you pleased. I had no money, and could not do as I pleased. He did care for me. He did love me.'

'He told you so?'

'Yes; or was about to.'

'And how did you answer him?'

'I had that very morning become engaged to Mr Kennedy. That was my answer.'

'And now, if he were to love me, you would grudge me his love?'

'Not for that reason; but because I look upon it as written in heaven that you are to be Oswald's wife.'

'Heaven's writings then are false,' said Violet.

.   .   .   .   .

Phineas Finn's servant girl came into his room in the morning. 'Sir,' said she, 'there's a gentleman here.' She handed him a card. 'Mr Quintus Slide. Banner Office, 137 Fetter Lane.' Mr Quintus Slide proved to be a young man, under thirty, not remarkable for clean linen. He was a well-known and not undistinguished member of a powerful class of men. He knew the ' 'Ouse' well, and was a writer for the press. And, though he talked of ' 'Ouses' and 'horgans', he wrote good English with great rapidity. It was Mr Slide's taste to be an advanced reformer. No man could do an article on the people's indefeasible rights with more pronounced vigour than Mr Slide. He was a 'people's friend'. It was his business to abuse Government, and to express on all occasions an opinion that as a matter of course the ruling powers were the 'people's enemies'.

'You come out strong, Mr Finn, and we'll see that you are properly reported. I'm on the *Banner*, sir, and I'll answer for that.' Such was the burden of Mr Slide's visit. 'You'll find, Mr Finn, that in public life there's nothing like having a horgan to back you. What is the most you can do in the 'Ouse? Nothing, if you're not reported. You're speaking to the country, ain't you? And you can't do that without a horgan, Mr Finn. You come among us on the *Banner*, Mr Finn. You can't do better.'

Then Phineas understood the nature of the offer made to him.

A few days later he visited the office of *The People's Banner* There he wrote a leading article for which he was to be paid a guinea. Mr Slide, however, was anxious that Phineas should rid himself of his heterodox political resolutions about the ballot. It was not that they cared much about his own opinions; and when Phineas attempted to argue on the merits of the ballot he was put down very shortly. 'We go in for it, Mr Finn.' If Mr Finn would go in for it too, Mr Slide seemed to think that Mr Finn might make himself very useful at the *Banner* office. Phineas stoutly maintained that this was impossible, and was therefore driven to confine his articles in the service of the people to those open subjects on which his opinions agreed with those of *The People's Banner*.

He found also that Mr Slide had ideas as to getting into the 'Ouse at some future time. 'I always look upon the 'Ouse as my oyster, and 'ere's my sword,' said Mr Slide, brandishing an old quill pen. 'What is it a man wants? It's only pluck.' Then Phineas asked him whether he had any idea of a constituency, at which Mr Slide named the borough of Loughton; and Phineas Finn, thinking of Saulsby, the Earl, Lady Laura, and Violet, walked away disgusted. Would it not be better that the quiet town should remain as it was, than that it should be polluted by the presence of Mr Quintus Slide?

There were some great speeches made on the final evening of the debate. Mr Gresham taunted Mr Turnbull with being a recreant to the people, of whom he called himself so often the champion. Mr Gresham knew well enough that Mr Turnbull was not to be moved by any words; but the words were not the less telling to the House and to the country. Mr Daubeny replied to him with equal genius and skill, if not with equal heart. Mr Gresham had asked for the approbation of all present and of all future reformers. Mr Daubeny denied him both. Then Mr Mildmay made his reply and uttered a futile prayer that this his last work on behalf on his countrymen might be successful. His bill was read a second time, in obedience to the casting vote of the Speaker—but a majority such as that was tantamount to a defeat.

April was over, and the much-needed Whitsuntide holidays were coming on. But little of the routine work of the Session had been done; and, as Mr Mildmay told the House, the country would suffer were the Queen to dissolve Parliament at this period of the year. The old Ministers would go on with the business of the country, and at the close of the Session writs should be issued for new elections.

Mr Turnbull told Mr Mildmay that he had lost his bill, good in other respects, because he had refused to introduce the ballot into his measure. Let him promise to be wiser for the future, and to obey the wishes of the country, and then all would be well with him. Mr Mildmay declared that if by the fresh election it should be shown that the ballot was in truth desired, he would at once leave the execution of their wishes to abler and younger hands.

There appeared leader after leader in *The People's Banner* urging the constituencies to take advantage of the Prime Minister's words, and to show clearly at the hustings that they desired the ballot. 'You had better come over to us, Mr Finn; you had indeed,' said Mr Slide. 'Now's the time to do it, and show yourself a people's friend. You'll have to do it sooner or later, whether or no.'

This advice was given to him about the end of May, and at that time Lord Chiltern was staying briefly with Phineas in his lodgings in Great Marlborough Street. Lord Chiltern when he came up to London was still in bandages, which were a sufficient excuse for his visiting the house neither of his father nor his brother-in-law. But Lady Laura went to him frequently; and there were messages taken from Violet, some of which she worded with more show of affection, perhaps as much for the discomfort of Phineas as for the consolation of Lord Chiltern.

'Of course you will come to us at Loughlinter when Parliament is up?' Lady Laura said to Phineas one day.

'I must go over to Ireland about my re-election.'

'We go down on the first of July. It will be August before the men of Loughshane are ready for you.'

'To tell you the truth, Lady Laura, I doubt whether the men of Loughshane will have anything more to say to me.'

'I was afraid there was but a bad chance,' said Lady Laura. 'I've got a plan of my own.'

'What plan?'

'Or rather it isn't mine, but Papa's. He wants you to come and try your luck at Loughton.'

'Lady Laura!'

'It isn't quite a certainty, you know, but I suppose it's as near a certainty as anything left.'

'I have no right to such a favour.'

'That is a matter entirely for Papa's consideration,' said Lady Laura, with an affectation of solemnity in her voice. 'My father feels that he has to do the best he can with his influence in the borough, and therefore he comes to you.'

Of course Phineas was persuaded. But he first discussed the matter with Lord Chiltern. 'Do not scruple about me,' said Lord Chiltern; 'you are quite welcome to the borough for me.'

'But if I did not stand, would you do so? There are so many reasons which ought to induce you to accept a seat in Parliament.'

'Whether that be true or not, Phineas, I shall not accept my father's interest at Loughton, unless it be offered to me in a way in which it never will be offered. You may go down to Loughton with a pure conscience as far as I am concerned.'

Phineas had his interview with the Earl on the following morning, and went down to Loughlinter early in July, taking Loughton in his way. He stayed there one night at the inn, and was introduced to sundry influential inhabitants of the borough. He told them he was a good sound Liberal and a supporter of Mr Mildmay's Government, of which their neighbour the Earl was so conspicuous an ornament.

He found Loughlinter nearly empty. Mr Kennedy himself was shut up with books and papers. The Earl also would read a little, and then would sleep a good deal. Lady Laura administered tea and read novels.

Phineas often wandered up and down the Linter and down to the lake. Once, as he was sitting at the top of the falls, he looked up, to see Lady Laura standing before him.

There was a little wooden seat nearby, and upon this Lady Laura sat down. 'How well I remember,' she said, 'the day when you and I were here last autumn!'

'You told me then that you were going to marry Mr Kennedy. How much has happened since then!'

'And yet how slow the time has gone!'

'I do not think it has been slow with me,' said Phineas.

'No; you have had your hands full of work. I am beginning to think that it is a great curse to have been born a woman.'

Phineas of course understood that she was complaining of her husband. He had perceived that Mr Kennedy was an autocrat in his own house, and he knew Lady Laura well enough to be sure that such masterdom would be very irksome to her. But he had not imagined that she would complain to him.

'The truth is, my friend,' she said, 'that I have made a mistake.'

'A mistake?'

'Yes, Phineas, a mistake. I have blundered as fools blunder.'
She had never called him Phineas before.

'You can tell no one who is more anxious for your happiness,' he said.

'Phineas,' she said, slowly, 'I wish you would go from here.'

'What, at once?'

'Not today, or tomorrow. Stay here now till the election; but do not return.'

'And why?' he asked.

'Because I am a fool,' she said. 'Is not that enough for you?'

'Laura . . .'

'No, no; I will have none of that. I am a fool, but not such a fool as to suppose that any cure is to be found there.'

'Only say what I can do for you and I will do it.'

'You can do nothing, except to keep away from me. Goodbye.' So she turned away and went back to the house by herself.

. . . . .

Phineas was elected Member for Loughton without any trouble. When he returned to London a letter awaited him.

Banner of the People Office,
3rd August, 186–

My dear Finn,

I must say I think you have treated me badly, and without that sort of brotherly fairness which we on the public press expect from one another. However, perhaps we can come to an understanding, and if so, things may yet go smoothly. Give me a turn and I am not at all averse to give you one. Will you come to me here, or shall I call upon you?

Yours always, Q.S.

He went to the office of *The People's Banner*, and found Mr Slide writing an article for the next day's copy.

'I suppose you're very busy,' said Phineas.

'Not so particular but what I'm glad to see you.' He threw down his pen and rushed at once at his subject.

'Well, now, Finn,' he said, 'don't you know that you've treated me badly about Loughton?'

'I don't know what you mean.'

'Didn't I tell you that I had Loughton in my heye?'

'How on earth could you have stood for Loughton? What interest would you have had there?'

'Now, I'll tell you what I'll do, Finn. I think you have thrown me over most shabby, but I won't stand about that. You shall have Loughton this Session if you'll promise to make way for me after the next election. If you'll agree to that we'll have a special leader to say how well Lord What's-his-name has done with the borough; and we'll be your horgan through the whole Session.'

'It's the most absurd proposal that was ever made.'

'Very well,' said Quintus Slide. 'Now we understand each other. I think I can show you what it is to come among gentlemen of the press, and then to throw them over. Good morning.'

Phineas shook off a little dust from his foot as he left the office of *The People's Banner*, and resolved that in future he would attempt to make no connection in that direction. On the second morning after his meeting he saw the result of his independence. There was a startling article showing the pressing necessity of immediate reform by an illustration of the borough-mongering rottenness of the present system. When such a patron as Lord Brentford could by his mere word put into the House such a stick as Phineas Finn, a man who had struggled to stand on his legs before the Speaker, but had wanted both the courage and the capacity, nothing further could surely be wanted to prove that the Reform Bill of 1832 required to be supplemented by some more energetic measure.

Phineas laughed as he read the article. But he suffered. Mr Quintus Slide, when he was really anxious to use his thong earnestly, could generally raise a weal.

On the 10th of August Phineas Finn did return to Loughton. He had received a letter from Lord Chiltern, in which there was a message for Lord Brentford. 'If you see my father, tell him that I am ready at any moment to do what is necessary for raising the money for Laura.' Taking this as his excuse he returned to Loughton, knowing full well that Violet Effingham and Lady Baldock were to spend the 11th there.

He met the Earl standing on the great steps before his own castle doors. He told his story there and then. 'Let him come here, and she shall be here also,' said the Earl, speaking of Violet. To this Phineas could say nothing out loud, but he told himself that he would take no dishonest advantage of Lord Chiltern. He would give the whole message as it was given to him by Lord Brentford. But how could he bid Lord Chiltern come home to woo Violet Effingham, and instantly go forth to woo her for himself? He found that he could not do so—unless he told the whole truth to Lord Chiltern.

Phineas wrote an elaborate letter, with words intended to bring the prodigal son back to his father's home. And everything was said about Miss Effingham that could or should have been said. 'Now,' he said, on the last page, 'I must speak of myself. I have loved her for six months, and I am here with the express intention of asking her to take me. I do not deprecate your anger, if you choose to be angry. But I cannot address myself to Miss Effingham without telling you. Do not quarrel with me if you can help it; but if you must I will be ready.' Then he posted the letter and went up to the Castle.

He had only the one day for his action, and he knew that Violet was watched by Lady Baldock as by a dragon. After lunch they were to ride. He was aware that he must greatly increase the distance between them and the others of their party before he could dare to plead his suit.

They had gone some half mile when they reached a spot on which a green ride led away from the main road through the trees to the left. 'You remember this place; do you not?' said Violet. Phineas declared that he remembered the woodman's cottage well.

'I always come here when I am at Saulsby,' said Violet, 'that I may teach myself to think kindly of Lord Chiltern.'

'I understand it all,' said Phineas.

158

'He used to be so nice, only he has taught himself to be so rough. Will he ever change, do you think?'

Phineas knew that it was his duty to be honest. 'I think he would be changed altogether if we could bring him here—so that he should live among his friends.'

'Mr Finn,' she said, 'I wonder whether I may ask a question?'

'Any question.'

'Is there any quarrel between you and Lady Laura?'

'None.'

'Then why are you not going to be at Loughlinter this autumn?'

He paused a moment before he replied: 'It did not suit.'

'Perhaps I can guess it,' she said. 'But I will not try.'

'I would have given my left hand to have been at Loughlinter.'

'Are you so fond of it?'

'I should have been staying there with you,' he said. He paused and for a moment there was no word spoken by either of them; but he could perceive that her hand was playing with her horse's mane with a nervous movement. 'When I found how it must be, and that I must miss you, I rushed down here that I might see you for a momnet. And now I am here I do not dare to speak to you of myself. Have you not a word to say to me?'

'No—no—no,' she replied, 'not a word when you speak to me like that. Come—we will join the others.' Then she cantered on, and he followed her.

Though he spent the evening with her, and stood over her as she sang at the Earl's request, and pressed her hand as she went to bed, and was up to see her start in the morning, he could not draw from her either a word or a look.

CHAPTER FOUR

FEBRUARY was far advanced, and the new Reform Bill had already been brought forward, before Lady Laura Kennedy came up to town. Phineas got a note to say that she was at home and would see him if he called. He did so, and sat there for half an hour, having spoken no word on any other subject than that of politics. 'Where is your brother?' he said at last.

'Oswald is in London.'

'Where is he staying?'

'At Mauregy's.'

'Did he say anything about me?' asked Phineas.

'We mentioned your name certainly.'

'He had got a letter from me?'

'He did not say so.'

'I will see him tomorrow if I can.'

On the following morning Phineas called at Mauregy's Hotel, but he found that Lord Chiltern was out. He wrote a note and left it with the porter:

Dear Chiltern,

I particularly want to see you with reference to a letter I wrote to you last summer. I must be in the House today from four till the debate is over. I will meet you anywhere at any hour tomorrow morning.

Yours, always, P.F.

During the debate a note was brought to him:

I have got your letter this moment. Of course we must meet. We shall require to be private, and I will therefore be at your rooms at one o'clock on Wednesday.—C.

Phineas at once perceived that the note was written in an angry spirit. He crushed it into his pocket, and determined that he would be in his rooms at the hour named.

In the course of the debate Phineas got upon his legs. Hitherto he had failed altogether as a speaker. But there arose within him a sudden courage as soon as the sound of his own voice in that room had made itself intimate to his ear; and after the few first sentences, all fear, all awe, was gone from him. Barrington Erle came up to him as they were leaving the House, with his old easy manner. 'So you have got into form at last,' he said. 'I always thought it would come.' The verdict of Barrington Erle sufficed to assure him that he had succeeded.

Punctually at one o'clock the next day Lord Chiltern arrived at his lodgings. Phineas went forward with his hand out to meet his visitor. 'Chiltern,' he said, 'I am very glad to see you.' But Lord Chiltern did not take his hand. Passing on to the table, he chucked a letter across. Phineas perceived that it was that which he, in his great attempt to be honest, had written from the inn at Loughton.

'I received it oddly enough together with your own note at Mauregy's. It has been round the world, I suppose, and reached me only then. As far as I can learn you have not acted upon it. But I must ask you in what position you now stand towards Miss Effingham.'

'I think she regards me as an intimate friend.'

'I presume I may understand that you have given up any idea of changing that position?'

'You may understand nothing of the kind, Lord Chiltern.'

'Why? What hope have you?'

'I shall not speak of that.'

'Then, sir, I require that you shall meet me. Will you do that?'

'You mean to fight?'

'Yes, to fight.'

'You want to bully me, Chiltern.'

'No, sir; I simply want you not to interfere with that which you have long known I claim as my own.'

'But it is not your own.'

161

'Then you can only fight me.'

And the duel did indeed come off. The two men, with a friend apiece and a doctor, crossed the Channel and met on the sands at Blankenberg in Belgium about nine o'clock one morning. One shot was exchanged, and Phineas wounded in the right shoulder. Lord Chiltern offered to shake hands in a true spirit of friendship, if only his late friend would say that he did not intend to prosecute his suit with the young lady. Phineas would give no such pledge, and made his way back to London. No bone had been broken, and on the Tuesday he went down to the House, telling those who had missed him during the debate that he had been in Kent, where he had had an accident to his arm. He stayed and voted, and then went painfully home to his lodgings.

By the time that Mr Mildmay's great Reform Bill was going into committee Phineas was able to move about London in comfort, with his arm, however, still in a sling. Day after day, and clause after clause, the Reform Bill was fought in committee, and few men fought with more constancy on the side of the Ministers than did the Member for Loughton. Now words came very easily to him. And then quickly came to him a reputation for practical usefulness.

Otherwise he would hardly have been asked to a semi-political dinner at Lady Glencora Palliser's. There was no man among the eight men at the dinner-party not in Parliament, and the only other except Phineas not attached to the Government was Mr Palliser's great friend, John Grey, the Member for Silverbridge. There were four Cabinet Ministers in the room—the Duke, Lord Cantrip, Mr Gresham, and the owner of the mansion. There was also Barrington Erle and young Lord Fawn, an Under-Secretary of State. But the wit and grace of the ladies present lent more of character to the party than even the position of the men. Lady Glencora Palliser herself was a host. There was no woman then in London better able to talk to a dozen people on a dozen subjects; and then, moreover, she was still in the flush of her beauty and the bloom of her youth. Lady Laura was there, by what means divided from her husband Phineas could not imagine; but Lady Glencora was good at such divisions. Violet Effingham was in the room also, giving Phineas a blow at the heart as he saw her smile. And there was Madame Max Goesler. Phineas found that it was his fortune to take down to dinner, not Violet Effingham, but Madame Max Goesler.

Up to that moment he had never heard of Madame Max Goesler. He could not surmise whence she had come, or why she was there. She was probably something over thirty years of age. She had thick black hair, which she wore in curls which hung down low beneath her face. Her eyes were large, of a dark blue colour, and very bright. She seemed to intend that she employed them to conquer—looking as a knight may have looked in olden days who entered a chamber with his sword drawn from the scabbard and in his hand. In colour she was abundant, and yet the fabric of her dress was black, with traceries of yellow and ruby silk which went in and out through the black lace, across her bosom, and round her neck, and over her shoulders, and along her arms, and down to the very ground at her feet, robbing the black stuff of all its sombre solemnity. She had rubies in her ears, and a ruby brooch, and rubies in bracelets on her arms. Phineas, as he took his place by her side, thought that fortune had done well with him—only that he should have liked it so much better could he have been seated next to Violet Effingham.

'Mr Finn,' she said, 'what would I not give to be a member of the British Parliament at such a moment as this!'

'Why at such a moment as this particularly?'

'Because there is something to be done.'

'It sometimes seems to me that there is too much to be done.'

'Too much of nothingness, Mr Finn. But now there is a real fight in the lists. The one great drawback to the life of women is that they cannot act in politics.'

'And which side would you take?'

'What, here in England?' said Madame Max Goesler. 'Politically I should want to vote for everything that could be voted for—ballot, manhood suffrage, womanhood suffrage, unlimited right of striking, tenant right, education of everybody. But then, Mr Finn, there is such a difference between life and theory, is there not?'

'And it is so comfortable to have theories that one is not bound to carry out,' said Phineas.

'Isn't it? Mr Palliser, do you live up to your political theories?' At this moment Mr Palliser was sitting perfectly silent and he gave a little spring in his chair as this sudden address was made to him. 'Your House of Commons theories, I mean, Mr Palliser. Mr Finn is saying that it is very well to have far-advanced ideas because one is never called upon to act upon them practically.'

'That is a dangerous doctrine, I think,' said Mr Palliser gravely. 'I think I may say that I always am really anxious to carry into practice all those doctrines of policy which I advocate in theory.' Mr Palliser, when he had made his little speech, turned to the Duke's daughter and asked some question about the conservatories at Longroyston.

'I have called forth a word of wisdom,' said Madame Max Goesler, almost in a whisper.

'Yes,' said Phineas, 'and taught a Cabinet Minister to believe that I am a most unsound politician. You may have ruined my prospects for life, Madame Max Goesler.'

'Let me hope not. But to put aside joking, they tell me that you are sure to become a Minister.'

'Your informants are very kind,' he replied awkwardly.

Ten minutes after this, when the moment was just at hand in which the ladies were to retreat, Madame Max Goesler again addressed Phineas, looking very full into his face as she did so. 'I wonder whether the time will ever come, Mr Finn, in which you will give me an account of that day's journey to Blankenberg?'

'To Blankenberg!'

'Yes, to Blankenberg.' Then Lady Glencora rose from her seat, and Madame Max Goesler went out with the others.

What had Madame Max Goesler to do with his journey to Blankenberg? thought Phineas. And why should a perfect stranger to him have dared to ask him such a question? But as the conversation round the table drifted into politics Phineas, for a while, forgot Madame Max Goesler and the Blankenberg journey, and listened to the eager words of Cabinet Ministers, now and again uttering a word of his own, and showing that he, too, was eager. But the session in Mr Palliser's dining-room was not long, and Phineas soon found himself making his way amidst a throng of coming guests into the rooms above. He first encountered Lady Laura. 'Do tell me one thing, Lady Laura—who is Madame Max Goesler?'

'She is the widow of an Austrian banker, and has lived the greater part of her life at Vienna. She is very rich, and has a small house in Park Lane, where she receives people so exclusively that it has come to be thought an honour to be invited by Madame Max Goesler. Her enemies say that her father was a German Jew, living in England, in the employment of the Viennese bankers, and they say also that she has been married a second time to an Austrian Count, to whom she allows ever so much a year to stay away from her. What they do know is that Madame Max Goesler spends seven or eight thousand a year, and that she will give no man an opportunity of even asking her to marry him.'

During the time that Lady Laura was giving him the history of Madame Max Goesler his eyes had wandered round, and he had perceived that Violet was talking to Lord Fawn, an unmarried peer of something over thirty years of age, with an unrivalled pair of whiskers, a small estate, and a rising political reputation. Lord Fawn had been talking to Violet through the whole dinner, and Phineas was beginning to think that he should like to make another journey to Blankenberg, with the object of meeting his lordship on the sands. When Lady Laura had done speaking, Phineas succeeded in making his way up to the place in which Violet was still standing, with Lord Fawn beside her. 'I have been making such a struggle, to get to you,' he said.

She received him with her genial smile, looking exactly as she had looked when he had parted from her on the morning after their ride. 'I have so longed to hear from you how you got on at Loughlinter,' he said.

'Yes, yes; and I will tell you something of it some day. What a happy man you were at dinner! You had Madame Max Goesler all to yourself for nearly two hours, and I suppose there was not a creature in the room who did not envy you. What did she talk about?'

'The ballot chiefly, and manhood suffrage.'

'She said something more than that, I am sure. Madame Max Goesler never lets any man go without entrancing him.'

'I think her very beautiful,' said Phineas.

'So do I,' said Violet. 'And she is a dear ally of mine. We were a week together last winter, and swore an undying friendship.'

Half an hour after this, when Phineas was preparing to fight his way out of the house, he was again close to Madame Max Goesler. He had not found a single moment in which to ask Violet for an answer to his old question, and was retiring from the field discomfited, but not dispirited. Lord Fawn, he thought, was not a serious obstacle in his way.

'I saw that you were successful this evening,' said Madame Max Goesler to him.

'I was not aware of any success.'

'I call it great success to be able to make your way where you will through such a crowd as there is here. You seem to me to be so stout a cavalier that I shall ask you to find my servant, and bid him get my carriage. Will you mind?' Phineas, of course, declared that he would be delighted, and, having returned, was standing with Madame Max Goesler in the cloak-room. She said, 'You know Lord Fawn, who was talking to Miss Effingham just now. You should have heard him trying to pay me a compliment before dinner. It was like a donkey walking a minuet, and yet they say he is a clever man and can make speeches.'

'He is a well-informed man,' said Phineas.

'But he is an oaf, is he not? And yet they say he is to marry that girl.'

'I do not think he will,' said Phineas stoutly.

'I hope not, with all my heart; and I hope that somebody else may—unless somebody else should change his mind. Mind you come and call on me—193 Park Lane. I daresay you know the little cottage.' Then he put Madame Max Goesler into her carriage, and walked away to his club.

.　　.　　.　　.　　.

One morning Phineas received a note from Lord Brentford:

My dear Mr Finn,

You are no doubt aware that Lord Bosanquet's death has taken Mr Mottram into the Upper House, and that Mr Lawrence Fitzgibbon has been offered his place as Under-Secretary for the Colonies. This will vacate the Irish seat at the Treasury Board, and I am commissioned by Mr Mildmay to offer it to you. Perhaps you will do me the pleasure of calling on me tomorrow between the hours of eleven and twelve.

Yours very sincerely,

Brentford.

Even as a junior lord he would have a thousand a year! Even as a junior lord he could make himself useful, and when once he should be known to be a good working man, promotion would come to him. No ladder can be mounted without labour; but he already had his foot upon it.

Lord Brentford had also asked the new Lord of the Treasury to make a certain communication on his behalf to his son. This Phineas had found himself obliged to promise to do.

'Dear Lord Chiltern,' he had commenced, 'I write at the instance of your father, who has heard nothing of our little affair.' Then he explained at length Lord Brentford's wishes as he understood them. 'Pray come home. Touching V.E., I feel that I am bound to tell you that I still mean to try my fortune, but that I have no ground for hoping that my fortune will be good. Since the day on the sands I have never met her but in society. I know you will be glad to hear that my wound was nothing; and I think you will be glad to hear that I have got my foot on to the ladder of promotion.'

By the middle of September there was assembled a large party at Matching Priory, the country mansion belonging to Mr Plantagenet Palliser. Phineas was invited, and when he arrived at Matching he found that half the Cabinet was there. Mr Kennedy was not there, nor was Lady Laura. Mrs Max Goesler was there also, and Violet Effingham was expected in two days, and Lord Chiltern at the end of the week; and on

167

the very day on which Phineas reached Matching the Duke of Omnium arrived; Mr Palliser was the Duke's nephew and heir. The Duke shook hands with Phineas, and made a little bow, and in a moment was speaking a word of condescension to some other favoured individual. Phineas retreated.

Violet Effingham, to the surprise of Phineas, was brought to Matching by Lord Brentford. Phineas at first thought that it was intended that the Earl and his son should meet and make up their quarrel at Mr Palliser's house. But Lord Brentford stayed only one night, and Phineas on the next morning heard the whole history of his coming and going from Violet. 'I have almost been on my knees to him to stay,' she said.

'And what did he say?'

'That if Chiltern can be made to go to Saulsby, fatted calves without stint will be killed. I shall do all I can to make him go; and so must you, Mr Finn.'

Lord Chiltern arrived, and Phineas was a little nervous as to their meeting. The last time he had seen this man they had met with pistols in their hands to shoot at each other. 'Well, old fellow,' Lord Chiltern greeted him, laughing. Then all doubt was over, and Phineas was shaking his former friend warmly by the hand. 'My father has been here, so Violet tells me.'

Phineas felt some hesitation in speaking of Miss Effingham to Lord Chiltern. 'And how do you get on with her?' asked Lord Chiltern. 'She has refused me three times. Have you been more fortunate?'

Lord Chiltern, as he asked his question, looked full into Finn's face. 'No,' said he at last, 'I have not been more fortunate.'

'Then we start fairly, Finn. Now we understand each other.'

That evening Lord Chiltern took Miss Effingham down to dinner. It was almost nothing to Phineas that Madame Max Goesler was intrusted to him.

.   .   .   .   .

Phineas and Lord Chiltern were to leave Matching together. Phineas was to remain at his office all October, and in November the general election was to take place.

There was a very tender parting between Phineas and Madame Max Goesler. She had learned from him pretty nearly all his history, and certainly knew more of his affairs than any of those in London who had been his most staunch friends. 'Of course you'll get a seat,' she said. 'They never throw over an ally so useful as you are.'

'The truth is, Madame Max, I do not know where I shall go. There is to be redistribution of the boroughs, and Loughton may go into the melting pot with the rest.'

'Mr Finn—I wonder whether I may say one thing,' she continued. Then, blushing and laughing as she spoke, in spite of her usual self-confidence, she told him that accident had made her rich, full of money. Money was a drug with her. Money she knew was wanted. Would he not understand her, and come to her, and learn from her how faithful a woman could be?

He still was holding her by the hand, and he now raised it to his lips and kissed it. 'The offer from you,' he said, 'is as high-minded, as generous, and as honourable as its acceptance by me would be mean-spirited, vile, and ignoble. But whether I fail or whether I succeed, you shall see me before the winter is over.'

London was very empty; but the approaching elections still kept some there who otherwise would have been looking after the first flush of pheasants. Barrington Erle was there, and was not long in telling Phineas his views.

'Let me see. Loughton is grouped with Smotherem, and Walker is a deal too strong at Smotherem to hear of any other claim. Would you have another chance at Loughshane? Of course you know that Morris is very ill.' This Mr Morris was the sitting Member for Loughshane.

Phineas wrote to his father, asking after the borough, and asking after the health of Mr Morris. Before Dr Finn had had an opportunity of answering his son's letter Mr Morris had been gathered to his fathers. Phineas came over and stood for the borough. The contest was very sharp, but Phineas was returned.

Again successful! Had not everything gone well with him —so well, as almost to justify him in expecting that even yet

169

Violet Effingham would become his wife? Dear, dearest Violet! Then he questioned himself as to what he would say to Miss Flood Jones, as he went to meet her that evening at a neighbour's house.

'I am so glad to see you, Mary,' he said.

'Thank you. We did not happen to meet last year, did we, Mr Finn?'

'Do not call me Mr Finn, Mary.'

'You are such a great man now!'

'Not at all a great man.'

'But it is a great thing to be in Parliament and in the Government too.'

'It is a great thing for me, Mary, to have a salary, though it may only be for a year or two. However, I will not deny that it is pleasant to have been successful.'

'It has been very pleasant to us, Phineas.'

Then there was a pause in the conversation for a moment. 'I often wonder when the time will come that I shall be quietly at home again. I have to be back in my office in London this day week, and yet I have not had a single hour to myself since I have been at Killaloe. But I will certainly ride over and see your mother.'

'Dear Mary,' he said as he pressed her hand that night, 'things will get themselves settled at last, I suppose.' He was behaving very ill to her, but he did not mean to behave ill.

He rode over to Floodborough, and saw Mrs Flood Jones. Mrs Flood Jones, however, received him very coldly, and Mary did not appear. Mary had communicated to her mother her resolutions as to her future life. 'The fact is, Mamma, I love him. I cannot help it. If he ever chooses to come for me, here I am. If he does not, I will bear it as well as I can.'

.　　　.　　　.　　　.　　　.

Before Christmas came there were various sources of uneasiness at Loughlinter. There had been, as a matter of course, great anxiety as to the elections. Mr Kennedy's own seat was quite safe; but there were the tidings from Ireland to be re-

170

ceived; and respecting one special borough in Ireland Lady Laura evinced more solicitude than her husband approved.

'He is in,' said Lady Laura, opening a telegram.

'Who is in?'

'Our friend Phineas Finn.'

'You over-do your anxiety on such a subject,' he said.

'What do you mean, Robert? This man is my friend, is your friend, has been my brother's best friend, is loved by my father—and is loved by me, very dearly.'

'I will not have you love any man—very dearly.'

'Robert!'

'I will have no such expressions from you. They are unseemly.'

'Am I to understand that I am insulted by an accusation?'

'There has been no accusation. If you will take my advice, you will cease to think of Mr Finn extravagantly; and I must desire you to hold no further direct communication with him.'

'I have held no communication with him,' said Lady Laura, advancing a step towards him. But Mr Kennedy simply pointed to the telegram in her hand. 'I need hardly say to you that I intend to accuse you of no impropriety of feeling in reference to this young man.'

'No, Robert, you need hardly say that. Such an allusion is an insult which I will not endure to have repeated again. If you say another word in any way suggesting the possibility of improper relations between me and Mr Finn I will write to my father and my brother and desire them to take me from your house. If you wish me to remain here, you had better be careful!'

He was cowed and left her. This had occurred about the end of November, and on the 20th December Violet Effingham reached Loughlinter. Life in Mr Kennedy's house had gone quietly during the intervening three weeks, but not very pleasantly. Lady Laura had triumphed; but on some other matters he continued to assert himself, taking his wife to church twice every Sunday, using longer family prayers than she approved, reading an additional sermon himself every Sunday evening, calling upon her for weekly attention to elaborate household accounts, till sometimes she almost longed to talk again about Phineas Finn so that there might be a rupture and she might escape. But her husband asserted himself within bounds, and she submitted, longing for the coming of Violet Effingham.

To Violet, very shortly after her arrival, she told her whole story. 'This is terrible,' said Violet. 'In any case, as far as I can see, Madame Max Goesler is Mr Finn's present passion.'

'I do not believe it in the least,' said Lady Laura, firing up.

'Why should he not marry Madame Max Goesler? It would be just the thing for him. She is very rich.'

'Never. You will be his wife.'

'Laura, you are the most capricious of women. You have two dear friends, and you insist that I shall marry them both. Which shall I take first?'

'Oswald will be here in a day or two, and you can take him if you like it. No doubt he will ask you. But I do not think you will.'

Lord Chiltern came on Christmas Eve, and was received with open arms by his sister, and with that painful irritating affection which such a girl as Violet can show to a man when she will not give him that other affection for which his heart is panting. The two men were civil to each other, but very cold. On the Christmas morning Mr Kennedy asked his brother-in-law to go to church. 'It's a kind of thing I never do,' said Lord Chiltern. Mr Kennedy looked a look of horror. Lady Laura showed that she was unhappy. Violet Effingham turned away her face, and smiled.

Christmas Day and the next day passed without any sign from Lord Chiltern, and on the day after that he was to go away. After breakfast on that last morning he was upstairs with his sister in her own room. 'Laura,' he said, 'go down like a good girl and make Violet come up here. And mind, you are not to come back yourself. I must have Violet alone.'

'But suppose Violet will not come?'

'I think she will have common sense enough to teach her that I have a right to ask for an interview.' Violet did come.

'Violet, this is very good of you,' said Lord Chiltern. 'It is the old story, and I am so bad at words.'

'I must have been bad at words too, as I have not been able to make you understand.'

'While you are single there must be hope—unless you tell me that you have given yourself to another man.'

'I have not done that.'

'Then how can I not hope?'

'But I am not the only woman.'

'To me you are, absolutely, as though there were none other on the face of God's earth. I live much alone; but you are always with me. I am thinking of you day and night. The more indifferent you show yourself to me, the more I love you. Violet, try to love me.' He came up to her, and took her by both her hands, and tears were in his eyes. 'Say you will try to love me. You used to love me—a little.'

'Indeed—indeed, I did.'

'And now? Is it all changed now?'

'No,' she said, retreating from him.

'How is it, then? Violet, speak to me honestly. Will you be my wife?' She did not answer him, and he stood for a moment looking at her. Then he rushed at her, and, seizing her in his arms, kissed her forehead, her lips, her cheeks, then both her hands, and then her lips again. Then he went back to the rug before the fire, and stood there with his back turned to her.

After a minute or two he turned round. He approached her and put his arm round her waist. 'Do you not believe me?'

'I do believe you. And you will be good?'

'Ah—I do not know that.'

'Try, and I will love you so dearly. Nay, I do love you dearly. I do. I do.'

'This is a great change,' he said. 'I hardly know myself in my new joy.'

'Remember, sir, that the first thing you have to do is to write to your father.'

He instantly went to the writing-table and took up paper and pen. 'Come along,' he said. 'You are to dictate it.' But this she refused to do. 'I cannot write it,' he said, throwing down the pen. 'My blood is in such a tumult that I cannot steady my hand.'

'You must not be so tumultuous, Oswald, or I shall have to live in a whirlwind.'

'You repent?'

'No, indeed; but you must not be rough to me, and outrageous, and fierce—will you, Oswald?'

'I will do my best, dearest. And you may at any rate be sure of this, that I will love you always. So much good of myself I can say.'

'It is very good,' she answered. 'And now I must go. And as you are leaving Loughlinter I will say good-bye. When am I to have the honour and felicity of beholding your lordship again?'

'Say a nice word to me before I am off, Violet.'

'I—love—you—better—than all the world beside; and I mean—to be your wife—some day. Are not those nice words?'

He would not prolong his stay at Loughlinter. 'I don't like Kennedy, and I don't like being in his house,' he said to Violet. His plan was to stop that night at Carlisle, and write to his father from thence. He would then go on to London and down to Willingford, and there wait for his father's answer. 'There is no reason why I should lose more of the hunting than necessary.'

'And so that is settled at last,' said Violet to Laura that night.

'I hope you do not regret it.'

'On the contrary, I am as happy as the moments are long. I have always loved him. But from the beginning, when I was a child, I have known that he was dangerous. And I could have lived without him. There have been moments when I thought I could learn to love someone else.'

'Poor Phineas, for instance.'

'We will mention no names. Your brother, Laura, is dangerous. A sense of danger does not make me unhappy, though the threatened evil may be fatal.'

Lady Laura Kennedy thereupon wrote a letter to her friend Phineas Finn.

174

My dear Friend,

Violet Effingham is here, and Oswald has just left us. I think it best to let you know immediately that she has accepted him—at last. If there be any pang in this to you, be sure that I will grieve for you. I believe I need say nothing more; except that it shall be among my prayers that you may obtain all things that may tend to make you happy, honourable, and of high esteem.

> Your most sincere friend,
> Laura Kennedy.

When Phineas received Lady Laura Kennedy's letter he was sitting in his gorgeous apartment in the Colonial Office. Then it was all over! The game was played out. As for the colonies, he would have parted with every colony belonging to Great Britain to have got the hand of Violet Effingham for himself. Now at this moment he told himself that he had never loved anyone but Violet Effingham.

On the fourth day after his sorrow had befallen him Phineas wrote a line to Madame Goesler to ask if she would be at home. 'I will be at home from five to six—and alone.' That was the answer and Phineas was of course at the cottage a few minutes after five, and told her his grief.

'You are very good-natured to let me come.'

'No; it is so good of you to trust me. It is better to speak it out. You will get over it quicker in that way than in any other. Mr Finn, there are other ladies in the world prettier than Miss Violet Effingham. Of course you will not admit that now. Just at this moment, and for a month or two, she is peerless, and you will feel yourself to be of all men the most unfortunate. Think of your politics, and your speeches, and your colonies, rather than of your love. You are at home there, and no Lord Chiltern can rob you of your success. And if you are down in the mouth, come to me.' She gave him her hand, which was very soft, and left it for a moment in his, and he was consoled.

.   .   .   .   .

Lord Chiltern did exactly as he said he would do. He wrote to his father as he passed through Carlisle, and at once went on to his hunting at Willingford. But his letter was very stiff and ungainly.

Railway Hotel, Carlisle,
December 27, 186–

My Lord,

I am now on my way from Loughlinter to London, and write this letter to you in compliance with a promise made by me to my sister and to Miss Effingham. I have asked Violet to be my wife, and she has accepted me, and they think that you will be pleased to hear that this has been done. Laura thinks that you will wish to see both Violet and myself at Saulsby. For myself, I can only say that, should you desire me to come, I will do so on receiving your assurance that I shall be treated neither with fatted calves nor with reproaches. I am not aware that I have deserved either.

I am, my lord, yours affect.,
Chiltern.

P.S. My address will be 'The Bull, Willingford'.

The Earl was of course disgusted by the pertinacious obstinacy of his son's letter, and for an hour or two swore to himself that he would not answer it. But before the evening had passed he had done so.

Saulsby, December 29, 186–

My dear Chiltern,

I have received your letter, and am truly delighted to hear that dear Violet has accepted you as her husband. You have long known my opinion of her. I shall be proud to welcome her as a daughter to my house.

I shall of course write to her immediately, and will endeavour to settle some early day for her coming here. When I have done so I will write to you again, and can only say

176

that I will endeavour to make Saulsby comfortable to you.

Your affectionate father,

Brentford.

Richards, the groom, is still here. You had perhaps better write to him direct about your horses.

By the middle of February arrangements had all been made. Lord Chiltern, on his arrival, went immediately to his father. 'My lord,' said he, walking up to the Earl with his hand out, 'I am very glad to come back to Saulsby. I suppose Violet is here.'

'Yes, she is here, and Laura. They will be very glad to see you. So am I.'

'Thank you, sir,' said Lord Chiltern, looking his father full in the face.

'I have been very much pleased by this engagement,' continued the Earl.

'What do you think I must be, then?' said the son, laughing. 'I have been at it, you know, off and on, ever so many years; and have sometimes thought I was quite a fool not to get it out of my head. And now she talks as though it were she who had been in love with me all the time!'

'Perhaps she was.'

'I don't believe it in the least. She may be a little so now.'

'I hope you mean that she always shall be so.'

'I shan't be the worst husband in the world, I hope; and I am quite sure I shan't be the best.'

Now that she had succumbed, Violet did not scruple to be as generous as a maiden should be who has acknowledged herself to be conquered. She would walk with him and ride with him, and take a lively interest in the performances of all his horses, and listen to hunting stories as long as he chose to tell them. All of which set Lady Laura thinking whether her friend had not been wiser than she had been. She had never known anything of that sort of friendship with her husband.

In her misery one day Lady Laura told her brother of the terrible dreariness of her life at Loughlinter, and of her inability to induce her husband to alter it for her sake.

177

'Do you mean that he ill-treats you?' said the brother, with a scowl.

'He does not beat me, if you mean that. He is hard, and dry, and just, and dispassionate, and he wishes me to be the same. That is all.'

'I never could understand why you married him. If you think well of it I will go off to Loughlinter tomorrow and tell him that you will never return to him. And if you are not safe from him here at Saulsby you shall go abroad with us.'

'I shall go back to Loughlinter,' she said. 'I will try it for another year.'

'If it does not succeed, come to us.'

'I cannot say what I will do. Never be a tyrant, Oswald; or at any rate, not a cold tyrant. Beating might often be a mercy.'

CHAPTER FIVE

THERE was a new trouble coming. The Reform Bill for England had passed; but now there was to be a Reform Bill for Ireland. Phineas had invited his senior colleague, Mr Monk, to visit Ireland with him, in view of certain ideas respecting tenant-right which Mr Monk was beginning to adopt and in which Phineas had pledged his support, despite his colleague's warning that it might prove unwise to do so at this stage. It was a great day in Killaloe, that on which Phineas arrived at the doctor's house leading a Cabinet Minister.

There was a large dinner-party at the doctor's on the day after Mr Monk's arrival.

'Oh, Mr Monk,' said Mrs Finn, 'it is such a blessing for Phineas that you should be so good to him.'

'I don't know any young man,' said he, 'in whose career I have taken so strong an interest.'

Phineas had taken out to dinner the mother of his devoted Mary, Mrs Flood Jones. 'What a pleasure it must be to the doctor and Mrs Finn to see you come back in this way,' said Mrs Flood Jones.

'With all my bones unbroken?' said he, laughing.

'Yes; with all your bones unbroken. You know, Phineas, when we first heard that you were to sit in Parliament we were afraid that you might break a rib or two.'

'I am not out of the wood yet, Mrs Flood Jones. There is still plenty of possibility for coming to grief.'

'As far as I can understand it you are out of the wood. All that your friends here want to see now is that you should marry some nice English girl, with a little money, if possible. Mary was saying, only the other day, that if you were once married we should all feel quite safe about you. We all take the most lively interest in your welfare.' Thus Mrs Flood Jones signified that she had forgiven him his thoughtlessness to her daughter; and showed him, also, that Mary's feelings were not now of a nature to trouble her.

Mr Monk's programme allowed him a week at Killaloe, and from thence he was to go to Limerick and to Dublin, in order that he might be entertained at public dinners and speak about tenant-right. Mr Monk had counselled Phineas to remain at Killaloe. But Phineas had refused to subject himself to such cautious abstinence. Mr Monk had come to Ireland as his friend, and he would see him through his travels.

'You might find it disadvantageous to you in London.'

'I must take my chance of that.'

Phineas went with Mr Monk first to Limerick and then to Dublin, and found himself at both places to be regarded as a hero only second to the great hero. At both places the one subject of debate was tenant-right—could anything be done to make it profitable for men with capital to put their capital into Irish land? The fertility of the soil was questioned by no one, nor the sufficiency of railroads and the like, nor the abundance of labour. The only difficulty was that the men who were to produce wealth from these things had no guarantee that it would be theirs when it was created. That was the question which Mr Monk pledged himself to keep in hand when Parliament should meet. Of course Phineas spoke also, and of course he pledged himself.

'I am sorry you went so far as that,' Mr Monk said to him. They were standing on the pier at Kingstown, and Mr Monk was preparing to return to England.

'And why not I as far as you?'

'Because I am prepared to resign my office tomorrow; and directly I can see Mr Gresham I shall offer to do so.'

'He won't accept your resignation.'

'He must accept it, unless he is prepared to instruct the Irish Secretary to bring in such a bill as I can support.'

'I shall be exactly in the same boat.'

'But you ought not to be in the same boat; nor need you. My advice to you is to say nothing about it till you get back to London, and then speak to Lord Cantrip. Tell him that you will not say anything on the subject in the House, but that in the event of there being a division you hope to be allowed to vote as on an open question. It may be that I shall get Gresham's assent, and if so we shall be all right. If I do not you must resign also.'

'Of course I shall,' said Phineas.

'But I do not think they will. You have been too useful, and they will wish to avoid the weakness which comes to a ministry from changing its team. Good-bye, my dear fellow; and remember my last word of advice to you is to stick by the ship. I am quite sure it is a career which will suit you.'

It was September when Phineas found himself back at Killaloe, and he was due to be at his office in London in November. The excitement of Mr Monk's company was now over and he had nothing to do but to receive pouches full of official papers from the Colonial Office, and study all the statistics which came within his reach in reference to tenant-right. He had not, since his arrival, been a moment alone with Mary Flood Jones. She had kept out of his way successfully, though she had constantly been with him in company. As for Phineas, he had felt that his old friend was very cold to him.

One evening he managed to be alone with Mary for a few

minutes. 'Mary,' he said to her suddenly, 'it seems to me that you have avoided me purposely ever since I have been at home. We used to be such great friends.'

'That was before you were a great man, Phineas. You know so many people now, and people of such a different sort, that of course I fall a little into the background.'

'I believe there is no one in the whole world,' he said, after a pause, 'whose friendship is more to me than yours is. I think of it so often, Mary. Say that it shall be between us as it used to be.'

'Of course we are friends. We have always been friends.'

'What would you say if you heard that I had resigned my office and given up my seat?' he asked. Of course she expressed her horror at such an idea, and then he told her everything.

'And do you mean that you would lose your salary?'

'Certainly I should. But what is a man to do? Would you recommend me to say that black is white?'

'I am sure you will never do that.'

'You see, Mary, it is very nice to be called by a big name and to have a salary. But there are drawbacks. There is this especial drawback.'

'What especial drawback, Phineas?'

'A man cannot do what he pleases with himself. How can a man marry, so circumstanced as I am?'

'A man may be very happy without marrying, I suppose.'

He paused for many moments before he spoke again. 'I wonder whether you would listen to me if I were to tell you a history?' Of course she listened, and the history he told her was the tale of his love for Violet Effingham.

'Then, Mr Finn, you must seek someone else who is equally blessed.'

'Mary, that is ill-natured. You have not believed that I loved Miss Effingham because she was rich. Love is involuntary. It does not often run in a yoke with prudence. I did love her very dearly.'

'Did love her, Mr Finn?'

'Yes—did love her. Is there inconstancy in changing one's love, and in loving again?'

'I do not know,' said Mary.

'If there be, dear, I am inconstant. But I could not speak of a new passion till I had told the story of that which has passed away. You have heard it all now, Mary. Can you try to love me, after that?'

When she essayed to speak she found that she was dumb. She was as happy as earth, as heaven could make her; but she did not know how to tell him that she was happy. He still sat looking at her, and now by degrees he had got her hand in his. 'Mary,' he said, 'will you be my wife?'

She said, 'If you came to me tomorrow and told me you had no income it would make no difference. I would sooner give up that than be a clog on you.' Then he took her in his arms and kissed her. 'Oh, Phineas!' she said, 'I do love you so entirely!'

'My own one!'

'Yes; your own one. But if you had known it always! Never mind. Now you are my own—are you not?'

'Indeed yes, dearest.'

'Oh, I do believe I am the happiest creature on the face of this earth!'

.   .   .   .   .

Before Phineas had returned to London his engagement with Mary Flood Jones was known to all Killaloe. That other secret of his, which had reference to the probability of his being obliged to throw up his office, was known only to Mary herself. December was half over before he saw Lord Cantrip. 'Yes, yes,' said Lord Cantrip, 'I see what you were about. I wish I had been at your elbow.'

'You think, then, I ought to resign?'

'As you wish it. Of course I'll speak to Gresham. Monk, I believe, has resigned already. I can only advise you to forget all that took place in Ireland. If you will do so, nobody else will remember it.'

He was with Madame Goesler frequently, and discussed his position with her. 'I think you are quite right, my friend,' she said. 'What—you are to be in Parliament and say that this black thing is white, or that this white thing is black, because you like to take your salary! That cannot be honest.' Then, when he came to talk to her of money, that he must give up Parliament itself, she offered to lend him money. When he pointed out that there would never come a time in which he could pay such money back she stamped her foot and told him that he had better leave her. 'You have high principle,' she said, 'but not principle sufficiently high to understand that this thing could be done between you and me without disgrace to either of us.'

But he whispered to this new friend no word of the engagement with his dear Irish Mary. His Irish life, he would tell himself, was a thing quite separate from his life in England. He said not a word about Mary Flood Jones to any of those with whom he lived in London. He began to reflect what sort of a blackguard he would be were he to desert Mary and marry Madame Max Goesler. Half a dozen people who knew him and her might think ill of him for his conduct to Mary, but when he thundered forth his Liberal eloquence as an independent Member, having the fortune of a charming wife to back him, giving excellent dinners at the same time in Park Lane, would not the world praise him very loudly?

There had come upon Madame Goesler a seriousness of gesture, and almost a solemnity of tone, which made him conscious that he should in no way trifle with her. She was so earnest in her friendship that he owed it to her to tell her everything. But before he could think of the words in which his tale should be told she had gone on to question him. 'Is it solely about money that you fear?' she said.

'It is simply that I have no income on which to live.'

'Have I not offered you money?'

'But Madame Goesler, you who offer it would yourself despise me if I took it.'

'No, I do deny it. Money is neither god nor devil, that it should make one noble and another vile. It is an accident, if honestly possessed. If I give to you a thousand pounds, now this moment, and you take it, you are base; but if I leave it you in my will, and die, you take it, and are not base. Explain to me the cause of that.'

'You have not said it quite all.'

'What have I left unsaid?'

'It is because you are a woman, and young, and beautiful, that no man may take wealth from your hands.'

'You will not take money from my hand?'

'No, Madame Goesler; I cannot do that.'

'Take the hand then first. When it and all that it holds are your own, you can help yourself as you list.' So saying, she stood before him with her right hand stretched out towards him. The temptation certainly was very strong. She was standing there with her hand stretching towards him. He took it.

'My friend,' he said.

'I will be called friend by you no more,' she said. 'You must call me Marie, your own Marie, or you must never call me by any name again. Which shall it be, sir?' He paused a moment, holding her hand. 'Speak to me! tell me! Which shall it be?'

'It cannot be as you have hinted to me,' he said at last. Instantly the hand was withdrawn, and she strode out of the room.

The day of the debate came, and Phineas Finn was still at the Colonial Office. But his resignation had been sent in and accepted. About noon his successor came, and he had the gratification of resigning his arm-chair to Mr Bonteen. There was a glance of triumph in his enemy's eyes, and an exultation in the tone of his enemy's voice, which were very bitter to him. He left him as quickly as he could. He knew that he could not venture to think of remaining in London as a Member of Parliament with no other income than that which his father could allow him, even if he could again secure a seat in Parliament. The Irish Reform Bill was scrambled through the two Houses, and then the Session was over, and they who knew anything of the private concerns of Mr Phineas Finn were aware that he was about to return to Ireland, and did not intend to reappear on the scene which had known him so well for the last five years.

Among those of whom he was bound to take a special leave the members of the family of Lord Brentford were, of course, the foremost. Lord Chiltern and Violet Effingham were to be married within a month.

'I shall try and make the best of it,' said Chiltern to Phineas. 'But I say, you'll come over and ride Bonebreaker again. He's down there at the Bull, and I've taken a little box close by. I can't stand the governor's county for hunting.'

'And will your wife go down to Willingford?'

'Of course she will, and ride to hounds a great deal closer than I can ever do. Mind you come, and if there's anything in the stable fit to carry you you shall have it.'

It was on the morning of the Sunday on which he was to leave London that he saw Lady Laura. He found her quite alone, and he could not but perceive how very much she was altered in appearance, so much had her troubles preyed upon her spirit. 'So you have come to say good-bye,' she said as she rose to meet him.

'Yes, Lady Laura; to say good-bye.' Then he was silent, with his hat dangling in his hands and his eyes fixed upon the floor.

'Do you know, Mr Finn,' she said, 'I am very angry with myself about you.'

'Then it must be because you have been too kind to me.'

'It is because I fear that I have done much to injure you. From the first day I knew you, when we were talking about the beginning of the Reform Bill, I wished that you should come among us and be one of us.'

'I have been with you to my infinite satisfaction, while it lasted.'

'But it has not lasted, and now I fear that it has done you harm.'

'Who can say whether it has been for good or evil? But I am very grateful to you for all the goodness you have shown me. Your father has told me that you are going to Dresden.'

'Yes; he will accompany me. It is a sad break up, is it not? But the lawyer says that if I remain here I may be subject to very disagreeable attempts from Mr Kennedy to force me to go back again.'

He wanted to part from her with some special expression of affection, but he did not know how to choose his words. He had wished that some allusion should be made, not to the Braes of Linter, but to the close confidence which had so long existed between them; but he found that the language to do this properly was wanting to him. Had the opportunity arisen he would have told her now the whole story of Mary Flood Jones; but the opportunity did not come, and he left her, never having mentioned the name of his Mary.

As he sat down to dine at his lodgings for the last time he saw a small note lying on the table. He knew the handwriting well, and he hesitated for a moment before at last he opened it.

I learn that you are going today, and I write a word which you will receive just as you are departing. It is to say merely this—that when I left you the other day I was angry, not with you, but with myself. Let me wish you all good wishes and that prosperity which I know you will win.

Yours very truly,

M.M.G.

Should he put off his journey and go to her this very evening and claim her? The question was asked and answered in a moment. He wrote to her a reply.

Thanks, dear friend. I do not doubt but that you and I understand each other thoroughly, and that each trusts the other for good wishes and honest intentions.

Always yours,

P.F.

When he had written this, he kept it till the last moment in his hand, thinking that he would not send it. But as he slipped into the cab, he gave the note to his late landlady to post.

On the first night of his arrival at Killaloe he sat for an hour downstairs with his father talking over his plans. The old doctor was not quite as well off as he had been when Phineas first started with his high hopes for London. Since that day he had abandoned his profession and was now living on the fruits of his life's labour. For the last two years he had been absolved from the necessity of providing an income for his son, and had allowed himself to feel that no such demand upon him would again be made. Now, however, it was necessary that he should do so. Could his son manage to live on two hundred a year? There would then be four hundred a year left for the wants of the family at home. Phineas swore that he could fight his battle on a hundred and fifty, and they ended the argument by splitting the difference. Tenant-right was a very fine thing, but could it be worth such a fall as this?

'And about dear Mary?' said the father.

'I hope it may not be very long,' said Phineas.

'I shall never be impatient—never,' Mary said to him. 'But of course we cannot be married for the next twenty years.'

'Say forty, Mary.'

'I will say anything you like. And, Phineas, I must tell you one thing. I am beginning to understand how much you have given up for me.'

He swore to her that he was prouder of winning her than anything he had ever done in all his life, and that of all the treasures that had ever come in his way she was the most precious. She went to bed that night the happiest girl in all Connaught.

Before the summer was over Phineas received a letter from Lord Cantrip.

Mr Gresham has been talking to me, and we both think that a permanent Government appointment may be acceptable to you. There is a vacancy for a poor-law inspector in Ireland, whose residence I believe should be in Cork. The salary is a thousand a year. Should the appointment suit you, Mr Gresham will be most happy to nominate you to the office. Let me have a line at your early convenience.

'A thousand a year!' said Mary Flood Jones, opening her eyes wide with wonder at the golden future before them.

'It is nothing very great,' said Phineas.

'Oh, Phineas; surely a thousand a year will be very nice.'

'It will be certain,' said Phineas, 'and then we can be married tomorrow.'

'But I have been making up my mind to wait ever so long,' said Mary.

'Then your mind must be unmade,' said Phineas.

The Eustace Diamonds

CHAPTER ONE

IT was admitted by all her friends, and also by her enemies—
who were in truth the more numerous and active body of the
two—that Lizzie Greystock had done very well with herself.
She was the only child of old Admiral Greystock, a man who
liked whist, wine and wickedness in general. She was hardly
nineteen when her father died, greatly in debt; but before
eight months were passed she was engaged to be married to
Sir Florian Eustace.

The match with Sir Florian Eustace was certainly very
splendid. He was about eight-and-twenty, very handsome, of
immense wealth, moving in the best circles, popular, with the
reputation of a gallant soldier, and a most devoted lover. He
was one who denied himself no pleasures, let the cost be what
it might in health, pocket, or morals. They told him that he
was like to die if he did not change his manner of living:
they had all been short-lived, the Eustaces, but they were
grand people, and never were afraid of death.

The marriage took place. They spent a honeymoon of six
weeks at a place he had in Scotland. They went abroad—
and before the end of the spring he was dead.

She was wretched and would see no one. But friends and
enemies did not hesitate to say that Lizzie Greystock had
done very well, for it was known that in the settlements made
she had been treated with unwonted generosity. In due course
a baby son was born to her. She opened a modest little house
in London, in Mount Street, and before long had acquired
a large circle of acquaintances. In the space of twelve months,
Lizzie Greystock had become Lady Eustace as a bride, and
Lady Eustace as a wealthy widow and a mother.

Frank Greystock, Lizzie's cousin, was the only son of the Dean of Bobsborough. He had been called to the Bar, and had begun pretty well. The Corporation of the City of London had brought an action against the Bank of England and a great deal of money had found its way among the lawyers, some of it into the pocket of Frank Greystock. It was attributed to him that the Bank of England was saved from the necessity of reconstructing all its bullion-cellars, and he had made his character for industry. In the year after that Frank Greystock was invited to stand as Conservative candidate for Bobsborough, and was duly elected. He was at this time nearly thirty years old. He was good-looking, but not strikingly handsome, with sharp grey eyes, a face clean shorn with the exception of a small whisker, with wiry, strong dark hair, which was already beginning to show a tinge of grey. He intended to get on in the world, and believed that happiness was to be achieved by success.

John Eustace and Greystock were very intimate. 'I tell you what I wish you'd do, Greystock,' Eustace said to him one day, as they were standing idle together in the lobby of the House, for John Eustace was also in Parliament. 'Just marry your cousin, my brother's widow.'

'But my dear fellow . . .'

'I know she's fond of you. You were dining there last Sunday.'

'And so was Fawn. Lord Fawn is the man to marry Lizzie.'

'She'll never be Lady Fawn,' said John Eustace confidently. 'She's worth nearly £5000 a year as long as she lives, and I really don't think she's much amiss.'

'Much amiss! I don't know whether she's not the prettiest woman I ever saw,' said Greystock.

'Yes—but I mean in conduct and all that. She is making herself difficult, and Camperdown, our lawyer, means to jump upon her; but it's only because she doesn't know what she ought to be at, and what she ought not. You could tell her.'

'It wouldn't suit me at all to have to quarrel with Camperdown,' said the barrister, laughing.

'You and he would settle everything in five minutes, and it

192

would save me a world of trouble,' said Eustace, as he walked back into the House.

John Eustace was right. Mr Camperdown was intent upon regaining possession of the Eustace family diamond necklace, supposed to be worth £10,000, and had written to Lizzie to that effect. Mr Camperdown was a gentleman of about sixty, who had been lawyer to Sir Florian's father, and whose father had been lawyer to Sir Florian's grandfather. His connexion with the property and with the family was of a nature to allow him to take almost any liberty with the Eustaces. To this letter Lizzie made no answer whatever, nor did she to a second note, calling attention to the first. When John Eustace told Greystock that Camperdown intended to 'jump on' Lady Eustace, a further letter had been written by the firm threatening legal proceedings. 'I'll file a bill in Chancery, if necessary,' the lawyer told John Eustace. 'It's as clear a case of stealing as I ever knew.'

After reading this letter once Lizzie read it a dozen times; and then made up her mind that her safest course would be not to answer it. But yet she felt sure that something unpleasant would come of it. Mr Camperdown was not a man to take up such a question and let it drop. Legal steps! If only there had been a friend whom she could consult; though not a simply respectable, high-minded friend, who would advise her as a matter of course to make restitution.

Then the door opened, and Lord Fawn was announced. Lord Fawn was a man of about thirty-five and an Under-Secretary of State, very diligent at his work but generally understood to be in need of marrying for money. 'How kind this is,' said Lizzie. Lord Fawn stood twiddling his hat. Then Lizzie, with a pretty eagerness, asked after his mother, Lady Fawn, and his sisters. She leaned forward her face as she asked her questions, and threw back her loose lustrous lock of hair, with her long lithe fingers covered with diamonds which Sir Florian had really given her. 'They are all quite well, thank you,' said Lord Fawn. And then he was silent for a few moments. 'Lady Eustace,' he said at last, 'I don't know what your views of life may be.'

'I have a child, you know, to bring up.'

'Ah, yes.'

'He will inherit a very large fortune, Lord Fawn—too large, I fear, to be of service to a youth of one-and-twenty—and I must endeavour to fit him for the possession of it. That is and always must be the chief object of my existence.'

'No doubt, no doubt.'

'They tell me the poor little dear will have forty thousand a year when he's of age; and when I look at him in his little bed, and press him in my arms, and think of all that money, I almost wish that his father had been a poor plain gentleman.' Then the handkerchief was put to her eyes, and Lord Fawn had a moment in which to collect himself.

'Ah—I myself am a poor man; for my rank I mean.'

'A man with your position, Lord Fawn, and your talents and genius for business, can never be poor.'

'You see, for a peer, my fortune is very small indeed. It's about five thousand a year, and out of that my mother has half for her life.'

'What an excellent arrangement,' said Lizzie. There was so long a pause made between each statement that she was forced to make some reply.

'Now,' said he, 'I have told you everything about myself which I was bound, as a man of honour, to tell before I—I—I ... In short, you know what I mean.'

'Oh, Lord Fawn!'

'I have told you everything. I owe no money, but I could not afford to marry a wife without an income. I admire you more than any woman I ever saw. I love you with all my heart.' He was now standing upright before her, with the fingers of his right hand touching his left breast, and there was something almost of dignity in his gesture and demeanour. 'It may be that you are determined never to marry again. I can only say that if you will trust yourself to me—yourself and your child —I will do my duty truly by you both, and will make your happiness the chief object of my existence. Lady Eustace, may I venture to entertain a hope?'

'May I not have an hour to think of it?' said Lizzie, just venturing to turn a glance upon his face.

'Oh, certainly. I will call again whenever you may bid me.'

But Lizzie was too magnanimous for this. 'Lord Fawn,' she said, rising, 'you have paid me the greatest compliment that a man can pay a woman. Coming from you it is doubly precious; first, because of your character and secondly— secondly, because I can love you.' This was said in her lowest whisper, and then she moved towards him gently, and almost laid her head upon his breast. Of course he put his arm round her waist, and then her head was upon his breast. 'Dearest Lizzie!' he said, kissing her forehead.

'Dearest Frederic!' she murmured.

'I shall write to my mother tonight,' he said.

'Do, do, dear Frederic.'

'And she will come to you at once, I am sure.'

'I will receive her and love her as a mother,' said Lizzie, with all her energy. Then he kissed her again—her forehead and her lips—and took his leave, promising to be with her at any rate on Wednesday.

'Lady Fawn!' she said to herself. The name did not sound so well as that of Lady Eustace. But it is much to be a wife; and more to be a peeress.

.   .   .   .   .

Lady Fawn was delighted to receive her son's news and lost no time in starting from Fawn Court, at Richmond, to pay the promised call. The carriage first stopped at the door of Lady Fawn's married daughter in Warwick Square. Now, Mrs Hittaway, whose husband was chairman of the Board of Civil Appeals, heard much more about things than did her mother. 'Mamma,' she said, 'you don't mean it! She is the greatest vixen in all London.'

'Oh, Clara!'

'And such a liar. It's my belief that she is over head and ears in debt. I've heard quite enough about Lady Eustace to feel certain that Frederic would live to repent it. I don't doubt they'd be separated before two years were over.'

'Oh dear, how dreadful!' exclaimed her mother.

Lady Fawn was, however, of opinion that she must still carry out her intention of calling upon her son's intended bride. Lord Fawn had sent a message to Mount Street, informing the lady of the honour intended for her. And in truth Lady Fawn was somewhat curious now to see the household of the woman who might perhaps do her the irreparable injury of ruining the happiness of her only son.

Lizzie was of course at home. She had taken great pains with her dress, studying not so much her own appearance as the character of her visitor. She was dressed richly, but very simply. Everything about her room betokened wealth; but she had put away the French novels and had placed a Bible on a little table, not quite hidden, behind her own seat. The long lustrous lock was tucked up, but the diamonds were still upon her fingers.

'Dear, dear Lady Fawn!' she said, throwing herself into the arms and nestling herself against the bosom of the old lady, 'this makes my happiness perfect.' Then she retreated a little, still holding the hand she had grasped between her own, and looking up into the face of her future mother-in-law. Her manner was almost perfect. Perhaps there was a little too much of gesture, too violent an appeal with the eyes, too close a pressure of the hand. No suspicion, however, of all this would have touched Lady Fawn had she come to Mount Street without calling in Warwick Square on the way. But those horrible words of her daughter were ringing in her ears.

'My dear,' Lady Fawn said, 'I hope you will make him a good wife.'

It was not very encouraging, but Lizzie made the best of it. 'Oh, Lady Fawn, I will so strive to make him happy. What would he wish me to do and to be? You know his noble nature, and I must look to you for guidance.'

'My dear, if you will endeavour to do your duty by him I am sure he will do his by you.'

'I know it. I am sure of it. And I will, I will.' She had heard that Lady Fawn was peculiarly religious. 'There,' she said, stretching out her hand backwards and clasping the book which lay upon the small table—'there; that shall be my guide. That will teach me how to do my duty by my noble husband.'

'You certainly can't do better, my dear, than read your Bible,' said Lady Fawn—but there was more of censure than of eulogy in the tone of her voice. She then asked Lady Eustace when it would suit her to come down to Fawn Court, having promised her son to give the invitation.

'Oh, I should like it so much,' said Lizzie. 'Whenever it will suit you I will be there at a minute's notice.' It was then arranged that she should be at Fawn Court on that day week, and stay for a fortnight. 'Of all things that which I most desire now,' said Lizzie, 'is to know you and the dear girls— and to be loved by you all.'

Lady Eustace, as soon as she was alone in the room, stood in the middle of it, scowling. As soon as Lord Fawn had left her after the engagement was made she had begun to tell herself that he was a poor creature, and that she had done wrong. Now that Lady Fawn had been cold to her she thought still less of the proposed marriage. In truth, she almost had made up her mind to break it off. But on the following Wednesday morning she received a note which threw her back violently upon the Fawn interest. 'Messrs. Camperdown and Son present their compliments to Lady Eustace. They have received instructions to proceed by law for the recovery of the Eustace diamonds, and will feel obliged to Lady Eustace if she will communicate to them the name and address of her attorney.' The lawyer's letter afflicted her with a sense of weakness, and there was strength in the Fawn connexion. As Lord Fawn was so poor, perhaps he would adhere to the jewels. She knew that she could not fight Mr Camperdown without assistance, and therefore her heart softened towards her betrothed.

Frederic came and was received very graciously. The conversation for a while was such as might be looked for between two lovers of whom one was a widow and the other an Under-Secretary of State from the India Office. They were loving, but discreetly amatory, talking chiefly of things material, each flattering the other, and each hinting now and again at certain little circumstances of which a more accurate knowledge seemed to be desirable.

'Of course there will be things to be settled,' he said, 'and my lawyer had better see yours. Mr Camperdown is a . . .'

'Mr Camperdown!' almost shrieked Lizzie. 'Mr Camperdown was Sir Florian's lawyer.'

'That will make it all the easier, I should think.'

'I don't know how that may be. Mr Camperdown has been very uncourteous to me. He wishes to rob me of a thing that is quite my own. There—you might as well read that note.'

Lord Fawn read Mr Camperdown's letter very attentively. 'What are these diamonds?' he asked.

'A necklace. They say its value is about—ten thousand pounds.'

'Ten thousand pounds! You don't keep it in the house, do you?'

'In an iron case upstairs.'

Lord Fawn was by now involved in a painful maze of doubt and almost of dismay. He was a poor man, and a greedy man, and he would have liked his wife to have ten thousand pounds' worth of diamonds very well; but he would rather go without a wife and a wife's fortune than marry a woman subject to an action for claiming diamonds not her own. 'I think,' said he at last, 'it would be best if you were to put them into Mr Camperdown's hands, and then someone would be appointed to decide whose property they were.'

'They're my property.'

'But he says they belong to the family.'

'Sir Florian Eustace gave them to me, and I shall keep them. If they don't belong to me they belong to my son; and who has so good a right to keep them for him as I have? But they belong to me. Mr Camperdown wants to rob me, and I shall look to you to prevent it.'

'I can do nothing,' said Lord Fawn, in a tremor. Then Lizzie looked at him, and her look called him a poltroon as plain as a look could speak. Then they parted, and the signs of affection between them were not satisfactory. But a day or two later Lord Fawn received letters congratulating him on his intended marriage. Lord Fawn was, therefore, well aware that Lady Eustace had published the engagement. It was known to everybody, and could not be be broken off without public scandal.

On the day fixed, 5 June, Lizzie arrived at Fawn Court. The Fawn ladies were not good hypocrites. Lady Fawn had said almost nothing to her daughters of her visit to Mount Street, but there was a general conviction that an evil thing had fallen upon them. Consequently, their affection to the new-comer, though spoken in words, was not made evident by signs and manners. Lizzie herself took care that the position in which she was received should be sufficiently declared. 'It seems so odd that I am to come among you as a sister,' she said. The girls were forced to assent to the claim, but they assented coldly.

When Lord Fawn came forward to greet her she put her cheek up, just a little, so that he might see that he was expected to kiss it. He did touch her cheek with his, blushing as he did so. She had her ungloved hand in his, and, still holding him, returned into the circle. She said not a word, and what he said was of no moment; but they had met as lovers, and any of the family who had allowed themselves to imagine that even yet the match might be broken now unconsciously abandoned that hope.

In the course of the evening, however, her lover did say a word to her in private. 'My dear Lizzie, since I last saw you I have been twice with Mr Camperdown.'

'You are not going to talk about Mr Camperdown today?'

'What I want to say is this. You must restore those dia-monds. It would not suit my views that my wife should be seen wearing the jewels of the Eustace family.'

'I don't want to wear them.'

'Then why keep them?'

'Because they are my own. Because I do not choose to be put upon. You should defend my right to them.'

'Do you mean to say that you will not oblige me by doing what I ask you?'

'I will not be robbed of what is my own.'

'Then I must declare'—and now Lord Fawn spoke very slowly—'that under these circumstances I must retract from the enviable position which your favour has given me.'

'What do you mean?' said Lizzie, flashing round upon him. 'Do you threaten me with deserting me?'

'I want you to understand me.'

'Understand you! You understand nothing yourself that a man ought to understand. If I told your mother to give up her diamonds, what would she say?'

'But they are not yours, unless you will submit that question to an arbitrator.'

'I will submit nothing to anybody. You have no right to speak on such a subject till after we are married.'

'I must have it settled first, Lady Eustace.'

'Then, Lord Fawn, it is settled already. I shall keep my own necklace, and Mr Camperdown may do anything he pleases. As for you—if you ill-treat me, I shall know where to go. You will be pleased, Lord Fawn, to let your mother know that I am indisposed.' Then she sailed through them all, without a word, and marched up to her bedroom.

During the rest of the evening Lord Fawn was closeted with his mother, and he went away to London next morning. He left a note for Lady Eustace.

Dearest Lizzie,

Think well of what I have said to you. It is not that I desire to break off our engagement; but that I cannot allow my wife to keep the diamonds which belong of right to her late husband's family. You may be sure that I should not be thus urgent had I not taken steps to ascertain that I am right in my judgement. In the meantime you had better consult my mother.

Yours affectionately,

Fawn.

Lady Fawn did manage to have an interview with Lady Eustace, but Lizzie altogether refused to listen to any advice on the subject of the necklace. 'It is an affair,' she said haughtily, 'in which I must judge for myself—or with the advice of my own particular friends.' Then she declared her intention of returning to her own house on the following day. To this Lady Fawn made no objection.

The burden of his position was so heavy on Lord Fawn's mind that after leaving Fawn Court he was hardly as true to the affairs of India as he himself would have wished. He was resolved to do what was right—if only he could find out what would be right. Not to break his word, not to be unjust, not to deviate by a hair's breadth from that line of conduct which would be described as 'honourable' in the circle to which he belonged, not to give his political enemies an opportunity for calumny—this was all in all to him. The young widow was very lovely and very rich, and it would suit him well to marry her. But he would give all this up rather than find himself in the mess of having married a wife who had stolen a necklace.

Frank Greystock was, he knew, Lizzie's nearest relative in London. He appealed to Greystock, and Frank came to him at the India House. But before he saw Lord Fawn Frank had been with his cousin. The lie which she had fabricated for the benefit of Lord Fawn she now repeated with increased precision to her cousin. Sir Florian, she said, in putting the trinket into her hands had explained to her that she was to regard it as her own peculiar property. 'If it was an heirloom he couldn't do it,' Frank had said, with all the confidence of a practising barrister. 'Sir Florian could only give away what was his own to give.'

'But Lord Fawn had no right to dictate.'

'Certainly not,' said Frank; and then he made a promise that he would stand by his pretty cousin in this affair. 'I don't see why you should assume that Lady Eustace is keeping property that doesn't belong to her,' he said to Lord Fawn.

'I will go by what Camperdown tells me,' said Lord Fawn.

'Mr Camperdown is a very excellent attorney, and a most respectable man,' said Greystock, 'but we cannot allow him to be judge and jury. If any claim be really made for these jewels by Mr John Eustace on the part of the heir, or on behalf of the estate, a statement had better be submitted to counsel and the family deeds must be inspected. In the meantime, I understand that you are engaged to marry my cousin?'

'I was engaged to her, certainly,' said Lord Fawn.

'You can hardly mean to assert, my lord, that you intend to be untrue to your promise because my cousin has expressed her wish to retain property which she believes to be her own! She has chosen to accept you as her future husband, and I am bound to see that she is treated with good faith and honour.'

Lord Fawn made some attempt at a stipulation that this assurance to Lizzie was to be founded on the counter-assurance given to him that the matter of the diamonds should be decided by proper legal authority; but Frank would not submit to this, and at last the Under-Secretary yielded. The engagement was to remain in force. Counsel were to be employed. The two lovers were not to see each other just at present. And when the matter had been decided by the lawyers Lord Fawn was to express his regret for having suspected his lady love.

About a week after this there was a meeting at Mr Camperdown's chambers. Greystock attended to hear what Mr Camperdown had to say in the presence of Lord Fawn and John Eustace. Before the meeting Mr Camperdown had been looking over old deeds. 'There is luckily no doubt as to the facts,' he declared. 'The diamonds formed a part of a set of most valuable ornaments settled in the family by Sir Florian Eustace in 1799. The deed was drawn up by my grandfather, and is now here. I do not know how we are to have further proof.'

'My dear sir,' said Frank, 'your experience must have told you that there is considerable difficulty in dealing with the matter of heirlooms.'

'People generally understand it clearly,' said Lord Fawn.

'The late Sir Florian does not appear to have understood it very clearly,' said Frank. As Mr Camperdown said to John Eustace afterwards, it was manifest enough that she meant 'to hang on to them'.

'I can only hope Lord Fawn will not be fool enough to marry her,' said Mr Camperdown. Lord Fawn himself was of the same way of thinking.

.   .   .   .   .

The London season was in its full splendour. During her widowhood Lady Eustace had been every inch a widow—as far as crape would go. Two years of retreat from the world is generally thought to be the proper thing for a widow. Lizzie had not quite accomplished her two years before she re-opened the campaign in Mount Street with her crape brought down to a minimum. She did not encounter much reproach. People called her a flirt, held up their hands in surprise at the late Sir Florian's foolish generosity—for the accounts of Lizzie's wealth were greatly exaggerated—and said that of course she would marry Lord Fawn.

'Poor dear Lord Fawn!' said Lady Glencora Palliser to her dear friend Madame Max Goesler. 'I suppose he is terribly in want of money.'

'But Lady Eustace is very pretty.'

'Yes, she is quite lovely to look at. And she is clever—very. And she is rich—very. But . . .'

'Well, Lady Glencora. What does your "but" mean?'

'You're a great deal too clever, Madame Goesler, to want any explanation. I can only say I'm sorry for poor Lord Fawn —who is a gentleman, but will never set the Thames on fire.'

This conversation took place in the house then occupied by Lady Chiltern in Portman Square—Lady Chiltern, with whom, as Violet Effingham, Lord Fawn had been much in love. 'I think it the nicest match in the world for him,' Lady Chiltern said.

'But have you heard of the diamonds?' asked Lady Glencora. Neither of the others had heard of the diamonds, and Lady Glencora was able to tell her story.

'You don't mean to say that Lord Fawn is off?' asked Madame Goesler.

'I do,' said Lady Glencora.

'I don't think he has courage enough for such conduct as that,' said Madame Goesler.

'I wonder she ever took him,' said Lady Glencora. 'There is no doubt about her beauty, and she might have done better.'

'Is she to be at your party on Friday, Lady Glencora?' asked Madame Goesler.

'She has said she would come—and so has Lord Fawn, for that matter.'

'She'll come for the sake of the bravado,' said Lady Chiltern. 'And wear the diamonds.'

Lady Eustace did go to Lady Glencora's evening party; and she did wear the diamonds.

'I like her for wearing them,' said Lady Glencora to Lady Chiltern.

Lady Eustace made the most of her opportunity. Soon after the quadrille was over she asked Lord Fawn to get her carriage for her. Of course he got it, and of course he put her into it. And of course all the world saw what he was doing.

The thirtieth of July came round, and Lizzie prepared to leave London for her Scottish property. There was a train leaving London for Carlisle at 11 a.m. by which she purposed to travel, so that she might sleep in that city and go on through Dumfries to Portray the next morning. She did not dare to leave the diamonds behind, nor to take them without the iron box. At a little after ten her carriage was at the door, and a cab for the servants. The luggage was brought down, and the iron case, which was very heavy, deposited as a footstool for Lizzie. At that very moment who should appear but Mr Camperdown. 'Lady Eustace!' said Mr Camperdown, taking off his hat, 'I believe you are now starting for Scotland.'

'We are, Mr Camperdown—and we are very late.'

'I only heard this morning that you were going so soon, and it is imperative that I should see you. Lady Eustace, I must insist on knowing where are the Eustace diamonds.' Lizzie felt the box beneath her feet, and, without showing that she did so, somewhat widened her drapery.

'I shall answer no questions. William, make the coachman drive on.'

'Then I shall be forced, on behalf of the family, to obtain a search-warrant, both here and in Ayrshire, and proceedings will be taken also against your ladyship personally.' So saying, Mr Camperdown withdrew, and at last the carriage was driven on.

At Euston Square station the footman struggled with the box into the waiting-room, and the porter struggled with it from the waiting-room to the carriage. The same thing happened at Carlisle, where the box was carried up into Lizzie's bedroom by the footman. In the morning people looked at her as she walked down the long platform with the box still struggling before her. But at last Lady Eustace, and the servants, and the iron box, reached Portray Castle in safety.

CHAPTER TWO

PORTRAY CASTLE was really a castle—with battlements and a round tower at one corner, and a gate which looked as if it might have had a portcullis, and narrow windows in a portion of it, and a cannon mounted up on a low roof, and an excavation called the moat, running round two sides of it. As a house it was not particularly eligible, the castle form of domestic architecture demanding that space, which in less ambitious houses can be applied to comfort, shall be surrendered to magnificence. There was a great hall, and a fine dining-room with plate-glass windows looking out upon the sea; but the other sitting-rooms were insignificant, and the bedrooms were here and there and were for the most part small and dark. That, however, which Lizzie had appropriated to her own use was a grand chamber, looking also out upon the open sea.

The Castle stood on a bluff of land, with a fine prospect of the Firth of Clyde, and with a distant view of the Isle of Arran. When the air was clear, as it often is clear there, the Arran hills could be seen from Lizzie's window, and she was proud of talking of the prospect. Behind the castle the estate stretched for some eight or ten miles, and the landscape became rough and grand.

Lizzie had never entertained her friends in style before.

She had had a few people to dine with her in London, and once or twice had received company on an evening, but now she meant to show her friends that she had got a house of her own. At the end of October a Mrs Carbuncle and one Lord George de Bruce Carruthers arrived at Portray Castle. And for a couple of days there was a visitor whom Lizzie was very glad to welcome, but of whose good nature on the occasion Mr Camperdown thought very ill indeed. This was John Eustace. His sister-in-law wrote to him in very pressing language and as—so he said to Mr Camperdown—he did not wish to quarrel with his brother's widow as long as might be avoided he accepted the invitation. If there was to be a law-suit about the diamonds, that must be Mr Camperdown's affair.

And she got a clergyman down from London, the Rev. Joseph Emilius, of whom it was said that he was born a Jew in Hungary, and that his name in his own country had been Mealyus. At the present time he was among the most eloquent of London preachers, and was reputed by some to have reached such a standard of pulpit-oratory as to have no equal within the memory of living hearers. But he did not get on very well with any particular bishop, and there was doubt in the minds of some people whether there was or was not any Mrs Emilius. He had come up quite suddenly within the last season, and had made church-going quite a pleasant occupation to Lizzie Eustace.

Mrs Carbuncle was a wonderful woman. She was the wife of a man with whom she was very rarely seen, whom nobody knew, who was something in the City, but somebody who never succeeded in making money; and yet she went everywhere. Audacity may be said to have been the ruling principle of her toilet; audacity in colour, in design, and in construction. Though nearly forty she would wear her jet-black hair streaming down her back, and when June came would drive about London in a straw hat. Mrs Carbuncle was certainly a handsome woman, and had learned so to walk as though half the world belonged to her.

The manner in which Lord George de Bruce Carruthers had attached himself to these ladies was a mystery; but then

Lord George was always mysterious. He was about forty-five years of age, hunted a great deal, had never owned a fortune, and had never been known to earn a shilling. But they who knew him well declared that he never borrowed a shilling and never owed a guinea. When in London he lodged in a single room, and dined at his club. He was a Colonel of Volunteers, having got up the Long Shore Riflemen, the roughest regiment of Volunteers in all England.

He was a long-legged, long-bodied, long-faced man, with rough whiskers and a rough beard on his upper lip, but with a shorn chin. His eyes were very deep set in his head, and his cheeks were hollow and sallow, and yet he was a powerful, healthy man. He liked to have good-looking women about him, and yet nobody presumed it probable that he would marry. For the last two or three years there had been friendship between him and Mrs Carbuncle; and during the last season he had become almost intimate with Lizzie. Lizzie thought that perhaps he might be the romantic Corsair whom, sooner or later in her life, she must certainly encounter.

The coming of John Eustace was certainly a great thing for Lizzie, though it was only for two days. It saved her from that feeling of desertion by those who naturally belonged to her. She could call him John, and bring down her boy to him, and remind him, with almost a tear in her eye, that he was the boy's guardian. 'So much depends on that little life —does it not, John?' she said.

'Lucky little dog!' said John, patting the boy's head. 'Of course he'll go to Eton.'

'Not yet,' said Lizzie with a shudder.

'Well, no; hardly—when he's twelve.' John Eustace was a thoroughly good-natured man of the world who could forgive many faults. He did not like Mrs Carbuncle, and was afraid of Lord George. He believed Mr Emilius to be an impostor. But he smiled and was gay, and called Lady Eustace by her Christian name. John was so very nice that she almost made up her mind to talk to him about the necklace; but she was cautious, and found it better to abstain. After breakfast on the second day he took his departure without an allusion to things that were unpleasant.

Then Frank Greystock arrived; and one day Lizzie went out hunting for the first time in her life, plucking up her courage and telling herself that a woman can die but once. Lord George rode by her side and instructed her in all the terms and practices, and before long she understood more than would nine or ten young women who had never ridden a hunt before. Lord George declared that she rode like a celestial Bird of Paradise. When they were back at the Castle, and had taken warm baths and glasses of sherry and got themselves dressed and had come down to dinner, they were all very happy. To Lizzie it had certainly been the most triumphant day of her life. She had found the thing she liked to do. She could remember every jump and her feeling of ecstasy as she landed on the right side. And she had by heart every kind word that Lord George had said to her—and she loved the pleasant Corsair-like intimacy that had sprung up between them.

They did not dine till past eight, and the ladies and gentlemen all left the room together. Coffee and liqueurs were brought into the drawing-room, and they were all intimate, comfortable, and at their ease.

'Now I don't mean to stir again,' said Lizzie, throwing herself into a corner of a sofa, 'till somebody carries me to bed. I never was so tired in all my life.'

'You only killed one fox,' said Mr Emilius, pretending a delightfully clerical ignorance, 'and on Monday you killed four. Why should you be tired?'

'I suppose it was nearly twenty miles,' said Frank, who was also ignorant.

'About ten, perhaps,' said Lord George. 'It was an hour and forty minutes, and there was a good bit of slow hunting after we had come back over the river.'

'I'm sure it was thirty,' said Lizzie.

But though Lizzie was in heaven, it behoved her to be careful. The Corsair was a very fine specimen of the Corsair breed—about the best Corsair she had ever seen, and had been devoted to her for the day. But these Corsairs are known to be dangerous, and it would not be wise that she should sacrifice any future prospects of importance on behalf of a feeling, which, no doubt, was founded on poetry, but which might too probably have no possible beneficial result. As far as she knew, the Corsair had not even an island of his own in the Aegean Sea. And, if he had, might not the island too probably have a Medora or two of its own?

Frank Greystock stayed till the following Monday at Portray, but could not be induced to hunt on the Saturday—on which day the other sporting men and women went to the meet. So he remained at the Castle and took a walk with Mr Emilius. Mr Emilius asked a good many questions about Portray and exhibited the warmest sympathy with Lizzie's widowed condition. He called her a 'sweet, gay, unsophisticated, light-hearted young thing.' 'She is very young,' replied her cousin. 'Yes,' he continued, in answer to further questions, 'Portray is certainly very nice. I don't know what the income is. Well, yes; I should think it is over a thousand. Eight! No, I never heard it said that it was as much as that.' Mr Emilius put it down in his mind as five.

After that Lord George went, and also Mr Emilius, but Mrs Carbuncle remained till after Christmas, greatly overstaying the original time fixed for her visit. A great friendship had sprung up between Mrs Carbuncle and Lizzie, so that both had become very communicative. On the great subject of the diamonds Lizzie had spoken her mind freely to Mrs Carbuncle early in the days of their friendship. 'Ten thousand pounds,' ejaculated Mrs Carbuncle, opening wide her eyes.

It was some days after this that there came by post some terribly frightful documents which were the first results of the filing of a bill in Chancery. Within eight days Lizzie was to enter an appearance towards showing why she should not surrender her diamonds to the Lord Chancellor, or to some other terrible myrmidon. She told Mrs Carbuncle, and Mrs Carbuncle evidently thought that the diamonds were as good as gone. 'I suppose you can't sell them?' said she.

'I could sell them tomorrow. What is to hinder me? Suppose I took them to jewellers in Paris.'

'The jewellers would think you had stolen them.'

'I didn't steal them,' said Lizzie; 'they're my very own.'

'I daresay it will all come right,' said Mrs Carbuncle.

In the first week in January Lord George returned to the Castle with the view of travelling up to London with the two ladies. Of course, he had heard of the diamonds. He had heard too of Lord Fawn, and knew why Lord Fawn had peremptorily refused to carry out his engagement. But till he was told by Mrs Carbuncle he did not know that the diamonds were kept within the Castle, nor did he understand that it would be part of his duty to guard them on their way back to London. 'They are worth ever so much; ain't they?' he said to her.

'Ten thousand pounds,' said Mrs Carbuncle.

'I don't believe a word of it,' said he.

Lord George owned to himself that such a necklace was worth having—as also were Portray Castle and the income arising from the estate, even though they could be held in possession only for a single life. Hitherto in his very chequered career he had escaped the trammels of matrimony, and among his many modes of life had hardly even suggested to himself the expediency of taking a wife with a fortune and then settling down. But now it did occur to him that Portray Castle was a place in which he could pass two or three months annually without ennui. And that if he were to marry, little Lizzie Eustace would do as well as any other woman with money. Lizzie certainly bestowed upon him many of her smiles, much of her poetry, and some of her confidence. But then she was such an 'infernal little liar'. Lord George was able to discover so much of her.

'She does lie, certainly,' said Mrs Carbuncle; 'but then who doesn't?'

On the morning of their departure the box with the diamonds was brought down into the hall. Lizzie had been with her diamonds that morning, and had seen them out of the box and into it. Few days passed on which she did not handle them and gaze at them.

'Supposing somebody were to steal that on the way,' said Lord George.

'I don't think it would make me a bit unhappy. You've heard about it all. There never was such a persecution.'

It had been arranged that the party should sleep at Carlisle.

It consisted of Lord George, the ladies, the man-servant, Lord George's own man, and the two maids. The iron box was again put into the carriage; and was used by Lizzie as a foot-stool.

'And now these weary diamonds again,' said Lord George, as the train stopped against the Carlisle platform. 'I suppose they must go into your bedroom, Lady Eustace?'

'I wish you'd let the man put the box in yours—just for this night,' said Lizzie.

'Not if I know it,' said Lord George, and explained that it would be quite as liable to be stolen when in his custody as it would in hers; but if stolen while in his would entail upon him a grievous vexation which would by no means lessen the effect of her loss. Lord George suggested that it should be entrusted to the landlord; but she decided that the box should go to her own room. 'There's no knowing what that Mr Camperdown mightn't do,' she whispered to Lord George.

The evening at Carlisle was spent very pleasantly. The ladies agreed that they would not dress—but of course they did so with more or less of care. Lizzie made herself look very pretty. Lord George was infinitely petted, and Lizzie called him a Corsair to his face.

Lizzie, when she was finally in her own room, found her maid, Patience Crabstick, waiting. She was anxious to get rid of her girl's attendance. It had been so this morning, and before dinner. She was secret in her movements, and always had some recess in her boxes and bags and dressing appara-tuses to which she did not choose that Miss Patience Crabstick should have access. She was careful about her letters, and very careful about her money. And then, as to that iron box, Patience Crabstick had never seen the inside of it.

Alongside Lizzie's chamber there was a small room which was devoted to Crabstick's accommodation. She departed from attendance on her mistress by the door which opened from the one room to the other; but this had no sooner been closed than Crabstick descended to complete the amusements of the evening. Lizzie bolted both the doors on the inside. Some short prayer she said, with her knees close to the iron box. Then she put certain articles of property under her pillow—

her watch and chain, and her rings, and a packet from her travelling-desk—and was soon in bed, thinking that, as she fell away to sleep, she would revolve in her mind that question of the Corsair; would it be good to trust herself and all her belongings to one who might perhaps take her belongings away, but leave herself behind? While she was considering it she fell asleep.

On the next morning Lizzie was awakened earlier than she had expected, and found not only Patience Crabstick in her bedroom but also the wife of the manager of the hotel. The story was soon told to her. Her room had been broken open while she slept and her treasure was gone.

Lady Eustace had hardly time to get her slippers on, and to wrap herself in her dressing-gown and make herself just fit for public view before the manager and Lord George were in her bedroom. The superintendent of the Carlisle police was there almost as soon as the others, and the head of the constabulary of the county.

Lizzie, when she first heard the news, was awestruck, rather than outwardly demonstrative of grief. 'There has been a regular plot,' said Lord George. Captain Fitzmaurice, the gallant chief, nodded his head. 'Plot enough,' said the superintendent, who did not mean to confide his thoughts to any man, or to exempt any human being from his suspicion. The manager of the hotel was very angry. Did not everybody know that if articles of value were brought into an hotel they should be handed over to the safe keeping of the manager? 'My dear fellow,' said Lord George, 'nobody is saying a word against you, or your house.'

At last the man retreated, and Lizzie was left with Patience and Mrs Carbuncle. But even then she did not give way to her grief, but sat upon the bed awestruck and mute.

'I feared how it might be,' said Mrs Carbuncle, holding Lizzie's hand affectionately.

'I always was a-telling my lady . . .' began Crabstick.

'Hold your tongue!' said Lizzie angrily.

'I think I'll lie down again for a little while. I feel so sick I hardly know what to do.' With much difficulty she got them to leave her. Then she bolted the door that still had a bolt, and turned the lock in the other. Having done this she took out from under her pillow the little parcel which had been in her desk—and, untying it, perceived that her dear diamond necklace was quite safe. The box, and nothing but the box, had fallen into the hands of the thieves.

Lizzie's silence when the abstraction of the box was made known to her was not at first deliberate fraud. She was ashamed to tell them that she brought the box empty from Portray, having the diamonds in her own keeping because she had feared the box might be stolen. And then it occurred to her, quick as thought could flash, that it might be well that Mr Camperdown should be made to believe that they had been stolen. And so she kept her secret. The reflections of the next half-hour told her how very great would now be her difficulties. But as she had not disclosed the truth at first she could hardly disclose it now.

Then she thought for a while that she would get rid of the diamonds altogether. If she could only think of a place fit for such purpose she would so hide them that no human ingenuity could discover them. Let the thieves, if they were taken, say what they might, her word would be better than theirs. She would declare that the jewels had been in the box when the box was stolen, and the thieves would be supposed, even by their own friends and associates, to have disposed of the diamonds. Mr Camperdown could do nothing further to harass her. Lord Fawn might probably be again at her feet. And in all the fuss and rumour which such an affair would make in London, there would be nothing of which she need be ashamed. She liked the idea, and she had grown to be very sick of the necklace.

But what should she do with it? Her acquaintance with a Mr Benjamin, a jeweller, was present to her mind. She might not be able to get ten thousand pounds from Mr Benjamin; but if she could get eight, or six, or even five, how pleasant would it be! If she could put away the diamonds for three or four years, surely after so long an interval they might be made available? But where should be found such hiding-place? A hole dug deep into the ground; would not that be the place? But then, where should the hole be dug? If anywhere,

213

it must be at Portray. But now she was going from Portray to London. It seemed to her to be certain that she could dig no hole in London that would be secret.

What she wanted was someone she could trust. But she had no such friend. She could not dare to give the jewels up to Lord George. So tempted, would not any Corsair appropriate the treasure? And if she were mistaken about him, and he was no Corsair, then would he betray her to the police? She thought of Frank Greystock, Mrs Carbuncle—even of Patience Crabstick; but there was no friend whom she could trust.

Both Mrs Carbuncle and Lord George had been astonished to find how well she bore her loss. Lord George gave her credit for real bravery. Mrs Carbuncle suggested, in a whisper, that perhaps she regarded the theft as an easy way out of a lawsuit. Then Lord George whistled, and declared that, if the little adventure had all been arranged by Lady Eustace herself with the view of getting the better of Mr Camperdown, his respect for that lady would be very greatly raised.

The box had been found, and a portion of the fragments were brought into the room while the party were still at breakfast. The news was taken up to Lizzie by Crabstick, together with a pheasant's wing and some buttered toast. The iron box had been forced, so said the sergeant of police, with tools of the finest steel, made for such purpose. The sergeant was quite sure that the thing had been done by London men at the very top of their trade. Every motion of the party must have been known to them. The very doors of the bedroom in the hotel had been measured by the man who had so silently cut out the bolt. The sergeant of police was almost lost in admiration.

The whole party were called upon to give their evidence to the Carlisle magistrates before they could proceed to London. This Lizzie did, having the necklace at that moment locked up in her little travelling desk at the inn. When she at last got into the train for London the little parcel was still in her desk, and the key of her desk was fastened round her neck.

'As I am alive,' said Lord George, as soon as the train had left the station, 'that head policeman thinks I am the thief!' Mrs Carbuncle laughed. Lizzie protested that this was absurd. 'It's a fact,' continued Lord George. 'They delight in suspicions. I don't doubt but that there is already a belief in some of their minds that you have stolen your own diamonds for the sake of getting the better of Mr Camperdown.'

'But what could I do with them if I had?'

'Sell them, of course. There is always a market for such goods.'

'But who would buy them?'

'If you have been so clever, Lady Eustace, I'll find a purchaser for them. One would have to go a good distance to do it—and there would be some expense. But the thing could be done. Vienna, I should think, would be about the place.'

'Very well, then,' said Lizzie. 'You won't be surprised if I ask you to take the journey for me.' Then they all laughed, and were very much amused. It was quite agreed among them that Lizzie bore her loss very well.

CHAPTER THREE

BEFORE the end of January everybody in London had heard of the great robbery at Carlisle—and various rumours were afloat.

There were strong parties formed—Lizzieites and anti-Lizzieites. The Lizzieites were of opinion that poor Lady Eustace was being very ill-treated; that the diamonds did probably belong to her; and that Lord Fawn clearly ought to be her own. These Lizzieites were all of them Conservatives; Frank Greystock had probably set the party on foot. Those newspapers which had devoted themselves to upholding the Conservative politicians of the day were very heavy indeed upon Lord Fawn. The whole force of the Government, however, was anti-Lizzieite; and as the controversy advanced every good Liberal became aware that there was nothing so wicked, so rapacious, so bold, or so cunning but that Lady

Eustace might have done it, or caused it to be done. Lady Glencora Palliser for a while endeavoured to defend Lizzie in Liberal circles—instigated, perhaps, by a feeling that any woman in society who was capable of doing anything extraordinary ought to be defended. But even Lady Glencora was forced to abandon her generosity, and to confess, on behalf of her party, that Lizzie Eustace was a very wicked young woman.

The party assembled at Matching Priory, the country house belonging to Mr Palliser in which Lady Glencora took much delight, was not large, because Mr Palliser's uncle, the Duke of Omnium, who was with them, was now a very old man, and did not like very large gatherings. Lord and Lady Chiltern were there—that Lord Chiltern who had been known so long and so well in the hunting counties of England, and that Lady Chiltern who had been so popular in London as the beautiful Violet Effingham; and Mr and Mrs Grey were there, very particular friends of Mrs Palliser's. Mr Grey was now sitting for the borough of Silverbridge, in which the Duke of Omnium was still presumed to have a controlling influence, in spite of all Reform Bills, and Mrs Grey was in some distant way connected with Lady Glencora. And Madame Max Goesler was there; and Mr and Mrs Bonteen, who had been brought there, not, perhaps, altogether because they were greatly loved, but in order that the gentleman's services might be made available by Mr Palliser in reference to some great reform about to be introduced in monetary matters. Mr Palliser, who was Chancellor of the Exchequer, was intending to alter the value of the penny. The future penny was to be made, under his auspices, to contain five farthings, and the shilling ten pennies. It was thought that if this could be accomplished, the arithmetic of the whole world would be so simplified that henceforward the name of Palliser would be blessed by all school-boys, clerks, shopkeepers, and financiers. But the difficulties were so great that Mr Palliser's hair was already grey from toil, and his shoulders bent by the burthen imposed upon them. Lord Fawn was also at Matching, a suggestion having been made to Lady Glencora by some leading Liberals that he should be supported in his difficulties by her hospitality.

The mind of Mr Palliser himself was too deeply engaged to admit of its being interested in the great necklace affair; but there was not one of the others who did not listen anxiously for news on the subject. As regarded the old Duke, it had been found to be quite a godsend, and from post to post as the facts reached Matching they were communicated to him.

'Duke,' Lady Glencora said, entering rather abruptly the small warm luxurious room in which her husband's uncle was passing his morning, 'they say now that after all the diamonds were not in the box when it was taken out of the room at Carlisle.' The Duke was reclining in an easy-chair, with his head leaning forward on his breast, and Madame Goesler was reading to him. But Lady Glencora's tidings awakened him completely.

'The diamonds not in the box!' he said, pushing his head a little more forward in his eagerness.

'Barrington Erle says Major Mackintosh is almost sure the diamonds were not there.' Major Mackintosh was an officer very high in the police force.

'Then she must have known it,' said Madame Goesler.

'That doesn't quite follow, Madame Max,' said Lady Glencora, and went on to add the information, which she had received from Barrington Erle, that Major Mackintosh was widely believed to be of opinion that Lord George had the diamonds, with or without Lady Eustace's knowledge. Lord George had offered to fight everybody or anybody, beginning with Lord Fawn and ending with Major Mackintosh.

On the next morning there came further news. The police had asked permission to search the rooms in which lived Lady Eustace and Lord George, and in each case had been refused. 'I am told that Lord George acts the indignant madman uncommonly well,' said Barrington Erle in his letter. As for poor Lizzie, she had fainted when the proposition was made to her. The request was renewed as soon as she had been brought to herself; and then she refused—on the advice, as she said, of her cousin, Mr Greystock.

Mr Palliser was of opinion that the attempt to search the lady's house was iniquitous. Mr Bonteen shook his head, and rather thought that, if he were Home Secretary, he would have had the search made. Madame Goesler was of opinion that a lady who could carry such a box about the country with her deserved to have it stolen. Lord Fawn, unfortunately, had been acquainted with the lady, and was constrained to say that her conduct had been such as to justify the suspicions of the police. 'Of course, we all suspect her,' said Lady Glencora; 'and, of course, we suspect Lord George too, and Mrs Carbuncle. But then, you know, if I were to lose my diamonds people would suspect me just the same—or perhaps Plantagenet. It is so delightful to think that a woman has stolen her own property and put all the police into a state of ferment.' Lord Chiltern declared himself to be heartily sick of the whole subject; and Mr Grey, who was a very just man, suggested that the evidence, as yet, against anybody, was very slight. 'Of course, it's slight,' said Lady Glencora. 'If it were more than slight, it would be just like any other robbery, and there would be nothing in it.'

All these matters were told to the Duke by Lady Glencora and Madame Goesler in his Grace's private room; for the Duke was now infirm and did not dine in company unless the day was very auspicious to him. But in the evening he would creep into the drawing-room, and on this occasion he had a word to say about the Eustace diamonds to everyone in the room. 'Wouldn't have her boxes searched, you know. That looks uncommonly suspicious. Perhaps, Lady Chiltern, we shall hear tomorrow morning something more about it.'

'Poor dear Duke,' said Lady Chiltern to her husband.

'Doting old idiot!' he replied.

·   ·   ·   ·   ·

No suggestion had in truth been made to Lord George de Bruce Carruthers as to the searching of his lordship's boxes and desks. That very eminent detective officer, Mr Bunfit, had, however, called upon Lord George more than once, and Lord George had declared very plainly that he did not like it. 'If you'll have the kindness to explain to me what it is you want, I'll be much obliged to you,' Lord George had said.

'Well, my lord,' said Bunfit, 'what we want is these diamonds.'

'Do you believe I've got them?'

'A man in my situation, my lord, never believes anything. We has to suspect, but we never believes.'

'You suspect that I stole them?'

'No, my lord; I didn't say that. But things are very queer; aren't they?'

The immediate object of Mr Bunfit's visit on this morning had been to ascertain from Lord George whether it was true that his lordship had been with Messrs Harter and Benjamin, the jewellers, on the morning after his arrival in town. Mr Bunfit had expressed a very strong opinion to Major Mackintosh that the necklace had in truth been transferred to them on that morning. That there was nothing 'too hot or too heavy' for Messrs Harter and Benjamin was quite a creed with the police of the West End of London. The question was asked, and Lord George did not deny the visit. 'Unfortunately, they hold acceptances of mine,' said Lord George, 'and I am often there.'

'We know as they have your lordship's name to paper,' said Mr Bunfit, thanking Lord George for his courtesy.

There had been many interviews between Lizzie and various members of the police force in reference to the diamonds, but the questions put to her had always been asked on the supposition that she might have mislaid the necklace. But when Mr Bunfit called upon her, perhaps for the fifth or sixth time, and suggested that he should be allowed, with the assistance of the female whom he had left behind him in the hall, to search all her ladyship's boxes, drawers, presses, and receptacles in London, the thing took a very different aspect. 'You see, my lady,' said Mr Bunfit, 'it may have got anywhere among your ladyship's things, unbeknownst.' Lady Eustace was now living at Mrs Carbuncle's house and Mrs Carbuncle was the first to protest. If Mr Bunfit thought that he was going to search her things, Mr Bunfit was very much mistaken. Her house was her own, and she gave Mr Bunfit to understand that his repeated visits were not agreeable to her. But when Mr Bunfit suggested that the search should be confined to the rooms used exclusively by Lady Eustace Mrs Carbuncle absolutely changed her views, and recommended that he should be allowed to have his way.

As soon as the words were out of Mrs Carbuncle's mouth poor Lizzie's courage deserted her entirely. There came some obstruction in her throat so that she could not speak. She felt as though her heart were breaking. She put out both her hands and could not draw them back again. She knew that she was betraying herself by her weakness. She could just hear the man explaining that the search was merely to satisfy everybody that there was no mistake—and then she fainted. Mrs Carbuncle and Mr Bunfit hurried to help her.

'The whole thing has been too much for her,' said Mrs Carbuncle severely, ringing the bell for further aid.

'No doubt, mum; no doubt. We has to see a deal of this sort of thing. Just a little air, if you please, mum—and as much water as'd go to christen a baby. That's always best, mum. Just dash the water on in drops like. They feels a drop more than they would a bucketful—and then when they comes to they hasn't to change theirselves.'

Bunfit's advice, founded on much experience, was good, and Lizzie gradually came to herself and opened her eyes. She immediately clutched at her breast feeling for her key. She found it unmoved, but before her finger had recognized the touch her quick mind had told her how wrong the movement had been. It had not been lost upon Mr Bunfit. He felt almost sure that there was something in her possession—probably some document—which would place him on the track of the diamonds. But he could not compel a search.

'Don't you think you'd better leave us now?' said Mrs Carbuncle to him.

'Indeed you had,' said Lizzie. 'I am fit for nothing just at present.'

'We won't disturb your ladyship the least,' said Mr Bunfit, 'if you'll only just let us have your keys. Your servant can be with us, and we won't move one tittle of anything. I don't demand it, Lady Eustace, but if you'll allow me to say so, I do think it will look better for your ladyship.'

'I can take no step without consulting my cousin, Mr Greystock,' said Lizzie; and having thought of this she adhered to it. Ill as she was, she could be obstinate, and Bunfit left the house without having been able to finger that key.

As he walked back to his own quarters in Scotland Yard Bunfit was by no means dissatisfied with his morning's work. He was now sure that her ladyship possessed, at any rate, some guilty knowledge. Bunfit was one of those who believed that the box was empty when taken out of the hotel. It was his opinion that the box had been opened and the door cut by the instrumentality of Lord George de Bruce Carruthers —with the assistance of some well-skilled mechanical thief. Bunfit believed that the diamonds were now either in the possession of Lord George or of Harter and Benjamin, and that Lord George and the lady were lovers. But Bunfit was almost alone in his opinion. There were men high in their profession as detectives who avowed that two very well-known thieves had been concerned in the business. That a certain Mr Smiler had been there, a gentleman for whom the whole police of London entertained a feeling which approached to veneration, and that most diminutive of full-grown thieves, Billy Cann—most diminutive but at the same time most expert—was not doubted by some minds. It was a known fact that Mr Smiler had left London from the Euston Square station on the day before that on which Lizzie and her party had reached Carlisle. If Mr Smiler and Billy Cann had both been at work at the hotel, then it was hardly conceivable that the robbery should have been arranged by Lord George. Was it probable that Lord George would have committed himself with such men, and incurred the very heavy expense of paying for their services, when he was—according to the Bunfit theory—able to get at the diamonds without any such trouble, danger, and expenditure?

Frank Greystock took up his cousin's part altogether in good faith. He entertained not the slightest suspicion that she was deceiving him. That the robbery had been a bona-fide robbery, and that Lizzie had lost her treasure, was to him beyond doubt. He had gradually convinced himself that Mr Camperdown was wrong in his claim, and was strongly of opinion that Lord Fawn had disgraced himself by his conduct to the lady. When he now heard, as he did hear, that some undefined suspicion was attached to his cousin—and when he heard also, as unfortunately he did hear—that Lord Fawn had encouraged that suspicion, he was very irate, and said grievous things of Lord Fawn. He busied himself very much in the matter, and even interrogated John Eustace as to his intentions.

'My dear fellow,' said Eustace, 'if you hated those diamonds as much as I do, you would never mention them again.' Greystock declared that this expression of aversion to the subject might be all very well for Mr Eustace, but that he found himself bound to defend his cousin.

'You cannot defend her against me,' said Eustace, 'for I do not attack her. I have never said a word against her. I went down to Portray when she asked me. As far as I am concerned she is perfectly welcome to wear the necklace, if she can get it back again. I will not make or meddle in the matter one way or the other.' Frank, after that, went to Mr Camperdown, but he could get no satisfaction from the attorney. Mr Camperdown would only say that he had a duty to do. Should the diamonds be recovered he would claim them on behalf of the estate. In his opinion, whether the diamonds were recovered or not, Lady Eustace was responsible to the estate for their value.

'If it goes on like this it will kill me,' Lizzie was saying to Lord George Carruthers.

'They are treating me in precisely the same way,' said Lord George.

'But think of your strength and of my weakness, Lord George.'

'By heavens, I don't know!' said Lord George. 'It was a good joke when we talked of the suspicions of that fellow at Carlisle as we came up by the railway—but it is no joke now. I've had men with me, almost asking to search among my things.'

'They have quite asked me!' said Lizzie piteously.

'You—yes. There's some reason in that. These infernal diamonds did belong to you, or, at any rate, you had them.

You are the last person known to have seen them. But what the mischief can I have had to do with them? Because I was civil enough to look after you coming up to town, and because one of you were careless enough to lose your jewels, I am to be talked about all over London as the man who took them!'

Lord George had escaped from conventional usage into rough, truthful speech, and Lizzie understood it and appreciated it, and liked it. It seemed fitting that a Corsair should be as uncivil as he pleased. Lizzie listened to it with a strange fascination. She looked up timidly into his deep-set eyes, as he came and stood over her. 'Tell me all that you know about it,' he said, in that deep low voice which, from her first acquaintance with him, had filled her with interest, and almost with awe.

Lizzie Eustace was speechless as she continued to look up into the Corsair's face. He waited perhaps a minute, looking at her, before he renewed his question; and the minute seemed to her to be her age. There gradually came a grim smile over his face and she was sure that he could read her very heart. Then he called her by her Christian name—as he had never called her before. 'Come, Lizzie,' he said, 'you might as well tell me all about it. You know.'

'Know what?' The words were uttered in the lowest whisper.

'About this damned necklace. Come—out with it! If you won't tell me you must tell someone else. There has been a deal too much of this already.'

'You won't betray me?'

'Not if you deal openly with me.'

'I will; indeed I will. And it was all an accident. When I took them out of the box I only did it for safety.'

'You did take them out of the box then?' She nodded her head. 'And have you got them now?' There was another nod. 'And where are they?'

'Upstairs.'

'In your bedroom?'

'In my desk in the little sitting-room.'

'The Lord be good to us!' ejaculated Lord George. 'All the police in London, from the chief downwards, are agog

223

about this necklace. Every well-known thief in the town is envied by every other thief because he is thought to have had a finger in the pie. I am suspected and half the jewellers in London and Paris are supposed to have the stones in their keeping. Every man and woman is talking about it and people are quarrelling about it till they almost cut each other's throats; and all the while you have got them locked up in your desk! How on earth did you get the box broken open and then conveyed out of your room at Carlisle?'

Then Lizzie in a frightened whisper, with her eyes often turned on the floor, told the whole story. 'If I'd had a minute to think of it,' she said, 'I would have confessed the truth at Carlisle. Why should I want to steal what was my own? But they came to me all so quickly, and I didn't like to say that I had them under my pillow.'

'Then you committed perjury at Carlisle. Major Mackintosh and the magistrates won't settle down, peaceable and satisfied, when they hear the end of the story. And I think Messrs Camperdown will have a bill against you. It's been uncommonly clever, but I don't see the use of it.'

'I've been very foolish; but you won't desert me?'

'Upon my word I don't know what I'm to do.'

He passed his arm round her waist, but more as though she were a child than a woman, as he stood thinking. Of all the affairs in which he had ever been engaged it was the most difficult. She submitted to his embrace, and leaned upon his shoulder, and looked up into his face. If he would only tell her that he loved her, then he would be bound to her and must share with her the burthen of the diamonds. 'George!' she said, and burst into a low, suppressed wailing, with her face hidden upon his arm.

'That's all very well,' said he, still holding her—for she was pleasant to hold—'but what the devil is a fellow to do? I don't see my way out of it. I think you had better go to Camperdown and give them up to him and tell him the truth.'

'I'll never give them up to Mr Camperdown. They are mine—my very own. My cousin, Mr Greystock, who is much more of a lawyer than Mr Camperdown, says so. Oh, George, do think of something! Don't tell me that I must give them up! Wouldn't Mr Benjamin buy them?'

'Yes—for half nothing; and then go and tell the whole story and get money from the other side. You can't trust Benjamin.'

'But I can trust you.' She wanted him to take the terrible packet from her there and then, and use his own judgement in disposing of it. But this he positively refused to do.

There was one other trouble on her mind. She had told the detective officer that she would submit her boxes and desks to be searched if her cousin Frank should advise it. If the policeman were to return with her cousin while the diamonds were still in her desk, what should she do? 'They would never ask to search your person,' suggested Lord George. 'Have them about you when he comes. Don't take them out with you; but keep them in your pocket while you are in the house during the day. They will hardly bring a woman to search you.'

'But there was a woman with the man when he came before.'

'Then you must refuse in spite of your cousin. Show yourself angry with him and with everybody. Swear that you did not intend to submit yourself to such indignity as that. They can't do it without a magistrate's order, unless you permit it. Of course they'll suspect you, but they do already. And your cousin will suspect you, but you must put up with that. It will be very bad, but I see nothing better. Of all things, say nothing of me.'

And then he took his leave of her. 'Oh, George,' she said, 'I have no friend now but you. You will care for me?' He took her in his arms and kissed her, and promised that he would care for her. How was he to save himself from doing so? When he was gone Lizzie sat down to think of it all, and felt sure that at last she had found her Corsair.

·   ·   ·   ·   ·

Mrs Carbuncle and Lizzie Eustace did not shut themselves up because there was trouble in the household. Mrs Carbuncle was very fond of the play, and made herself acquainted with every piece as it came out. Every actor and actress of note on the stage was known to her, and she dealt freely in criticisms on their respective merits. The ladies had a box at the Haymarket taken for this very evening. Lizzie, when she was left by Lord George, had many doubts whether she would go or stay at home. But to be alone—with her necklace in the desk upstairs, or in her pocket, was terrible to her. And then, they could not search her or her boxes while she was at the theatre. She must not take the necklace with her there. He had told her to leave it in her desk when she went from home.

The play, *The Noble Jilt*, was a failure; at least so said Mrs Carbuncle. 'A noble jilt is a contradiction in terms. There can be no such thing. A woman, when she had once said the word, is bound to stick to it.'

'I'd never marry a man merely because I said I would,' Lizzie disagreed. 'If I found I didn't like him I'd leave him at the altar. I'd leave him any time I found I didn't like him.' This was said just as the carriage stopped at Mrs Carbuncle's door. They at once perceived that the hall door was open, and that there were policemen in the hall, with the cook and housemaid and Mrs Carbuncle's own maid. A policeman in uniform stepped forward and touched his hat. 'My lady,' he said, addressing Mrs Carbuncle, 'there's been a robbery here.'

'A robbery!'

With a horrid spasm across her heart, which seemed ready to kill her, so sharp was the pain, Lizzie recovered the use of her legs and followed Mrs Carbuncle into the dining-room. 'We've been upstairs, my lady,' said the policeman, 'and they've been in most of the rooms. There's a desk broke open.' Lizzie gave an involuntary little scream. 'Yes, mum, a desk, and a bureau, and a dressing-case. What's gone your ladyship can tell when you sees. And one of the young women is off. It's she as done it.' Then the cook explained. She and the housemaid and Mrs Carbuncle's lady's maid had just stepped out, only round the corner to what they called a tea-party, at a public-house, and by previous agreement Patience Crabstick had remained in charge. When they came back Patience Crabstick was gone, and the desk, and bureau, and dressing-case, were found to have been opened. 'She had a reg'lar thief along with her, my lady,' said the policeman, ' 'cause of the way the things was opened.'

'I always knew that young woman was downright bad,' said Mrs Carbuncle in her first expression of wrath.

They made their way upstairs, with the two policemen following. On the stairs Lizzie explained that in her desk, of which she always carried the key round her neck, there were two ten-pound notes, and four five-pound notes, and three sovereigns; in all, forty-three pounds. Her other jewels—the jewels which she had possessed over and above the fatal diamond necklace—were in her dressing-case. Patience, she did not doubt, had known that the money was there, and certainly knew of her jewels. So they went upstairs. The desk was open and the money gone. Five or six rings and a bracelet had been taken also from Lizzie's dressing-case, which she had left open. The necklace was of course gone; but Lizzie of course made no mention of it.

Of Mrs Carbuncle's property sufficient had been stolen to make a long list in that lady's handwriting. The superintendent of police was there before they went to bed, and was of opinion that the thieves had expected to find more plunder. The superintendent had heard of the diamond necklace, and expressed an opinion that poor Lady Eustace was especially marked out for misfortune. 'It all comes of having such a girl as that about her,' said Mrs Carbuncle.

Lizzie, when the policemen were gone, and the noise was over, and the house was closed, slunk away to her bedroom. She had talked of giving away her necklace, and had seriously thought of getting rid of it by burying it deep in the sea. But now that it was in very truth gone from her the loss of it was horrible to her. Ten thousand pounds, for which she had struggled so much and borne so many things, which had come to be the prevailing fact of her life, gone from her for ever! But the feeling came upon her that her own disgrace was every hour being brought nearer to her. Her secret was no longer quite her own. One man knew it, and he had talked to her of perjury. Patience must have known it, too; and now someone else also knew it.

She tried to form some idea in her mind of what might be

the truth. Of course, Patience Crabstick had known her secret, but how long had the girl known it? And how had the girl discovered it? The Corsair knew the facts, and no one but the Corsair. She had offered the necklace to the Corsair, but he had refused to take it. She could understand that he should see the danger of accepting the diamonds from her hand, and yet should be desirous of having them. And might not he have thought that he could best relieve her from the burthen of their custody in this manner? She felt no anger against the Corsair as she weighed the probability of his having taken them in this fashion. A Corsair must be a Corsair. Were he to come to her and confess the deed, she would almost like him the better for it—admiring his skill and enterprise. But how very clever he must have been, and how brave!

When the morning came she said that she was ill, and refused to leave her bed. Policemen, she knew, were in the house early. If it were absolutely necessary, she said, the men must come into her room. If her deposition must be taken, she would make it in her bed. In the course of the day the magistrate did come into her room and the deposition was taken. Forty-three pounds had been taken from her desk, and certain jewels, which she described, from her dressing-case. As far as she was aware, no other property of hers was missing. And so, a second time, she had sworn falsely.

Lord George was in the house for a great part of the day, but he did not ask to be admitted to Lizzie's room; nor did she ask to see him. Frank Greystock was there late in the afternoon, and went up at once to his cousin. Frank, into whose mind no glimmer of suspicion against his cousin had yet entered, was very tender with her and remained for more than an hour. 'Oh, Frank, what had I better do?' she asked.

'I would leave London, if I were you.'

'Yes—of course. Oh yes, I will!'

'If you don't fear the cold of Scotland . . .'

'I fear nothing—nothing but being where these policemen can come to me. Oh!'—and then she shuddered and was in truth hysterical. As she remembered the magistrates, and the detectives, and the policemen in their uniforms, the thoughts that crowded on her were more than she could bear.

'Your child is there, and it is your own house. Go there till all this passes by,' he told her. She promised him that as soon as she was well enough she would at once go to Scotland.

In the meantime the Eustace diamonds were locked up in a small safe fixed into the wall at the back of a small cellar beneath the establishment of Messrs Harter and Benjamin, in Minto Lane, in the City. Messrs Harter and Benjamin always kept a second place of business. Their great shop was at the West End; but they had accommodation in the City.

.   .   .   .   .

When the Hertford Street robbery was three days old and was still the talk of the town Lizzie Eustace was really ill. She had promised to go down to Scotland; but as her presence of mind returned she remembered that even at Portray she would not be out of danger, and that she could do nothing in furtherance of her plans if once immured there. Lord George was in London, and Lord Fawn was in London. It was more than ever necessary to her that she should find a husband who would not be less her husband when the truth of that business at Carlisle should be known to all the world. Her husband might take her abroad, and the whole thing would die away.

She was most anxious to see Lord George; but if what Mrs Carbuncle said to her was true, Lord George refused to see her. Of course there were difficulties. That her cousin Frank should see her in her bedroom was a matter of course. But the Corsair was not a cousin—nor as yet an acknowledged lover. 'You see, my dear,' said Mrs Carbuncle, 'there can be no real reason for his seeing you up in your bedroom. If there had been anything between you, as I once thought there would . . .' There was something in the tone of Mrs Carbuncle's voice which grated on Lizzie's ear—something which seemed to imply that all that prospect was over.

'You know, my dear,' she added, 'Mr Emilius is to come to you this afternoon.'

'Mr Emilius! I had quite forgotten. He is coming here to read to me.'

Mr Emilius did come and read to Lady Eustace that afternoon. A clergyman is as privileged to enter the bedroom of a sick lady as is a doctor or a cousin. Mr Emilius first said a prayer, kneeling at Lizzie's bedside; then he read a chapter in the Bible, and after that he read the first half of the fourth canto of *Childe Harold* so well that Lizzie felt for the moment that, after all, poetry was life and life was poetry.

CHAPTER FOUR

PARLIAMENT had now met, and Lady Glencora Palliser's party in the country had been to some extent broken up. On 13th of February Mr Palliser made his first great statement in Parliament on the matter of the five-farthinged penny, and pledged himself to do his very best to carry that stupendous measure through Parliament in the present Session. Some said that the penny with five farthings, the penny of which a hundred would make ten shillings, the penny which would make all future pecuniary calculations easy to the meanest British capacity, could never become the law of the land. Others were willing to believe that gradually the thing would so sink into the minds of Members of Parliament, of writers of leading articles, and of the active public generally, as to admit of a decimal system being desirable. But it was probable, many said, that Mr Palliser might kill himself by labour which would be herculean. It behoved Lady Glencora to see that her Hercules did not kill himself.

In this state of affairs Lady Glencora—into whose hands the custody of Mr Palliser's uncle, the Duke of Omnium, had now altogether fallen—had a divided duty between Matching and London. But though she was burthened with great care, Lady Glencora by no means dropped her interest in the Eustace diamonds; and when she learned that on the top of the great Carlisle robbery a second robbery had been superadded, she took it into her head to make a diversion in Lady Eustace's favour. She called in Hertford Street. She was told by the servant that Lady Eustace was in bed, but she sent up her card. The compliment was one much too great to be refused. Lady Glencora stood so high in the world; if Lord George would keep her secret, thought Lizzie, and Lady Glencora would be her friend, might she not still be a successful woman? So Lady Glencora Palliser was shown up to Lizzie's chamber. Lizzie was found with her nicest shawl and prettiest handkerchief, with a volume of Tennyson's poetry, and a scent-bottle. She knew that it behoved her to be very clever at this interview.

'Lady Eustace,' said Lady Glencora with a smile, 'I have just come to offer you my sympathy.'

'The loss has been as nothing to the vexation that has accompanied it, Lady Glencora. I don't know how to speak of it. Ladies have lost their jewels before now, but I don't know that any lady before me has ever been accused of stealing them herself.'

'There has been no accusation, surely.'

'I haven't exactly been put in prison, Lady Glencora, but I have had policemen here wanting to search my things; and you know yourself what reports have been spread.'

'Oh, yes; I do.' Then Lady Glencora poured out her sympathy—perhaps with more eloquence than discretion. 'As for the loss of the diamonds, I think you bear it wonderfully,' said Lady Glencora.

'If you could imagine how little I care about it!' said Lizzie with enthusiasm. 'Ah—you can never have known trials such as mine. Perhaps you may have heard that in the course of last summer I became engaged to marry a nobleman with whom you are acquainted.'

'Oh, yes; Lord Fawn. We all heard of it.'

'And you have heard how he has treated me?'

'Yes—indeed.'

'I will say nothing about him, Lady Glencora. It would not be proper. But all that came of this wretched necklace. Can

231

you wonder that I should say that I wish these stones had been thrown into the sea?'

'I suppose Lord Fawn will—will come all right again now?' said Lady Glencora. 'His objection to the marriage will now be over.'

'I'm sure I do not in the least know what are his lordship's views,' said Lizzie in scorn, 'and, to tell you the truth, I do not very much care.'

'What I mean is, that he didn't like you to have the Eustace diamonds . . .'

'They were not Eustace diamonds. They were my diamonds.'

'But he did not like you to have them; and as they are now gone, his objection is gone too. Why don't you write to him, and make him come and see you? That's what I should do.'

Lizzie, of course, repudiated vehemently any idea of forcing Lord Fawn into a marriage which had become distasteful to him—let the reason be what it might. 'His lordship is perfectly free, as far as I am concerned,' said Lizzie with a little show of anger. But all this Lady Glencora took at its worth. Lady Glencora determined that she would remake the match.

The five-farthing bill had been laid upon the table on a Tuesday, and on the Wednesday there was a little dinner at Mr Palliser's house. The Prime Minister was to be there, and Mr Bonteen, and Barrington Erle. A question, perhaps of no great practical importance, had occurred to Mr Palliser —by what denomination should the fifth part of a penny be known? Someone had, ill-naturedly, whispered to Mr Palliser that a farthing meant a fourth. Should he stick by the word farthing; or should he call it a fifthing, a quint, or a semitenth? Mr Gresham had expressed an opinion, somewhat offhand, that English people would never be got to talk about quints, and so there was a difficulty. A little dinner was therefore arranged, and Mr Palliser, as was his custom, put the affair of the dinner into his wife's hands. When he was told that she had included Lord Fawn among the guests he opened his eyes. Lord Fawn, who might be good enough at the India Office, knew literally nothing about the penny. 'He'll take it as the greatest compliment in the world,' said Lady Glencora. 'I don't want to pay Lord Fawn a compliment,' said Mr Palliser. 'But I do,' said Lady Glencora. And so the matter was arranged.

It was a very nice little dinner, and the great question of the day was settled in two minutes, before the guests were out of the drawing-room. 'Stick to your farthing,' said Mr Gresham.

'I think so,' said Mr Palliser.

'Quint's a very easy word,' said Mr Bonteen.

'But squint is an easier,' said Mr Gresham, with all a Prime Minister's jocose authority.

'They'd certainly be called cock-eyes,' said Barrington Erle.

'Stick to the old word,' said Mr Gresham. And so the matter was decided, while Lady Glencora was flattering Lord Fawn.

'Whom do you think I saw the other day?' said Lady Glencora, when she got her victim into a corner. 'I called upon poor Lady Eustace, and found her in bed.' Lord Fawn blushed up to the roots of his hair. 'I do feel for her so much. I think she has been so hardly used.'

He was obliged to say something. 'My name has, of course, been much mixed up with hers.'

'Yes, Lord Fawn, I know it has. And it is because I am so sure of your high-minded generosity and thorough devotion that I have ventured to speak to you. All manner of stories have been told about her, as I believe without the slightest foundation. They tell me now that she had an undoubted right to keep the diamonds; that even if Sir Florian did not give them to her, they were hers under his will. Those lawyers have given up all idea of proceeding against her.'

'Mr Camperdown thought that the property should be given up.'

'Oh yes, that's the man's name; a horrid man. I am told that he was really most cruel to her. And then, because a lot of thieves had got about her, and took first her necklace and then her money, they were impudent enough to say that she had stolen her own things.'

'I don't think they quite said that, Lady Glencora.'

'Something very much like it, Lord Fawn. I have no doubt in my own mind who did steal all the things.'

'Who was it?'

'Oh—one mustn't mention names in such an affair without evidence. At any rate, she has been very badly treated, and I shall take her up. If I were you I would go and call upon her; I would indeed.'

'I don't know what to think,' said Lord Fawn. After that he escaped as quickly as he could. He knew well enough how strong was Lady Glencora.

On the next morning Lord Fawn took an opportunity of seeing Mr Camperdown.

'My dear lord,' said Mr Camperdown, 'I shall wash my hands of the matter altogether. The diamonds are gone.'

'You will drop the bill in Chancery then?'

'What good can the bill do us when the diamonds are gone? In fact, the trustees have decided that they will do nothing more, and my hands are tied.'

On the next morning, Friday, there came to Lord Fawn the note which Lady Glencora had recommended Lizzie to write. It was very short. 'Had you not better come and see me? You can hardly think that things should be left as they are now.' He had hoped that things might be left, and that they would arrange themselves; that he could throw aside his engagement without further trouble, and that the subject would drop. But it was not so.

On the next day, Saturday, he went down, as was his custom, to Richmond, and did not once mention Lizzie's name; Lady Fawn and her daughters never spoke of her now. But on his return to London on the Sunday evening he found another note from Lizzie. 'You will hardly have the hardihood to leave my note unanswered. Pray let me know when you will come to me.' Should it be known that he had received two such notes from a lady and that he had not answered or noticed them the world would judge him to have behaved badly. So he wrote fixing a day for his visit to Hertford Street.

'I am going to see her in the course of this week,' he said in answer to a further question from Lady Glencora, who, chancing to meet him in society, had again addressed him on the subject. He lacked the courage to tell Lady Glencora to mind her own business and to allow him to do the same. Lady Glencora was the social queen of the party to which he belonged, and Mr Palliser was Chancellor of the Exchequer, and would some day be Duke of Omnium.

'As you are great, be merciful, Lord Fawn,' said Lady Glencora. 'You men, I believe, never realize what it is that women feel when they love. It is my belief that she will die unless you are reunited to her. And then she is so beautiful!'

'It is a subject that I cannot discuss, Lady Glencora.'

'I daresay not. And I'm sure I am the last person to wish to give you pain. But you see, if the poor lady has done nothing to merit your anger it does seem rather a strong measure to throw her off and give her no reason whatever. How would you defend yourself, suppose she published it all?' Lady Glencora's courage was very great, and her impudence also. This last question Lord Fawn left unanswered, walking away in great dudgeon.

The Saturday morning came at last for which Lord Fawn had made his appointment with Lizzie. He was shown up, and she received him very gracefully. She rose from her chair, and put out her hand for him to take. She spoke no word of greeting, but looked at him with a pleasant smile, and stood for a few seconds with her hand in his. She certainly had no intention of lessening his embarrassment. 'I hope you are better than you have been,' he said at last.

'I am getting better, Lord Fawn. Will you not sit down?' He then seated himself, placing his hat beside him on the floor, but at the moment could not find words to speak. 'I have been very ill.'

'I have been so sorry to hear it.'

'There has been much to make me ill—has there not?'

'About the robbery, you mean?'

'About many things. The robbery has been by no means the worst, though it frightened me much. There were two robberies, Lord Fawn.'

'Yes—I know that.'

'And it was very terrible. And then, I had been threatened with a lawsuit. You have heard that, too?'

'Yes—I had heard it.'

'I believe they have given that up now. I understand from my cousin, Mr Greystock, that the stupid people have found out at last that they had not a leg to stand on. My cousin, who is a brother rather than a cousin, has known how to protect me from the injuries done to me—or, rather, has known how to take my part when I have been injured. My lord, I have had great wrong done me.'

'Do you mean by me?'

'Yes, by you. I am to be thrown over simply because your lordship chooses to throw me over. Can you justify yourself—in your own heart?'

Unfortunately for Lord Fawn, he was not sure that he could justify himself. Lizzie was waiting for an answer to her question. Having paused for some seconds, she repeated her question in a stronger and more personal form. 'Now, Lord Fawn, what do you mean to do?'

'I had thought, Lady Eustace, that any regard you might ever have entertained for me—had been dissipated.'

'Have I told you so? And now let me ask, Lord Fawn, on what ground you and I stand together. When my friend, Lady Glencora, asked me, only this morning, whether my engagement with you was still an existing fact, and brought me the kindest possible message on the same subject from her uncle, the Duke of Omnium, I hardly knew what answer to make to her. I told her that we were engaged, but that your lordship's conduct to me had been so strange that I hardly knew how to speak of you among my friends.'

'After all that has passed, perhaps we had better part,' said Lord Fawn miserably.

'Then I shall put the matter into the hands of the Duke of Omnium,' said Lizzie boldly. 'I will not have my whole life ruined, my good name blasted . . .'

'I have not said a word to injure your good name.'

'On what plea, then, have you dared to take upon yourself to put an end to an engagement which was made at your own pressing request? On what ground do you justify such conduct? You are a Liberal, Lord Fawn; and everybody regards the Duke of Omnium as the head of the Liberal nobility in

England. He is my friend, and I shall put the matter into his hands.'

Lord Fawn felt the absurdity of the threat, and yet it had effect upon him. The Duke of Omnium, or the Duke's name, was a power in the nation. Lady Glencora was certainly very powerful and might make London almost too hot to hold him if she chose to go about everywhere saying that he ought to marry the lady.

'Lady Eustace,' he said, 'I am most anxious not to behave badly in this matter.'

'But you are behaving very badly.'

'With your leave I will tell you what I would suggest. I will submit to you in writing my opinion on this matter'— Lord Fawn had been all his life submitting his opinion in writing and thought that he was rather a good hand at the work. 'I will then endeavour to explain to you the reasons which make me think that it will be better for us both that our engagement should be at an end. If, after reading it, you shall disagree with me, and still insist on the right which I gave you when I asked you to become my wife, I will perform the promise which I certainly made.' To this most foolish proposal on his part Lizzie, of course, acquiesced. She bade him farewell with her sweetest smile. It was now manifest to her that she could have her husband—or her revenge, just as she might prefer.

This had been a day of triumph to her, and she was talking of it in the evening to Mrs Carbuncle when she was told that a policeman wanted to see her downstairs. She descended slowly, and was then informed by the man in uniform that her late servant, Patience Crabstick, had given herself up as Queen's Evidence, and was now in custody in Scotland Yard. It had been thought right that she should be so far informed; but the man was able to tell her nothing further.

CHAPTER FIVE

On the Monday morning there appeared in one of the daily newspapers the following paragraph: 'We are given to understand that a man well known to the London police as an accomplished housebreaker has been arrested in reference to the robbery which was effected on the 30th of January last at Lady Eustace's house in Hertford Street. No doubt the same person was concerned in the robbery of her ladyship's jewels at Carlisle on the night of the 8th of January. The mystery which has so long enveloped these two affairs will now probably be cleared up.'

Poor Lizzie felt that fresh trouble was certainly coming upon her. She had learned now that the crime for which she might be prosecuted and punished was that of perjury— that even if everything was known she could not be accused of stealing, and that if she could only get out of the way till the wrath of the magistrate and policemen should have been evaporated she might, possibly, escape altogether. At any rate, they could not take her income away from her. But how could she get out of the way, and how could she endure to be cross-examined, and looked at, and inquired into, by all those who would be concerned in the matter? She thought that, if only she could have arranged her matrimonial affairs before the bad day came upon her, she could have endured it better. If she might see Lord George she could ask for advice —could ask for advice, not as she was always forced to do from her cousin on a false statement of facts, but with everything known and declared.

On that very day Lord George came to Hertford Street. He had never whispered her secret to anyone and had still been at a loss about the second robbery when he too saw the paragraph in the newspaper. He went direct to Scotland Yard and made inquiry there. His name had been so often used in the affair that such inquiry from him was justified. 'Well, my lord; yes; we have found out something,' said Bunfit. 'Mr Benjamin is gone off, you know. But what's the good, now we has the telegraph?'

Lord George had been very careful, asking no question which would have shown that he knew that the necklace had been in Hertford Street when the robbery took place there; but it seemed to him now that the police must be aware that it was so. The arrest had been made because of the robbery in Hertford Street, and because of that arrest Mr Benjamin had taken his departure. Mr Benjamin was too big a man to have concerned himself deeply in the smaller things which had then been stolen.

From Scotland Yard Lord George went direct to Hertford Street. He was in want of money, in want of a settled home, in want of a future income, and altogether unsatisfied with his present mode of life. Lizzie Eustace, no doubt, would take him. To have his wife, immediately on her marriage, or even before it, arraigned for perjury, would not be pleasant. There was very much in the whole affair of which he would not be proud as he led his bride to the altar; but a man does not expect to get four thousand pounds a year for nothing.

'So you have come at last,' she said.

'Yes, I've come at last. It would not have done for me to come up to you when you were in bed. Those women downstairs would have talked about it everywhere.'

'I suppose they would.'

'And now tell me what you know about this second robbery.'

'I know nothing, Lord George.'

'Oh yes, you do. You know, at any rate, that the diamonds were there.'

'Yes—I know that.'

'And were they taken?'

'Of course they were taken.'

'You are sure of that? Because, you know, you have been very clever. It might, you know, have been a little game to get them out of your own hands—between you and your maid.'

'I don't know what you take me for, Lord George.'

'I take you for a lady who, for a long time, got the better of the police and the magistrates, and who managed to shift all the trouble off your own shoulders on to those of other people. You have heard that they have taken one of the thieves?'

'And they have got the girl.'

. 'Have they? I didn't know that. That scoundrel Benjamin has cleared off, too. Of course the whole truth will come out.'

'You won't tell. You promised that you would not.'

'If they put me in a witness-box of course I must tell. Patience Crabstick will tell it all, without any help from me. She'll say where the diamonds were found—and how did they come there if you didn't put them there? You've only two things to do.'

'What are they, Lord George?'

'Go off, like Mr Benjamin; or else make a clean breast of it. Send for John Eustace and tell him the whole. It will all be published, and then, perhaps, there will be an end of it.'

'I couldn't do that!' said Lizzie, bursting into tears.

'People who are rich and are connected with rich people, and have great friends, have great advantages over their inferiors when they get into trouble. If you were nobody, you would be indicted for perjury and would go to prison. As it is, if you will tell all your story to one of your swell friends I think it very likely that you may be pulled through. I should say that Mr Eustace, or your cousin Greystock, would be the best.'

'Why couldn't you do it? You know it all. I told you because—because—because I thought you would be the kindest to me.'

He had suggested a second alternative—that she should go off, like Mr Benjamin. In that case ought she not to go under the protection of her Corsair? 'Might I not go abroad—just for a time?' she asked.

'It is possible,' he said. 'Not that it would blow over altogether. Everybody would know it; and if you meant to be off you should be off at once.'

'Oh dear!'

She remembered, with a pang of agony, that she had already overdrawn her account at the bankers. She was the possessor of an income of four thousand pounds a year, and now, in her terrible strait, she could not stir because she had not money with which to travel.

Lord George sat looking at her and thinking whether he would make the plunge and ask her to be his wife. He had been careful to reduce her to such a condition of despair that she would undoubtedly have accepted him, so that she might have someone to lean upon in her trouble; but, as he looked at her, he doubted. She was such a mass of deceit that he was afraid of her. She might say that she would marry him, and then, when the storm was over, refuse to keep her word. She might be in debt—almost to any amount. He did know that she was subject to all manner of penalties for what she had done. He looked at her, and told himself that she was very pretty. But, in spite of her beauty, his judgement went against her. 'That's my advice,' he said, getting up from his chair.

'Are you going?'

'I don't know what else I can do for you.'

'You are so unkind!'

He shrugged his shoulders, just touched her hand, and left the room without saying another word to her.

.　　.　　.　　.　　.

It was now the twentieth of March, and a fortnight had gone since an intimation had been sent to Lady Eustace from the headquarters of the police that Patience Crabstick was in their hands. Nothing further had occurred, and it might be that Patience Crabstick had told no tale against her. It might be that Patience would find it to her interest to tell no tale against her late mistress. At any rate, there was silence and quiet, and the affair of the diamonds seemed almost to be passing out of people's minds. Greystock had twice called in Scotland Yard but had been able to learn nothing. Thus encouraged, Lizzie determined that she would remain in London till after she should have received the promised letter from Lord Fawn.

It took Lord Fawn a long time to write his letter, but at last he wrote it. But he was not able to do this without interference from others. Frank Greystock interfered, and Lady Glencora Palliser. Even John Eustace had been worked upon to write to Lord Fawn, stating his opinion, as trustee for his late brother's property, that the Eustace family did not think that there was ground of complaint against Lady Eustace in reference to the diamonds which had been stolen. Lady Glencora had the effrontery to ask him when a day would be fixed for the marriage. At last he wrote his letter.

My dear Lady Eustace,

In accordance with the promise which I made to you, I take up my pen with the view of communicating to you the result of my deliberations respecting the engagement of marriage which, no doubt, did exist between us last summer.

Since that time I have taken upon myself to say that that engagement was over; and I am free to admit that I did so without any assent or agreement on your part to that effect. My defence is as follows:

I learned that you were in possession of a large amount of property, vested in diamonds, which was claimed by the executors under your late husband's will as belonging to his estate. Had I married you in these circumstances I could not but have become a participator in the lawsuit which I was assured would be commenced. I could not be a participator with you, because I believed you to be in the wrong.

Since that time the property has been stolen and the lawsuit against you has been withdrawn. I am no longer justified in declining to keep my engagement because of the prejudice to which I should have been subjected by your possession of the diamonds; and, therefore, as far as that goes, I withdraw my withdrawal.

But now there arises the question whether, in both our interests, this marriage should go on. There has no doubt sprung up between us a feeling of mutual distrust, which has led to recrimination, and which is hardly compatible with that perfect confidence which should exist between a man and his wife. I confess that for my own part I do not now desire a union which was once the great object of my ambition. As to your own feelings, you best know what they are; but if you have ceased to love me I think you should not insist upon a marriage simply because by doing so you would triumph over a former objection.

You have rank and wealth, and, therefore, I can comfort myself by thinking that if I dissuade you from this marriage I shall rob you of neither. I acknowledge that I wish to dissuade you, as I believe that we should not make each other happy. As, however, I do consider that I am bound to keep my engagement to you if you demand that I shall do so, I leave the matter in your hands for decision.

I am, and shall remain,

Your sincere friend,

Fawn.

Lizzie told her friend Mrs Carbuncle, 'My lord has come down from his high horse at last.'

'Lord Fawn? What does he say?'

'Just that he has behaved very badly, and that he hopes I shall forgive him. Of course, there is ever so much of it— pages of it. It wouldn't be Lord Fawn if he didn't spin it all out like an Act of Parliament, with "whereas" and "where- is" and "whereof". But the meaning of it is that I may pick him up if I choose to take him. I'd show you the letter, only perhaps it wouldn't be fair to the poor man.'

'Then why not have him and have done with it?'

'He is such an ass; such a load of Government waste-paper.'

'Come, my dear—you've had troubles. They may come again. As to Lord George, we all know that he has not got a penny piece in the world that he can call his own.'

'If he had as many pennies as Judas Lord George would be nothing to me,' said Lizzie.

'Of course you know your own business, but if I were you I would take Lord Fawn. After all, what does love signify?'

243

'So that's your advice,' said Lizzie. 'I'm half inclined to take it, and perhaps I shall. Either one way or the other, I shall let him know that I like my triumph. I was determined to have it, and I've got it.'

She was considering her answer when Major Mackintosh was shown into her room. 'Lady Eustace,' said the Major, 'I am very sorry to trouble you. But I think we have found out the whole truth. We have had very clever people to deal with, and I fear that, even now, we shall never get back the property.'

'I do not care about the property, sir. Nobody has lost anything but myself; and I really don't see why the thing should not die out, as I don't care about it.'

'We have two persons in custody, Lady Eustace, who we shall use as witnesses, and I am afraid we shall have to call upon you also—as a witness. Of course, Lady Eustace, you are not bound to say anything to me unless you like it—and you must understand that I by no means wish you to criminate yourself.'

'I don't know what that means.'

'I suppose we may take it for granted that the diamonds were in your desk when the thieves stole the money out of it?' The man's voice was very gentle, and very kind. 'The woman Crabstick has confessed, and will state on her oath that she saw the necklace in your hands in Hertford Street, and that she saw it placed in the desk. She then gave information of this to Benjamin—as she had before given information as to your journey up from Scotland—and she was introduced to the two men whom she let into the house. One of them, indeed, she had before met at Carlisle. She then was present when the necklace was taken out of the desk. The man who opened the desk and took it out, who also cut the door at Carlisle, will give evidence to the same effect. The man who carried the necklace out of the house, and who broke open the box at Carlisle, will be tried—as will also Benjamin, who disposed of the diamonds. I have told you the whole story, as it has been told to me by the woman Crabstick. Of course, you will deny the truth of it if it be untrue.' Lizzie sat with her eyes fixed upon the floor, but said nothing.

She could not speak. 'If you will allow me, Lady Eustace, to give you advice—really friendly advice . . .'

'Oh, pray do.'

'You had better admit the truth of the story, if it is true.'

'They were my own,' she whispered.

'But you had taken them out of the box before you went to bed at the inn at Carlisle?'

'They frightened me by saying the box would be stolen.'

'Exactly; and then you put them into your desk here, in this house?'

'Yes—sir.'

'I should tell you, Lady Eustace, that I had not a doubt about this before I came here.'

'What will they do to me, Major Mackintosh?'

'I am afraid that you must undergo the annoyance of being one of the witnesses. They will ask you to tell the truth. And you will probably be asked to repeat it, this way and that, in a manner that will be troublesome to you. You see, here in London and at Carlisle you have—given incorrect versions.'

'When they came to me at Carlisle I was so confused that I hardly knew what to tell them. And when I had once—given an incorrect version, you know, I didn't know how to go back.'

'I can understand all that,' he said.

How much kinder he was than Lord George had been when she confessed the truth to him. And such a handsome man as he was, too—not exactly a Corsair, as he was great in authority over the London police, but a powerful, fine fellow, who would know what to do with swords and pistols as well as any Corsair; and one, too, no doubt, who would understand poetry. Any such dream, however, was altogether unavailing, as the Major had a wife at home and seven children. 'If you will only tell me what to do I will do it,' she said, looking up into his face with entreaty and pressing her hands together in supplication.

Then he explained to her that if she were summoned and used as a witness there would be no attempt to prosecute her for the 'incorrect versions' of which she had undoubtedly been guilty. He could not assure her that it would be so, but he had no doubt of it. However, he recommended her very

245

strongly to go at once to Mr Camperdown and make a clean breast of it to him. 'The whole family should be told,' said the Major, 'and it will be better for you that they should know it from yourself than from us. My dear Lady Eustace, the sooner you get back into straight running, the sooner you will be comfortable.'

That evening Mr Emilius dined with the ladies. He was peculiarly gracious and smiling. To Lizzie he was almost affectionate, and Mrs Carbuncle he flattered to the top of her bent. Mr Emilius discoursed with an unctuous mixture of celestial and terrestrial glorification, which was proof, at any rate, of great ability on his part. He told them how a good wife was a crown, or rather a chaplet of aetherial roses, to her husband, and how high rank and great station in the world made such a chaplet more beautiful and more valuable. His work in the vineyard, he said, had fallen lately among the wealthy and nobly born; and though he would not say that he was entitled to take glory on that account, still he gave thanks daily in that he had been enabled to give his humble assistance towards the running of a godly life to those who, by their example, were enabled to have so wide an effect upon their poorer fellow-creatures.

. . . . .

Early on the Wednesday morning, two or three hours before the time fixed for Lizzie's visit to Mr Camperdown, her cousin Frank came to call upon her.

'I do not at all wish to pry into your secrets,' he began, 'but I hear rumours which seem to be substantiated.'

'Major Mackintosh was here—a most kind man, and I was so glad to see him. They have found out everything. It was the jeweller, Benjamin, who concocted it all. That horrid sly girl I had, Patience Crabstick, put him up to it. And there were two regular housebreakers. They have found it all out at last.'

'But the diamonds are gone?'

'Oh yes; those weary, weary diamonds. Do you know, Frank, that, though they were my own, as much as the coat you wear is your own, I am glad they are gone at last.'

'I always supposed that they were taken at Carlisle,' said Frank. Lizzie fell on her knees, with her hands clasped together and her one long lock of hair hanging down so as to touch his arm. Her eyes were bright with tears, but were not, as yet, wet and red with weeping.

'Only the box. Oh! Frank, don't cross-question me about it. I have got to go to Mr Camperdown's this very day. I offered to do that at once, and I shan't have strength to go through it if you are not kind to me now. Dear, dear Frank—do be kind to me.'

And he was kind to her. He lifted her up to the sofa and did not ask her another question about the necklace. Of course she had lied to him and to all the world. From the very commencement of his intimacy with her, he had known that she was a liar. He could not but smile as he looked at her. 'Oh, Frank, do not laugh at me,' she said.

'I am not laughing, Lizzie; I am only wondering.'

'And now, Frank, what had I better do?'

He explained to her how she would be required to tell the truth in opposition to the false evidence which she had formerly given; and that she would herself be exempted from prosecution for perjury only on the ground that she would be giving evidence against criminals whose crimes had been deeper than her own. And he urged her to go away to Scotland as soon as the examination by the magistrate was over. 'I suppose they can't quite eat me,' she said, smiling through her tears.

'No, they won't eat you.'

'And will you go with me?'

'Yes—I suppose I had better do so.'

'Ah; that will be so nice. I shall not mind what they say to me as long as you are by my side.'

She had ordered the carriage to take her to Mr Camperdown's chambers, but before she started she had just a word with Mrs Carbuncle. 'I think I shall go down to Scotland shortly,' she said.

'That is if they let you go,' said Mrs Carbuncle.

'What do you mean?'

'The police. I know all about it, Lady Eustace. Lord George has told me the whole story, and informs me that you will probably be locked up today or tomorrow.'

'If he did, he knows nothing about it.'

'He ought to know, considering all you have made him suffer. That you should have gone on, with the necklace in your own box all the time, letting people think that he had taken them, and accepting his attentions all the while, is what I cannot understand! You are quite right in getting off to Scotland as soon as possible—if they will let you go. Of course you could not stay here.'

Lizzie was much flustered and weakened by Mrs Carbuncle's ill-usage, and had difficulty in restraining herself from tears. But the carriage was waiting, and as she passed through the hall she so far recovered herself as to conceal her dismay from the servants.

CHAPTER SIX

LIZZIE, in her fears, had been very punctual in arriving at Mr Camperdown's chambers. She was attired as became a lady of rank who had four thousand a year and was the intimate friend of Lady Glencora Palliser. She was a little taken aback when she saw her brother-in-law also in the room. 'Ah, John,' she said, 'I did not expect to find you.'

'I thought it best that I should be here—as a friend.'

'It makes it much pleasanter for me, of course,' said Lizzie. 'I am not quite sure that Mr Camperdown will allow me to regard him as a friend.'

'You have never had any reason to regard me as your enemy, Lady Eustace,' said Mr Camperdown. 'Will you take a seat? I understand that you wish to state the circumstances under which the Eustace family diamonds were stolen while they were in your hands.'

'My own diamonds, Mr Camperdown.'

'They have been stolen, at any rate,' said the lawyer. 'And now will you tell us how?'

Lizzie looked round upon her brother-in-law and sighed. She had never yet told the story in all its nakedness, although it had been three or four times extracted from her by admission. She paused, hoping that questions might be asked her which she could answer by easy monosyllables, but not a word was uttered to help her. 'I suppose you know all about it,' she said at last, and proceeded to tell a version which, so far as she was capable of telling the truth, was a true version.

'How was I to think what I told people when I was so frightened and confused that I didn't know where I was or what I was doing?' she concluded.

'But the diamonds were not stolen at Carlisle,' said Mr Camperdown. 'Did you tell the police what you had lost—or the magistrate—after the robbery in Hertford Street?'

'Yes; I did. There was some money taken, and rings, and other jewellery.'

'Did you tell them that the diamonds had been really stolen on that occasion?'

'They never asked me, Mr Camperdown. There—I have told you everything. I suppose I may go now?'

'I have no reason for wishing to detain you, Lady Eustace. If I were to talk for ever I should not, probably, make you understand the extent of the injury you have done, or teach you to look in a proper light at the position in which you have placed yourself and all those who belong to you.'

'I ain't a bit ashamed of anything,' said Lizzie. 'Good-bye, John,' and she put out her hand to her brother-in-law.

'Good-bye, Lizzie.'

'Mr Camperdown, I have the honour to wish you good morning.' Lizzie made a low curtsey to the lawyer and was then attended to her carriage by the lawyer's clerk.

'The barrister who will have the cross-examining of her at the Central Criminal Court,' said Mr Camperdown, as soon as the door was closed behind her, 'will have a job of work on his hand. There's nothing a pretty woman can't do when she has got rid of all sense of shame.'

On her return to Hertford Street Lizzie found a note from Mrs Carbuncle. 'I have made arrangements for dining out today, and shall not return till after ten. I will do the same tomorrow, and on every day till you leave town, and you can breakfast in your own room. You will kindly leave this house by Monday.'

Lizzie therefore wrote to her late friend.

Madam,

I certainly am not desirous of continuing an acquaintance into which I was led by false representations, and in the course of which I have been almost absurdly hospitable to persons altogether unworthy of my kindness. You and your especial friend Lord George Carruthers were entertained at my country-house as my guests for some months. I am here by arrangement; and as I pay more than a proper share of the expenses of the establishment I shall stay as long as I please, and go when I please.

Lizzie had come back from the attorney's chambers in triumph; but her elation was considerably repressed by a short notice which she read in the evening paper which told the whole story and expressed a hope that Lady Eustace would be able to explain that part of her conduct which at present was quite unintelligible. Lizzie threw the paper from her, asking what right newspaper-scribblers could have to interfere with the private affairs of such persons as herself. Was it not almost a certainty that Lord Fawn would retreat from his offer on learning the facts which were now so well known?

On the next morning a letter was brought to her from Lord Fawn, dated from his club the preceding evening. 'Lord Fawn presents his compliments to Lady Eustace. Lady Eustace will be kind enough to understand that Lord Fawn recedes altogether from the proposition made by him in his letter to Lady Eustace dated March 28th last. Lord Fawn thinks it best to express his determination under no circumstances to communicate again personally with Lady Eustace on this subject—or, as far as he can see at present, on any other.'

The letter was a blow to her, although she had assured herself a dozen times that a marriage with such a one as Lord Fawn, a man who had not a grain of poetry in his composition, would make her unutterably wretched. But she would still write to him, and date her letter before the time that his was dated. He probably would not believe her date, but writing on this pretence she would avoid the necessity of alluding to his last letter.

My Lord,
    I have taken a week to answer the letter which your lordship has done me the honour of writing to me, because I have thought it best to have time for consideration in a matter of such importance. I think I never read a letter so false, so unmanly, and so cowardly, as that which you have found yourself capable of sending to me.
    You became engaged to me when, as I admit with shame, I did not know your character. You have since repudiated me and vilified my name, simply because, having found that I had enemies, and being afraid to face them, you wished to escape from your engagement. It has been cowardice from the beginning to the end. Your whole conduct to me has been one long, unprovoked insult, studiously concocted, because you have feared that there might possibly be some trouble for you to encounter. Nobody ever heard of anything so mean, either in novels or in real life.
    And now you again offer to marry me—because you are again afraid. You need not be afraid. No earthly consideration would induce me to be your wife.
E. Eustace.

This was to be the last week of her sojourn in town, and then she was to go down and bury herself at Portray. She had been notified that she must go and give evidence before the magistrate on Friday. As she was thinking of this, Mr Emilius was announced. In her loneliness she was delighted to receive any visitor, and she knew that Mr Emilius would be at least courteous to her.
    'I heard that you were going to Scotland, and I wished to have an opportunity of saying—just a word to you, in private,

before you go.' He drew his chair near to Lizzie and leaned over towards her with his two hands closed together between his knees. He was a dark, hookey-nosed, well-made man, with an exuberance of greasy hair, who would have been considered handsome by many women, had there not been something almost amounting to a squint amiss with one of his eyes. When he was preaching it could hardly be seen, but in the closeness of private conversation it was disagreeable.

'Lady Eustace, you and I have known each other now for many months, and I have received the most unaffected pleasure from the acquaintance—may I not say from the intimacy which has sprung up between us?' Lizzie bowed. 'I think that, as a devoted friend and a clergyman, I shall not be thought to be intruding on private ground in saying that circumstances have made me aware of the details of the robberies by which you have been so cruelly persecuted. I do not know how far your friends or the public may condemn you, but . . .'

'Nobody has dared to condemn me, except this impudent woman here.'

'I am delighted. I was on the point of observing to you that according to the view of the matter which I, as a clergyman, have taken, you were altogether justified in the steps which you took for the protection of property which was your own.'

'Of course I was justified,' said Lizzie.

'You know best, Lady Eustace, whether any assistance I can offer will avail you anything.'

'I don't want any assistance, Mr Emilius, thank you.'

'I certainly have been given to understand that they who ought to stand by you with the closest devotion have, in this period of what I may, perhaps, call—tribulation, deserted your side with cold selfishness.'

'But there isn't any tribulation, and nobody has deserted my side.'

'I was told that Lord Fawn . . .'

'Lord Fawn is an idiot.'

'Quite so—no doubt.'

'And I have deserted him. I wrote to him this very morning, in answer to a pressing letter from him to renew our engagement, to tell him that that was out of the question. I despise Lord Fawn, and my heart can never be given where my respect does not accompany it.'

'A noble sentiment, Lady Eustace, which I reciprocate completely. And now, to come to what I may call the inner purport of my visit to you this morning, the sweet cause of my attendance on you, let me assure you that I should not now offer you my heart unless with my heart went the most perfect respect and esteem which any man ever felt for a woman.'

'What on earth do you mean, Mr Emilius?'

'I mean to lay my heart, my hand, my fortunes, my profession, my career at your feet. I make bold to say of myself that I have, by my own unaided eloquence and intelligence, won for myself a great position in this swarming metropolis. Lady Eustace, I know your great rank. I feel your transcendent beauty—ah, too acutely. I have been told that you are rich. But I, myself, who venture to approach you as a suitor for your hand, am also somebody in the world. The blood that runs in my veins is as illustrious as your own, having descended to me from the great and ancient nobles of my native country. The profession which I have adopted is the grandest which ever filled the heart of man with aspirations. I have barely turned my thirty-second year, and I am known as the greatest preacher of my day, though I preach in a language which is not my own. Your House of Lords would be open to me as a spiritual peer, would I condescend to come to terms with those who crave the assistance which I could give them. I can move the masses. I can touch the hearts of men. And in this great assemblage of mankind which you call London I can choose my own society among the highest of the land. Lady Eustace, will you share with me my career and my fortunes? I ask you, because you are the only woman whom my heart has stooped to love.'

The man was a nasty, greasy, lying, squinting preacher, over forty years of age. Yet, presuming as she did that something of what he said was false, she liked the lies. There was a dash of poetry about him; and poetry, as she thought, was not compatible with humdrum truth. She liked his audacity. Nevertheless, though she admired his manner and his language, she was quite aware that he was in pursuit of her money.

'I was told, Mr Emilius,' she said, 'that some time since you used to have a wife.'

'It was a falsehood, Lady Eustace. From motives of pure charity I gave a home to a distant cousin. I was then in a land of strangers and my life was misinterpreted. I sent the lady back to her native country. My compassion could supply her wants there as well as here.'

'Then you still support her?'

'I did do so, till she found a congenial home as the wife of an honest man.'

'Oh, indeed. I'm quite glad to hear that.'

'And now, Lady Eustace, may I venture to hope for a favourable answer?'

Lizzie made him a speech as long and almost as well turned as his own. Her heart had of late been subject to many vicissitudes. She had lost the dearest husband that a woman had ever worshipped. She had ventured, for purposes with reference to her child which she could not now explain, to think once again of matrimony with a man of high rank, but who had turned out to be unworthy of her. After that she was unwilling to entertain any further idea of marriage. Upon hearing this Mr Emilius bowed low, and before the street-door closed against him had begun to calculate how much a journey to Scotland would cost him.

.   .   .   .   .

On the Wednesday and Thursday Lizzie had been triumphant; for she had certainly come out unscathed from Mr Camperdown's chambers, and a lady may surely be said to triumph when a gentleman lays his hand, his heart, his fortunes, and all that he has got, at her feet. But when the Friday came, though she was determined to be brave, her heart did sink within her bosom. She understood well that she would be called upon to admit in public the falseness of the oaths she had sworn upon two occasions; and that she would be subject to very damaging remarks from the magistrate, and probably also from some lawyers employed to defend the prisoners. She dressed from head to foot in black, with a heavy black veil. She breakfasted early and then took a large glass of wine to support her. When Frank called for her at a quarter to ten she was quite ready and grasped his hand almost without a word. 'It will soon be over,' he said. 'The case will come on at once, so that you will not be kept waiting.'

There was so great a crowd about the courthouse that Lizzie's brougham could hardly make its way up to the door. But the policemen were as courteous to her as though she had been the Lord Chancellor's wife. She was led at once into a private room and told that she would be kept there only a very few minutes. Frank made his way into the court and found that two magistrates had just seated themselves on the bench.

The jeweller, Mr Benjamin, had been sent back in durance vile from Vienna. With him in the dock stood Mr Smiler, the housebreaker, a huge, ugly, resolute-looking scoundrel, possessed of enormous strength. He stood, perfectly straight, looking at the magistrate, and never for a moment leaning on the rail before him during the four hours that the case consumed. Once, when his friend, Billy Cann, was brought into court to give evidence against him, dressed up to the eyes, serene and sleek, Smiler turned a glance upon him which, to the eyes of all present, contained a threat of most bloody revenge. But Billy knew the advantages of his situation, and nodded at his old comrade, and smiled.

The case was outlined very shortly and very clearly by the gentleman who was employed for the prosecution. It would all, he said, have laid in a nutshell, had it not been complicated by a previous robbery at Carlisle. Were it necessary, there would be no difficulty in convicting the prisoners for that offence also, but it had been thought advisable to confine the prosecution to the act of burglary committed in Hertford Street. He stated the facts of what had happened at Carlisle, merely for explanation. Then Frank Greystock left the court, and returned with Lizzie on his arm.

After she was sworn she was told that she might sit down; but she was requested to remove her veil. The first question asked her was very easy. Did she remember the night at Carlisle? Would she tell the history of what occurred on that night? When the box was stolen, were the diamonds in it? No; she had taken the diamonds out for security, and had kept them under her pillow. Then came a bitter moment, in which she had to confess her perjury before the Carlisle bench; but even that seemed to pass off smoothly. The magistrate asked one severe question. 'Do you mean to say, Lady Eustace, that you gave false evidence on that occasion—knowing it to be false?' 'I was in such a state, sir, from fear, that I did not know what I was saying,' exclaimed Lizzie, bursting into tears and stretching forth towards the bench her two clasped hands with the air of a suppliant. From that moment the magistrate was altogether on her side, and so were the public. Poor, ignorant, ill-used young creature; and then so lovely! That was the general feeling. But she had not as yet come beneath the harrow of the learned gentleman on the other side, whose best talents were due to Mr Benjamin. Then she told all she knew about the other robbery. She certainly had not said, when examined on that occasion, that the diamonds had been taken. She had omitted to name the diamonds in her catalogue of the things stolen. But she was sure that she had never said that they were not then taken. She had said nothing about the diamonds, knowing them to be her own and preferring to lose them. Such was her evidence for the prosecution, and then she was turned over to the learned and acute gentleman whom Mr Benjamin had hired to show cause why he should not be sent for trial.

This gentleman addressed Lady Eustace as though he hardly dared to speak to a woman so eminent for wealth, rank, and beauty. 'Was he to understand that she went of her own will before the bench of magistrates at Carlisle, with the view of enabling the police to capture certain persons for stealing certain jewels, while she knew that the jewels were actually in her own possession?' Lizzie, confounded by the softness of his voice as joined to the harshness of the question, could hardly understand him, and he repeated it thrice, becoming every time more and more mellifluous. 'Yes,' said Lizzie at last. 'Your ladyship did send the Cumberland police after men for stealing jewels which were in your ladyship's own hands when you swore the information?' 'Yes,' said Lizzie. 'And your ladyship knew all the time that the poor men were altogether innocent of taking the jewels?' 'But they took the box,' said Lizzie, through her tears. Soft as he was in his manner, he nearly reduced Lizzie Eustace to fainting.

The two men were committed for trial at the Central Criminal Court, and Lizzie Eustace was bound by certain penalties to come forward when called upon, and give her evidence again.

'I am glad that it is all over,' said Frank, as he left her at Mrs Carbuncle's hall door.

'Oh Frank, where should I be if it were not for you?'

Lady Eustace did not leave the house during the Saturday and Sunday, and engaged herself exclusively with preparing for her journey. She had no further interview with Mrs Carbuncle, and on the Monday she and her maid travelled to Portray, taking an early train which conveyed them there within that one day.

.   .   .   .   .

The trial of Mr Benjamin and Mr Smiler was fixed to take place at the Central Criminal Court about the middle of May. Early in May the attorneys for the prosecution applied to Greystock, asking him to make arrangements for his cousin's appearance on the occasion, whereupon he wrote to Lizzie, offering to go with her into court and naming an hotel at which to stay during the very short time she need remain in London. She answered at once. She was sorry to say that she was much too ill to travel, or even to think of travelling. Such was her present condition that she doubted greatly whether she would ever again be able to leave the two rooms to which she was at present confined. All that remained to her in life was to watch her own blue waves from the casement of her dear husband's castle—that casement at which he had loved to sit, and to make herself happy in the smiles of her child. A few months would soon see the last of it all, and

257

then, perhaps, they who had trampled her to death would feel some pangs of remorse as they thought of her early fate.

Lizzie had two strings to her bow. A lawyer from Ayr had told her that the summons sent to her was not worth the paper on which it was printed in regard to a resident in Scotland; and she also got a doctor from the neighbourhood who was satisfied that she was far too ill to travel up to London. Depressed vitality in all the organs and undue languor in all the bodily functions was the complaint from which she was suffering. A certificate to this effect was got in triplicate. One copy she sent to the prosecuting attorneys, one to Frank, and one she kept herself.

It was considered that the trial could not be postponed till the next sitting at the Criminal Court, because certain witnesses in respect to the diamonds had been procured from Hamburg and Vienna, at very great cost. The diamonds had been traced first to Hamburg, and then to Vienna; they were now adorning the bosom of a certain enormously rich Russian princess, from whose grasp it was found impossible to rescue them.

A confidential clerk was sent to Portray, but altogether failed in making his way into Lizzie's presence. Word was brought to him that nothing but force could take Lady Eustace from her bed-chamber; and that force might take her out dead, but certainly not alive. He made inquiry about the doctor, and found that he certainly was a doctor. The attorneys for the prosecution were almost beside themselves. They sent down a doctor of their own, but Lizzie would not see the doctor, though threats of most frightful consequences were conveyed to her. She would be exposed, fined thousands of pounds, committed to gaol for contempt of court, and prosecuted for perjury into the bargain. But she was firm, and the trial went on without her.

It appeared that though her evidence was very desirable it was not absolutely essential, as the statement which she had made at the police-court could be brought up and used against the prisoners. All the facts of the robbery were, moreover, proved by Patience Crabstick and Billy Cann. And the transfer of the diamonds by Mr Benjamin to the man who recut them at Hamburg was also proved. Many other morsels of collateral evidence had also been picked up by the police—so that there was no possible doubt as to any detail of the affair in Hertford Street.

Lizzie's absence was a great disappointment to the sight-seers of London, but nevertheless the court was crowded. It was understood that the learned serjeant who was retained on this occasion to defend Mr Benjamin would be rather severe upon Lady Eustace, even in her absence, and many came to hear him. They were not disappointed.

'If justice had really been done in this case, gentlemen, it is Lady Eustace who should now be on her trial before you, and not my unfortunate client. But, gentlemen, she is not here. She is at her own castle in Scotland, and sends to us a medical certificate. Had she the feelings of woman in her bosom she ought indeed to be sick unto death. I say again that she ought to be here in that dock—in that dock in spite of her fortune, in that dock in spite of her title, in that dock in spite of her castle, her riches, her beauty, and her great relatives. It is she whom public opinion will convict as the guilty one in this marvellous mass of conspiracy and intrigue. In her absence, and after what she has done herself, can you convict any man either of stealing or of disposing of these diamonds?' Nevertheless, the jury did find both Benjamin and Smiler guilty, and the judge did sentence them to penal servitude for fifteen years.

Although many threats had been uttered against Lizzie, not only by Mr Camperdown and the other attorneys, but even by the judge himself, no attempt was made to punish her. The affair was over, and men were glad to avoid the necessity of troubling themselves further with the business.

Mr Emilius travelled from London to Kilmarnock. He had watched the case against Benjamin and Smiler very closely. When he first heard of Lady Eustace's illness he wrote to her a most affectionately pastoral letter, strongly adjuring her to think of her health before all things, and assuring her that in his opinion she was quite right not to come up to London. She wrote him a very short but gracious answer, thanking him for his solicitude. 'I don't suppose anybody knows how ill I am; but it does not matter. When I am gone they will know what they have done.' Then Mr Emilius resolved that he would go down to Scotland.

From Kilmarnock he wrote to her, saying that business connected with his ministrations had brought him into her beautiful neighbourhood and that he could not leave it without paying his respects to her in person. He trusted that the state of her health would not prevent her from seeing him. He gave her no address, as he rather wished to hinder her from answering him, but at the appointed hour on the day he had named he knocked at the Castle door.

An appearance of sickness Lizzie did maintain, even with her own domestics. To do as much as that was due even to the doctor whom she had cajoled out of the certificate, and who was afterwards frightened into maintaining it. But Mr Emilius was her clergyman—her own clergyman, as she took care to say to her maid—who had come all the way from London to be present with her in her sickness; and of course she would see him.

The conversation was at first, of course, confined to the lady's health. She thought that she was, perhaps, getting better, though, as the doctor had told her, the reassuring symptoms might too probably only be too fallacious. She could eat nothing—literally nothing. Her only delight was in reading and in her child's society. Sometimes she thought that she would pass away with the boy in her arms and her favourite volume of Shelley in her hand. Mr Emilius expressed a hope that she would not pass away yet, for ever so many years. 'Oh, my friend,' said Lizzie, 'what is life, that one should desire it?' Mr Emilius of course reminded her that, though her life might be nothing to herself, it was very much indeed to those who loved her. 'Yes, to my boy,' said Lizzie. Mr Emilius informed her, with confidence, that it was not only her boy that loved her. There were others—or, at any rate, one other. She might be sure of one faithful heart, if she cared for that. Lizzie only smiled.

With widows, he had been told, the wooing should be brisk. 'Dearest Lady Eustace,' he said suddenly, 'may I be allowed to renew the petition which I was once bold enough to make to you in London? I did venture to tell you—that—I loved you.'

'Mr Emilius, so many men have told me that.'

'I can well believe it. Some have told you so, perhaps, from base, mercenary motives. I shall never pay you any compliments, Lady Eustace. You will only hear words of truth from my lips. Some, no doubt, have spoken from the inner depths of their hearts. But none, Lady Eustace, has spoken with such adamantine truth, with so intense an anxiety, with so personal a solicitude for your welfare in this world and the next, as that—or I should rather say those—which glow within this bosom.' Mr Emilius gesticulated, and struck his breast, and brought out his words as though he meant them.

'I know well the value of such a heart as yours, Mr Emilius.'

'Accept it then, dearest one.'

She had no belief whatever in his love. And yet she liked it. She liked lies, thinking them to be more beautiful than truth.

'Mr Emilius,' she said, throwing herself back upon her couch, 'you press me very hard. You take advantage of my illness.'

'In attacking a fortress do not the besiegers take all advantages? Dear Lady Eustace, allow me to return to London with the right of protecting your name at this moment, in which the false and the thoughtless are attacking it. My beloved is subject to the malice of the world. My beloved is a flower all beautiful within and without, but one whose stalk is weak, whose petals are too delicate, whose soft bloom is evanescent. Let me be the strong stall against which my beloved may blow in safety.'

A vague idea came across Lizzie's mind that this glowing language had a taste of the Bible about it. She did not relish piety at such a crisis as this; but she liked being called a flower.

'Do you expect me to give you answer now, Mr Emilius?'

'Yes—now.' And he stood before her in calm dignity, with his arms crossed upon his breast.

She did give him his answer, but first she turned her face to the back of the sofa, and burst into a flood of tears. She sobbed forth something about her child, something about her sorrows, something as to the wretchedness of her lot in life, something of her widowed heart—something also of that duty to others which would compel her to keep her income in her own hands; and then she yielded herself to his entreaties.

Early in the month of June, Lady Eustace was led to the altar by her clerical bridegroom. The wedding took place at the Episcopal church at Ayr, far from the eyes of curious Londoners. Mr Emilius could be persuaded to agree to no settlements prejudicial to that marital supremacy which should be attached to the husband; but Lizzie, knowing that her betrothal had been made public to all the world, did not care to recede from another engagement.

On that same day Lady Glencora Palliser entertained a large company of guests at Matching Priory. That the Duke of Omnium was there was quite a matter of course. Madame Max Goesler was also at Matching; and Mr Palliser was there, taking the rest that was so needful to him—which meant that after having worked all day he was able to eat his dinner and then only write a few letters before going to bed, instead of attending the House of Commons till two or three o'clock in the morning. His mind was still deep in quints and semi-tenths. His great measure was now in committee. His hundred and second clause had been carried, with only nine divisions against him of any consequence. Mr Bonteen was there, too, with his wife, and Barrington Erle, and Lord Chiltern, with his wife. Lord Fawn was not there. Lord Fawn, whose health had temporarily given way beneath the pressing labours of the India Board, was visiting his estates in Tipperary.

'She is married today, Duke, down in Scotland,' said Lady Glencora, sitting close to the Duke's ear. They were in the small morning sitting-room, and no one else was present except Madame Max Goesler.

'Married today—down in Scotland. Dear, dear! What is he?'

'He's some sort of a clergyman, Duke.'

'A clergyman! I wonder what made a clergyman marry her?'

'Money, Duke,' said Lady Glencora, speaking very loud.

'Oh, ah, yes; money. And what's the clergyman like?'

'An impostor who has come over here to make a fortune,' said Madame Goesler. 'We hear that he has a wife in Prague. But he has got poor little Lizzie Eustace and all her money into his grasp.'

'Dear, dear, dear!' said the Duke. 'And the diamonds never turned up after all. I think that was a pity, because I knew the late man's father very well. We used to be together a good deal at one time. He had a fine property, and we used to live—but I can't just tell you how we used to live. He, he, he!'

'You had better tell us nothing about it, Duke,' said Madame Max.

The affair was again discussed that evening in the billiard-room. 'It was a most unworthy conclusion to such a plot,' said Mr Bonteen. 'It always happens that they catch the small fry and let the large fish escape.'

'Whom did you specially want to catch?' asked Lady Glencora.

'Lady Eustace and Lord George de Bruce Carruthers.'

'I quite agree with you, Mr Bonteen, that it would be very nice to send the brother of a marquis to Botany Bay, or wherever they go now; and that it would do a deal of good to have the widow of a baronet locked up in the Penitentiary; but, you see, if they didn't happen to be guilty it would be almost a shame to punish them.'

'They ought to have been guilty,' said Barrington Erle.

Mr Palliser was enjoying ten minutes of recreation before he went back to his letters. 'I can't say I attended to the case very closely,' he observed. 'But as far as I could hear, Lord George Carruthers cannot possibly have had anything to do with it. Coldfoot told me so.' Sir Harry Coldfoot was Secretary of State for Home Affairs, and in a matter of such importance had an opinion of his own.

'Why didn't he come forward as a witness when he was summoned?' asked Mr Bonteen triumphantly. 'And as for the woman, does anybody mean to say that she should not have been indicted for perjury?'

'The woman, as you are pleased to call her, is my particular friend,' said Lady Glencora. When Lady Glencora made

263

any such statement as this—and she often did make such statements—no one dared to answer her. It was understood that Lady Glencora was not to be snubbed, though she was very much given to snubbing others. She had attained this position for herself by a mixture of beauty, rank, wealth, and courage; but the courage had, of the four, been her greatest mainstay.

Lord Chiltern rapped his cue down on the floor and made a speech. 'I never was so sick of anything in my life as I am of Lady Eustace. People have talked about her now for the last six months.'

At that moment Madame Max Goesler entered the room and whispered a word to the hostess. She had just come from the Duke, who could not bear the racket of the billiard-room. 'Wants to go to bed, does he? Very well, I'll go to him.'

'He seems to be quite fatigued with his fascination about Lady Eustace.'

'I call that woman a perfect godsend. What should we have done without her?' This Lady Glencora said almost to herself as she prepared to join the Duke. The Duke had only one more observation to make before he retired for the night. 'I'm afraid, you know, that your friend hasn't what I call a good time before her, Glencora.'

Phineas Redux

CHAPTER ONE

THE general election of 18— will be well remembered by all who take an interest in the political matters of the country. Mr Gresham, the Liberal, had been Prime Minister. There had come to be a split among his followers on the question of the open ballot. Then Mr Daubeny for twelve months had sat upon the throne, distributing the good things of the Crown amidst Conservative birdlings. And Mr Daubeny was still so sitting, to the infinite dismay of the Liberals. So the men who had quarrelled agreed to quarrel no more. Mr Daubeny's enemies were resolved to knock him altogether on the head at the general election which he had himself called into existence, having been disgracefully out-voted upon a motion brought forward by Mr Palliser, the late Liberal Chancellor of the Exchequer, respecting decimal coinage.

One thing was manifest to the Liberals. In the next Parliament they must have men good and true. Now no Liberal had been known to be more good and true than Mr Finn, the Irishman, who had retired from office because he had found himself compelled to support a measure which had since been carried by those very men from whom he had been obliged to divide himself. He had been twelve months in advance of his party, and had consequently been driven out into the cold.

Phineas Finn, when last seen by the public, two years earlier, was departing from parliamentary life in London to a modest place under Government in his own country. After various turmoils he had married the girl of his heart. But now his wife was dead. He had lost his father as well as his wife, and had inherited about four thousand pounds. He was not at this time much over thirty; and since he had retired from

London his very soul had sighed for the lost glories of West-minster and Downing Street. When, therefore, he received the following letter from his friend, Barrington Erle, he neighed like the old warhorse.

My dear Finn,

You have no doubt heard that there will be a general election about the end of September. Have you a mind to try again? I would suggest Tankerville in Durham.

I am very sorry to hear of your great loss, as also was Lady Laura Kennedy, who, as you are aware, has left her husband and is still abroad with her father. We have all thought that the loneliness of your present life might per-haps make you willing to come back among us.

Yours, ever faithfully,

Barrington Erle.

Phineas resigned his place before the month was over, and returned to London, where he was able to re-engage his old lodgings in Great Marlborough Street. One morning there he received a letter from Lady Laura Kennedy.

Dresden, November 18, ——

My dear Mr Finn,

I have heard with great pleasure that you are back in politics. My cousin Barrington writes me word that you will certainly get the seat. I cannot conceive of you as living any other life than that of the House of Commons, Downing Street, and the clubs.

As to myself, I and my father live here a sad, solitary life. He does nothing. He is here because he cannot bear that I should live alone.

Of my husband, Mr Kennedy, it is singular how little I ever hear. I suppose that he lives exclusively at Lough-linter. From time to time I am implored by him to return to my duty beneath his roof. He says no word of happiness. He offers no comfort. He makes his claim simply on Holy Writ and duty. I leave his letters unanswered.

Cannot you come and see us? Papa would be delighted.

I cannot explain to you what it would be to me to be able to talk again to one who knows my past life as you do. Do come if you can.

Most sincerely yours,
Laura Kennedy.

He made up his mind to spend the Christmas with Lord Brentford and Lady Laura Kennedy at Dresden. But his departure was postponed by another invitation which surprised him much.

November 9th, Loughlinter.

Dear Sir,

I am informed that you intend spending some days with the Earl of Brentford.

Since my wife, Lady Laura Kennedy, left me I have had no means of communicating with her by the assistance of any common friend. Having heard that you are about to visit her I feel a great desire to see you that I may be enabled to send by you a personal message. My health renders it difficult that I should proceed to London, and I therefore ask it of your Christian charity that you should visit me here.

Yours truly,
Robert Kennedy.

Phineas felt that he had no alternative but to go. A thousand memories crowded on his brain as he made the journey. He had first gone to Loughlinter, not as Lady Laura's guest —for Lady Laura had not then even been engaged to be married. When there he had asked Lady Laura to be his own wife, and she had then told him that she was to become the wife of the owner of that domain. He remembered the blow as though it had been struck but yesterday. Now he was about to see them both again, separately; and to become the medium of some communication between them. He knew, or thought he knew, that no communication could avail anything.

It was dark night when he was driven up to the door of Loughlinter House in a fly from the town of Callander. The door was opened by an old servant in black. He looked round the vast hall, which, when he had before known it, was ever filled with signs of life, and felt at once that it was empty and deserted. It struck him as intolerably cold, and he saw that the huge fireplace was without a spark of fire. Dinner, the servant said, was prepared for half-past seven. And as it was already past seven he hurried upstairs to his room. Here again everything was cold and wretched; and yet Mr Kennedy was one of the richest commoners of Great Britain.

But he dressed, and made his way downstairs. The man explained that Mr Kennedy's state of health did not admit of late dinners. He was to dine alone, and Mr Kennedy would receive him after dinner. A very poor dinner it was. There was a morsel of flabby white fish, as to the nature of which Phineas was altogether in doubt, a beef steak as to the nature of which he was not at all in doubt, and a little crumpled-up tart. There was a bottle of claret, which Phineas declined to have anything to do with after the first attempt.

When dinner was over he was at once led across the hall and introduced to the chamber known as the 'laird's ain room'. Robert Kennedy rose to receive him. He was still under fifty, but he looked as though he were seventy. He was very grey, and stooped so much, that though he came forward a step or two to greet his guest, it seemed as though he had not taken the trouble to raise himself to his proper height. 'You find me a much altered man,' he said. 'It is trouble of the mind, not of the body, Mr Finn. It is her doing. What did I do that she should leave me? Did I strike her? Was I faithless? Did I frighten her by hard words, or exact hard tasks? Mr Finn, do you know what made her go away?'

'I imagine that she was not happy.'

'Happy? What right had she to expect to be happy? Are we not told that we are to look for happiness there, and to hope for none below?' He stretched his left hand to the ceiling. 'But why shouldn't she have been happy? Did she ever say anything against me?'

'Nothing but that your temper and hers were incompatible.'

'I thought at one time that you advised her to go away?'

'Never!'

'She told you about it?'

'Not till she had made up her mind. I had known, of course, that things were unpleasant.'

'How were they unpleasant? When she did what was wrong, of course I had to tell her. She would not go to church on Sunday afternoon, but had meetings of Belial at her father's house instead.' Phineas well remembered those meetings of Belial, in which he with others had been wont to discuss the political prospects of the day.

'I am not sure, Mr Kennedy, that a husband is justified in demanding that a wife shall think just as he thinks on matters of religion.'

'I never told her so. I never spoke a hard word to her in my life. I wanted her to do her duty. You were in love with her once, Mr Finn?'

'Yes, I was.'

'Ah! Yes. When anything of that kind happens, people had better keep out of each other's way afterwards. I don't see why you should go all the way to Dresden to pay her a visit. It isn't a decent thing for a young unmarried man to go half across Europe to see a lady who is separated from her husband, and with whom he was once in love.'

'Lady Laura Kennedy is living with her father, the Earl of Brentford,' said Phineas.

'Who was it wrote and asked you?'

'The letter was from Lady Laura.'

'Yes, from my wife. What right had my wife to write to you when she will not even answer my appeals? She is my wife—my wife! Mr Finn, as the husband of Lady Laura Kennedy, I desire that you abstain from seeking her presence.'

'I shall certainly go to Dresden,' said Phineas. 'If you have a message to send, I will take it.'

'Then you will be accursed among adulterers. By such a one I will send no message.'

'Good night,' said Phineas, and then he left the room. He left the house early on the following morning without again seeing Mr Kennedy.

.   .   .   .   .

271

Phineas found Lord Brentford living in a spacious house, close upon the northern confines of the cheerful city of Dresden. He was hardly in the house before Lady Laura Kennedy was in his arms, and had put up her cheek to his lips. 'Oh, my friend,' she said; 'oh my friend! How good you are to come to me!' And then she led him into a large room, in which a table had been prepared for breakfast, close to an English-looking open fire.

As yet he had hardly looked at her, but he felt that she had become old and worn, angular and hard-visaged. When he had first known her she had been a woman with a noble presence—not soft and feminine as had been Violet Effingham, but handsome and lustrous, with a healthy youth. He and she were of the same age, past their thirty-second birthday. He felt himself to be still a young man, but he could not think of her as of a young woman.

'Now sit down,' she said, 'and be comfortable. You will have a cutlet, won't you? I breakfasted an hour ago, and more. Tell me first about Violet. She is happy?'

'She has a baby. She says Lord Chiltern is the finest fellow in the world.'

'So Oswald is quite tame?'

'I should think always.'

'She refused him again and again, because she thought it wrong to run a great risk, but I knew she would never marry anyone else. And now, Phineas, we will put it off no longer. Tell me all that you have to tell me about—him.'

Phineas and Lady Laura sat talking earnestly till the servant told them that 'My lord' was ready to receive Mr Finn. 'You will find him much altered,' said Lady Laura. So saying she led him into a room, in which he found the Earl. Phineas saw at once that Lord Brentford had passed from manhood to senility. He almost tottered as he came forward, and he wrapped his coat around him with that air of studious self-preservation which belongs only to the infirm.

'It is very good of you to come and see me, Mr Finn. It's a terrible long journey from London, isn't it?'

'Too long to be pleasant, my lord.'

'Pleasant! There's no pleasantness about it. So you're going

272

into Parliament again? They tell me the Tories are going to disestablish the Church. I'm very glad I'm out of it all. Things have come to such a pass that I don't see how a gentleman is to hold office nowadays.'

After a while, when Phineas had told the Earl all there was to tell of politics and of his son and his grandson, Lady Laura suddenly interrupted them. 'You knew, Papa, that he has been to Loughlinter, and has seen Mr Kennedy.'

'Oh, indeed.'

'He is quite assured that I should not return to live with my husband.'

'Not a shadow of doubt,' said Phineas. 'I will not say that Mr Kennedy is mad; but I do not think she could live with him in safety. He is crazed about religion. He repudiates all belief in happiness. He wishes her to return to him chiefly because it is right that a man and wife should live together.'

'So it is,' said the Earl.

'But not to the utter wretchedness of both of them,' said Lady Laura. 'I certainly will not return to Loughlinter.'

Two days after this was the day fixed for Finn's departure. On the intermediate day the Earl begged for a few minutes' private conversation with him. Did Phineas think that his return would be of any use to the party? With all his desire to be civil, Phineas could not say that the Earl's presence would materially save the interests of the Liberal party.

And then, with the tardiness of old age, the Earl proposed his little plan. 'Why should she not make an attempt to live once more with her husband?'

'I am quite sure she ought not to do so. The marriage was a misfortune.' After that the Earl did not dare to say another word about his daughter; but discussed his son's affairs. Did not Phineas think that Chiltern might now be induced to go into Parliament? 'Nothing would make him do so,' said Phineas.

'But he might farm? Other men keep hounds and farm too.'

'But Chiltern is not like other men. He gives his whole mind to it, and finds full employment. He is quite happy, and

273

so is she. What more can you want for him? Everybody respects him now.'

'That goes a very great way,' said the Earl. Then he thanked Phineas cordially.

On the last morning Laura gave him his breakfast by candle-light, and went down with him to the station. The morning was black, and the frost was as hard as iron, but she was thoroughly good-humoured and apparently happy.

'It has been so much to me to have you here, that I might tell you everything,' she said. 'I want you to marry again, and if I can I will love her almost as much as I do you.'

'If I ever intend such a thing, I will tell you.'

'Now, good-bye. God bless you, Phineas.' She held his hand tight within her own for some seconds. Then she drew down her veil, and went and stood apart till the train had left the platform.

CHAPTER TWO

ON the 20th January Phineas travelled down to Tankerville to fight his election campaign. He was gloriously entertained by the Liberals, the campaign proceeded triumphantly, and he was Member for the borough. The moment the decision was announced Phineas hurried to the post-office and sent his message to Lady Laura Kennedy at Dresden: 'I have got the seat.' He almost thought that this was in truth the proudest and happiest moment of his life. He was again a member of the British House of Commons—was again in possession of that privilege for which he had never ceased to sigh since the moment in which he lost it.

'I never knew a fellow with such luck as yours,' said Barrington Erle to him, on his return to London. 'But, Phineas, we must have no tricks on this Church reform matter. We mean to do all we can to throw out the second reading.'

'You know what I said at the hustings.'

'Damn the hustings. You were against the Church at the hustings. You will vote just the other way. There will be a little confusion, but the people of Tankerville will never remember the particulars.'

'I don't know that I can do that.'

'By heavens, if you don't you shall never more be officer of ours.'

Lady Laura Kennedy had written to her sister-in-law, Lady Chiltern. She could not bear to think that Phineas should be left alone in London till Parliament should meet, and had therefore appealed to Lady Chiltern. An invitation at once went to him to visit Harrington Hall. If any woman loved her husband beyond all things Lord Chiltern's wife did. But there had been a tenderness in regard to the young Irish Member of Parliament which the former Violet Effingham had in old days shared with Lady Laura, and which made her now think that all good things should be done for him. He was a widower, and she remembered of old that he was fond of pretty women, and she knew that in coming days he might probably want money; and therefore she asked Madame Max Goesler to spend a fortnight at Harrington Hall. Madame Max Goesler and Phineas Finn had been acquainted before, as Lady Chiltern was well aware.

She had decided that it would be expedient that she should say something when those two old friends first met each other again in her drawing-room. 'Madame Max,' she said, 'you remember Mr Finn.'

'Very well indeed,' said Madame Max, putting out her hand with her sweetest smile. 'And I hope Mr Finn will not have forgotten me.'

But poor Phineas was not happy. 'I shall never forget you,' said he; and that unavoidable blush suffused his face, and the blood began to career through his veins.

'I am so glad you are in Parliament again,' said Madame Max.

'When I saw you last in London,' said Phineas, 'I certainly did not think that we should meet again so soon.'

'No; I left you as though I had grounds for quarrelling; but there was no quarrel. I wrote to you, and tried to explain that.'

'You did; and I was very grateful.'

'And here you are back among us; and it does seem so odd. Lady Chiltern never told me that I was to meet you. It is better so, for otherwise I should not have come. You see I can be quite frank with you, Mr Finn. I am heartily glad to see you, but I should not have come had I been told.'

'Are you still living in Park Lane?'

'Oh yes—and shall be most happy to see you.'

'Then I shall be most happy to call.'

.   .   .   .   .

Mr Quintus Slide's newspaper was still *The People's Banner*, and Mr Slide still professed to protect the existing rights of the people, and to demand new rights for the people. But he now did so as a Conservative. He had watched the progress of things, and had perceived that duty called upon him to be the organ of Mr Daubeny. The somewhat difficult task of veering round without inconsistency and without flaw to his infallibility was eased by Mr Daubeny's views on Church matters. *The People's Banner* could still be a genuine *People's Banner* in reference to ecclesiastical policy.

Thus it became Mr Slide's duty to speak of men as heaven-born patriots whom he had designated a month or two since as bloated aristocrats and leeches fattened on the blood of the people. Mr Slide was certainly well adapted for his work. Perhaps his great value was shown most clearly in his distinct appreciation of the low line of public virtue with which his readers would be satisfied. 'If there is any beastliness I 'ate it is 'igh-faluting,' he had been heard to say to his underlings.

One Sunday morning he called at Great Marlborough Street and asked for Phineas Finn. Phineas remembered when they had last met—but he knew that enmities are foolish things, and that it did not become him to perpetuate a quarrel with such a man as Mr Quintus Slide. The editor grasped the young Member's hand and congratulated him as though he had never been all but kicked out of that very same room by its present occupant. 'Now you want to know what I'm come about. Do you know the Right Honourable Robert Kennedy, of Loughlinter, in Scotland?'

'I do.'

'Very well. Mr Kennedy has I believe been greatly wronged.'

'I am not prepared to talk about Mr Kennedy's affairs,' said Phineas.

'But he is prepared to talk about them. He has been ill-used, and he has come to *The People's Banner* for redress.' Whereupon the editor handed Phineas a long scrap of printed paper containing a letter to the editor signed by Robert Kennedy.

Mr Kennedy had told the whole story of his wrongs as far as he himself understood the truth. He spoke of his wife as having been, and being, under the influence of Mr Phineas Finn; spoke of his own former friendship for that gentleman, and then accused Phineas of treachery in betraying that friendship. He spoke of the injury done him by his wife's father in affording a home to his wife when her proper home was at Loughlinter. And then he declared himself willing to take the sinning woman back to his bosom. He quoted both the Old and New Testament in proof of his assertions, and went on to say that, owing to some gross insufficiency in the laws of extradition, he could not call upon the magistracy of a foreign country to restore to him his erring wife. But he thought that public opinion, if loudly expressed, would have its effect both upon her and upon her father.

'You don't mean to say that you'll publish it.'

'Why shouldn't we publish it?'

'It's a private quarrel between a man and his wife. What on earth have the public got to do with that?'

'The morale of our aristocracy would be at a low ebb indeed if the public press didn't act as their guardians.'

'And you call yourself a Conservative?'

'We go in for morals and purity of life, and we mean to do

277

our duty by the public without fear or favour. Your name is mentioned there in a manner that you won't quite like, and I think I am acting uncommon kind by you in showing it to you before we publish it.'

As regarded himself, Phineas was inclined to kick Mr Slide and his *Banner* into the street. But he was bound to think first of Lady Laura. On her behalf he was bound to prevent this publicity if it could be prevented.

'It is a libel of the grossest kind, and of course there would be a prosecution. Both Lord Brentford and I would be driven to that.'

'We should be quite indifferent. Mr Kennedy would hold us harmless. We're straightforward. My showing it to you would prove that. Now I'll tell you what we'll do, on behalf of what I call purity. We'll delay the publication if you'll undertake that the lady shall go back to her husband.'

'The lady is not in my hands.'

'She's under your influence. She'd go sharp enough if you told her.'

'You never made a greater mistake in your life.'

'You won't interfere, then?' said Mr Quintus Slide, taking back the slip.

'I will—if you'll give me the time. Let me first see Mr Kennedy.'

Mr Slide thought a while over that matter. 'Well, you can see Mr Kennedy if you will. He came up to town four or five days ago, and he's staying at an hotel in Judd Street. Macpherson's. I don't think he ever goes out of the house, and he's waiting in London till this thing is published.'

'I will go and see him,' said Phineas.

'And I shall hear from you?'

'Yes, you shall hear from me.'

'If we see that we can induce the lady to go back to her husband we shall habstain from publishing, and virtue will be its own reward. I needn't tell you that such a letter as that would sell a great many copies.' Then Mr Slide departed.

Judd Street is a highly respectable street, but it can hardly be called fashionable. Phineas, when he called on Sunday afternoon, was informed by Mrs Macpherson that Mr Kennedy was 'nae doubt at hame, but was nae willing to see folk on the Saaboth'. Phineas pleaded the extreme necessity of his business, and sent up his card. At last he was desired to walk upstairs.

Mr Kennedy, as Phineas entered the drawing-room, slowly rose from his chair, putting down the Bible which had been in his hands. There was no shaking of hands.

'I should not have come to you on such a day as this, Mr Kennedy . . .'

'It is a day very unfitted for the affairs of the world,' said Mr Kennedy.

'Had not the matter been most pressing in regard both to time and its own importance.'

'Therefore I have consented to see you.'

'You know a man of the name of Slide, Mr Kennedy— the editor of *The People's Banner*. This Mr Slide has just been with me, having in his hand a printed letter from you, which—you will excuse me, Mr Kennedy—is very libellous.'

'I will bear the responsibility of that.'

'But you would not wish to publish falsehood about your wife, or even about me.'

'Falsehood! How dare you use that word to me? Is it false to say that she has left my house? Is it false to say that she is my wife, and cannot desert me, as she has done, without breaking her vows, and disregarding the laws both of God and man? Am I false when I offer to take her back, let her faults be what they may have been? Falsehood is villainy, and it is not I that am the villain.'

'You have joined my name in the accusation.'

'Because you are her paramour. I laid my command upon you that you should not visit my wife and you disobeyed, and you are an adulterer. Who are you to come for ever between me and my wife?'

'I never injured you in thought or deed. I come to you now because I have seen a printed letter which contains a gross libel upon myself and should not be published. You cannot hope to regain your wife by publishing false accusations against her.'

'I can prove every word I have written. She dare not come

279

here and submit herself to the laws of her country. She is a renegade from the law, and you abet her in her sin. But it is not vengeance that I seek. "Vengeance is mine, saith the Lord".'

'It looks like vengeance, Mr Kennedy.'

'Is it for you to teach me how I shall bear myself in this time of my great trouble? But I'll tell you what I'll do. If you will say that she shall come back again I'll have it cancelled.'

'Why should I ask her to submit herself to misery?'

'Misery! Must a woman need be miserable because she lives with her husband? Let her come back to me and she shall live in peace and quiet, and hear no word of reproach.'

'I can have nothing to do with it, Mr Kennedy.'

'Then, sir, you shall abide my wrath.' With that he sprang quickly round, grasping at something which lay upon a shelf near him, and Phineas saw that he was armed with a pistol. Phineas, who had hitherto been seated, leaped to his legs; but the pistol in a moment was at his head and the madman pulled at the trigger. But the mechanism required that some bolt should be loosed before the hammer would fall, and the unhandy wretch for an instant fumbled over the work so that Phineas, still facing his enemy, had time to leap backwards towards the door. But Kennedy, though he was awkward, still succeeded in firing before Phineas could leave the room. He was not struck, however. With three or four steps he leaped down the stairs, and, finding the front door closed, took shelter within Mrs Macpherson's bar. 'The man is mad,' he said; 'did you not hear the shot?' The woman was too frightened to reply, but stood trembling, holding Phineas by the arm. There was nobody in the house, she said, but she and the two lasses.

Phineas had not as yet resolved whether he would get a policeman when the bell from the room was rung furiously. 'It's the laird,' said Mrs Macpherson, 'and if naebody waits on him he'll surely be shooting ane of us.' The two girls were now outside the bar shaking in their shoes, unwilling to face the danger. At last the door of the room above was opened, and Phineas's hat was sent rolling down the stairs.

It was clear to him that the man was so mad as to be not

even aware of the act he had perpetrated. 'He'll do nothing more with the pistol,' he said. At last it was determined that one of the girls should be sent to fetch Macpherson home from the Scotch Church, and that no application should be made at once to the police. It seemed that the Macphersons knew the circumstances of their guest's family, and that there was a cousin of his in London who was the only one with whom he seemed to have any near connexion. The thing that had occurred was to be told to this cousin, and Phineas left his address, so that if it should be thought necessary he might be called upon to give his account of the affair. Then he asked for a glass of brandy, and, having swallowed it, was about to take his leave. 'The brandy wull be saxpence, sir,' said Mrs Macpherson, as she wiped the tears from her eyes.

CHAPTER THREE

I T was rumoured all over London that the Duke of Omnium was dying. For three days Mr Palliser was at Matching and visited his uncle twice a day. But not a syllable was ever said between them beyond the ordinary words of compliments. The rest of his time Mr Palliser spent with his private secretary, toiling for unapproachable results in reference to decimal coinage. To him his uncle's death would be a great glow, as in his eyes to be Chancellor of the Exchequer was much more than to be Duke of Omnium. For herself Lady Glencora was nearly equally indifferent, though she did in her heart of hearts wish that her son should go to Eton with the title of Lord Silverbridge.

The Duke seemed to be without discomfort, and was certainly free from fear. A clergyman gave him the sacrament. He took it—as the champagne prescribed, or the few mouthfuls of chicken broth. As to the future, he neither feared much nor hoped much; but was, unconsciously, supported by a general trust in the goodness and the greatness of the God who had made him what he was. He himself had never done any good, but he had always carried himself like a duke, and like a duke he carried himself to the end.

So the Duke died, and Lady Glencora Palliser became Duchess of Omnium. But the change was much greater to Mr Palliser than to his wife. As to rank, he was raised from that of a simple commoner to the very top of the tree. He was made master of almost unlimited wealth, and all the added grandeurs which come from high influence when joined to high rank were sure to be his. But he was no more moved by these things than would have been a god, or a block of wood. His uncle was dead; but his uncle had been an old man, and his grief on that score was moderate. As soon as his uncle's body had been laid in the family vault at Gatherum, men would call him Duke of Omnium; and then he could never sit again in the House of Commons. To his uncle it had been everything to be Duke of Omnium. To Plantagenet Palliser it was less than nothing. He had lived among men and women with titles all his life, himself untitled, but regarded by them as one of themselves, till the thing had come to seem almost nothing. He had won for himself by his own aptitudes and his own industry one special position in the empire—and that position, and that alone, was incompatible with the rank which he was obliged to assume. 'I suppose you must give up the Exchequer,' his wife said to him. He made no reply. Even to her he could not explain his feelings.

She did regret the change in her name, though she was by no means indifferent to the rank. As Lady Glencora Palliser she was known to everyone, and had always done exactly as she had pleased. She must lay down her mischief, and abandon her eccentricity, and in some degree act like other duchesses.

The Duke was buried and the will was read, and Plantagenet Palliser was addressed as Duke of Omnium by all the tenantry and retainers of the family in the great hall of Gatherum Castle. Planty Pall had come to the throne, and half a county was ready to worship him. But he did not know how to endure worship. At every 'Grace' that was flung at him he winced and was miserable, and declared to himself that he should never become accustomed to his new life.

. . . . .

Phineas Finn had been successful in obtaining an injunction to restrain the publication of Mr Kennedy's letter, upon his own affidavit as to what had occurred at Macpherson's Hotel. To say that Mr Quintus Slide was aghast is but a poor form of speech for the expression of his emotion. He had been 'done', 'sold', absolutely robbed by that wretchedly false Irishman whom he had trusted with all the confidence of a candid nature and an open heart! Treachery was no adequate word for the injury inflicted on him.

A paragraph was shown to him in a morning paper of that day which must, he thought, refer to Mr Kennedy and Phineas Finn. 'A rumour has reached us that a Member of Parliament, calling yesterday afternoon upon a member of a late Government, at his hotel, was shot at by the latter. Whether the rumour be true or not we have no means of saying, and therefore abstain from publishing names. We are informed that the gentleman who used the pistol was out of his mind. The bullet did not take effect.' How cruel it was that such information should have reached the hands of a rival, and not fallen in the way of *The People's Banner*! And what a pity that the bullet should have been wasted!

'I'll crush you,' said Quintus Slide, in a stage whisper; 'I will, as sure as my name is Slide.'

No public or official inquiry was made into the circumstance. Mr Kennedy, under the care of his cousin, retreated to Scotland; and, as it seemed, there was to be an end of it. Throughout the month of March various bolts were thrust both at Phineas and at the police by the editor of *The People's Banner*, but they seemed to fall without much effect.

Nevertheless, these missiles had their effect. Everybody knew that there had been a 'row' between Mr Kennedy and Phineas Finn, and that the 'row' had been made about Mr Kennedy's wife. There was a very romantic story afloat as to an engagement which had existed between Lady Laura and Phineas Finn before the lady had been induced by her father to marry the richer suitor. Was it not known that the Earl had purchased the submission of Phineas Finn by a seat for his borough of Loughton? Was it not known that Lord Chiltern, the brother of Lady Laura, had fought a duel with Phineas Finn?

While all these things were being said Phineas became something of a hero. But there were some who said that the Member for Tankerville had injured his prospects with his party.

'I never saw such a fellow as you are,' said Barrington Erle to him. 'You are always getting into a mess.'

'Nobody ought to know better than you how false all these calumnies are.'

'Of course they are calumnies; but you had heard them before, and what made you go poking your head into the lion's mouth?'

Mr Bonteen was very much harder upon him than was Barrington Erle. 'I never liked him from the first, and always knew he would not run straight. No Irishman ever does. It's out of the question that he should come in again. At any rate if he does, I don't. I shall tell Gresham so very plainly.' Phineas heard of it; and he thought that Mr Gresham was hardly as cordial to him as he might be when they met in the House.

Phineas had written to Lady Laura, giving her an account of the occurrence, and had received from her a short thanksgiving that his life had not been sacrificed. Then on the last day of the month he received another letter.

Dresden, March 27th, 18—

My dear Friend,

At last we have resolved that we will go back to England. Papa's lawyer, Mr Forster, tells him that it will be best.

284

He cannot bear to think that my position should be withheld from me by Mr Kennedy while I have done nothing wrong. He thinks that if my unfortunate husband be insane, there can be no difficulty in my obtaining a separation.

We have sent to have the house in Portman Square got ready for us, and I suppose we shall be there about the 15th of next month. Perhaps I ought to tell you that Mr Forster has expressed surprise that you did not call on the police when the shot was fired. Of course I can understand it all. God bless you.

Your affectionate friend,

L.K.

Phineas was obliged to console himself by reflecting that his first and great duty in the matter had been to her. That he was to be punished he began to perceive too clearly. Within the little inner circles of the Liberal party the usual discussions were made as to the Ministry which Mr Gresham would soon be called upon to form. But in the midst of it all no office was assigned to Phineas Finn; and there was a general feeling, not expressed, but understood, that his affair with Mr Kennedy stood in his way.

There was great injustice in all this, Phineas thought, not only from Mr Slide but also from those who ought to have been his staunch friends. He had been enticed over to England almost with a promise of office, and he was sure that he had done nothing which deserved punishment, or even censure. On one matter, however, he was determined to be firm. When Barrington Erle had absolutely insisted that he should vote upon the Church Bill in opposition to all that he had said upon the subject at Tankerville, he had stipulated that he should have an opportunity in the debate of explaining his conduct. 'That will be all right, of course,' said Barrington Erle to him.

There was at this time existing a small club which had entitled itself the Universe. The name was supposed to be a joke, as it was limited to ninety-nine members. It was domiciled in one simple apartment. It was kept open only when Parliament was sitting. Its attractions were not numerous, the conversation was generally listless and often desultory. But the thing had been a success, and men liked to be members of the Universe. Mr Bonteen was a member, and so was Phineas Finn. On Sunday evening, as Phineas entered the room, he perceived that his enemy was seated alone on a corner of a sofa. On that very morning Mr Gresham had suggested to Mr Bonteen that in the event of a Liberal Government being formed he should hold the office of Chancellor of the Exchequer. This, perhaps, had not been done in the most flattering manner, as Mr Gresham had deeply bewailed the loss of Mr Palliser, and had almost demanded a pledge of Mr Bonteen that he would walk exactly in Mr Palliser's footsteps; but the offer had been made, and Mr Bonteen already felt the warmth of the halo of perfect divinity.

Phineas was presumed to be on terms of intimacy with the man, and he took his seat beside him, asking some question as to the debate. Now Mr Bonteen had more than once expressed an opinion among his friends that Phineas Finn would throw his party over, and vote with the Government. It suited him to affect something more than doubt on the present occasion.

'I presume that you, as usual, will vote against us.'

'I never voted against my party but once,' said Phineas, 'and then I did it with the approbation of every man in it for whose good opinion I cared a straw.' There was something near to insult in his words.

'You must do it again now, or break every promise that you made at Tankerville.'

'Do you know what promise I made at Tankerville? I shall break no promise.'

'You must allow me to say, Mr Finn, that the kind of independence which is practised by you and Mr Monk, grand as it may be, is a little dangerous. I like to be sure that the men who are in the same boat with me won't take it into their heads that their duty requires them to scuttle the ship.' Having so spoken, Mr Bonteen rose from his seat on the corner of the sofa, and joined a small congregation.

The man, Phineas thought, had been determined to affront him. And then there was all the additional bitterness which arose from the conviction that Bonteen had spoken the opinion of other men as well as his own, and that he had plainly indicated that the gates of the official paradise were to be closed against the presumed offender.

On the next day Phineas, with his speech before him, was obliged for a while to forget, or at least to postpone, Mr Bonteen and his injuries. At half-past four he was on his legs in the midst of a crowded House. He began by saying that no man was more anxious than he, an Irish Roman Catholic, to abolish that which he thought to be the anomaly of a State Church, and he did not in the least doubt that he should now be doing the best in his power with that object in voting against the second reading of the present Bill. That such a measure should be carried by the gentlemen opposite, in their own teeth, at the bidding of the right honourable gentleman who led them, he thought to be impossible. Upon this he was hooted at from the other side with many gestures of indignant denial, and was, of course, equally cheered by those around him. Someone asked him in fury by what right he took upon himself to judge of the motives of gentlemen on that side of the House of whom personally he knew nothing. Phineas replied that the whole country was convinced that the Conservative party as a body was supporting this measure, unwillingly, and at the bidding of one man; and, for himself, he was bound to say that he agreed with the country.

The vehemence with which his insolence was abused by one after another of those who spoke later from the other side was ample evidence of his success. But nothing occurred then or at the conclusion of the debate to make him think that he had won his way back to Elysium. During the whole evening he exchanged not a syllable with Mr Gresham. Erle said a few good-natured words to him, and Mr Monk praised him highly. But in reading the general barometer of the party as regarded himself he did not find that the mercury went up.

At five o'clock in the morning the division took place, and the Government was beaten by a majority of 72. This was much higher than any man had expected. When the parties were marshalled in the opposite lobbies it was found that in the last moment the number of those Conservatives who dared to rebel against their leaders was swelled by the course which the debate had taken. There were certain men who could not endure to be twitted with having deserted the principles of their lives, when it was clear that nothing was to be gained by the party by such desertion.

CHAPTER FOUR

'So you've had a great victory,' said Madame Max Goesler, when Phineas called on her later that day.

'Yes—greater than we expected.'

'According to Mrs Bonteen the chief result to the country will be that the taxes will be so very safe in her husband's hands.'

'I don't like her, or her husband.'

'I do like a woman that can thoroughly enjoy her husband's success. I don't think Lady Glencora ever cared in the least about her husband being Chancellor of the Exchequer.'

'Because it added nothing to her own standing.'

'That's very ill-natured, Mr Finn; you used to be the best-humoured of men.'

'I hadn't so much to try my temper as I have now, and then you must remember, Madame Goesler, that I regard these people as being especially my enemies.'

'Lady Glencora was never your enemy.'

'Nor my friend, especially.'

'Then you wrong her. If I tell you something you must be discreet. She does not like Mr Bonteen, or his wife. She has had too much of them at Matching. Her Grace is determined to fight your battle for you.'

'I want her to do nothing of the kind, Madame Goesler.'

'You will know nothing about it. If you have enemies behind your back, you must have friends behind your back also.'

'For Heaven's sake, not.'

'You'll be called the ladies' pet, but you mustn't mind that. Lady Laura will be here before it's arranged and she will get hold of Mr Erle.'

'If that kind of thing is done I shall not accept place even if it is offered me.'

'Are you going to let a man like Mr Bonteen bowl you over? Did you ever know Lady Glen fail in anything that she attempted?'

'You have been very wrong to tell me.'

'Perhaps I have, Mr Finn. But we believe that falsehoods have been used which are as disparaging to Lady Laura Kennedy as they are injurious to you. Someone has told Mr Gresham that you have been the means of breaking the hearts both of Lord Brentford and Mr Kennedy and he must be made to understand that this is untrue. If only for Lady Laura's sake you must submit.'

'And you do not feel that all this is derogatory to me?'

'Not a whit. It is not done with the object of obtaining an improper appointment on behalf of an unimportant man.'

'I'd rather fight above ground.'

'That's all very well, but your enemies won't stay above ground. Is that newspaper man above ground? And for a little job of clever mining, believe me, there is not a better engineer going than Lady Glen.'

.   .   .   .   .

The Prime Minister is elected by the nation, but is burdened with the necessity of selecting his colleagues. On the present occasion it was known at the end of a week that Mr Gresham had not filled all his offices, and that there were difficulties. It was announced that the Duke of St Bungay could not quite agree on certain points with Mr Gresham, and that the Duke of Omnium would do nothing without the other Duke. The

Duke did not approve of Mr Bonteen. Mr Gresham, so it was said, insisted on Mr Bonteen, appealing to the other Duke. But that other Duke, Planty Pall that was, instead of standing up for Mr Bonteen, was cold and unsympathetic. He could not join the Ministry without his friend the Duke of St Bungay, and as to Mr Bonteen, he thought that perhaps a better selection might be made.

Lady Glencora, as people would still persist in calling her, was at the bottom of it all. She had sworn an oath inimical to Mr Bonteen, and did not leave a stone unturned in her endeavours to accomplish it. If Phineas Finn might find acceptance, then Mr Bonteen might be allowed. For this she struggled, speaking her mind boldly to this and that member of her husband's party, but she struggled in vain. She could obtain no assurance on behalf of Phineas Finn. The Duke of St Bungay would do nothing for her. Barrington Erle declared himself powerless. Then she went sedulously to work.

'Plantagenet, of all your men that are coming up, your Mr Bonteen is the worst. I often think that you are going downhill, both in character and intellect, but if you go as low as that I shall prefer to cross the water and live in America.' This she said in the presence of the two Dukes.

'What has Mr Bonteen done?' asked the elder, laughing.

'He was boasting this morning openly of whom he intended to bring with him into the Cabinet.' Mr Bonteen had talked largely and with indiscretion, but had made no such boast as that of which the Duchess accused him.

What she had said was not thrown away. 'Your wife is almost right about that man,' the elder Duke said to the younger.

'It's Mr Gresham's doing, not mine,' said the younger.

That evening Mr Bonteen was singled out by the Duchess for her special attention, and in the presence of all who were there assembled he made himself an ass. He could not save himself from talking about himself when he was encouraged. On this occasion he offended all those feelings of official discretion and personal reticence which had been endeared to the old Duke by the lessons which he had learned from former statesmen and by the experience of his own life. To be quiet, unassuming, almost affectedly modest in any mention of himself, low-voiced, reflecting always more than he resolved, and resolving always more than he said, had been his aim. That he had really been indispensable to many he must have known, but not to his closest friend would he have said so in plain language. To such a man the arrogance of Mr Bonteen was intolerable.

'I am not sure that you are not going a little too quick in regard to Mr Bonteen,' said the elder Duke to Mr Gresham shortly afterwards.

'Palliser wishes it,' said Mr Gresham, shortly.

'He and I think that there has been some mistake about that.' Then the Duke made a suggestion. 'Could not some special office at the Treasury be constructed for Mr Bonteen's acceptance, having special reference to the question of decimal coinage?'

'But how about the salary?' asked Mr Gresham. 'I couldn't propose a new office with a salary above £2,000.'

'Couldn't we make it permanent,' suggested the Duke, 'with permission to hold a seat if he can get one?'

'I fear not,' said Mr Gresham.

But Mr Gresham was too wise to treat as of no account the objections of such a one as the Duke of St Bungay. He saw Mr Bonteen, and he saw the other Duke, and Mr Bonteen made himself very disagreeable indeed. In his heart he accused the young Duchess, though he mentioned her name to no one. Then there was made an insidious proposition to Mr Gresham—which reached him at last through Barrington Erle—that matters would go quiet if Phineas Finn were placed in his old office at the Colonies instead of Lord Fawn, whose name had been suggested, and for whom, as Barrington Erle declared, no one cared a brass farthing. Mr Gresham, when he heard this, thought that he began to smell a rat. Why should the appointment of Mr Phineas Finn make things go easier in regard to Mr Bonteen? There must be some woman's fingers in the pie. Now Mr Gresham was firmly resolved that no woman's fingers should have anything to do with his pie.

The thing went from bad to worse. Neither of the two Dukes absolutely refused to join the Ministry; but they were persistent in their objection to Mr Bonteen. At last Mr Bonteen was absolutely told that he could not be Chancellor of the Exchequer. If he would consent to give his very valuable services to the country with the view of carrying through Parliament the great measure of decimal coinage he should be President of the Board of Trade, but without a seat in the Cabinet. He would thus become the Right Honourable Bonteen, which, no doubt, would be a great thing for him. 'Mr Bonteen,' said Mr Gresham, 'if you can act with us I shall be very grateful to you. If you cannot, I shall regret the loss of your services.' Mr Bonteen took twenty-four hours to consider, and was then appointed President of the Board of Trade without a seat in the Cabinet. Mr Legge Wilson became Chancellor of the Exchequer. When the lists were completed, no office whatever was assigned to Phineas Finn.

Before the Ministry had been a week in office almost everybody knew that the Duchess had done it. The Duchess was the bosom friend of Lady Laura Kennedy, who was in love with Phineas Finn. She had gone on her knees to Mr Gresham to get a place for her friend's favourite, and Mr Gresham had refused. Consequently, at her bidding, half-a-dozen embryo Ministers—her husband among the number—had refused to be amenable to Mr Gresham. Mr Gresham had at last consented to sacrifice Mr Bonteen, who had originally instigated him to reject the claims of Phineas Finn. That the degradation of the one man had been caused by the exclusion of the other all the world knew.

The quarrel between Phineas Finn and Mr Bonteen had now become the talk of the town and an organ came forward to support Mr Bonteen—not very creditable to him as a Liberal, being a Conservative organ—but not the less gratifying to his spirit, inasmuch as the organ not only supported him, but exerted its very loudest pipes in abusing the man whom of all men he hated the most. *The People's Banner* was the organ, and Mr Quintus Slide was, of course, the organist. The following was one of the tunes he played:

One piece of advice which we have ventured to give Mr Gresham he has been wise enough to follow. We took upon ourselves to tell him that if he ventured to place the Member for Tankerville again in office the country would not stand it—and he has abstained. The jaunty footsteps of Mr Phineas Finn are not heard ascending the stairs of any office, as used to be the case about three years since. The good-looking Irish Member of Parliament who had been put in possession of a handsome salary by feminine influences will not, we think, again become a burden on the public purse. But we cannot say that we are as yet satisfied in this matter, or that we believe that the public has got to the bottom of it—as it has a right to do. We have never yet learned why it is that Mr Bonteen, after having been nominated Chancellor of the Exchequer, was afterwards excluded from the Cabinet. We believe that we are justified in saying that it was managed through the influence of the Member for Tankerville. Mr Phineas Finn, with his female forces, has again interfered. We cannot but feel that it is a disgrace to the Government, a disgrace to Parliament, and a disgrace to the country that such results should come from the private scandals of two or three people among us by no means of the best class.

.   .   .   .   .

For a few months after his marriage with Lady Eustace, that fashionable preacher of dubious extraction, Mr Joseph Emilius, enjoyed a halcyon existence. He drew more largely upon her money than was pleasing to her, and appeared to have requirements for cash which were both secret and unlimited. At the end of twelve months Lady Eustace had run away from him, and Mr Emilius had made overtures, by accepting which his wife would be enabled to purchase his absence at the cost of half her income. Lady Eustace declared passionately that any possible sacrifice would be preferable to the company of Mr Emilius. There had, however, been a rumour before her marriage that there was still living in his old country a Mrs Emilius when he married Lady Eustace. If it could be proved that Mr Emilius had a wife living in Bohemia, a cheaper mode of escape would be found for the persecuted lady.

It had happened that Lady Eustace had become intimate with Mr Bonteen and his wife. She had a most desirable residence in the country, Portray Castle in Scotland. She was rich, beautiful, and clever; and, though her marriage with Mr Emilius had never been looked upon as a success, still, in the estimation of some people, it added an interest to her career. The Bonteens had taken her up, and now both Mr and Mrs Bonteen were hot in pursuit of evidence which might prove Mr Emilius to be a bigamist.

When the disruption of conjugal relations was commenced Lady Eustace threw herself into the hands of the Bonteens. With that energy for which he was so conspicuous Mr Bonteen had made a visit to Bohemia during his short Christmas holidays, and had there set people to work. At Prague he had found the woman whom he believed to be Mrs Emilius, now living somewhat merrily under another name. She acknowledged that in old days she had been acquainted with a certain Yosef Mealyus, at a time in which he had been in the employment of a Jewish money-lender in the city; but, she declared, she had never been married to him. Then Mr Bonteen had returned home, and had become engaged in matters of deeper import than the deliverance of Lady Eustace from her thraldom.

Mr Emilius made no attempt to obtain the person of his wife while she was under Mr Bonteen's custody, but he did renew his offer to compromise. If the estate could not afford to give him the two thousand a year which he had first demanded, he would take fifteen hundred. He explained all this personally to Mr Bonteen, who condescended to see him. But when Mr Bonteen somewhat rashly told him that the evidence of a former marriage and of the present existence of the former wife would certainly be forthcoming, he defied Mr Bonteen and his evidence, and swore that if his claims were not satisfied he would make use of the power which the English law gave him for the recovery of his wife's person.

And as to her property, it was his, not hers. From this time forward if she wanted to separate herself from him she must ask him for an allowance. But the lawyers of the Eustace family, who were not, indeed, very fond of Lady Eustace personally, came forward for the sake of the property. So the Reverend Mealyus, as everybody now called him, went to law; and Lady Eustace went to law; and the Eustace family went to law; but still, as yet, no evidence was forthcoming sufficient to enable Mr Bonteen as the lady's friend to put the gentleman into prison.

After his interview with Mr Bonteen he made a journey to Prague. It was thought that he would not return, and that Lady Eustace would be obliged to carry on the trial which was to liberate her and her property, in his absence. But he did return, declaring aloud that he would have his rights. People then began to doubt. It was known that a very clever lawyer's clerk had been sent to Prague to complete the work there which Mr Bonteen had commenced. But the clerk did not come back as soon as was expected, and news arrived that he had been taken ill. There was a rumour that he had been poisoned at his hotel, but people hardly believed the rumour. It became necessary, however, to send another lawyer's clerk, and the matter was gradually progressing to a very interesting complication.

Mr Bonteen, to tell the truth, was becoming sick of Lady Eustace. When the man came back, bolder than ever, she again betook herself to the shelter of Mr Bonteen's roof. She expressed the most lavish affection for Mrs Bonteen, and professed to regard Mr Bonteen as almost a political god, and became very loud in her wrath when he was robbed of his seat in the Cabinet.

'I always hated the very name of that Phineas Finn.'

'Did you know him?' said Mrs Bonteen.

'Not exactly. Poor Lord Fawn used to talk of him. He was one of those conceited Irish upstarts that are never good for anything.'

'Very handsome, you know,' said Mrs Bonteen.

'It is dreadful to think that a creature like that should be able to interfere with such a man as Mr Bonteen.'

This was on Wednesday afternoon, the day on which Members of Parliament dine out. On that same Wednesday evening Phineas Finn dined at the house of Madame Goesler, and went from thence to the Universe Club in better spirits than he had known for some weeks past. The Duke and Duchess had been at Madame Goesler's, and Lord and Lady Chiltern, who were now up in town, and Barrington Erle. The dinner had been very pleasant. Barrington Erle had expressed a regret that Phineas was not at his old post at the Colonies, and the young Duke had echoed it. Phineas thought that the manner of his old friend Erle was more cordial to him than it had been lately, and even that comforted him.

Barrington Erle and Phineas went off to the Universe together, and as they went up the stairs, they heard the hum of many voices in the room. 'Mr Phineas Finn, or some such fellow as that, would be after her at once,' said Mr Bonteen. Then Phineas walked immediately among the knot of men and showed himself. 'What is it, Mr Bonteen, that Phineas Finn will do?' he asked.

Mr Bonteen had been—dining. He was not a man by any means habitually intemperate. But he was flushed with much wine, and he was a man whose arrogance in that condition was apt to become extreme. Mr Bonteen looked Phineas full in the face a second or two before he answered, 'You have crept upon us unawares, sir. Listeners never hear any good of themselves.'

'I wish to hear no good of myself from you,' said Phineas. 'Who is it that you said I should be after?' The room was full, and everyone there knew that Lady Eustace was the woman. Everybody at present was talking about Lady Eustace.

'What a row about nothing!' said Mr Bonteen. 'We were speaking of a very pretty woman, and I was saying that some young fellow generally supposed to be fond of pretty women would soon be after her. If that offends your morals you must have become very strict of late.'

There was something in the explanation which, though very bad and vulgar, it was almost impossible not to accept. Such at least was the feeling of those who stood around Phineas Finn.

'There are reasons, Mr Bonteen,' he said, 'why I think you should abstain from mentioning my name in public. Your playful references should be made to your friends, and not to those who, to say the least of it, are not your friends.'

When the matter was discussed afterwards it was thought that Phineas Finn should have abstained from making the last speech. It was certainly evidence of great anger on his part. And he was very angry. Fate at the moment was so far propitious that outward circumstances saved Mr Bonteen from any immediate reply. Expected Royalty arrived. The Prince, with some well-known popular attendant, entered the room, and for a moment every gentleman rose from his chair. It was but for a moment, and then the Prince became as any other gentleman, talking to his friends; but the quarrel had been trodden underfoot.

When the Prince went, which he did when his cigar was finished, a ruck of men left the club. Phineas went down the stairs with Barrington Erle, and they stood for a moment at the door talking to each other. Finn's way lay eastward from the club, whereas Erle would go westwards. 'How well the Prince behaves at these sort of places!' said Erle.

'Princes ought to behave well,' said Phineas. 'Somebody else didn't.'

'Don't bother your mind about it, old fellow.'

'I tell you what it is, Erle, I don't think I'm a vindictive man by nature, but with that man I mean to make it even some of these days.'

As they were speaking Mr Bonteen came out from the front door alone, and seeing the two men standing, passed on towards the left. 'Good night, Erle,' he said. It was about one o'clock and the night was very dark. 'By George, I do dislike that man,' said Phineas. Then, with a laugh, he took a life-preserver out of his pocket, and made an action with it as though he were striking some enemy over the head. In those days there had been much garotting in the streets, and writers in the press had advised those who walked about at night to be armed with sticks. As soon as he had spoken, he bade good night to Barrington Erle, and followed Mr Bonteen down the street, at the distance of perhaps a couple of hundred yards.

.   .   .   .   .

On the next morning at seven o'clock a superintendent of police called at the house of Mr Gresham and informed the Prime Minister that Mr Bonteen had been murdered as he was returning from his club late at night, in the darkness of the mouth of a passage. The superintendent had heard from Lady Eustace—and from Mrs Bonteen, as far as that poor woman had been able to tell her story—some account of the cause of quarrel between the respective husbands of those two ladies, and the Reverend Mr Emilius was already in custody. He had been found in bed at his lodgings and had given himself up without difficulty. He had seemed to be horror-struck when he heard of the man's death, but had openly expressed his joy. 'He has endeavoured to ruin me,' he said to the policeman. But nothing had been found tending to implicate him in the crime. The servant declared that he had gone to bed before eleven o'clock, and had not left the house afterwards. Was he in possession of a latch-key? It appeared that he did usually carry a latch-key, but that it was often borrowed from him by members of the family when it was known that he would not want it himself—and that it had been so lent on this night. Nobody in fact had left the house after ten. Nevertheless his clothes were examined minutely, but without affording any evidence against him. That Mr Bonteen had been killed with some blunt weapon, such as a life-preserver, was assumed by the police, but no such weapon was in the possession of Mr Emilius, nor had any yet been found. He was, however, in custody, with no evidence against him except his acknowledged enmity to Mr Bonteen.

At eleven o'clock Mr Gresham heard much more. At that time there were present with him two officers of the police force, his colleagues in the Cabinet, Lord Cantrip and the Duke of Omnium, two of his junior colleagues in the Government, Lord Fawn and Barrington Erle, and Major Mackintosh, the chief of the London police.

Erle described the quarrel at the club, and also the anger which Finn had expressed as he stood talking at the club door, though Erle expressed his strongest conviction that the murder had not been committed by him. But he told also of the life-preserver which Finn had shown him, and they marvelled at the coincidences of the night. Major Mackintosh thought that this evidence was very unfortunate as regarded Mr Finn. 'It is on the cards,' said the Major, 'that he may have chosen to attack Mr Bonteen without intending to murder him. The murder may have been an accident.'

Phineas was accordingly visited at his rooms by two constables, who proceeded to take possession of the life-preserver and certain articles of his clothing, and then escorted him to Bow Street. At the police-office everybody was very civil to him, and he was asked whether he would not wish to have professional advice while the charge was being made against him. But this he declined, at any rate for the present. He was allowed to tell his own story, after repeated cautions. There had been some words between him and Mr Bonteen in the club; after which, standing at the door of the club with his friend, Mr Erle, he had seen Mr Bonteen walk away towards Berkeley Square. He had soon followed, but had never overtaken Mr Bonteen. He had not heard the sound of any struggle, or of words. He had carried the life-preserver because of the danger of garotters. He had not seen anyone on his way from the Square to his own house with sufficient observation to enable him to describe such person.

The statement both by Erle as to what had taken place in the club, and afterwards at the door, tallied exactly with that afterwards given by Phineas. An accurate measurement of the streets and ways concerned was already furnished. Taking the duration of time a constable proved that the prisoner would have had time to hurry to the passage where Mr Bonteen had been attacked in time to waylay him.

It was considered that the evidence given was sufficient to make a remand imperative, and Phineas Finn was committed to Newgate. He was assured that every attention should be paid to his comfort, and was treated with great consideration. The evidence adduced to prove that Mr Emilius could not have been on the spot was so very strong that the magistrate told the police that he must be released on the next examination unless something could be adduced against him.

The tidings of what had taken place first reached Lady Laura Kennedy from her brother, Lord Chiltern.

'I must see Phineas,' said Lady Laura frantically.

'You cannot see him.'

'Who will hinder me?'

'I will see that you are hindered. What is the man to you that you should run the risk of evil tongues, for the sake of visiting him in gaol. It will make people think that the things are true which have been said.'

'And they will hang him because I love him? I do love him.'

'Shame should prevent your telling it,' said Lord Chiltern.

'There is no disgrace in love. I did disgrace myself when I gave the hand for which he asked to another man, because—because . . .' But she was too noble to tell her brother even then that she had married the rich man, rejecting the poor man's hand, because she had given up all her fortune to the payment of her brother's debts.

'Be calm, Laura,' said her sister-in-law, 'and Oswald will do all that can be done.'

'But they will hang him.'

'Nonsense!' said her brother. 'It is as likely as not that in three days' time he will be out at large, and all the world will be running after him just because he has been in Newgate. He has plenty of friends. I will see that he is not left without everything that he wants.' So saying Lord Chiltern went, leaving the two women together.

'If it be true I will hang myself,' said Lady Laura. 'There will be nothing left to live for. You think it shameful that I should love him.'

'I have not said so.'

'I saw it in your eye when he accused me. And I know that it is shameful. But I can bear my own disgrace better than his danger.' After a long pause she spoke again. 'If Robert should die—what would happen then?'

'It would be—a release, I suppose,' said Lady Chiltern.

'A release indeed; and I would become that man's wife

the next day, at the foot of the gallows—if he would have me. But he would not have me.'

In fact Robert Kennedy was dying; and in the first week of May, when the beauty of the spring was beginning to show itself on the braes of Loughlinter, he did die, believing, as he had ever believed, that the spirit of evil was stronger than the spirit of good.

The telegram announcing that event came to her at her father's house in Portman Square on the day after that on which Phineas had been arrested. The news delighted the old Lord, and he was almost angry with his daughter because she also would not confess her delight.

'Oh, Papa, he was my husband.'

'Yes, yes, no doubt. I was always against it, you will remember.'

'Pray do not talk in that way now, Papa. I know that I was not to him what I should have been.'

'You used to say it was all his fault.'

'We will not talk of it now, Papa. He is gone, and I remember his past goodness to me.'

At the end of ten days from the death of Mr Kennedy there came the tidings of the will. This reached her lawyer, Mr Forster, and he brought it personally to Portman Square.

'He has bequeathed to you the use of Loughlinter for your life, Lady Laura.'

'To me!'

'Yes, Lady Laura. The will is dated in the first year of his marriage, and has not been altered since.'

'What can I do with Loughlinter? I will give it back to them.' Then Mr Forster explained that the legacy referred not only to the house and grounds, but to the whole estate known as the domain of Loughlinter. Were she to give it up, the world would of course say that she had done so from a feeling of her own unworthiness. 'Why should I feel myself to be unworthy?' she asked. The lawyer smiled, and told her that of course she would retain Loughlinter.

Then he was taken to the Earl's room. Lady Laura preferred not to hear her father's exultations. But while this was being done she also exulted. Might it not still be possible that there should be before her a happy evening to her days; and that she might stand once more beside the falls of Linter, contented and hopeful, with her hand in his to whom she had once refused her own on that very spot?

·   ·   ·   ·   ·

Phineas Finn was at last committed to be tried for the murder of Mr Bonteen. Little more had been learned, or even surmised, by the police. As to Mr Emilius, he did not attempt to run away, for which attempt certain pseudo-facilities were put in his way by police ingenuity. Mr Emilius stood his ground and courted inquiry. Mr Bonteen had been to him, he said, a very bitter, unjust, and cruel enemy, had endeavoured to rob him of his dearest wife, had charged him with bigamy, had got up false evidence in the hope of ruining him. He had undoubtedly hated Mr Bonteen, and might probably have said so. But, as it happened, through God's mercy, he was enabled to prove that he could not possibly have been at the scene of the murder when the murder was committed. The reverend gentleman was taken to half-a-dozen shops at which life-preservers had lately been sold, but at none of them was Mr Emilius remembered, and then all further inquiry in that direction was abandoned. 'I forgive my persecutors from the bottom of my heart,' he said, 'but God will requite it to them.'

Phineas was taken to Newgate, and confined almost with the glory and attendance of a State prisoner. This was no common murder, and no common murderer. Nor were they who interested themselves in the matter the ordinary rag, tag, and bobtail of the people, but also Dukes and Earls, Duchesses and Countesses, Members of the Cabinet, and beautiful women, amongst them the Duchess of Omnium—and Madame Max Goesler.

'The man Mealyus went back to his home in Poland not long ago,' said Madame Goesler. 'Perhaps he got the life-preserver there, and brought it with him.'

'And if he bought a bludgeon there, it would weaken the effect of Mr Finn's bludgeon,' the Duchess agreed. 'And if he bought rope to make a ladder it would show that he had got out of his lodgings after the door was locked.'

'Or had a false key made,' said Madame Goesler.

On the following day a lady, who had got out of a cab at the corner of Northumberland Street, in the Marylebone Road, knocked at a door just opposite to the deadest part of the dead wall of the Marylebone Workhouse. Here lived Mrs and Miss Meager to whom Mr Emilius had for a while trusted for his domestic comforts. When he was liberated by the police he had returned to the house, taken his two boxes away in a cab, and been seen no more by the ladies of Northumberland Street.

But a further gleam of prosperity fell upon them in consequence of the tragedy which had been so interesting to them. Hitherto the inquiries made at their house had had reference solely to the habits and doings of their lodger during the last few days; but now came this visitor of their own sex. It was Madame Goesler. She dealt out sovereigns— and soon had Mrs and Miss Meager at her feet.

'Yes, ma'am,' said Mrs Meager, 'he did take the key abroad with him. Amelia remembers we were a key short at the time he was away.'

Madame Goesler was convinced that a dozen other latchkeys might have been made after the pattern without any apparent detection by the London police.

Madame Goesler thanked the women and left. She knew that her interest was romantic and unpractical. Nevertheless, the conviction of the guilt of that other man, towards which she still thought that much could be done if the maker of a secret key were found, was so strong upon her that she would not allow herself to drop it.

'Do you mean that you are going to go yourself?' the Duchess said to her that afternoon.

'Yes, I am.'

'Then you must be very far gone in love, indeed. I shouldn't like to go to Prague in June.'

'I'd go to Siberia in January if I could find out that that horrid man really committed the murder.'

'Who are going with you?'

'We shall be quite a company. We have a detective police-man, and an interpreter who understands Greek and German, and a lawyer's clerk, and there will be my own maid.'

'Everybody will know all about it before you get there.'

'We are not to go quite together. The policeman and the interpreter are to form one party, and I and my maid another. The clerk is to be alone.'

'I think it is very grand of you, my dear; and for your sake I hope he may live to be Prime Minister.'

And so Madame Goesler started for Prague with the determination of being back, if possible, before the trial began. It was to be commenced at the Old Bailey towards the end of June. It was already known that the Attorney-General, Sir Gregory Grogram, was to lead the case for the prosecution, and that the Solicitor-General, Sir Simon Slope, was to act with him. The defence was to be entrusted to the well-practised but now aged hands of that most experienced practitioner Mr Chaffanbrass, than whom no barrister ever rescued more culprits from the fangs of the law.

But the glory of this trial would not depend chiefly on the array of counsel, nor on the fact that the Lord Chief Justice himself would be the judge, so much as on the social position of the murdered man and of the murderer. Noble lords and great statesmen would throng the bench of the court to see Phineas Finn tried. When Mr Gresham, hard pressed by Mr Turnbull for a convenient day, offered that gentleman Thursday, the 24th of June, for suggesting to the House a little proposition of his own with reference to the English Church establishment, Mr Turnbull openly repudiated the offer, because on that day the trial of Phineas Finn would be commenced. 'I hope,' said Mr Gresham, 'that the work of the country will not be impeded by that unfortunate affair.' 'I am afraid,' said Mr Turnbull, 'that the right honourable gentleman will find that the Member for Tankerville will on that day monopolize the attention of this House.'

In the meantime it was necessary that Mr Bonteen's late place at the Board of Trade should be filled. Mr Bonteen had been appointed chiefly because it was thought that he might in that office act as a quasi House of Commons deputy to the

Duke of Omnium in carrying out his great scheme of a five-farthinged penny and a ten-pennied shilling. The Duke was determined to go on with his great task of decimal coinage. He suggested to Mr Gresham that he would himself take the place left vacant by Mr Bonteen—of course retaining his seat in the Cabinet.

'I should hardly have ventured to suggest such an arrangement to your Grace,' said the Prime Minister.

This great nobleman, who was now asking for Mr Bonteen's shoes, had been Chancellor of the Exchequer, and would have remained Chancellor of the Exchequer and was now Lord Privy Seal, a Lordship of State which does carry with it a status and a seat in the Cabinet, but does not necessarily entail any work. But the present Lord, who cared nothing for status, had almost envied Mr Bonteen the realities of the Board of Trade. 'I think upon the whole it will be best to make the change,' he said to Mr Gresham. And Mr Gresham was delighted.

When it was publicly known that the Duke of Omnium had stepped into Mr Bonteen's shoes, the general opinion was that he should not have consented to succeed a man so insignificant as Mr Bonteen. He strove to bear his wife's sarcasms without showing that they pained him.

'They say that poor Lord Fawn is losing his mind,' she said to him.

'Lord Fawn! I haven't heard anything about it.'

'He was engaged to Lady Eustace once, you remember. They say that he'll be made to declare why he didn't marry her if this bigamy case goes on. I hope he won't have to resign.'

'I hope not, indeed.'

'Because, of course, you'd have to take his place as Under-Secretary.'

'Glencora,' he said to her. 'I wish that you could drop the subject of this trial till it be over.'

'No more than you can avoid your decimals. Out of the full heart the mouth speaks, and my heart is very full. What harm do I do?'

'You set people talking of you.'

'They have been doing that ever since we were married;

but I do not know that they have made out much against me. We must go after our nature, Plantagenet. Your nature is decimals. I run after units.'

At the time of the murder, Lady Eustace, the wife of Mr Emilius, was living as the guest of Mr Bonteen. When the first days of agony and despair had passed by, Mrs Bonteen became fixed in her certainty that Phineas Finn had murdered her husband. But Lizzie had her own opinion, though she was forced to leave it unexpressed in the presence of Mrs Bonteen. She knew the man who claimed her as his wife. Her Yosef Mealyus, as she had delighted to call him since she had separated herself from him, was, she thought, the very man to commit a murder. He was by no means degraded in her opinion by the feeling. There was a dash of adventure about it which was almost gratifying.

Then one morning a servant announced that Mr Camperdown, the attorney, was below. In former days there had been an old Mr Camperdown, who was vehemently hostile to poor Lizzie Eustace; but now, in her new troubles, the firm that had ever been true to her first husband had taken up her case for the sake of the family and her property, and for the sake of the heir, Lizzie Eustace's little boy; and Mr Camperdown, junior, was therefore shown upstairs to Mrs Bonteen's drawing-room.

'We have found it all out, Lady Eustace,' said Mr Camperdown.

'Found out what?'

'We've got Madame Mealyus over here.'

'No!'

'Yes, indeed; and photographs of the registry of the marriage from the books of the synagogue at Cracow. His signature was Yosef Mealyus, and his handwriting isn't a bit altered. I think we could have proved it without the lady; but of course it was better to bring her if possible.'

'But I shall be free! Oh, Mr Camperdown, I shall be free from the power of that horrid man who has entangled me in the meshes of his sinful life.' Mr Camperdown went on to say that Yosef Mealyus had already been arrested, and was again in prison.

CHAPTER FIVE

At a quarter past ten on the 24th of June, the Chief Justice was on the bench at the Old Bailey, with a second judge to help him, and with lords and distinguished commoners and great City magnates crowding the long seat between him and the doorway; the court was full; and Phineas Finn, the Member for Tankerville, was in the dock.

A crowd of witnesses were heard on the first days, but none of them were of much interest to the public. The three doctors were examined as to the state of the dead man's head when he was picked up, and as to the nature of the instrument with which he had probably been killed; and the facts of the quarrel with Mr Bonteen, and Phineas Finn's life-preserver, were proved.

The case for the prosecution was completed on the Saturday evening. On the Monday morning the trial was recommenced, and the whole day was taken up by the address which Mr Chaffanbrass made to the jury. It was not his intention, he said, to accuse anyone of the murder. It was his business to defend the prisoner, not to accuse others. But, as he should prove to them, two persons had been arrested as soon as the murder had been discovered, two persons totally unknown to each other, and who were never for a moment supposed to have acted together—and the suspicion of the police had in the first instance pointed, not to his client, but to the other man. That other man had also quarrelled with Mr Bonteen, and that other man was now in custody on a charge of bigamy chiefly through the instrumentality of Mr Bonteen, who had been the friend of the victim of the supposed bigamist. With the accusation of bigamy they would have nothing to do, but he must ask them to take cognizance of that quarrel as well as of the quarrel at the club. He then named that formerly popular preacher, the Rev. Mr Emilius.

After lunch he occupied nearly three hours in giving to the jury, and to the whole assembled court, the details of about two dozen cases in which apparently strong circumstantial evidence had been wrong in its tendency. In some of the cases quoted, the persons tried had been acquitted; in some, convicted and afterwards pardoned; and in one the poor victim had been hung. On this he insisted with a pathetic eloquence which certainly would not have been expected from his grubby, unkempt appearance, and spoke with tears in his eyes—real unaffected tears—of the misery of those wretched jurymen who, in the performance of their duty, had been led into so frightful an error. Through the whole of this long recital he seemed to feel no fatigue. At six o'clock he completed his speech, and it was computed that the old man had been on his legs very nearly seven hours. It was said of him afterwards that he was taken home speechless by one of his daughters and immediately put to bed, that he roused himself about eight and ate his dinner and drank a bottle of port in his bedroom, that he then slept, refusing to stir even when he was waked, till half-past nine in the morning, and that then he scrambled into his clothes, breakfasted, and got down to the court in half an hour. At ten o'clock he was in his place, and nobody knew that he was any the worse for the previous day's exertion.

This was on a Tuesday, the fifth day of the trial, when a long array of distinguished persons was brought up to give to the jury their opinion as to the character of Mr Finn. The Duchess of Omnium had been anxious to be one, but the Duke had forbidden it, telling his wife that she really did not know the man, and that she was carried away by a foolish enthusiasm. Those selected included Lord and Lady Cantrip, Lord and Lady Chiltern, and Mr Monk. Perhaps the few words which fell from Mr Monk were as strong as any that were spoken. 'He is a man whom I have delighted to call my friend, and I have been happy to think that his services have been at the disposal of his country.'

Sir Gregory Grogram replied. It seemed to him that the evidence was as he had left it. It would be for the jury to decide, under such directions as his lordship might be pleased to give them, how far that evidence brought the guilt home to the prisoner. He would use no rhetoric in pursuing the case against the prisoner. It was late in the afternoon when Sir Gregory had finished his speech, and the judge's charge was reserved for a sixth day.

On the following morning it was observed that before the judges took their seats Mr Chaffanbrass entred the court with a manner much more brisk than was expected from him now that his own work was done. Mr Chaffanbrass was on his feet before the Chief Justice had taken his seat, but the judge was the first to speak. 'I am informed, Mr Chaffanbrass, that you wish to address the court before I begin my charge.'

'Yes, my lud; and I am afraid, my lud, that I shall have to ask your ludship to delay your charge for some days—either to do that or to call upon the jury to acquit the prisoner. I venture to assert that no jury can convict the prisoner after hearing me read that which I hold in my hand.

'This telegram has reached us only this morning,' continued Mr Chaffanbrass. ' "Mealyus had a house door-key made in Prague. We have the mould in our possession, and will bring the man who made the key to England." Now, my lud, the case in the hands of the police, as against this man Mealyus, or Emilius, broke down altogether on the presumption that he could not have let himself in and out of the house in which he had put himself to bed on the night of the murder. We now propose to prove that he had prepared himself with the means of doing so, and had done so after a fashion which is conclusive as to his having required the key for some guilty purpose. We assert that your ludship cannot allow the case to go to the jury without taking cognizance of this telegram; and we go further, and say that those twelve men, as twelve human beings, with hearts in their bosoms and ordinary intelligence at their command, cannot ignore the message, even should your ludship insist upon their doing so with all the energy at your disposal.'

Then there was a scene in court, and out spoke the foreman of the jury. Was it proposed that they should be locked up till somebody should come from Prague, and that then the trial should be recommenced? Then a most irregular word was spoken. One of the jurymen declared that he was quite willing to believe the telegram. 'Everyone believes it,' said Mr Chaffanbrass. Then the Chief Justice scolded the juryman, and Sir Gregory Grogram scolded Mr Chaffanbrass. It seemed as though all the rules of the court were to be set at defiance. Everybody was talking.

Something, however, must be done. The Chief Justice was of opinion that the jury were entitled to have before them the facts now tendered in evidence before they could be called upon to give a verdict, and that therefore they should submit themselves in the service of their country to the very serious additional inconvenience which they would be called upon to endure. He accordingly adjourned the proceedings for one week.

The trial had been adjourned on Wednesday, the 24th of June. Madame Goesler reached London on the Sunday morning, and on the Monday the whole affair respecting the key was unravelled in the presence of the Attorney-General, and with the personal assistance of Major Mackintosh. Without a doubt the man Mealyus had caused to be made for him in Prague a key which would open the door of the house in Northumberland Street. A key was made in London from the model now brought which did open the door. The Attorney-General seemed to think that it would be his duty to ask the judge to call upon the jury to acquit Phineas Finn, and that then the matter must rest for ever, unless further evidence could be obtained against Yosef Mealyus. It would not be possible to hang a man for murder simply because he had fabricated a key. There was no tittle of evidence to show that he had actually been out of the house on that night.

On the Tuesday another discovery was made more wonderful than that of the key. A little boy was seen playing in one of those gardens through which the passage runs with a short loaded bludgeon in his hand. Luckily it attracted attention, and his little lordship took two gardeners and a coachman and all the nurses to the very spot at which he found it. Before an hour was over he was standing at his father's knee, detailing the fact with great open eyes to two policemen, having by this time become immensely proud of his adventure. The instrument was submitted to persons experienced in such matters, and it was declared on all sides that the thing was not of English manufacture.

Mealyus was confronted with the weapon in the presence of Major Mackintosh. He took the thing in his hand.

'You don't know anything about it, Mr Mealyus?' said one of the policemen present, looking closely into his face. 'Of course you need not criminate yourself.'

'What should I know about it? I never had such a stick, or, as I believe, saw one before.' He did it very well, but he could not keep the blood from rising to his cheeks. The policemen were sure that he was the murderer—but what could they do?

On the Wednesday morning Phineas Finn was again brought into the court, and again placed in the dock. There was a general feeling that he should not again have been so disgraced. When he was brought up the steps into the dock after the judges had taken their seats there was almost a shout of applause. The crier was very angry, and gave it to be understood that everybody would be arrested unless everybody was silent; but the Chief Justice said not a word.

Phineas himself was pale and haggard. It was observed that he leaned forward on the rail of the dock all the day, not standing upright as he had done before; and they who watched him closely said that he never once raised his eyes on this day to meet those of the men opposite to him on the bench, although heretofore throughout the trial he had stood with his face raised.

Mr Chaffanbrass, rising in his place, proceeded at once to the details about the key and the bludgeon. He concluded with a little speech—with which he took up the greatest part of an hour, amounting to his confident assertion that there was not a single person in the court who was not now convinced of the innocence of his client. When Mr Chaffanbrass sat down the Attorney-General waived any right of further reply.

It was half-past three when the judge began his charge. It occupied four hours of which by far the greater part was taken up in recapitulating and sifting evidence. 'Gentlemen,' he said at last, 'I think you will find no difficulty in acquitting the prisoner of the murder laid to his charge,' whereupon the jurymen put their heads together, and the foreman, without half a minute's delay, declared that they were unanimous, and that they found the prisoner Not Guilty. 'And we are of opinion,' said the foreman, 'that Mr Finn should not have been put upon his trial on such evidence as has been brought before us.'

And Phineas was discharged. When he was led down from the dock he hardly knew whither he was being taken, and found himself in a small room attached to the court. He made an effort to carry himself with his ordinary tranquillity. 'It will be all right now, I dare say,' he said. 'I wonder whether I could have a glass of water.'

He sat down while the water was brought to him. Then Lord Cantrip made his way into the room. 'My friend,' said he, 'the bitter day has passed over you, and I hope that the bitterness will soon pass away also.' Phineas attempted to smile as he held the hand of the man with whom he had formerly been associated in office. 'I am requested by Mr Gresham to express to you his entire sympathy, and his joy that all this is at last over.' Phineas tried to make some little speech, but utterly failed.

Then there was a question asked as to what he would do. 'I think I'll go to my—own room—in Marlborough Street.' And to that resolution he adhered. And then at last he was alone. He stood up in the middle of the room, stretching forth his hands. Could it be that the last week had been real— that everything had not been a dream? Had he in truth been suspected of a murder and tried for his life?

And now what should be his future life? One thing seemed certain to him. He had been so hacked and hewed about, so exposed to the gaze of the vulgar, so mauled by the public, that he could never more be anything but the wretched being who had been tried for the murder of his enemy. The pith had been taken out of him, and he was no longer a man fit for use. He could never more enjoy that freedom from self-consciousness, that inner tranquillity of spirit, which are essential to public utility. Then he remembered certain lines which had long been familiar to him, and he repeated them aloud, with some conceit that they were apposite to him:

> The true gods sigh for the cost and pain,
> For the reed that grows never more again
> As a reed with the reeds in the river.

He tried to make out for himself some other plan for his future life—but, interspersed with any idea that he could weave, were the figures of two women. Lady Laura Kennedy and Madame Max Goesler. The former could be nothing to him but a friend; and though no other friend would love him as she loved him, yet she could not influence his life. She was very wealthy, but her wealth could be nothing to him. She would heap it all upon him if he would take it. He understood and knew that. Taking no pride to himself that it was so, feeling no conceit in his love, he was conscious of her devotion to him—yet could her devotion avail him nothing!

But how might it be with that other woman? Were she, after all that had passed between them, to consent to be his wife—and it might be that she would consent—how would the world be with him then? He would be known as Madame Goesler's husband, and have to sit at the bottom of her table, and be talked of as the man who had been tried for the murder of Mr Bonteen. Look at it in which way he might, he thought that no life could any longer be possible to him in London.

Ten days passed by, and Phineas Finn had not been out of his lodgings till after daylight, and then he only prowled about and saw no one, even in his own room, but two or three of his most intimate friends. Among those, Lord Chiltern, Barrington Erle and Mr Monk. To Madame Goesler he had written a letter of thanks—a letter which had in truth cost him some pains. 'I know,' he said, 'for how much I have to thank you, but I do not know in what words to do it. I ought

313

to be with you telling you in person of my gratitude; but I must own to you that for the present what has occurred has so unmanned me that I am unfit for the interview. I should only weep in your presence like a school-girl, and you would despise me.' Her answer to him was very short.

My dear Mr Finn,

I can well understand that for a while you should be too agitated by what has passed to see your friends. Remember, however, that you owe it to them as well as to yourself not to sink into seclusion. Send me a line when you think that you can come to me that I may be at home.

Most sincerely yours,

M.M.G.

His friends who did see him urged him constantly to bestir himself. Lord Chiltern was especially urgent with him to return to his usual mode of life, telling him plainly that he was weak and womanly—or rather that he would be were he to continue to dread the faces of his fellow-creatures.

'When I used to look at you in the dock, by heaven I envied you your pluck and strength,' he told him.

'I was burning up the stock of coals, Chiltern.'

'You'll come all right after a few weeks. You've been knocked out of time—that's the truth of it.'

Mr Monk came to him often, pressing him very much to come down to the House. 'I have made up my mind to one thing,' Phineas said to him at the end of the ten days.

'And what is the one thing?'

'I will give up my seat.'

'I do not see a shadow of a reason for it.'

'Nevertheless I will do it. There may be and probably are men down at Tankerville who still think that I am guilty. There is an offensiveness in murder which degrades a man even by the accusation.'

'No doubt there will be expressions of great regret, and my belief is that they will return you again.'

'If so, they'll have to do it without my presence.'

And within a fortnight of his restoration to liberty Phineas

Finn was no longer a Member of Parliament. Both Mr Gresham and Mr Daubeny expressed their regret in the House, and Mr Monk said a few words respecting his friend, which were very touching. He ended by expressing a hope that they soon might see him there again, and an opinion that he was a man peculiarly fitted by the tone of his mind, and the nature of his intellect, for the duties of Parliament.

Then at last, when all this had been settled, he went to Lord Brentford's house in Portman Square. Lady Laura was at home. In those days she never went into society.

'Oh, Phineas, I am so glad you have come. So you have given up your seat.'

'Yes, I am no longer a Member of Parliament.'

'Barrington says that they will certainly re-elect you.'

'We shall see. You may be sure at any rate of this, that I shall never ask them to do so. What does it matter who sits in Parliament? The fight goes on just the same. The same falsehoods are acted. The same mock truths are spoken. The same wrong reasons are given. The same personal motives are at work.'

'And yet, of all believers in Parliament, you used to be the most faithful.'

'One has time to think of things, Lady Laura, when one lies in Newgate. It seems to me to be an eternity of time since they locked me up. And as for that trial, which they tell me lasted a week, I look back at it till the beginning is so distant that I can hardly remember it. But I have resolved that I will never talk of it again. And you? What will you do?'

'I cannot say. They seem to think that I should live at Loughlinter; but I cannot live there alone.'

He soon took his leave of her, and did so with no warmer expressions of regard. Then he crept back to his lodgings, and she sat weeping alone in her father's house. When he had come to her during her husband's lifetime it had been better than this.

.   .   .   .   .

A deputation of Tankerville electors waited upon Phineas two days after his resignation.

'You'll miss the House if you give it up; you will, after a bit, Mr Finn,' he was assured. 'You've got to come round again, Mr Finn, and you shouldn't put yourself out of the way of coming round comfortably.'

Phineas knew that there was wisdom in the words. Though at this moment he was low in heart, disgusted with the world, and sick of humanity, yet he knew that it would not be so with him always. As others recovered so would he, and it might be that he would live to 'miss the House', should he now refuse the offer made to him. He accepted the offer.

So Phineas Finn was re-elected for Tankerville without opposition and without expense. For six weeks after the ceremony parcels were showered upon him by the ladies of the borough who sent him worked slippers, scarlet hunting waistcoats, pocket handkerchiefs, with 'P.F.' beautifully embroidered, and chains made of their own hair; and even Mr Quintus Slide and *The People's Banner* were compelled to trim their sails and join in the general satisfaction.

The interest in the murder by no means came to an end when Phineas Finn was acquitted. The new facts which served so thoroughly to prove him innocent tended with almost equal weight to prove another man guilty. And the other man was already in custody on a charge which had subjected him to the peculiar ill-will of the British public. He, a foreigner, by name Yosef Mealyus—as everyone was now very careful to call him —had come to England, had got himself to be ordained as a clergyman, and had married a rich wife with a title, although he had a former wife still living in his own country. There certainly did exist also a strong desire to prove Mr Emilius to have been a murderer, so that there might come a fitting termination to his career in Great Britain.

The police seemed to think that they could make but little capital, if any, out of the key—unless other evidence should be found. No doubt Mr Bonteen had been his enemy, but so great had been the man's luck that no real evidence seemed to touch him. In the meantime the trial for bigamy proceeded, and before the end of July he was convicted and sentenced to penal servitude for five years. All this happened in the middle of the efforts which were being made to trace the purchase of the bludgeon. They did not succeed; and the Bonteen murder has remained one of those crimes which are unavenged by the law.

Lizzie Eustace still had her income almost untouched. And she had her title, and her castle down in Ayrshire. Nor had she done anything which of itself must necessarily have put her out of the pale of society. As a married woman she had had no lovers; and, when a widow, very little fault in that line had been brought home against her. While it was thought that Phineas Finn had committed the murder, with Mrs Bonteen she had remained. But it was impossible that the arrangement should be continued when it became known—for it was known—that Mr Bonteen had been murdered by the man who had been Lizzie's reputed husband.

She went forth into lodgings in Half Moon Street, and was once more alone in the world. She had a child indeed, the son of her first husband, but such had been Lizzie's manner of life that neither her own relations nor those of her husband could put up with her. And yet she was conscious of no special sins, and regarded herself as one who, with a tender heart of her own and a too-confiding spirit, had been much injured by the cruelty of those with whom she had been thrown. Now she was alone, pitying herself with deepest compassion; but it never occurred to her that there was anything in her conduct that she need alter. She would still continue to play her game as before, would still scheme, would still lie; and might still, at last, land herself in that Elysium of life of which she had been always dreaming. Was it nature or education which had made it impossible to her to tell the truth, when a lie came to her hand? Lizzie, the liar! Poor Lizzie!

.   .   .   .   .

It was Mr Monk who at last drew from Phineas a promise that he would go down to the House and be sworn in early on a certain Tuesday afternoon. 'I am quite sure of this,' Mr

Monk had said, 'that the sooner you do it the less will be the annoyance.'

There were not a dozen Members present, and the speaker had not as yet taken the chair. Mr Monk stood by him while he took the oath, and in two minutes he was on a back seat below the gangway, with his friend by him, while the Members, in slowly increasing numbers, took their seats. One or two shook hands with him, but no one said a word to him of the trial, and after half an hour he almost ceased to be afraid.

'It wasn't so bad after all,' said Mr Monk.

'Perhaps not. I'll endeavour to get the matter off my mind. I will resolve, at any rate, that nothing shall make me talk about it any more.'

For about a week Phineas attended Parliament and then prepared to journey down to Matching Priory, in response to the often-repeated invitation of the Duchess of Omnium. He knew that Madame Goesler would be at Matching. But how should he meet her, and in what way should he greet her when they met?

When Phineas entered the hall at Matching he was at once ushered by a silent man in black into the little sitting-room on the ground floor in which the old Duke used to take delight. Here he found two ladies waiting to receive him. The Duchess came forward to welcome him, while Madame Goesler remained in the background, with composed face. 'Yes, there she is,' said the Duchess, laughing. She had already told him that he was welcome to Matching, and had spoken some short word of congratulation at his safe deliverance from his troubles. 'If ever one friend was grateful to another, you should be grateful to her, Mr Finn.' He did not speak, but walking across the room to the window by which Marie Goesler stood, took her right hand in his, and passing his left arm round her waist, kissed her first on one cheek and then on the other. The blood flew to her face and suffused her forehead, but she did not speak, or resist him or make any effort to escape from his embrace. As for him, he had no thought of it at all. No idea of kissing her when they should meet had occurred to him till the moment came. 'Excellently well done,' said the Duchess, still laughing with silent pleasant laughter. 'And now tell us how you are, after all your troubles.'

Throughout that whole evening he was unable to speak to Madame Goesler, but to the other people around him he found himself talking quite at his ease, as though nothing peculiar had happened to him. Almost everybody, except the Duke of Omnium, made some slight allusion to his adventure, and he, in spite of his resolution, found himself driven to talk of it. A few days ago he had thought that these allusions would kill him; but now he smiled and chatted, and was quiet and at ease.

'Good night, Mr Finn,' the Duchess said to him, 'I know the people have been boring you.'

'Everybody has treated me very well,' said Phineas.

'We—that is, Marie and I, you know—thought it would be the best thing for you to come down and get through it all here. We could see that you weren't driven too hard. By the by, you have hardly seen her—have you?'

'Hardly, since I was upstairs with your Grace.'

'My Grace will manage better for you in due course. I didn't like to tell you to take her out to dinner, because it would have looked a little particular after her very remarkable journey to Prague. If you ain't grateful you must be a wretch.'

'But I am grateful.'

'Well; we shall see. Good night. You'll find a lot of men going to smoke somewhere, I don't doubt.'

When Phineas Finn had been about a week at Matching, he received a very short note, from the Prime Minister, asking him to go up to London. He arrived in town in the evening, and his appointment with Mr Gresham was for the following morning. The great man received him with an excellent courtesy. He began by making a little speech about Mr Bonteen. That was almost unavoidable. And he praised in glowing words the attitude which Phineas had maintained during the trial. He had been delighted with the re-election at Tankerville, and thought that the borough had done itself much honour. Then came forth his proposition. Lord Fawn had retired, and the office of Under-Secretary for the Colonies, which Phineas had before held, was there for his acceptance. Mr Gresham went on to express his ardent hope that he might have the benefit of Mr Finn's services.

Phineas had come primed with his answer. 'I hope, Mr Gresham, that you will be able to give me a few hours to think of this.' Mr Gresham's face fell.

'I had hoped that the office was one which you would like.'

'So it is, Mr Gresham.'

'And I was told that you are now free from any political scruples which might make it difficult for you to support the Government.'

'Since the Government came to our way of thinking, a year or two ago—about Tenant Right, I mean—I do not know that there is any subject on which I am likely to oppose it. Perhaps I had better tell you the truth, Mr Gresham.'

'Oh, certainly,' said the Prime Minister.

'When you came into office, after beating Mr Daubeny on the Church question, no man in Parliament was more desirous of place than I was. It was aggravated by various circumstances—by calumnies in newspapers, and by personal bickerings. I need not go into that wretched story. These things have changed me very much. I have a feeling that I have been ill-used—not by you, Mr Gresham, but by the party; and I look upon the whole question of office with altered eyes.'

'In filling up the places at his disposal, a Prime Minister, Mr Finn, has a most unenviable task.'

'I can well believe it.'

'We shall neither of us get on by complaining, shall we, Mr Finn? You can let me have an answer perhaps by this time tomorrow.'

'If an answer by telegraph will be sufficient.'

'Quite sufficient. Yes or No. Nothing more will be wanted. You understand your own reasons, no doubt. Good morning.'

As he took his ticket back to Matching Phineas sent his message to the Prime Minister, taking that personage literally at his word. The message was, No. When he reached Matching it was already known that he had refused to accept Mr Gresham's offer, and he was met at once with regrets and condolements. 'I am sorry that it must be so,' said the Duke.

'You are still young, and will have further opportunities,' said Lord Cantrip.

'So you have decided for freedom?' said Madame Goesler that evening.

'Now that it is done, of course I am full of regrets,' said Phineas.

'That is simple human nature, I suppose.'

'Simple enough. The thing was offered to me not because I was thought to be fit for it, but because I had become wonderful by being brought near to a violent death!'

'Do you think that public life then is altogether a mistake, Mr Finn?'

'For a poor man it is, in this country. A man of fortune may be independent; and because he has the power of independence those who are higher than he will not expect him to be subservient. A man who takes to parliamentary office for a living may live by it, but he will have but a dog's life of it.'

'If I were you, Mr Finn, I certainly would not choose a dog's life.'

He said not a word to her on that occasion about herself. There had been talk of love between them before, on which occasion he had been compelled to tell her that he could not accept that which she offered to him. His feelings now were altogether changed, and why should not the feelings of Madame Goesler have undergone a similar change? In spite of her friendship would not revenge be dear to her—revenge of that nature which a slighted woman must always desire? He lay awake for many hours that night, thinking of it.

At a little before noon the next morning he knocked at her door, and was told to enter.

'I have come . . .'

'I know why you have come.'

'I doubt that. I have come to tell you that I love you.'

'Oh, Phineas—at last, at last!' And in a moment she was in his arms.

It seemed to him that from that moment all the explanations, and all the statements, and most of the assurances were made by her and not by him. After this first embrace he found

321

himself seated beside her, holding her hand. 'I do not know that I am right,' said he.

'Why not right?'

'Because you are rich and I have nothing.'

'If you ever remind me of that again I will strike you,' she said, raising up her little fist and bringing it down with gentle pressure on his shoulder. 'Between you and me there must be nothing more about that. It must be an even partnership. There must be ever so much about money, and you'll have to go into dreadful details, and make journeys to Vienna to see that the houses don't tumble down; but there must be no questions between you and me of whence it came.'

'You will not think that I have to come to you for that?'

'I know you love me. But, Phineas, I have not been sure till very lately that you would ever tell me so. As for me . . . ! Oh, heavens! when I think of it.'

'Tell me that you love me now.'

'I have never ceased to love you since I first knew you well enough for love. And you are the only man I ever loved. My husband was very good to me—and I was, I think, good to him. But he was many years my senior, and I cannot say I loved him, as I do you.' Then she turned to him, and put her head on his shoulder.

At half-past twelve the door was opened and the Duchess entered the room. 'Oh dear!' she exclaimed. 'Shall I retire?'

Madame Goesler rose from her seat. 'It's only a trifle. Mr Finn has asked me to be his wife.'

'Well?'

'I couldn't refuse Mr Finn a little thing like that.'

'I should think not, after going all the way to Prague to find a latch-key! I congratulate you, Mr Finn, with all my heart.'

'Thanks, Duchess.'

Before dinner on that day every one of the guests at Matching Priory knew that the man who had refused to be made Under-Secretary of State had been accepted by that possessor of fabulous wealth who was well known to the world as Madame Goesler of Park Lane.

The marriage did not take place till October, and then

322

they went abroad for the greater part of the winter, Phineas having received leave of absence officially from the Speaker and unofficially from his constituents. They went first to Vienna, and then back into Italy, and were unheard of by their English friends for nearly six months. In April they reappeared in London, and the house in Park Lane was opened with great *éclat*. Of Phineas everyone says that of all living men he has been the most fortunate.

The Prime Minister

CHAPTER ONE

IT was admitted that Ferdinand Lopez was a 'gentleman'. It was not generally believed that Ferdinand Lopez was well born. He had been at a good English private school. At the age of seventeen he had been sent to a German University, and at the age of twenty-one had appeared in a London stockbroker's office, where he was soon known as a very clever fellow, but having a taste for being a master rather than a servant. He was soon believed to be making a fortune. Then it was supposed that he had lost all that he had ever made or possessed. But not even his bankers or his lawyer really knew the state of his affairs.

He was certainly handsome; nearly six feet tall, very dark, very thin, with well-cut features indicating the great gift of self-possession. He wore an absolutely black moustache, and his teeth were perfect in form and whiteness. He dressed with perfect care. It was known to some few that he occupied rooms in Westminster—but to very few exactly where the rooms were. In a moderate way he was given to hospitality, but some club, tavern, or in the summer, some river bank would be chosen as the scene of these festivities.

A great portion of the London world was out of town taking its Easter holiday, when Ferdinand Lopez walked into a dingy little court called Little Tankard Yard, and into a little office in which there sat a greasy gentleman about forty years old. This was Mr Sextus Parker—commonly called Sexty Parker —well known on the Stock Exchange. 'What, Lopez!' said he. 'Uncommon glad to see you. What can I do for you?'

'I'll tell you what I want you to do. I want your name to this bill for £750 for three months.'

'Accommodation bill!' said Sexty. 'Why, you ain't hard up, are you?'

'I happen to have taken a share in a loan a little beyond my immediate means, and therefore want a few hundreds. If you ain't afraid about it, just sign it.'

'Oh, I ain't afraid,' said Sexty, writing his name across the bill.

'You've nothing to make and nothing to lose by this. Good day and many thanks.' Then Ferdinand Lopez took his departure and Sexty Parker was left alone in his bewilderment.

That same day Lopez dined with his friend Everett Wharton at the Progress Club, of which they were both members. The Progress had intended to do great things for the Liberal party. It had been believed that through this institution men of genius and spirit, but without wealth, would be supplied with sure seats in Parliament. But no such results had been achieved.

'For myself,' said Lopez, 'I can conceive no vainer object or ambition than a seat in the British Parliament. But if you want to get in why don't you arrange it with your father?'

'My father wouldn't pay a shilling for such a purpose.'

Everett Wharton was a trouble to his father. He was a good-looking, manly fellow, six feet high, with broad shoulders, with light hair, wearing a large silky bushy beard. Six months had taught him that banking was 'an abomination'. At twenty-five he had found that the Stock Exchange was the mart for such talents as he possessed; but at six-and-twenty the Stock Exchange was also abandoned; and now, at eight-and-twenty, Everett Wharton had discovered that a parliamentary career was that for which his genius had intended him. He had all that refers to unions, strikes, and lock-outs quite at his fingers' ends. He knew how the Church of England should be disestablished and recomposed. In the meantime he could never contrive to pay his tailor's bill regularly out of the allowance of £400 a year which his father made him.

The father did in truth give his offspring credit for greater talent than he possessed. And Everett was very dear also to a sister, Emily. Now Lopez aspired to the hand of that sister. Of her regard he had already thought himself nearly sure. Of the father's sanction to such a marriage he had reason to be more than doubtful. But the brother was his friend.

They strolled out of the club together, a little after ten o'clock. 'I wish I could make out your father more clearly,' Lopez said.

'You have dined three times within the last three months in Manchester Square.'

'Nevertheless, he looks upon me as a friend of yours rather than his own. I don't suppose he ever said a word in my favour in my absence.'

'He says he knows nothing about you.'

'Oh, that's it, is it? When next he says so ask him of how many of the men who dine at his house he can say as much. I can tell you this—if between us we can manage to handle him rightly, you may get your seat in Parliament and I may get my wife; that is, of course, if she will have me.'

Mr Abel Wharton had for a great many years been a barrister practising in the Equity Courts, and had amassed a large fortune. His wife had now been two years dead. He had been nearly fifty when his daughter was born. He was a spare, strongly made man, with spare light brown hair, hardly yet grizzled, with small grey whiskers, clear eyes, bushy eyebrows, and with considerable vehemence of talk when he was opposed. He was a man of whom men were generally afraid.

At about noon on the day following that on which Lopez had dined with Everett Wharton he was shown into the lawyer's room.

'How do you do, sir?' said Mr Wharton. 'I hope I see you well, sir.' His tone and manner were very cold. 'Is there anything I can do for you?'

Ferdinand Lopez made his plunge. 'Mr Wharton, I have taken the liberty to call upon you because I want to speak to you about your daughter.'

'About my daughter!'

'Yes, sir. Having ventured to entertain a hope I have thought it best to come to you at once.'

'Does she know anything of this?'

'Of my visit to you? Nothing.'

'Of your intentions—your preference for her.'

329

'I have endeavoured to commend myself to your daughter, but I have never spoken a word of love to her.'

'Does Everett know of all this?'

'Yes. He would not I think object to call me his brother.'

'Mr Lopez,' said the old lawyer, 'you must forgive me if I say that I should wish to see my daughter marry not only in my own sphere but with someone of my own class. I don't know who your father was—whether he was an Englishman, whether he was a Christian—and I know nothing of your means.'

'My father was a Portuguese. My mother was an English lady. I was an orphan before I understood what it was to have a parent.'

'I do not know what your profession is.'

'I am engaged in foreign loans.'

'Very precarious I should think.'

'It is the business by which many of the greatest mercantile houses in the city have been made.'

'And by which many come to ruin. I ain't sure that I wish to marry my daughter in the City. I have always been for absolute toleration in matters of religion—have always advocated admission of Roman Catholics and Jews into Parliament, and even to the bench . . .'

'I have always belonged to the Church of England,' said Ferdinand Lopez.

'Lopez is a bad name to go to a Protestant church with, and I don't want my daughter to bear it. I am very frank with you. Marrying into a family is a very serious thing indeed.'

'No man feels that more strongly than I do, Mr Wharton.'

'There had better be an end of it.'

'I wish you would give me a reason.'

'Because you are not English. It doesn't suit my ideas. I suppose I may have my own ideas about my own family, Mr Lopez? Good morning to you, sir. If I have said anything that has seemed to be unkind put it down to my anxiety as a father and not to my conduct as a man.' Then the door was closed behind his visitor. Mr Wharton was by no means satisfied with himself. He felt that he had been rude and at the same time not decisive. Then he remembered that sooner or later his girl would have at least £60,000, a fact of which no one but himself was aware. How would it be with him if he should find that the girl was really in love with this swarthy foreigner?

After dinner that evening Everett departed to his club, leaving his father and sister alone. Mr Wharton at once began. 'Emily, my dear, do you know what I am going to speak to you about?'

'Yes, Papa; I think it is about—Mr Lopez.'

'Your brother has told you, I suppose. Yes; it is about Mr Lopez. I have been very much astonished today by Mr Lopez.'

'Why, Papa?'

'Because he is a stranger and a foreigner. Would you have wished me to encourage him?'

'Yes, Papa. Papa, I love him.'

'Emily, it must not be.'

'Why not, Papa?'

'He is a foreigner. He has no relatives, no family. He is what we call an adventurer. You have made him no promise?'

'Oh no, Papa.'

'Nor spoken to him of your regard for him?'

'Not a word. Nor he to me—except in such words as one understands even though they say nothing.'

'I wish he had never seen you.'

'Is he a bad man, Papa?'

'Who knows? How is one to know whether a man be bad or good when one knows nothing about him?'

'You know, Papa, that I trust you,' she said. 'If you tell me that I am not to see him, I shall not see him. But I shall be very unhappy. I shall never love anyone else in the same way.'

'That is nonsense, Emily. There is Arthur Fletcher.'

'I am sure you will never ask me to marry a man I do not love, and I shall never love Arthur Fletcher. I think you should inquire about Mr Lopez, Papa, and be quite certain before you pronounce such a sentence against me. I am sure you believe me when I promise not to see him without your permission.'

'Of course I believe you.'

'But if I do that for you, Papa, I think that you ought to

be very sure, on my account, that I haven't to bear such un-happiness for nothing. Good night, now, Papa. You will think about it?'

'I will. Of course I will.'

And he began the process of thinking about it immediately. But he already began to fear that he lacked the power to steel his heart against his daughter.

.   .   .   .

'And what are they going to make you now?'

This question was asked of her husband by the Duchess of Omnium. Just at this time the political affairs of the nation had got themselves tied up into truly desperate knots. The heads of parties were at a standstill. Mr Daubeny, the Conservative, had been in power—was in power though he had resigned. But a Prime Minister cannot escape till he has succeeded in finding a successor who consents to make an attempt and succeeds in that attempt.

The Duke did not answer his wife's question in his usual manner. He would customarily smile gently at her badinage, and perhaps say a word intended to show that he was not in the least moved by her raillery. But in this instance he was very grave, and stood before her a moment making no answer at all.

'What is it, Plantagenet?' she exclaimed.

'I have received her Majesty's orders to go down to Windsor at once. I must start within half-an-hour.'

'You are going to be Prime Minister!' As she spoke she threw her arms up and then rushed into his embrace. Never since their first union had she been so demonstrative either of love or admiration.

'Stop a moment, Cora. I do not know how it may be yet. But this I know, that if I could avoid this task, I would certainly avoid it. I doubt whether I have any gift for governing men.'

'It will come.'

'I shall make the attempt if I am directed to do so.' Then he took his departure before she could say another word.

332

At about nine the Duke returned. 'I have told her Majesty that I would do the best I could,' he said.

'Then you are Prime Minister.'

'I have undertaken to form a Coalition Ministry, if I find it practicable. I never felt before that I had to lean so entirely on others as I do now. My own efficacy for the task depends on the co-operation of others, and unfortunately upon some others with whom I have no sympathy, nor have they with me.'

'Leave them out,' said the Duchess boldly.

'But they are men whose services the country has a right to expect.'

'Then bring them in, and think no more about it. It is no good crying for pain that cannot be cured.'

By the time the Easter holidays were over, the work of getting a team together had been accomplished. The work in Parliament began under the new auspices with great tranquillity. 'I have appointed a friend of yours,' the Duke said to his wife one evening.

'What friend?'

'Mr Finn is to go to Ireland.'

'You don't mean as Chief Secretary?'

'Yes, I do. Not in the Cabinet, though.'

It may be a question whether on the whole the Duchess did not work harder than he did in those first weeks. She set herself to work after her own fashion, arranging dinners and evening receptions, so that within six weeks all the world had begun to talk of the receptions given by the Prime Minister's wife. There were people who complained that she had everybody; that there was no selection whatever as to politics, principles, rank, morals—or even manners.

There had been a business deputation from the City to the Prime Minister and Lopez had contrived to be one of the number. He had contrived also to say a word on his own account to the Minister. The Duke had remembered him, and had suggested that he should have a card. And now he was among the flowers and greatness, the beauty, the politics, and the fashion of the Duchess's gatherings for the third time.

'This is fairyland,' said Lopez to the Duchess.

She answered, very graciously, 'We are always on the wing about this hour on Wednesday night.' The words contained a general invitation for the season. She would have said, if interrogated, that she had taken the man up in obedience to her husband. But in truth she had liked the look and the voice of the man.

CHAPTER TWO

MR WHARTON heard from his son of the man's attendance at the Duchess of Omnium's parties, and this troubled him. If the man did live with the great and wealthy it must be because they thought well of him. He could hardly maintain his opposition to one of whom the choice spirits of the world thought well. But it was wonderful to him that his girl should like such a man well enough to choose him as the one companion of her life. She had been brought up to prefer English men, and English thinking, and English ways.

It was now July, and the custom of the family was that the house in Manchester Square should be left for two months. They were, as usual, expected at Wharton Hall, the handsome old family place on the Wye in Herefordshire of his baronet cousin, Sir Alured Wharton, where, her father reflected with relief and hope, Emily would be likely to be thrown into the society of Arthur Fletcher.

Arthur Fletcher was the second brother of a Herefordshire squire with whom he lived at Longbarns, a large property some twelve miles from Wharton Hall. Almost since they were children he had been known to be in love with Emily Wharton. Though born to comfortable circumstances he had worked so hard as to have already made for himself a name at the bar. He was a fair-haired, handsome fellow; and yet

Emily Wharton, in the way of love, would have nothing to say to him, preferring—as her father once said in his extremest wrath—a greasy adventurer out of the gutter!

About a week before the departure of the Whartons for Herefordshire, Lopez called at the chambers of Mr Wharton.

'Well, Mr Lopez, what can I do for you?' The more he looked at the man the less he liked him.

'There is only one thing you can do for me.'

'Then I do not think that I can do anything for you, Mr Lopez. Did I not explain myself before?'

'I was not able to say then, as I can say now, that your daughter has accepted my love.'

'You ought not to have spoken to my daughter on the subject after what passed between us.'

'Before I directly asked her for her love, I came to you.'

'What's the use of that, if you go to her immediately afterwards in manifest opposition to my wishes? I will not give her my consent to become your wife.'

'I think it no more than honest, Mr Wharton, to declare that I regard myself as irrevocably engaged to your daughter; and she is, I am certain, as firmly fixed in her choice as I am in mine. Her happiness must be much to you.'

'It is everything.' Then he rang the bell and Lopez went his way.

.   .   .   .   .

'What do you think of Ferdinand Lopez?' asked the Duchess of her husband one day with studied abruptness.

'Why should I think of him?'

'I want you to think of him. I think he's a very pleasant fellow, and I'm sure he's a rising man. I suppose it's true that Mr Grey is going on this mission to Persia?' Mr Grey was at this time Member for the neighbouring borough of Silverbridge.

'He is to go after Christmas. I think he will give up his seat, though I think it is unnecessary.'

'Let Mr Lopez have it.'

'Mr Lopez!'

'Yes; he is a clever man who will be of use to you. You Ministers go on shuffling the old cards till they are so worn out that one can hardly tell the pips on them.'

'I am one of the old cards myself.'

'A man who is at the head of affairs can't be included among the pack. What you want is new blood. Take my advice and try this man.'

'But I do not know what may be the worth of Mr Lopez.'

'I will guarantee that,' said the Duchess. Whereupon the Duke laughed, and then left her.

On that same day she again encountered Mr Lopez at one of her receptions.

'You have never been in Parliament, I think,' said the Duchess.

'I have never even tried to get there.'

'Then why don't you try it?'

'I suppose I shall try to get into Parliament some day. Seats in Parliament don't grow like blackberries on bushes.'

'Pretty nearly,' said the Duchess.

'Are you alluding to anything?'

'Well—yes, I am. But I do not like to do more than allude. I fancy that Mr Grey, the Member for Silverbridge, is going to Persia. Therefore, Mr Grey will cease to be Member for Silverbridge. That's logic; isn't it?'

'Has your Grace any logic equally strong to prove that I can follow him in the borough?'

'No—or if I have it must for the present be kept to myself.' She certainly had a little syllogism in her head as to the Duke ruling the borough, the Duke's wife ruling the Duke, and therefore the Duke's wife ruling the borough; but she did not think it prudent to utter this on the present occasion. 'I think it much better that men in Parliament should be unmarried,' said the Duchess.

'But I am going to be married,' said he.

'Going to be married, are you?'

'I have no right to say so, because the lady's father has rejected me.' Then he told her the whole story.

'And why does the rich barrister object?' she asked.

'The rich barrister, Duchess, is an out-and-out old Tory,

336

who thinks that his daughter ought to marry no one but an English Tory.'

'A man does not hamper his daughter these days by politics.'

'There are other reasons. He does not like a foreigner. Now I am an Englishman, but I have a name so meanly Latin as Lopez.'

'The lady does not object to the Latinity?'

'I fancy not.'

'Or to the bearer of it?'

'Ah, there I must not boast.'

'Then,' said the Duchess, 'the old gentleman may as well give way at once.'

And the old gentleman did give way; if not at once, then in due course. The engagement was made in October, and the marriage took place in the latter part of November. When Lopez pressed for an early day Emily raised no difficulties, and her father gave way again. As the thing was to be done, what was to be gained by delay? Lopez proposed to take his bride into Italy for the winter months, alleging that he must be back in town by the beginning of February; and this was taken as a fair plea for hastening the marriage.

When the matter was settled he managed to interest her Grace in all his proceedings. She promised that she would call on his bride, and even went so far as to send her a costly wedding present.

But there was some delay as to the seat for Silverbridge. The Duke had not made any promise of supporting his wife's favourite. 'Don't set your heart upon it too much, Mr Lopez,' the Duchess said; 'but you may be sure I will not forget you.' Then it had been settled between them that should the vacancy occur during his absence, and should the Duke consent, he would return at once.

There were various little incidents which did not tend to make the happiness of Emily Wharton complete. She had written to her old lover, whose professional duties had, in fact, kept him from meeting her in Herefordshire that summer.

My dear Arthur,

There has been so much true friendship and affection between us that I do not like that you should hear from anyone but myself the news that I am going to be married to Mr Lopez on the 28th of November.

Yours affectionately,

Emily Wharton.

To this she received a very short reply.

Dear Emily,

I am as I always have been,

Yours,

A.F.

When Lopez left London not a word had been said between him and his father-in-law as to money. And this silence certainly suited Ferdinand Lopez. Though he was not absolutely penniless, he was altogether propertyless. He had been speculating in money without capital, and though he had now and again been successful, he had also now and again failed. It was not, therefore, surprising that Ferdinand Lopez should volunteer no statements to the old lawyer about money. He was quite confident that Mr Wharton had the wealth which was supposed to belong to him, and was willing to trust to his power of obtaining a fair portion of it as soon as he should in truth be Mr Wharton's son-in-law. But he did love the girl whom he was about to marry. He was willing to cheat all the world, so that he might make a fortune; but he did not wish to cheat her. It was his ambition now to carry her up with him.

Of course there arose the question where they should live. But he was ready with an immediate answer to this question. He had been to look at apartments in the Belgrave Mansions. When he took Emily to see them old Mr Wharton condescended to go with them. Though his heart was not in the business, still he thought he was bound to look after his daughter's comfort.

'Oh, Ferdinand, are they not too grand?' said Emily.

'You have only to say you don't like them, and you shall never be asked to put your foot in them again.'

'But I do like them.'

And then they were married, then went back to the house in Manchester Square, and within a couple of hours were on their road to Dover. Through it all not a word was said about money. At the last moment, Lopez had hoped that the old man would say something. 'You will find so many thousand pounds at your bankers,' or 'You may look to me for so many hundreds a year.' But there was not a word. The girl had come to him without the assurance of a single shilling. In his great endeavour to get her he had been successful. As he thought of this in the carriage, he pressed his arm close round her waist. If the worst were to come to the worst, he would fight the world for her.

And yet, before he reached Dover, he said, 'I wonder what your father means to do about money? He never told you?'

'Not a word. Does it matter, dear?'

'Not in the least.'

Before he went to the altar, Lopez had made certain arrangements which had caused Sextus Parker to stare with surprise and to sweat with dismay. Bills were drawn to run over to February, and ready money to a moderate extent was forthcoming, and fiscal tranquillity was insured for a certain short period. When he was in Paris he received a letter from Parker: 'Please to bear in mind that I can't and won't arrange for the bills for £1500 due 3rd February.' So it was necessary to him that a considerable sum of money should be extracted from the father-in-law before the end of January. They had hurried on southwards from Paris, and before the end of the first week had passed over the Simplon, and were at a pleasant inn on the shores of Como. Everything in their travels had been as yet delightful to Emily. A husband who is also an eager lover must be delightful to a young bride. And hitherto no lover could have been more tender than Lopez.

'Your father has not written to you since you started?' he said.

'Did you expect him to write?'

'To tell you the truth, I rather did. As, on a certain sub-

339

ject, he never opened his mouth to me, I thought he would write.'

'You want him to give you some money?'

'It would not be unusual, dear. He knows already that I have taken a home for you and paid for it.'

'What do you want me to do?'

'To write to him.'

'And ask him for money?'

'I think you should say that we should be glad to know what he intends to do, also saying that a certain sum of money would at present be of use to me.'

'Would it not be better from you?'

'I would rather you should write, if you do not mind it. Write your own letter, and show it me.'

Emily did not like the idea of telling her father anything which he might not like to hear; but her husband's behests were to her in these, her early married days, quite imperative. Mrs Lopez begged her father to address his reply to her at Florence, where they expected to find themselves within a fortnight. On their arrival at Florence he went at once to the post-office before breakfast, and returned with a letter in his hand. It was very short.

My dear Emily,

What you have said under your husband's instruction about money, I find upon consideration to be fair enough. I will pay £3000 to his account, if he would tell me where he would have it lodged. Then I shall think I have done my duty by him.

Everett is as idle as ever. Everything is very quiet and lonely here.

Your affectionate father,
A. Wharton.

He ate his breakfast in a state of exultation, and talked as though he had the command of almost unlimited means. He ordered a carriage and drove her out, and bought expensive presents for her.

'Shall I write and thank Papa?' she said that evening.

'I have been thinking of that,' he said. 'But I also will write, a post or two before you. As he has come round I suppose I ought to show myself civil. No doubt after a bit he will make permanent arrangements.'

In the first week in February they appeared in Belgrave Mansions, and Emily Lopez took possession of her new home with a heart as full of love for her husband as it had been when she walked out of the church.

CHAPTER THREE

ON his return to London Lopez found a letter waiting for him from the Duchess of Omnium.

My dear Mr Lopez,
We understand that the election will take place in April. No candidate will appear as favoured from hence. We used to run a favourite, and our favourite would sometimes have a walk over; but those good times are gone. There is no reason that I know why you should not stand as well as anyone else. There will be no Gatherum interest, but I fancy it had already leaked out that you would have been the favourite if there had been a favourite, which might be beneficial.

I need hardly say that I do not wish my name to be mentioned in the matter.

Sincerely yours,
Glencora Omnium.

'Shall you try it?' said Emily.
'Nothing venture nothing have. You don't think your father

341

would help me in doing it? It would add almost as much to your position as to mine.'

Emily shook her head. She had always heard her father ridicule the folly of men who spent more than they could afford in the vanity of writing two letters after their name.

'Perhaps I had better address him myself,' he said. 'Then I shall find out whether he really has our interest at heart.'

It was not long before he made the experiment. They dined with Mr Wharton in Manchester Square, and certainly the old man was courteous to Lopez. After dinner the two men were left together. 'I have been invited, sir,' Lopez said with his sweetest smile, 'to stand for Silverbridge.'

'You too!' said Mr Wharton. Then the name of the opposition candidate was mentioned to Lopez. It was Arthur Fletcher! The Fletchers were connected with the De Courcys, and the De Courcy interest had invited that rising barrister to stand for the Conservatives. 'I have beaten him once,' said Lopez to himself, 'and I think I can beat him again.'

Some little time after this, when they had been settled in London about a month, a letter was brought to Emily.

My dear Mrs Lopez,

I find that your husband and I are to be opponents at Silverbridge. I wish to say that I had pledged myself to the borough before I had heard his name as connected with it. I should not, however, have come forward had I known that Mr Lopez was to stand. I think you had better tell him so, and tell him also, with my compliments, that I hope we may fight our political battle with mutual good-fellowship and good-feeling.

Yours very sincerely,
Arthur Fletcher.

Emily was very much pleased by this letter. The moment her husband came in she showed it to him with delight. There came a dark scowl across his brow. 'His writing to you is a piece of infernal impudence. He deserves to be horsewhipped, and if I come across him he shall have it.'

'Oh, Ferdinand!'

'A man who was your rejected lover presuming to commence a correspondence with you!'

'You will not quarrel with him?'

'Certainly I will. I never thought much of these Herefordshire swells.'

But he came and kissed her brow, and she knew that his temper was again smooth. 'I'm going down to Silverbridge in the morning. I shall stay there a day or two and settle when I am to go down for the absolute canvass. I shall have to go with my hat in my hand to every blessed inhabitant in that dirty little town, and ask them all to be kind enough to drop in a paper for the most humble of their servants, Ferdinand Lopez.'

'And the expense?' suggested Emily.

'Oh, ah. When you come to talk of the expense I can't help feeling that I've been a little let in among them. The Duchess first promised me it was to be a simple walk over. Now they go back from that and open the thing to any comer. And then the political committee at the club coolly say that they've got no money. It isn't honest, you know.'

'Oh, Ferdinand,' she said, 'I do so hope you may be successful.'

'If the Castle is true to me. I shall know more about it when I come back.'

Lopez was at Silverbridge for a couple of days, and then returned, as his wife thought, by no means confident of success. He remained in town nearly a week, and during that time he managed to see the Duchess. But the account he gave to his wife of the visit did not express much satisfaction. 'She's a sly creature after all,' he said.

'I had always thought that she was too open rather than sly,' said his wife.

'People always try to get a character just opposite to what they deserve. She hummed and hawed and would not say a word about the borough. She went so far as to tell me that I wasn't to say a word about it to her.'

It may be understood why the Duchess had had very little to say to Mr Lopez about the election. She was aware that she owed something to Mr Lopez, whom she had certainly

343

encouraged to stand for the borough, but her husband had expressly forbidden her to declare publicly that he was in any way the favoured candidate. She had therefore sent her card to Mrs Lopez and was prepared to invite them both to her parties; but just at present she was a little tired of Ferdinand Lopez.

Lopez had been by no means gratified with his canvass or with the conduct of the borough generally. He had already begun to feel that the Duchess and the borough had thrown him over shamefully. Immediately on his arrival in Silverbridge a local attorney had with the blandest possible smile asked him for a cheque for £500. Of course there must be money spent at once, and of course the money must come out of the candidate's pocket. He gave the cheque, but showed clearly by his manner that he resented the application. This did not tend to bind to him more closely the services of those who were present when the demand was made. And then, as he began his canvass, he found that he could not conjure at all with the name of the Duke, or even with that of the Duchess. Still he persevered, and did not scruple to affirm in his speeches that the success of his canvass had been complete.

On the third day of his canvass Arthur Fletcher with his gang of agents and followers met Lopez with his gang in the street. Fletcher had already resolved what he would do. He walked up to Lopez, and with a kindly smile offered his hand. But Lopez had come to a resolution of a very different nature. He put his arms akimbo, resting his hands on his hips, and altogether declined the proffered civility. 'You had better walk on,' he said, and then stood, scowling, on the spot till the other should pass by. Fletcher looked at him for a moment, then bowed and passed on.

In the evening, as Lopez was sitting alone, he wrote a letter and sent it over to the opposition hotel.

Sir,
    Before this election began you were guilty of gross impertinence in writing a letter to my wife, to her extreme annoyance and to my most justifiable anger. And now, since

you have been here, you have presumed to offer to shake hands with me in the street, though you ought to have known that I should not choose to meet you on friendly terms after what has taken place. I now write to tell you that I shall carry a horsewhip while I am here, and that if I meet you in the streets again before I leave the town I shall use it.

Ferdinand Lopez.

That same night as Arthur Fletcher walked down the High Street he saw Lopez standing at his hotel door with a cutting whip in his hand. He was at that moment quite alone, but on the opposite side of the street there was a policeman, very slowly making his way along the pavement. Then Lopez advanced with his whip raised; but as he did so the policeman came across the street quickly, but very quietly, and stood right before him.

'Do you usually walk about attended by a policeman?' said Lopez, with all the scorn which he knew how to throw into his voice.

About two o'clock on the afternoon of the next day Mr Lopez appeared before the Silverbridge bench of magistrates, and was sworn to keep the peace to Mr Fletcher for the next six months.

On the day but one after this the ballot was taken, and at eight o'clock in the evening Arthur Fletcher was declared elected.

Lopez, as he returned to town, recovered something of his senses. Though he still fancied that Arthur Fletcher had done him a positive injury by writing to his wife, he began to feel that he had been wrong about the horsewhip. He was very low in spirits. The money which he had spent had been material to him, and the loss of it left him nearly bare. While he had had before his eyes the hope of being a Member of Parliament he had been able to buoy himself up. The position would have gone very far with Sexty Parker, and would, he thought, have had some effect even with his father-in-law. But now he was returning a beaten man.

On the next morning Lopez was at Mr Wharton's chambers early. Mr Wharton was himself at this moment very unhappy. He had renewed his quarrel with Everett about money lost at cards and had driven his son from his presence. His daughter had left him, not as he thought under happy auspices. Now he felt himself to be alone and destitute.

'So you have come back from Silverbridge?' he said to Lopez.

'Yes, sir; I have come back, not exactly triumphant. A man should not expect to win always.'

'You seem to have got into some scrape down there, besides losing your election.'

'Oh; you have seen that in the papers already. I have come to tell you of it. As Emily is concerned in it you ought to know.'

'Emily concerned! How is she concerned?'

Then Lopez told the whole story—after his own fashion, and yet with no palpable lie.

'I know the man so well,' said Mr Wharton, 'that I cannot and do not believe him to have harboured an improper thought in reference to my child.'

'Perhaps it was an indiscretion only.'

'I suppose it ruined your chance at Silverbridge?'

'I suppose it did.' This gave him the opening that he wanted, and he described the manner in which the £500 had been extracted from him. 'You can't play that game for nothing,' said Mr Wharton.

'The Duchess, when she spoke to me about it, was so certain.'

'I will pay the £500,' said Mr Wharton.

'Oh, sir, that is generous!' Then he got up and took the old man's hands. 'Some day, when you are at liberty, I hope you will allow me to explain to you the exact state of my affairs. You do not object?'

'No,' said the lawyer, but with hesitation in his voice. 'I don't object. But I do not know how I could serve them. If you and Emily have nothing better to do, come and dine tomorrow.' Lopez with real tears in his eyes took the cheque, and promised to come on the morrow. 'And in the meantime I wish you would see Everett.' Of course he promised he would see Everett.

346

Again he was exalted, on this occasion by the growing conviction that his father-in-law was a cow capable of being milked. And the quarrel between Everett and his father might clearly be useful to him. He might either serve the old man by reducing Everett to proper submission, or he might manage to creep into the empty space which the son's defection would make in the father's life. He might at any rate make himself necessary to the old man, and become such a part of the household in Manchester Square as to be indispensable. He thought that he saw the way to worm himself into confidence, and, so on, into possession.

He saw Sexty Parker in the city that day, and used his cheque for £500 in some triumphant way, partly cajoling and partly bullying his poor victim. Then he found Everett at the club.

'What's all this between you and your father?'

'Simply this. I sometimes play a game of whist, and therefore he called me a gambler. Then I reminded him that he also sometimes played a game of whist, and I asked him what deduction was to be drawn.'

'If you ask me,' said Lopez, 'I think he would take it kindly of you if you were to go and see him. Come and dine today, just as if nothing had happened.'

'If he wants me, he can ask me.'

That evening, after dinner in Manchester Square, the conversation between Mr Wharton and Lopez turned almost exclusively on Everett. 'He wants you to withdraw some name you called him,' said Lopez.

'Does he expect his father to send him a written apology?'

Lopez shrugged his shoulders. 'I asked him to come and dine today, but he didn't seem to like it.'

'He likes nothing but that infernal club.'

When the evening was over Lopez felt that he had done a good stroke of work.

From day to day Mr Wharton seemed to lean more upon his son-in-law. Everett declared to Lopez a dozen times that he would go to his father if his father wished it, and Lopez as often reported to the father that Everett would not go to him unless the father expressed such a wish. And so they had been kept apart. The old man always asked after his daughter, and at last another evening was fixed. Lopez told Emily that they were to dine in the Square on the following day, taking her in his arms and kissing her.

'I don't think your father is looking very well.'

'He is not ill?'

'Oh no. He feels the loss of your society. He is so much alone.'

'What can I do?'

'You should see him every day. I don't know whether we had not better leave this and go and live near him.'

'I would go and stay with him if he wanted me.'

'I have thought of that too. And if we were both there we could hardly fail to know how he was doing. You could offer that, couldn't you?'

'I could ask him if he wished it.'

'Say that it occurs to you that he is lonely by himself, and that we will both go to the Square at a moment's notice if he thinks it will make him comfortable. I have already had an offer for these rooms, and could get rid of the things we have bought to advantage.'

This was terrible to her. She had been invited to buy little treasures to make their home comfortable, and now she was told that her household goods had had a price put upon them and that they were to be sold. She had suggested that she would pay her father a visit, and her husband immediately proposed that they should quarter themselves permanently on the old man! She endeavoured not to read her husband's mind too closely—but there it was, opened to her wider day by day, and she knew that the lessons which it taught were vulgar and damnable.

The husband was jovial the following day when he came home. Then, when they were in the brougham, he began a course of very plain instructions. 'Look here, dear; you had better get him to talk to you before dinner. I'll take up a book while you are talking to him.'

'What do you wish me to say to him, Ferdinand?'

'I have been thinking of your own proposal, and I am quite sure that we had better join him in the Square. Begin

348

by saying that you are afraid he is desolate. Put your arm over him, and kiss him, and all that sort of thing.' She shrunk from him into the corner of the brougham, and yet he did not perceive it. 'Be sure to let him understand that the idea began with you.'

'But it did not.'

'Tell him just that. And if he should say anything about sharing the house expenses, you can tell him that I would do anything he might propose. You say as much as you can of all this before dinner, so that when we are sitting below he may suggest it if he pleases. It would suit me to get in there next week if possible.'

Mr Wharton was alone when they entered the drawing-room. It was not long before Lopez began to play his part by seating himself close to the open window and looking out into the Square; and Emily when she found herself close to her father, with her hand in his, could hardly divest herself of a feeling that she also was playing her part. 'I see so very little of you,' said the old man plaintively.

'I'd come up oftener if I thought you'd like it.'

'Of course you have to live with your husband. Isn't this sad about Everett?'

'Papa,' said Emily, 'would you like us to come and live here?'

'What—you and Lopez; here, in the Square?'

'He is thinking of giving up the place in Belgrave Mansions.'

'I thought he had them for ever so many months.'

'If you would wish it, we would come here—for a time.' He looked at her almost suspiciously; and she blushed as she remembered how accurately she was obeying her husband's orders. 'It would be such a joy to me to be near you again.'

There was something in her voice which instantly reassured him. 'Well . . .' he said; 'come and try it if it will suit him. Come and try it.'

It astonished her that the thing should be done so easily. Here was all that her husband had proposed to arrange by deep diplomacy settled in a few words. And yet she felt as though she had taken her father in. 'Papa,' she said, 'do not do this unless you feel sure that you would like it.'

'I feel sure of one thing, that it will be a great saving to your husband. There is plenty of room here, and it will at any rate be a comfort to me to see you sometimes.'

During dinner not a word was said on the subject. Lopez exerted himself to be pleasant, and told all that he had heard as to the difficulties of the Cabinet. Sir Orlando Drought had resigned as Leader of the House, and the general opinion was that the Coalition was going to pieces. The old man from time to time said sharp little things, showing that his intellect was not senile, all of which his son-in-law bore imperturbably. It was not that he liked it, or was indifferent, but that he knew that he could not get the good things which Mr Wharton could do for him without making some kind of payment. He must take the sharp words of the old man—and take all that he could get besides.

When the two men were alone together after dinner, Mr Wharton used a different tone. 'If you are to come,' he said, 'you might as well do it as soon as possible.'

'A day or two will be enough for us.'

'There are one or two things you should understand. I shall be very happy to see your friends at any time, but I shall like to know before they come.'

'Of course, sir.'

'And don't let there ever be any question of money between us.'

'Certainly not.'

'This arrangement will be tantamount to an allowance to Emily. You have also had £3500. I hope it has been well expended; except the £500 at that election.'

'The other was brought into the business.'

'I don't know what the business is. But you and Emily must understand that the money has been given as her fortune.'

'Oh, quite so; part of it, you mean.'

'I mean just what I say.'

'I call it part of it, because, as you observed just now, our living here will be the same as though you made Emily an allowance.'

350

'Ah well, you can look at it in that light if you please. I don't know that there's anything else to be said. I hope we shall get into the way of understanding each other, and being mutually comfortable. Shall we go upstairs to Emily?'

CHAPTER FOUR

SIR ORLANDO DROUGHT must have felt bitterly the quiescence with which he sank into obscurity on the second bench on the opposite side of the House. One great occasion he had on which it was his privilege to explain the insuperable reasons which caused him to break away from those right honourable friends to act with whom had been his comfort and his duty, his great joy and his unalloyed satisfaction. Then he occupied the best part of an hour in abusing those friends and all their measures. But Mr Monk who was to assume his place as Leader of the House only took five minutes to answer him; then the business of the House went on just as if Sir Orlando Drought had not moved his seat at all.

The end of the Session came, very quietly and very early. By the end of July there was nothing left to be done, and the world of London was allowed to go down into the country almost a fortnight before its usual time. The Duke of St Bungay declared that he had never known a Session of Parliament more thoroughly satisfactory to the Ministers, but in his own bosom was compelled to confess that there was a cloud in the heavens. The Prime Minister had become so moody, so irritable, and so unhappy, that the old Duke was forced to doubt whether things could go on much longer as they were. He was wont to talk of these things to Lord Cantrip, who was not a member of the Government, but whom the old Duke regarded with peculiar confidence. 'I cannot explain it to you,' he said to Lord Cantrip. 'There is nothing that ought to give him a moment's uneasiness. I don't remember such a state of things so easy for the Prime Minister since the days of Lord Liverpool.'

'I suppose it is his health,' said Lord Cantrip.

'He's well enough as far as I can see. The fault is that he takes things too seriously. If he could be got to believe that he might eat, and sleep, and go to bed, and amuse himself like other men, he might be a very good Prime Minister. England wouldn't come to an end because the Duke of Omnium shut himself up at Matching. But I love the man, and, with some few exceptions, am contented with the party. It cuts me to the heart when I see him suffering, knowing how much I did myself to make him undertake the work.'

'I suppose,' said Lord Cantrip, 'the Duchess is a little troublesome.'

'She's the dearest woman in the world,' said the Duke of St Bungay. 'And she is most zealous to serve him.'

'I fancy she overdoes it.'

'No doubt.'

'And that he suffers from perceiving it.'

'But a man hasn't a right to expect that his wife shall know everything and do everything without a mistake. And then he has such faults of his own! His skin is so thin.'

The Duke of St Bungay, though he declared that he wouldn't give up hope, was very uneasy on the matter. 'Why won't you let me go?' the Prime Minister had said to him.

'What—because such a man as Sir Orlando Drought throws up his office?'

'It's not Sir Orlando, but a sense of general failure,' said the Prime Minister. 'There seems to have come a lethargy upon the country.' Then the Duke of St Bungay knew that his friend had read a pernicious article in *The People's Banner*, and remembered that phrase, and understood at once how the poison had rankled.

It was a week before the Prime Minister would consent to fill the vacancy of First Lord of the Admiralty, which post Sir Orlando Drought had also held. He would not allow suggestions to be made to him and yet would name no one himself. With all his timidity he was becoming autocratic and peevishly imperious. At last he asked Phineas Finn to move to the Admiralty, and when Phineas somewhat reluctantly obeyed he had the same difficulty in filling the office Finn had held. Other changes became necessary, and Mr Quintus Slide, who hated Phineas Finn even worse than the poor Duke, found ample scope for his patriotic indignation.

Then one morning there reached Matching a letter which greatly added to the Duke's bitterness of spirit. He gave it to his wife to read. 'See what you have brought upon me,' he said, 'by your interference.'

My Lord Duke,

I consider myself entitled to complain to your Grace of the conduct with which I was treated at the last election at Silverbridge, whereby I was led into very heavy expenditure without the least chance of being returned for the borough. I am aware that I had no direct conversation with your Grace on the subject, and that I had no authority from yourself for supposing that I should receive your Grace's support. But I was distinctly asked by the Duchess to stand, and was assured by her that if I did so I should have all the assistance that your Grace's influence could procure for me.

Immediately on my arrival an application was made to me for £500. I cannot think that your Grace will be willing that a poor man like myself, in his search for an entrance into public life, should be mulcted to so heavy an extent in consequence of an error on the part of the Duchess. Should your Grace be able to assist me in my view of getting into Parliament for any other seat I shall be willing to abide the loss I have incurred. I hardly, however, dare to hope for such assistance. In this case I think your Grace ought to see that I am reimbursed.

I have the honour to be,
My Lord Duke,
Your Grace's very faithful Servant,
Ferdinand Lopez.

353

'Well,' said he, 'what do you say to that?'

'Do you want to make me roll in the gutter because I mistook him for a gentleman?'

'That was not all—nor half. In your eagerness to serve such a miserable creature as this you forgot my position! My enemies I can overcome, but I cannot escape the pitfalls which are made for me by my own wife.'

She had no joke ready, no sarcasm, no feminine counter-grumble. 'I'm sorry,' she ejaculated at last. 'What more can I say?'

'What am I to do? What can be said to the man?'

'Tear his letter in pieces, and let there be an end of it.'

'I do not feel sure but that he has right on his side. He is taking advantage of the mistake made by a good-natured woman through her folly and her vanity, and he knows very well that he is doing so. But still he has a show of justice on his side.'

'Send him the £500 without a word.'

'A question might be asked about it in the House.'

'Say that I did it. I shall not blench. Your saying it all in the House of Lords won't wound me half so much as your looking at me as you did just now.'

'God knows I would not hurt you willingly. If my anger were at the hottest I would not confess to a human being that you were not perfect—except to yourself.'

'Oh, thank you!'

'If I pay this money I shall take the consequences. But I wish you would remember that in all that you do you are dealing with my feelings, with my reputation. You say that I am thin-skinned.'

'Certainly you are. What people call a delicate organization, whereas I am rough and thick and monstrously commonplace.'

'Then should you too be thin-skinned for my sake.'

'I wish I could make you thick-skinned for your own. It's the only way to be decently comfortable in such a coarse, rough-and-tumble world as this is.'

'Let us both do our best,' he said, now putting his arm round her and kissing her. 'I think I shall send the man his money at once. It is the least of two evils. And now let there never be a word more about it between us.'

He went to his desk, drew a cheque for £500 in favour of Ferdinand Lopez, and then caused his secretary to send it in a note:

Sir,

The Duke of Omnium, feeling that you may have been induced to undertake the late contest at Silverbridge by misrepresentations made to you, directs me to enclose a cheque for £500, that being the sum stated by you to have been expended in carrying on the contest at Silverbridge.

I am, Sir,
Your obedient servant,
Arthur Warburton.

When Lopez received the reply he was sitting opposite his father-in-law at breakfast. Lopez read the few words which the private secretary had written, and then put the document with its contents into his pocket. 'So you think, sir, of going down to Herefordshire on the 15th,' he said in a very cheery voice.

'I suppose I shall,' said the barrister.

'I think we have made up our mind,' said Lopez, 'to take a cottage at Dovercourt. It is not a very lively place, nor yet fashionable. But it is very healthy, and I can run up to town easily. Unfortunately my business won't let me be altogether away this autumn.'

'I did not understand that you had made up your mind to go to Dovercourt,' said Emily.

'It suits my business, and we might as well consider it settled.' So saying, he left the room and went off to the city. Mr Wharton had seen a cloud on his daughter's face. He had been aware since they had both come into his house that the young wife's manner and tone to her husband were not that of perfect conjugal sympathy. But there had never fallen from her lips a syllable of complaint. 'Do you like the idea of going to this place?' he said.

'I don't know what it will be like. Ferdinand says it will be cheap.'

'Is that of such vital consequence?'

'I fear it is.'

Lopez had already had from him a considerable sum of money, having not yet been married twelve months, and was now living in London almost free of expense. Before his marriage he had always spoken of himself as a wealthy man.

'Do you understand his money matters, Emily?' he asked.

'Not at all, Papa.'

'What is his business?'

'He has a partner of the name of Parker. I believe they buy and sell.'

'I wish he would be open with me, and tell me everything.'

'Shall I let him know that you say so?'

'If you think that he will not be annoyed with you. Tell him that it will be better that he should let me know the whole condition of his affairs. God bless you, dear.' Then he stooped over her, and kissed her, and went his way.

It was evident on that day to Sexty Parker that his partner was a man of great resources. Money always 'turned up'. Some of their buyings and sellings had answered pretty well. Some had been great failures. No great stroke had been made as yet, but then the great stroke was always being expected. On this day, when the Duke's £500 was turned into the business, Sexty yielded in a large matter which his partner had been pressing upon him for the last week. On that day Lopez returned home in high spirits, for he did believe in his own intelligence and good fortune.

On that afternoon his wife spoke to him as her father had desired. 'Papa was talking about our affairs after you left this morning, and he thinks that it would be so much better if you would tell him all about them.'

'Why should you be discussing my affairs behind my back?'

'To my own father? And that too when you are telling me every day that I am to induce him to help you!'

'You have been talking of—my poverty.'

'I can't tell him in the same breath that you are rich and that you want money.'

'Money is the means by which men make money. If he was confident of my business he'd shell out his cash quick enough!'

'You won't speak to him then?'

'If I find that it will answer my own purpose I shall speak to him. But it would be very much easier to me if I could get you to be cordial in helping me. You know that you can trust me to do the best with your money if I could get hold of it, I suppose?'

'I could only tell him to judge for himself.'

'What you mean is that you'd see me damned before you would open your mouth for me to the old man!'

He had never sworn at her before. She burst into tears. 'You provoke me to be violent,' he said. 'I come away from the city tired with work and troubled with a thousand things, and you have not a kind word to say to me. If your father has anything to say to me, let him say it.' Then he paused. 'Come, old girl, cheer up! Don't pretend to be broken-hearted because I used a hard word.'

'I was so startled, Ferdinand.'

'Don't think anything more about it; but do bear this in mind, that, situated as we are, your influence with your father may be the making of or the marring of me.'

On the next morning there came a message to him as he was dressing. Mr Wharton wished to speak to him. Would he call on Mr Wharton at his chambers? He went there at the hour fixed.

'If I understand,' said Mr Wharton, 'rightly, you are a general merchant, buying and selling goods?'

'That's about it, sir.'

'What capital have you in the business?'

'Altogether I have had about £8000 in it.' In truth he had never been possessed of a shilling.

'Does that include the £3000 you had from me?'

'Yes, it does.'

'Then you have married my girl and started into the world with a business based on £5000, and which had so far miscarried that within a month or two after your marriage you were driven to apply to me for funds!'

'I wanted money for a certain purpose.'

'Have you any partner, Mr Lopez?'

'Yes. I have a partner who is possessed of capital. His name is Parker.'

'What is the name of your firm?'

'We haven't a registered name.'

'Then, sir, it seems to me that you are a commercial adventurer?'

'I watch the markets and buy goods, and sell them at a profit. We can very easily call ourselves merchants, and put up the names of Lopez and Parker over the door.'

'One other question, Mr Lopez. On what income have you paid income-tax for the last three years?'

'On £2000 a year.' This was a direct lie.

'Can you make out any schedule showing your exact assets and liabilities at the present time?'

'Certainly I can.'

'Then do so, and send it to me before I go into Herefordshire. My will as it stands at present would not be to your advantage. But I cannot change it till I know more of your circumstances.'

By his will he had left two-thirds of his property to Everett, and one-third to his daughter, with arrangements for settling her share on her children, should she be married and have children at the time of his death. This will had been made many years ago, and he had long since determined to alter it, in order that he might divide his property equally between his children; but he had postponed the matter, intending to give a large portion of Emily's share to her directly on her marriage with Arthur Fletcher. She had not married Arthur Fletcher, but still it was necessary that a new will should be made.

When he left town for Herefordshire he had not yet made up his mind how this should be done. The requested schedule had not been rendered, nor spoken of again. Before the end of the month the father-in-law wrote a line to his son-in-law.

Dear Lopez,

When we were discussing your affairs I asked you for a schedule of your assets and liabilities. I can make no new

358

arrangement of my property till I receive this. I tell you this that you may understand that it is for your own interest to comply with my requisition.

Yours,

A. Wharton.

Lopez received Mr Wharton's letter at Dovercourt. On that evening he did write to Mr Wharton and dated it from Little Tankard Yard, so that Mr Wharton might suppose that that was really his own place of business, and that he was there, at his work.

My dear Sir,

You have asked for a schedule of my affairs, and I have found it quite impossible to give it. My property at this moment consists of certain shares of cargoes of jute, Kauri gum, guano, and sulphur, worth altogether at the present moment something over £26,000, of which Mr Parker possesses the half; but then of this property only a portion is paid for. For the other half our bills are in the market. But in February next these articles will probably be sold for considerably more than £30,000. If I had £5000 placed to my credit now, I should be worth about £15,000 by the end of next February. I am engaged in sundry other smaller ventures, all returning profits.

I am undoubtedly in the condition of a man trading beyond his capital. When I married your daughter I no doubt thought that her means—whatever they might be— would be joined to my own. I know that a sum of £20,000, with my experience in the use of money, would give us a noble income. It is certainly the case that Emily's fortune, whatever you may choose to give her, would be of infinitely greater use to me now, and consequently to her, than at a future date which I sincerely pray may be very long deferred.

Believe me to be, your affectionate son-in-law,

Ferdinand Lopez.

This letter he himself took up to town on the following day, and there posted, addressing it to Wharton Hall.

When the respective parties had ended their vacations and had been back in Manchester Square about a week Mr Wharton announced to his son-in-law his final determination as to money. 'I had better tell you, Lopez, so that you may not be left in doubt—I shall not intrust any further sum of money into your hands on behalf of Emily. You have had what to me is a very considerable sum, though I fear that it did not go for much in your large concerns.'

'It was not very much, Mr Wharton.'

'I dare say not. At any rate, there will be no more. At present I wish Emily to live here, and you, of course, are welcome here also. If things are not going well with you this will, at any rate, relieve you from immediate expense.'

'My calculations, sir, have never descended to that.'

'Mine are more minute. When I am dead there will be provision for Emily made by my will, the income going to trustees for her benefit, and the capital to her children after her death.'

'And you will do nothing for me?'

'I should have thought that your present maintenance and the future support of your wife and children would have been regarded as something.'

'You are very explicit with me, sir. And I will be equally so to you now. Both I and your daughter are absolutely ruined unless you reconsider your purpose.'

'I certainly shall not reconsider it.'

'Then, sir, I must leave England, and try my fortune in Central America. There is an opening for me at Guatemala, though not a very hopeful one. I have not broken it to Emily yet.'

'You will not take her to Guatemala!'

'Not take my wife, sir? Indeed I shall. Do you think that she would wish to desert her husband?'

'I wish you had never known her.'

'That is neither here nor there, sir. As I have told you before, £20,000 at the present moment would enable me to surmount all my difficulties, and make me a very wealthy man. But unless I can command some such sum by Christmas everything here must be sacrificed.'

'Never in my life did I hear so base a proposition,' said Mr Wharton. 'As to my daughter, she must do as she thinks fit.'

'She must do as I think fit, Mr Wharton. As I understand that you intend to try to use authority over her, I shall take steps for removing her at once from your house.'

Lopez had thought the matter over, and had determined to 'brazen it out'. Nothing further was, he thought, to be got by civility and obedience. His idea of going to Guatemala was not devoid of truth. There were mines in Guatemala which wanted a resident director. Lopez had made application and received a letter saying that the thing might probably be arranged. 'I am quite in earnest,' Lopez said as he showed this letter to Mr Wharton. 'I suppose Emily will be able to start two months after her confinement. They tell me that babies do very well at sea.'

During this time, in spite of his threat, he continued to live with Mr Wharton in Manchester Square, and went every day into the city. He never spoke about his affairs to either of them, but daily referred to her future expatriation as a thing that was certain. At last there came up the actual question whether she were to go or not. Her father told her that though she was doubtless bound by law to obey her husband, in such a matter as this she might defy the law. 'I do not think that he can actually force you on board the ship,' her father said.

Emily discussed the matter with Lopez himself. 'My father thinks that I should refuse to go.'

'Do you think that it is a fine thing for a man to live in such a country as that all alone?'

'I think he would be better so than with a wife he does not —love.'

'Who says I do not love you?'

'Or with one who does—not—love him.'

'Do you tell me that to my face?'

'Yes; what good can I do now by lying? You have not been to me as I thought you would be.'

361

'And so, because you have built up some castle in the air that has fallen to pieces, you tell your husband that you do not love him. The fact is that your father and you have found out that I am not a rich man, and you want to be rid of me.'

'It is not true.'

'You will have to settle down and do your work as my wife in whatever place it may suit me to live. If your father would give me the fortune which ought to be yours there need be no going abroad.'

Just before Christmas her baby was born, but the poor child did not live a couple of days. She herself was so worn with care, so thin and wan and wretched, that looking in the glass she hardly knew her own face. Then she would look at all the preparations she had made—the happy work of her fingers when her thoughts of their future use were her sweetest consolation—and weep till she would herself feel that there never could be an end to her tears.

.   .   .   .   .

In the first week in January the Duke was at Matching with his wife and a very small party. There was the Duke of St Bungay and the Duchess, and Phineas Finn and his wife, and Lord and Lady Cantrip, Barrington Erle, and one or two others. One morning as the Duke sat in his own room after breakfast he read an article in *The People's Banner* of which the following was a part. 'We wish to know by whom were paid the expenses incurred by Mr Ferdinand Lopez during the late contest at Silverbridge. It may be that they were paid by that gentleman himself. It may be that they were paid by a new political club of which we have lately heard much. If an assurance can be given to us by Mr Lopez that such was the case we shall be satisfied. But a report has reached us which makes it our duty to ask this question. Were those expenses paid out of the private pocket of the present Prime Minister? If so, we maintain that we have discovered a blot in that nobleman's character which it is our duty to the public to expose. We will go farther and say that if it be

362

so, the Duke of Omnium is not fit any longer to hold the high office which he now fills.'

The statement made was at any rate true to the letter. He had paid the man's electioneering expenses; but he could not explain his motives without exposing his wife. It was open to him to take no notice of the matter. But he knew Mr Quintus Slide. The charge would be repeated in *The People's Banner* till it was copied into other papers; and then the further question would be asked—why had the Prime Minister allowed such an accusation to remain unanswered? He was not ashamed of the thing he had done; but he was ashamed that it should be discussed in public.

As he mused, the Duke of St Bungay was announced. In his hand he held a copy of *The People's Banner*.

'I did pay the man's expenses,' the Prime Minister told him without questioning.

'But why?'

'The man had, I fear, promised certain support from my house which certainly was not given him when the time came.'

'Was it the Duchess?'

'Upon the whole, my friend, I think I would rather not discuss it, even with you.'

'You could say that the payment had been made because your agents had misapprehended your instructions.'

'It would not be true.'

So the affair was left for the present, though the allusions to it in *The People's Banner* continued, until everybody in the House, and almost everybody in the country who read the newspapers, had heard of Mr Lopez and his election expenses—except the Duchess. She saw the newspapers daily, but did not read them very attentively. Nevertheless she knew that something was wrong. 'What is it that's going on?' she said one day to Mrs Phineas Finn.

'You know that the Duke paid the expenses that man Lopez says he incurred.'

'I know that.'

'And you know that Slide has found it out and published it all in *The People's Banner*?'

'No!'

363

'Yes, indeed. And a whole army of accusations has been brought against him. I have never liked to tell you.'

'Everybody deceives me,' said the Duchess angrily. 'I think you will kill me among you. It was my doing. Why do they attack him? I encouraged the man after Plantagenet had determined that he should not be assisted—and because I had done so he paid the man his beggarly money. What is there to hurt him in that? Let me bear it. My back is broad enough.'

'The Duke is very sensitive.'

'I hate people to be sensitive. It makes them cowards. But I shall have it out with Plantagenet. If I have to write letters to all the newspapers myself, I'll put it right.'

'I have just heard,' she said, having knocked at the door of his own room, 'that there is a row about the money you paid to Mr Lopez. Why had you not told me?'

'Why should I tell you?'

'If anything troubled me much I should tell you.'

'I couldn't do it, Cora. I will not have your name mentioned. We have had enough of this now.' Then she turned to go away, but he called her back. 'Kiss me, dear,' he said. Then she stooped over him and kissed him. 'Do not think I am angry with you because the thing vexes me. I am dreaming always of some day when we may go away together with the children, and live as other people live.'

'It would be very stupid,' she muttered to herself as she left the room.

There was certainly no resignation. The old Duke and Phineas Finn and Barrington Erle were all of opinion that the best plan for the present was to do nothing. Parliament had already met before Mr Slide had quite determined in what way he would carry on the war.

When the statement was first made in *The People's Banner* Lopez had come to Mr Slide at once and had demanded his authority for making it. Lopez had been paid his election expenses twice over, making a clear profit of £500 by the transaction. Now Mr Wharton would know that he had been cheated.

'Is it true, Lopez?' asked the editor. 'If it's true, I have got every right to publish it. If it's not true, I've got the right to ask the question. If you will 'ave to do with Prime Ministers you can't 'ide yourself under a bushel. You can't 'urt yourself. And if you oppose me, why, I shall oppose you.'

'It was true,' said Lopez.

'You asked him for the money—and threatened him.'

'I told him that I had been put to expense through the misrepresentations of the Duchess. He sent a cheque, and of course I took it.'

'Of course, of course. You couldn't give me a copy of your letter?'

'Never kept a copy.' He had a copy in his breast coat-pocket at that moment.

'He did write a note, I suppose?'

'Just a few words.'

'Could you let me 'ave that note?'

'I destroyed it at once.' This was also in his breast-pocket at the time.

'If you'll give me those two letters, Lopez, I'll stick to you through thick and thin.'

'You won't publish them?'

'I shall only refer to them.'

Then Lopez pulled the papers out of his pocket. 'Well,' said Slide, when he had read them; 'it is one of the rummest transactions I ever 'eard of.'

On the next morning there came out another article in *The People's Banner*, which ended: 'The Prime Minister may deny the fact. And therefore we at once inform the noble Duke that the entire correspondence is in our hands.' In saying this Mr Quintus Slide thought that he had quite kept the promise that he would only refer to the letters.

CHAPTER FIVE

THAT scheme of going to Guatemala had been in the first instance propounded by Lopez with the object of frightening Mr Wharton into terms. When under this threat neither Wharton nor Emily gave way, and when, with the view of strengthening his threat, he renewed his inquiries as to Guatemala and found that there might still be an opening for him in that direction, the threat took the shape of a true purpose. During all this time Mr Wharton was very wretched. If he could have freed his daughter from her marriage by half his fortune he would have done it without a second thought. If he could have assuredly purchased the permanent absence of her husband he would have done it at a large price. He spoke to Emily about it.

'Papa, I will never again ask you to give him a single penny. That must be altogether between you and him.'

Then Mr Wharton heard of the payment alleged to have been made to Ferdinand Lopez by the Duke of Omnium. 'Lopez,' he asked, 'what is this that the newspapers are saying about your expenses at Silverbridge? I paid your electioneering expenses.'

'You certainly subscribed £500 towards them, Mr Wharton.'

'I subscribed nothing, sir. You told me that the contest cost you £500 and that sum I handed to you.'

'Have it your own way, sir.'

'If you are not more precise, I shall think that you have defrauded me.'

'Defrauded you!'

'Yes, sir; me, or the Duke of Omnium. I shall take steps to let the Duke know. And I am obliged to say that the sooner you leave this house, the better. Emily can remain here.'

'That will not suit me,' said Lopez. When he left Manchester Square that morning he went to the rooms in Coleman Street of the San Juan Mining Association. The present project was that Lopez was to start on behalf of the Company early in May, that the Company was to pay his own expenses out to Guatemala, and that they should allow him while there a salary of £1000 a year for managing the mine. But there was one very serious stipulation. He must become proprietor of 50 shares in the mine, for £100 each. The payment must be made in advance. Now there was nobody to whom he could apply but Mr Wharton. He was, indeed, forced to declare at the office that the money was to come from Mr Wharton. In spite of all that had come and gone he still hoped that he might get the money. Surely Mr Wharton would sooner pay such a sum than be troubled at home with such a son-in-law.

But, even yet, he was not quite resolved as to going to Guatemala. Sexty Parker had been sucked nearly dry, and was at this moment so violent with indignation and fear and remorse that Lopez did not dare to show himself in Little Tankard Yard: but still there were certain hopes in that direction from which great results might come. If a certain new spirit which had just been concocted from the bark of trees in Central Africa, and which was called Bios, could only be made to go up in the market everything might be satisfactorily arranged. The hoardings of London were already telling the public that if it wished to get drunk without any of the usual troubles of intoxication it must drink Bios.

And so the days went on till the first week of February had passed, and it was now essential that the money for the shares should be paid up.

'Mr Wharton,' Lopez said, 'you and I have not been very good friends lately.'

'No, indeed.'

'There was a time during which I thought that we might hit it off together, and I did my best. Had I received from you during the last year that assistance which I think I had a right to expect as your son-in-law, I also might have been a rich man now. Now you know what has come to me and to your daughter. We are to be expatriated.'

367

'Is that my fault?'

'I think it is, but I mean to say nothing further of that. This Company which is sending me out is to pay me a salary of £1000 a year as resident manager at San Juan. Guatemala, I take it, is not the cheapest country in the world in which a man can live. But I am to own fifty shares and draw another £1000 a year as dividend on the profit of those shares.'

'And will double your salary.'

'Just so. But there is one little ceremony to be perfected before I can be allowed to enter upon so halcyon a state of existence. I must have the £5000 to invest in the undertaking before I can start.'

'And you are asking me for that £5000? Look here, sir. Between you and me there can be a bargain, and nothing but a bargain. I will go with you to the office of this Company and will pay for the shares if I can receive assurance there that the matter is as you say, and that the shares will not be placed in your power before you have reached Guatemala.'

'You can come today, sir.'

'And I must have a written undertaking from you that you will never claim my daughter's society again.'

'You mistake me, Mr Wharton. My wife goes with me to Guatemala.'

'If you want the money, you must leave her. Good morning.'

Ferdinand Lopez had once loved his wife, and would have loved her still could he have trained her to think as he thought. He did not know that he was a villain. When he was exhorting her to 'get round her father' he was not aware that he was giving her lessons which must shock a well-conditioned girl. He did not understand that everything she had discovered of his moral disposition since her marriage was of a nature to disgust her. But he still thought that the fortune must come if he would only hold on to his wife.

He was apt, when thinking over his difficulties, to attribute much of them to the hesitation and parsimony of Sexty Parker. None of their late ventures had been successful. And now Sexty was in a bad condition, drinking hard, declaring himself a ruined man, and swearing revenge. As the Guatemala scheme really took form Lopez endeavoured to keep out of Sexty's way. But Sexty too had heard of Guatemala, and hunted Lopez about the city. 'By God,' he said one day, having caught his victim in front of the Exchange, 'you're not going out of the country if I know it.'

'You're an ass, Sexty, and always were. If I can carry on as though I were going to this place I can draw £5000 from old Wharton. As you and I stand, pretty nearly the whole of that will go to you. But don't you spoil it all by making an ass of yourself.'

Sexty, who was three parts drunk, looked up into his face for a few seconds, and then made his reply. 'I'm damned if I believe a word of it.' Upon this Lopez affected to laugh, and made his escape.

·　　·　　·　　·　　·

Now that Parliament was sitting a great deal was being said in many quarters about the last Silverbridge election. The papers had taken the matter up generally. Mr Slide, day after day, repeated his question, 'We want to know whether the Prime Minister did or did not pay the election expenses of Mr Lopez at the last Silverbridge election; and if so, why he paid them. We shall continue to ask this question till it has been answered.' When Mr Slide found how hard it was 'to draw his badger', as he expressed it, he at last openly alluded to the Duchess.

Against the Duchess herself we wish to say not a word. She is known as exercising a wide if not a discriminate hospitality. We believe her to be a kind-hearted, ambitious lady, to whom any little faults may easily be forgiven on account of her good-nature and generosity. But we cannot accept her indiscretion as an excuse for a most unconstitutional act performed by the Prime Minister of this country.

No one ventured to speak to the Prime Minister as to the

accusation. Coming away from the Cabinet that day he took Mr Monk's arm. 'Have you happened to see an article in *The People's Banner* this morning?' he asked. Mr Monk replied that he had.

'If a question were asked about this in the House of Commons, who would be the best man to answer it?'

Mr Monk considered awhile. 'I think,' he said, 'that Mr Finn would do it. He has tact in such matters. Get some independent Member to ask the question. The matter would then be brought forward in no carping spirit, and you would be enabled, through Mr Finn, to set the matter at rest.'

At the instigation of Mr Monk, Sir James Deering, an independent Member who generally voted with the Coalition, asked the question. He trusted, he said, that the House would not think that the question was instigated by any personal desire on his part to inquire into the conduct of the Prime Minister. But a great deal had been talked and written lately about the late election at Silverbridge, and there were those who thought that something should be said to stop the mouths of cavillers.

The House was full to the very corners of the galleries. In one corner of the reporters' gallery sat Mr Slide, pencil in hand. It was a great day for him. He by his own unassisted energy had brought a Prime Minister to book. It was he who had watched over the nation! The Duchess had been most anxious to be present, but her husband had most peremptorily refused her permission.

Phineas Finn rose to reply. Perhaps, he said, no falser accusation than this had ever been brought forward against a Minister of the Crown. Had the noble Duke simply nominated a candidate, as candidates had been nominated at Silverbridge for centuries past, that candidate would have been returned with absolute certainty, and there would have been no word spoken on the subject. But when the vacancy had been declared the Duke had abstained altogether from the exercise of any privilege or power in the matter.

A man whom he would not name, but who he trusted would never succeed in his ambition to occupy a seat in that House, had been brought forward, and certain tradesmen in Silverbridge had been asked to support him as the Duke's nominee. The House perhaps could understand that the local adherents and neighbours of a man so high in rank and wealth as the Duke of Omnium would not gladly see the privileges of their lord diminished. There would always be worthy men in boroughs who liked to exercise some second-hand authority. At any rate it was the case that this candidate was encouraged. Then the Duke had heard it, and had put his foot upon the little mutiny, and had stamped it out at once. So far, he thought, the Duke had been free from blame; but now he came to the gravamen of the charge. The Duke had paid the money, when asked for it, because he felt that the man had been injured by incorrect representations made to him. 'I need hardly pause to stigmatize the meanness of that application,' said Phineas, 'but I may perhaps conclude by saying that, whether the last act done by the Duke in this matter was or was not indiscreet, I shall probably have the House with me when I say that it savours much more strongly of nobility than of indiscretion.'

When Phineas Finn sat down no one arose to say another word on the subject. After a short pause the ordinary business of the day was recommenced. The thing was over, and people were astonished that so great a thing should be over with so little fuss.

'Mr Finn,' said the Duke afterwards, 'I feel indebted to you for the trouble you have taken.'

'It was only a pleasant duty.'

The abuse which was now publicly heaped on the name of Ferdinand Lopez hit the man very hard. He would certainly go to Guatemala now. 'I wish to speak to you, sir,' he said to Mr Wharton that night.

'Well, sir?'

'The £5000 you promised me must be paid tomorrow. It is the last day.'

'I promised it only on certain conditions.'

'Mr Wharton, it surprises me that you should think it right to separate a husband from his wife.'

'I think it right, sir, to separate my daughter from such a one as you are. I will not pay a penny without it. I can meet

371

you at the office in Coleman Street tomorrow. If they do not object to employ such a man as their manager, I shall pay the money, if you will sign a document assuring your wife that you will not hereafter call upon her to live with you.'

'To the last you are hard and cruel to me,' said Lopez; 'but I will meet you in Coleman Street at eleven tomorrow.'

On the following morning the appointment was kept.

'Well, Hartlepod, how are you today?' Lopez addressed the Manager of the Company. 'So this little affair is to be settled at last. Mr Wharton, I believe I am right in saying that you are ready to pay the money.'

'As soon as I am assured that you are on your route to Guatemala.'

Then Mr Hartlepod spoke. 'Gentlemen,' he said, 'the matter within the last few days has assumed a different complexion. The Directors have changed their mind as to sending out Mr Lopez as their local manager. The Directors intend to appoint another gentleman.'

Lopez began to fume and to be furious. What! After all that had been done did the Directors mean to go back from their word? After he had been induced to abandon his business in his own country, was he to be thrown over in that way? 'By God, you have ruined me among you,' said Lopez; 'ruined me in the most shameful manner. There is no mercy, no friendship, no kindness, no forbearance anywhere! Why am I to be treated in this manner?'

'If you have any complaint to make,' said Mr Hartlepod, 'you had better write to the Directors. I have nothing to do but my duty.'

.   .   .   .   .

When Lopez and Mr Wharton were having their interview with Mr Hartlepod there came a visitor to Mrs Lopez in Manchester Square. She had sent a message of farewell to Arthur Fletcher. It had of course been understood by both of them that they were not to be allowed to see each other. But now, when Arthur Fletcher sent up his name, she did not hesitate to see him.

'I could not let you go without coming to you,' he said.

'It is very good of you. Guatemala sounds a long way off, Arthur. But they tell me it is a beautiful country. After all, why should I not be as happy in Guatemala as in London? As to friends, I do not know that it will make much difference, except Papa. At any rate I am very glad to be able to say good-bye to you before I start.' All this she said rapidly, forcing herself to speak so that she might save herself, if possible, from breaking down in his presence.

'Oh, Emily! Leave him! Why don't you leave him?'

'What!'

'You cannot deceive me.'

'I will hear nothing of the kind, sir. There is nothing to be said that can serve us at all.'

'Then it shall be said without serving. When I bid you leave him it is not that you may come to me. Though I love you better than all the world put together, I do not mean that.'

'Oh, Arthur, Arthur!'

'But let your father save you. Only tell him that you will stay with him and he will do it. Though I should never see you again I could hope to protect you.'

'I cannot stay,' she said. 'He has told me that I am to go, and I am in his hands. Good-bye, dear friend.'

She put her hand out and he grasped it, and stood for a moment looking at her. Then he seized her in his arms and kissed her brow and her lips. 'Oh, Emily, why were you not my wife? My darling, my darling!'

She had hardly extricated herself when the door opened and Lopez stood in the room. 'Mr Fletcher,' he said, very calmly, 'what is the meaning of this?'

'He has come to bid me farewell,' said Emily. 'When going on so long a journey one likes to see one's old friends, perhaps for the last time.' There was something of scorn in her tone.

'I am here to tell her that she has a friend to trust if she ever wants a friend,' said Fletcher.

'And you think that such trust as that would be safer than

373

trust in her husband? I desire you to leave at once.'

'Good-bye, Mr Fletcher,' she said, again putting out her hand.

But Lopez struck it up, not violently so as to hurt her, but still with roughness. 'Not in my presence,' he said.

'God bless you, my friend,' said Arthur Fletcher. 'I pray that I may live to see you back in the old country.'

'He was kissing you,' said Lopez, as soon as the door was shut.

'I did not bid him kiss me.'

'But afterwards you took his part as his friend.'

'I have no friend older than Arthur Fletcher, and none who are dearer to me. You must remember, Ferdinand, you are taking me across the world from all my friends.'

'Psha,' he said, 'that is all over. You are not going anywhere that I know of, unless it be out into the streets when your father shuts his door on you.'

'You are not going?'

'The fact is, your father has delayed so long the payment of the promised money that the thing has fallen through.'

'And now,' she said, 'what do you mean to do?'

'I am quite as much in the dark as you can be.'

'That is nonsense, Ferdinand. You must have some scheme of life?'

'I have none. I have had intentions, and they have failed— from want of that support which I had a right to expect. I have struggled and I have failed, and now I have got no intentions.'

'I must tell Papa what our plans are.'

'You can tell him what you please. If he will settle an adequate income on us, payable to me, I will go and live elsewhere. If he turns me into the street without provision he must turn you too. That is all I have to say. It will come better from you than from me. I am sorry, of course, that things have gone wrong. You are not very cheerful, my dear, and I think I'll go down to the club. I must be off tomorrow to Birmingham, to see a friend on business. I will breakfast at the station. As you said, something must be done. If it's to sweep a crossing, I must sweep it.'

374

As she lay awake while he slept she thought that those last words were the best she had heard him speak since they were married. There seemed to be some indication of a purpose in them. If he would only sweep a crossing she would stand by him and do her duty to him, in spite of all that had happened.

Early the following morning he kissed his wife. 'Good-bye, old girl,' he said; 'don't be down-hearted.'

'If you have anything before you to do I will not be down-hearted.'

'Tell your father that I will not trouble him here much longer. But tell him, also, that I have no thanks to give him for his hospitality.'

'I will not tell him that, Ferdinand.'

'He shall know it, though. But I do not mean to be cross to you. Good-bye, love.' Then he stooped over her and kissed her again—and so he took his leave of her.

At Euston Station he ordered breakfast. He was a good-looking man, of fashionable appearance, and the young lady who attended him was courteous to him. 'Upon my word, I should like to breakfast here every day of my life,' he said. The young lady assured him that, as far as she could see, there was no objection to such an arrangement. Then there were various little jokes between them.

After a while he took a first-class return ticket, not for Birmingham, but for the Tenway Junction. Tenway Junction is a spot some six or seven miles from London where lines diverge round the metropolis in every direction. It is a place quite unintelligible to the uninitiated, with sloping points, and cross passages, and mysterious meandering sidings, till it seems to the stranger to be impossible that the best trained engine should know its own line. Not a minute passes without a train going here or there, some rushing by without noticing Tenway in the least, crashing through like flashes of substantial lightning, and others stopping, disgorging and taking up passengers by the hundreds. From dusky morn and almost throughout the night the air is loaded with a succession of shrieks.

At Tenway Junction there are half-a-dozen long platforms

on which men and women and luggage are crowded. On one of these Ferdinand Lopez walked backwards and forwards as though waiting for the coming of some especial train. The crowd is ever so great that a man might walk there from morning to night without exciting special notice. As Lopez was walking up and down, with smiling face and leisurely pace, there came a shriek louder than all the other shrieks, and the morning express down from Euston to Inverness was seen coming round the curve. Lopez turned round and looked at it, and walked towards the edge of the platform, where there was an inclined plane leading down to the level of the rail. As he did so someone called to him. But Lopez heeded not the call. With quick, but still with gentle and apparently unhurried steps, he walked down before the flying engine— and in a moment had been knocked into bloody atoms.

CHAPTER SIX

THE last days of July had passed, and it had been at last decided that the Session should close on the 11th of August.

'Well, what do you think of it all?' the Duke of Omnium said one day to Mr Monk, affecting an air of cheery good humour.

'I think,' said Mr Monk, 'that the country is very prosperous. I don't know that I ever remember trade to have been more evenly satisfactory. We have not had a majority against us this Session on any Government question.'

'We have had narrowing majorities. What will the House do as to the County Suffrage Bill?'

Mr Monk did not dare tell him what he believed would be

the fate of the Bill. In truth no one dared to tell him exactly what he thought. It was known that the Prime Minister was painfully anxious as to the fate of the Ministry. In all the clubs it had been declared that this was the rock by which the Coalition would probably be wrecked. 'We shall be beaten, certainly,' said Mr Monk to Phineas Finn.

'What makes you so sure?'

'I smell it in the air. I see it in men's faces.'

'And yet it's a moderate bill.'

'It's not the bill that they'll reject, but us. We have served our turn, and we ought to go.'

'The House is tired of the Duke?'

'I fear it is so. His Ministry has been of great service to the country. But I think that to him it has been a continual sorrow.'

That evening the Prime Minister came to his wife's apartment. 'I have had the Duke of St Bungay with me,' he said.

'And what does his Grace say?'

'He thinks our days are numbered.'

'I could have told him that ever so long ago. There isn't a porter at one of the clubs who doesn't know it.'

'Then there will be the less surprise. Will it make you unhappy, Cora?'

'What—your going?'

'The change altogether.'

She looked him in the face for a moment before she answered, with a peculiar smile in her eyes to which he was well used, a smile half ludicrous and half pathetic, having in it also a dash of sarcasm. 'Yes, it will make me unhappy. And you?'

'I do not like to think that I shall be without work.'

'Yes; Othello's occupation will be gone—for awhile.' Then she came up to him and put both her hands on his breast. 'But yet, Othello, I shall not be all unhappy.'

The night of the debate on the bill arrived, but before the debate was commenced it would perhaps have been well for everybody if the measure could have been withdrawn and the Ministry could have resigned without the debate, as everybody was convinced that would be the end of it. There was something due to the Duke, but not enough to maintain him as Prime Minister.

Early in the night the House divided. The Opposition was beaten, but only by nine. The House was adjourned and Mr Monk went at once to Carlton Terrace.

'I wish it had only been three or four,' said the Duke, laughing.

'Why so?'

'Because there would have been less doubt. There is little more to be said, I suppose.'

'Very little, your Grace.'

'We had better meet tomorrow at two, and if possible I will see her Majesty in the afternoon. My reign is ended. You are a good deal older man than I, and yet probably yours has yet to begin.' Mr Monk smiled and shook his head as he left the room, not trusting himself to discuss so large a subject at so late an hour of the night.

Without waiting a moment after his colleague's departure the Prime Minister went into his wife's room, knowing that she was waiting up till she should hear the result of the division, and there he found Mrs Finn with her. 'Is it over?' asked the Duchess.

'We have beaten them, of course, as we always do,' said the Duke, attempting to be pleasant. 'You didn't suppose there was anything to fear?'

'Tell me what has been done, Plantagenet.'

'I shall cease to be Prime Minister tomorrow.'

'You don't mean to say that it's settled?'

'Quite settled. The play has been played, and the curtain has fallen, and the lights are being put out, and the poor weary actors may go home to bed.'

'But surely any majority would have done.'

'No, my dear. Nine will not do.'

'Then everything is over for me. I shall settle down in the country and build cottages. You, Marie, will still be going up the tree. If Mr Finn manages well he may come to be Prime Minister some day.'

'He has hardly such ambition, Lady Glen.'

'What beasts, what brutes, what ungrateful wretches men

are!—worse than women when they get together in numbers enough to be bold. Don't you feel like Wolsey, Plantagenet?'

'Not in the least, my dear. No one will take anything away from me that is my own.'

'For me, I am almost as much divorced as Catherine, and have had my head cut off as completely as Anne Bullen and the rest of them. Go away, Marie. I am going to have a cry by myself.'

The Duke put Mrs Finn into her carriage; and as he walked with her downstairs he asked her whether she believed the Duchess to be in earnest in her sorrow. 'She so mixes up her mirth and woe together,' he said, 'that I myself sometimes can hardly understand her.'

'I think she does regret it, Duke.'

'She told me but the other day that she would be contented.'

'A few weeks will make her so. As for your Grace, I hope I may congratulate you.'

'Oh yes; I think so. We none of us like to be beaten when we have taken a thing in hand. But, upon the whole, it is better as it is.'

Then he went alone to his own room, and sat for a couple of hours. Surely it was a great thing to have been Prime Minister of England for three years, but to have done something was nothing to him, unless there was also something left to do. How should it be with him now—how for the future? He feared that it was all over for him, and that for the rest of his days he must simply be the Duke of Omnium.

. . . . .

Soon after the commencement of the Session Arthur Fletcher became a constant visitor in Manchester Square, dining with the old barrister frequently. Mr Wharton quite understood that the young Member of Parliament was earnestly purposed to marry his daughter, and Fletcher was sure of all the assistance and support which Mr Wharton could give him.

'Her fortune will not be what I once promised you,' said the old man plaintively once.

'I do not remember that I ever asked you as to her fortune,' Arthur replied.

'If you had I should not have told you. But it is right that I should explain to you that that man succeeded in lessening it by six or seven thousand pounds.'

'If that were all!'

'And I have promised Sir Alured that Everett, as his heir, should have the use of a considerable portion of his share without waiting for my death. It is odd that the one of my children from which I certainly expected the greater trouble should have reformed and fallen so entirely on his feet.' Everett had surprised his father by becoming engaged to his cousin Mary Wharton, had applied himself eagerly to the duties of a country gentleman in Herefordshire, and had effected an affectionate reconciliation with the father who had once resigned all hope in him.

Arthur Fletcher had determined that he would renew his suit as soon as a year should have expired since the tragedy which had made his love a widow, and that year had now passed away. When he sought her out at last she knew what it was that he was about to ask; which he did ask, adding the assurance of her father's sanction.

'I cannot do it,' she said.

'And why?'

'I cannot be other than the wretched thing I have made myself.'

'But do you love me?'

'I have always loved you. Everything about you is dear to me. I can triumph in your triumphs, weep at your sorrows, be ever anxious that all good things may come to you; but, Arthur, I cannot be your wife.'

'Not though it would make us all happy—Fletchers and Whartons all alike?'

'Do you think I have not thought it over? Do you think I have never told myself what I had thrown away? But it is gone, and it is not now within my reach.'

'It is; it is,' he said, throwing himself on his knees and twining his arms round her. 'I know you love me. Whatever the feeling was that overcame you as to that other man, it has gone. I cannot be tender and soft in my words. The thing to be said is too serious to me. Every friend you have wants you to marry the man you love and to put an end to the desolation which you have brought on yourself. There is not one among us all, Fletchers and Whartons, whose comfort does not more or less depend on your sacrificing the luxury of your own woe.'

'Luxury!'

'Yes; luxury. No man ever had a right to say more positively to a woman that it was her duty to marry him than I have to you. And I do say it. I won't talk of my own love now, because you know it. I won't even talk of yours, because I am sure of it. But I say that it is your duty to give up drowning us all in tears, burying us in desolation. There! I have said what I've got to say, and I will not take your answer now. I will come to you again tomorrow, and then you shall answer me.'

He had been very rough with her, speaking of his own love as a thing too certain to need further words, and had declared himself to be so assured of her love that there was no favour for him now to ask. He had given her four-and-twenty hours. He was there at the time named. 'Well?' he said.

'I should disgrace you,' she said, not firmly as before, but whispering the words.

He waited for no other assent. In a moment his arms were round her, and her veil was off, and his lips were pressed to hers; and when she could see his countenance the whole form of his face was altered to her. It was bright as it used to be bright in the old days, and he was smiling on her as he used to smile.

'My own,' he said; 'my wife—my own!' And she had no longer the power to deny him.

·   ·   ·   ·   ·

On the Sunday after the fatal division the Duchess came across her husband somewhere in the house. 'Well,' she said; 'how is it all going to be?'

381

'Her Majesty has seen both Mr Gresham and Mr Daubeny as well as myself. It does not seem a very easy thing to make a Ministry just at present.'

'Why should not you go back? I thought you were going to break your heart because people even talked of your going.'

'I was going to break my heart, as you call it, not because people talked of my ceasing to be Prime Minister, but because the feeling of the House of Commons justified people in so saying. I hope you see the difference.'

'No, I don't.'

'It is no use our discussing it, Cora.'

'Of course I understand nothing, because I'm a woman.'

'You may at any rate understand this—that our troubles are at an end. You were saying but the other day that the labours of being a Prime Minister's wife had been almost too many for you.'

'As long as you didn't give way no labour was too much for me. I would have slaved morning and night so that we might have succeeded. I hate being beat.'

'Oh, Cora!'

'I can only speak as I feel.'

Then he slowly left her. As he went she was almost tempted to yield, and to throw herself into his arms, and promise that she would be soft to him, and to say that she was sure that all he did was for the best. If he had only been a little stronger, a little thicker-skinned, a little other than he was, it might all have been so different!

In the evening the Duke of St Bungay came to Carlton Terrace with the information that Mr Gresham would attempt to form a Ministry if the Duke of Omnium would join him.

'It is impossible,' said the younger Duke.

'Listen to me before you answer with such certainty. There are three or four gentlemen who, after the work of the last three years, feel themselves disinclined to join Mr Gresham unless you will do so also. I may specially name Mr Monk and Mr Finn. Gresham can hardly make a Ministry as things are now unless Mr Monk will join them. I do not think that any other Chancellor of the Exchequer is at present possible.'

'If you wish it I will see Mr Monk, and do all that I can to get him to go with you. But for myself it would be useless.'

Mr Monk did consent, making one or two stipulations as he did so. He required that his friend Phineas Finn should be included in the Government. Mr Gresham yielded. And so the Government was formed, and the crisis was again over. The triumph of *The People's Banner*, as to the omission of the Duke, was of course complete. The editor had no hesitation in declaring that he, by his own sagacity and persistency, had made certain the exclusion of that very unfit candidate for office.

Now that he had put his own decision beyond his own power the Duke was anxious to let his wife know how it was to be with them. 'It is settled at last,' he said. 'I am a private gentleman who will now be able to devote more of his time to his wife and children than has hitherto been possible with him.'

'How very nice! Do you mean to say that you like it?'

'I am sure that I ought to like it. I am thinking more of what you will like.'

'If you ask me, Plantagenet, after drinking brandy so long I hardly think that cheap claret will agree with my stomach. You ask for the truth, and there it is—very plainly.'

'I don't think you're gone so far, Cora, that the remedy will be fatal.'

'I am thinking of you rather than myself. What will you do? It's all very well to talk of me and the children, but you can't bring in a Bill for reforming us. You can't make us go by decimals. You can't increase our consumption by lowering our taxation. I wish you had gone back to some Board.'

'I was thinking that we could spend some months in Italy, Cora.'

'What; for the summer! After that we could utilize the winter by visiting Norway.'

'We might take Norway first.'

'I've got to be too old to like travelling.'

'What do you like, dear?'

'Nothing, except being the Prime Minister's wife; and upon my word there were times when I didn't like that very much. I don't know anything else that I'm fit for.'

But the ex-Prime Minister did not carry out his purpose of leaving London in the middle of the season and travelling either to Italy or Norway. He gradually allowed himself to open his mouth on this or that subject in the House of Lords with the dignity which should belong to a retired Prime Minister. The Duchess recovered much of her good temper, and abstained from reproaching her husband for his pusillanimity.

'I'm getting used to it,' she said one day to Mrs Finn.

'Of course you'll get used to it. We get used to anything in a marvellously short time.'

'What I mean is that I can go to bed, and sleep, and get up and eat my meals without missing the sound of the trumpets so much as I did at first. I remember hearing of people who lived in a mill and couldn't sleep when the mill stopped. It was like that with me at first. I had got myself so used to the excitement of it that I could hardly live without it. And here we are as humdrum as anyone else. Even if they should have him back again it would be a very lame affair to me then. I could never again rouse myself to the effort of preparing food and lodging for half the Parliament and their wives. I shall never again think that I can help to rule England by coaxing unpleasant men. It is done and gone, and can never come back again.'

Not long after this the Duke asked the new Chancellor of the Exchequer what he thought of the present state of public affairs.

'For my own part, there is only one thing in it that I regret, and that is your retirement from official life. If the country is to lose your services for the long course of years during which you will probably sit in Parliament then I shall think that the country has lost more than it has gained.'

The Duke sat for a while silent. Then he made his answer. 'Mr Monk, I should be false if I were to deny that it pleases me to hear you say so. I have thought much of all that for the

384

last two or three months. I shall certainly never desire to be
at the head of a Government again. For a few years I would
prefer to remain out of office. But I will endeavour to look
forward to a time when I may again perhaps be of some
humble use.'

The Duke's Children

CHAPTER ONE

No one, probably, ever felt himself to be more alone in the world than the Duke of Omnium when the Duchess died. When this sad event happened he had ceased to be Prime Minister. During the first nine months after he had left office he and the Duchess remained in England. Then they had gone abroad, taking with them their three children. The eldest, Lord Silverbridge, had been at Oxford, but had had his career there cut short by some more than ordinary youthful folly, which had been cause of very great sorrow to the Duke. The other boy was to go to Cambridge. Lady Mary was the youngest of the family, aged nineteen. The Duke had gone to work at his travels with a determination to create occupation out of a new kind of life. He had studied Dante and had striven to arouse himself to ecstatic joy amidst the loveliness of the Italian lakes. But he had failed. The Duchess had made no such resolution; in truth, they had both sighed to be back among the war-trumpets. He told himself from day to day that as a peer he had a seat in Parliament; and that he might still be useful as a legislator. She, in her career as a leader of fashion, had met with some trouble, but she had often felt that there was no happiness except in London society.

Then, in the early spring of 187–, they came back to England. Lord Gerald, the younger son, was at once sent up to Trinity. For the eldest son a seat was to be found in the House of Commons. In March they spent a few days in London, and then went down to Matching Priory. When she left town the Duchess was complaining of cold, sore throat, and debility. A week after their arrival at Matching she was dead.

It was not only that his heart was torn to pieces; it was as though a man should be suddenly called upon to live without hands or even arms. He was helpless, and knew himself to be helpless. Though he had loved his wife dearly he had at times been inclined to think that in the exuberance of her spirits she had been a trouble to him. But now it was as though all outside appliances were taken away from him.

A more loving father there was not in England, but nature had made him so undemonstrative that his children had hardly known his love. In all their joys, troubles, desires and disappointments they had ever gone to their mother. She had been conversant with everything about them. She had known with the utmost accuracy the nature of the scrapes into which Lord Silverbridge had precipitated himself, and also how probable it was that Lord Gerald would do the same. The results of such scrapes she, of course, deplored; but with the spirit that produced the scrapes she fully sympathized. The father disliked the spirit almost worse than the results, and was therefore often irritated and unhappy.

And the difficulties about the girl were almost worse to bear than those about the boys. She had given no signs of extravagance or other juvenile misconduct. But she was beautiful and young. How was he to bring her out into the world? How was he to guide her through the shoals and rocks which lay in the path of such a girl before she can achieve matrimony?

There had been one very dear ally staying in the house with them when the Duchess died. This was Mrs Phineas Finn. On the afternoon of the day after the funeral the Duke and she met. He was dressed of course in black. That, indeed, was usual with him, but now the tailor by his funeral art had added some deeper dye of blackness to his appearance. When he rose and turned to her she thought that he had at once become an old man. He was thin, and had acquired a habit of stooping which, when he was not excited, gave him an appearance of age. He who was not yet fifty might have been taken to be over sixty.

'Silverbridge,' he said, 'tells me that you go back to London tomorrow.'

'Of course I would stay, Duke, if I could be of any service.'

'Perhaps you would not mind reading this letter,' the Duke said. It was from Lady Cantrip, and contained an invitation for his daughter to spend some time with her.

'Would you wish her to go there, Duke?'

'I suppose she ought to go somewhere,' he said.

'I had not thought of it,' said Mrs Finn.

Mrs Finn knew something of Lady Mary which was not known to the father. The last winter abroad had been passed at Rome, and there Lady Mary Palliser had become acquainted with a certain Mr Francis Oliphant Tregear, the younger son of a Cornish gentleman, who had become Lord Silverbridge's friend at Oxford. Mrs Finn had perceived that the Duchess had become fond of Mr Tregear. Mrs Finn had found herself unable to ask whether the girl had given her heart to this young Tregear. The one was nineteen and the other as yet but two-and-twenty. But she knew that the father was quite in the dark on the matter.

Mrs Finn made the proposition to Lady Mary in respect to Lady Cantrip's invitation. Lady Mary Palliser was very like her mother, having exactly her mother's tone of voice, her quick manner of speech, and her sharp intelligence. She had also her mother's eyes, large and round, and almost blue, full of life and full of courage, eyes which never seemed to quail, and her mother's thick dark brown hair. She could, however, already assume a personal dignity of manner which had never been within her mother's reach. She had become aware of a certain brusqueness of speech in her mother, a certain aptitude to say sharp things without thinking whether the sharpness was becoming to the position which she held, and, taking advantage of the example, the girl had already learned that she might gain more than she would lose by controlling her words.

'Why does he want to send me away, Mrs Finn?'

'He feels that it would not be well that you should live without the companionship of some lady.'

'I am not afraid of being alone. I am sure he ought not to be here quite by himself.'

It was decided that Mrs Finn should remain at Matching for at least a fortnight. Very quickly there came to be close intimacy between her and Lady Mary. Then gradually came absolute confidence. Yes; she loved Mr Tregear. She had told him so.

'Then, my dear, your father ought to know it,' said Mrs Finn.

'I know all about that,' said Lady Mary. 'I am not a bit ashamed of being in love with Mr Tregear. He is a gentleman, highly educated, very clever, of an old family—older, I believe, than Papa's. And he is manly and handsome; just what a young man ought to be. Only he is not rich.'

'If he be all that you say, ought you not to trust your papa?'

'Of course he must be told; but it is Mr Tregear that should speak to him first.'

In Mrs Finn's opinion nothing could be more unwise. But in all her arguments she was opposed by the girl's reference to her mother. 'Mamma knew it.' And it did seem to Mrs Finn as though the mother had assented to this imprudent concealment. She felt almost sure that the Duchess, with all her courage, had been afraid to propose to her husband that their daughter should marry a commoner without an income.

Tregear was staying at the Duke's house in Carlton Terrace. Silverbridge, on leaving Matching, had asked the Duke's permission to have his friend with him. The Duke was not well pleased with his son as to a matter of politics, and gave his son's friend credit for the evil counsel which had produced this displeasure. The young man was a strong Conservative; and now Silverbridge had declared his purpose of entering the House of Commons, if he did enter it, as one of the Conservative party.

On the Saturday Silverbridge appeared at breakfast with a letter in his hand. 'The governor is coming up to town. I suppose he hopes to be able to talk me into obedience. He wants me to stand for the county as a Liberal, of course. I am very sorry to annoy him, and all that kind of thing. But if a man has got political convictions he must stick to them.'

'So it is, if he has really got any. However, as your father is coming to London I need not go down to Matching.'

The Duke arrived at his house in Carlton Terrace about

five o'clock in the afternoon and immediately went to his study. Tregear, thinking that nothing could be got by delay, sent his name in to the Duke before he had been an hour in the house and asked for an interview.

'Sir,' Frank said, as soon as the door was closed behind him; 'I have come to you to ask you to give me the hand of your daughter.'

'The hand of my daughter!'

'I know how very great is the prize,' said Frank, 'and how unworthy I am of it. But—as she thinks me worthy . . .'

'She thinks you worthy!'

Tregear had prepared to bow humbly before the late Prime Minister; but he had not prepared himself to be looked at as the Duke looked at him. 'The truth, my Lord Duke, is that your daughter loves me, and that we are engaged to each other—as far as that engagement can be made without your sanction as her father.'

'It cannot have been made at all,' said the Duke. 'Has any other one of my family known of this?'

'The Duchess, sir. We had all her sympathy and approval.'

The Duke was almost beside himself with emotion. He did know that his dear wife had been the most imprudent of women. And he recognized in her encouragement of this most pernicious courtship a repetition of that romantic folly by which she had so nearly brought herself to shipwreck in her own early life.

'That will do, sir,' he said. 'I have been greatly pained as well as surprised by what I have heard. Of the real state of the case I can form no opinion till I see my daughter. You, of course, will hold no further communication with her. Good morning, sir.'

Tregear bowed, turned upon his heel, and left the room.

The Duke sat for an hour looking up at the ceiling. Why was it that, for him, such a world of misery had been prepared? In his sons hitherto he had not taken pride. They were gallant, well-grown, handsome boys, with a certain dash of cleverness—more like their mother than their father; but they had not as yet done anything as he would have had them do it. But the girl had seemed to be all that he had desired. And

393

now she had engaged herself, behind his back, to the younger son of a little country squire!

.   .   .   .   .

Major Tifto had lately become a member of the Beargarden Club, under the auspices of his friend Lord Silverbridge. He was one of the best horsemen in England. There were some who said that as a judge of a hunter few excelled him. He was Master of the Runnymede Foxhounds, and was thus enabled to write the letters M.F.H. after his name. How he was to hunt five days a fortnight, finding servants and horses and feeding the hounds for eight hundred pounds a year, no one could understand. But Major Tifto did it, and succeeded in obtaining for the Runnymede a degree of popularity which for many years previous it had not possessed.

He was a well-made little man, light-haired and blue-eyed. But his eyes were small and never tranquil, and rarely capable of looking at the person who was speaking to him. He had small, well-trimmed, glossy whiskers, with the best-kept moustache, and the best-kept tuft on his chin which were to be seen anywhere. His face still bore the freshness of youth, which was a marvel to many who declared that Tifto must be far on the wrong side of forty. Yet he could jump over the backs of four chairs in a dining-room after dinner. That Major Tifto should make money by selling horses was, per-haps, a necessity of his position. But there were some who considered that they had suffered unduly under his hands.

This very moment was the culmination of the Major's life. He was Master of the Runnymede Hounds, he was partner with the eldest son of a Duke in the possession of that magni-ficent colt the Prime Minister, and he was a member of the Beargarden. He was taken there under Lord Silverbridge's wing. There were already four or five assembled, among whom was Mr Adolphus Longstaff, a young man of about thirty-five years of age, who spent very much of his time at the Beargarden. 'Do you know my friend Tifto?' said the Lord. 'Tifto, this is Mr Longstaff, whom men sometimes call

Dolly.' Whereupon the Major bowed and smiled graciously.

'I have heard of Major Tifto. Last season I was always intending to get down to your country and have a day with the Tiftoes,' said Dolly. 'Well, Silverbridge, how's the Prime Minister?'

'How is he, Tifto?' asked the noble partner.

'I don't think there's a horse in England just at present enjoying a very much better state of health,' said the Major pleasantly.

'Safe to run?' asked Dolly.

'I think we mean him to start, don't we, Silverbridge?' said the Major.

There was something perhaps in the tone in which the last remark was made which jarred a little against the young lord's dignity. At any rate he got up and declared his purpose of going to the opera. He should look in, he said, and hear a song from Mdlle Stuffa, the nightingale of the season. Major Tifto had some whisky-and-water, lit his third cigar, and began to feel the glory of belonging to the Beargarden.

'I never thought so much about her good looks,' he said, talking of the singer.

'Did you ever see her off the stage?' asked Dolly.

'Oh dear yes. We've been pals ever since she has been over here,' said Tifto, with an enormous lie.

'How do you get on with her husband?' asked Dolly, in the simplest voice.

'Husband!' exclaimed the Major, who was not possessed of sufficient presence of mind to suppress all signs of his ignorance.

'Ah,' said Dolly; 'you are not probably aware that your pal has been married to Mr Thomas Jones for the last year and a half.' Soon after that Major Tifto left the club—with considerably enhanced respect for Mr Longstaff.

.   .   .   .   .

'Silverbridge,' the Duke said next morning, 'I hope you have thought better of what we were talking about as to these coming elections. I trust you will not find yourself obliged

to desert the school of politics to which your family has belonged for many generations.'

'I could not call myself a Liberal, sir.'

'Why not?'

'Because I am a Conservative.'

'I believe it to be that most arrogant ill-behaved young
man who was with me yesterday who has done this evil,' his
father said angrily.

'You mean Frank Tregear?'

'I do. He has been speaking to me about your sister. Did
you know of this?'

'I knew there was something between them.'

'And why did you not tell me?'

'My dear mother, sir, thought well of him. I always told
him that you would never consent. In the meantime, they
were not seeing each other.'

'There must be an end of this,' said the Duke. 'I will speak
to your sister. In the meantime, the less you see of Mr Tregear
the better. Of course it is out of the question he should be
allowed to remain in this house.'

'Oh, certainly,' said Silverbridge.

The Duke returned to Matching an almost broken-hearted
man. When Lady Mary came to welcome him, he kissed her
and bade her come to him after his dinner.

'Come and sit down, Mary,' he said, pointing to the seat
on the sofa beside himself.

She took one of his hands within her own. 'Will Silverbridge
be a Liberal, Papa?'

'I am afraid not. It is a cause of great unhappiness to me;
but a man is entitled to his own opinion, even though he be
a very young man.'

'I am so sorry that it should be so, Papa, because it vexes
you.'

'I have many things to vex me. Mr Tregear came to me
yesterday, and told me . . . Oh, Mary, can it be true?'

'Yes, Papa,' she said, with her eyes turned down.

'Do you mean to tell me that you have engaged yourself
to that young man without my approval?'

'Of course you were to have been asked, Papa.'

'Then, Mary, it becomes my duty to tell you that it is quite impossible. Will you tell me that you will not see him again?'

'I don't think that I can say that.'

'Why not?'

'Oh Papa, how can I, when of all the people in the world I love him the best?'

'Do you not know that he is not fit to be your husband?'

'He is a gentleman, Papa.'

'The word is too vague to carry with it any meaning. I cannot but think you must have known that you were not entitled to give your love to any man without being assured that the man would be approved of by—by—by me.' He was going to say, 'your parents', but was stopped by the remembrance of his wife's imprudence. She saw it all, and was too noble to plead her mother's authority.

'Papa, I love Mr Tregear, and as I have told him so I will be true to him.'

Then it occurred to him how difficult it would be for him to have the charge of such a daughter—how impossible that he should conduct such a charge with sufficient firmness, and yet with sufficient tenderness.

'There shall be no writing,' he said, 'no visiting, no communication of any kind. As you refuse to obey me now, you had better go to your room.'

.   .   .   .   .

'And so poor Frank has been turned out of heaven,' said Lady Mabel Grex to young Lord Silverbridge. Lady Mabel was the daughter of the Earl of Grex, and their conversation was taking place at the Earl's home in Belgrave Square. 'You might as well tell me all about it. We are cousins, you know.' Frank Tregear, through his mother's family, was second cousin to Lady Mabel; as was also Lord Silverbridge.

'The governor merely seemed to think that he would like to have his own house to himself, like other people.'

'Lord Silverbridge, do you mean to say that there is not something in the wind about Lady Mary?'

397

'If there were I should not talk about it,' said Lord Silver-bridge.

'You are a very innocent young gentleman.'

'And you are a very interesting young lady.'

'You are going to dine here, Lord Silverbridge?'

'Not that I know of. Nobody has asked me, and I hate family dinners on Sunday.'

'I ask you. And you are an uncivil young—young—I should say cub if I dared, to tell me that you don't like dining with me any day of the week.'

'I don't like troubling your father.'

'I shall tell him you are coming, and Frank too. Of course you can bring him.' So at eight o'clock Lord Silverbridge reappeared in Belgrave Square with Frank Tregear.

Frank Tregear, having been known by the family as a boy, was Frank to all of them, as was Lady Mabel Mabel to him. Silverbridge, being Silverbridge to all his own people, hardly seemed to have a Christian name. He was Lord Silverbridge to Lady Mabel. Lady Mabel, by her very intimate friends called Mab, had allowed herself to be addressed by him as Lady Mab. There was thus between them all considerable intimacy.

'Lord Silverbridge is going to stand for the Duke's borough in the Conservative interest,' Lady Mabel told her father.

'I didn't know the Duke had a borough,' said the Earl.

'He had one till he thought it proper to give it up,' said the son, taking his father's part.

'And you are going to pay him off by standing against him. It's just the sort of thing for a son to do in these days.'

'I know it vexes him. But he doesn't quarrel with me. He even wrote to say that all my expenses at Silverbridge were to be paid.'

'I shall be on tenterhooks now till I know how it is to be at Silverbridge,' said Lady Mabel. 'When is it to be?'

'They say that the elections will be over before the Derby.'

'And which do you care for the most?'

'I should like to pull off the Derby, I own.'

'I do so hope you'll get the seat—and win the Derby,' were her last words to him later, as she wished him good night.

CHAPTER TWO

THE Conservative side was the popular side among the tradesmen of Silverbridge. Silverbridge had been proud to be honoured by the services of the heir of the house of Omnium, even while that heir had been a Liberal, and had the Duke chosen to continue to send them Liberals when he went into the House of Lords there would have been no question as to the fitness of the men so sent. But when the Duke declared that he would not interfere any more the borough had elected a certain Mr Fletcher, Conservative. Now Mr Fletcher was wanted elsewhere, and Lord Silverbridge was elected unopposed. When it was over he wrote a line to the Duke.

My dear Father,
    I am Member of Parliament for Silverbridge—as you used to be. I hope you won't think that it does not make me unhappy to have differed from you. Indeed it does. I don't think that anybody has ever done so well in politics as you have. But when a man does take up an opinion I don't see how he can help himself.
                    Your affectionate Son,
                      Silverbridge.

There was something in the letter which softened the Duke's heart to the young man. The thing had been done pleasantly enough, and the young Member's letter had been written with some good feeling.

The new Member for Silverbridge, when he entered the House to take the oath, was congratulated by his father's staunch friend Mr Monk, who of all Liberals was the firmest. And then the Member for Silverbridge was bustled up to the table between two staunch Tories.

'There seemed to be a great deal of bustle, and I didn't

understand much about it,' said the member to Lady Mabel Grex later.

'I do so hope that you will do well,' she said.

'I don't think I shall ever do much. I shall vote with my party of course.'

'Much more than that. If you didn't care for politics you couldn't have taken a line of your own. If you do not do it for your own sake, you will for the sake of your friends.'

'There are not very many I suppose who care about it.'

'Do you think I don't care a straw about it?'

'I don't know why you should. I always think that nobody is so full of chaff as you are, Lady Mab.'

'I am not chaffing now in recommending you to go to work in the world like a man.' As she said this she put out her hand, meaning perhaps to touch lightly the sleeve of his coat. But as she did so he put out his hand and took hold of hers. She drew it away, not angrily, or hurriedly, or with any flurry.

'If you will say that you care about it, you yourself, I will do my best.' As he made this declaration blushes covered his cheeks and forehead.

'I do care about it—very much,' said Lady Mabel, not blushing at all. Then there was a knock at the door, and Lady Mabel's maid putting her head in declared that my Lord had come in and had already been some time in his dressing-room. 'Good-bye, Lord Silverbridge,' she said quite gaily, and rather more aloud than would have been necessary, had she not intended that the maid also should hear her.

.   .   .   .   .

Prime Minister stood very well for the Derby. He was second favourite. Now had come the night before the Derby, and Tifto, having seen the horse conveyed to Epsom, had come up to London to dine with his partner and hear what was being said about the race at the Beargarden. The party dining there consisted of Silverbridge, Dolly Longstaff, and Tifto.

The dinner was very joyous. Of course the state of the betting in regard to Prime Minister was the subject generally popular for the night. Mr Lupton came in, a gentleman well known in all fashionable circles, parliamentary, social, and racing. 'I never keep these things dark,' said Tifto. 'Of course he's an uncertain horse.'

'Most horses are,' said Lupton.

'Just so, Mr Lupton. What I mean is, the Minister has got a bit of temper. But if he likes to do his best I don't think any three-year-old in England can get his nose past him. Is there any gentleman here who would like to bet me fifteen to one in hundreds against the two events—the Derby and the Leger?' The odds were at once offered by Mr Lupton, and the bet was booked.

This gave rise to other betting and before the evening was over Lord Silverbridge had taken wagers to such an extent that he stood to lose twelve hundred pounds. The champagne he had drunk, and the news that Quousque, the first favourite, had gone to pieces had so inflated him that he would almost have wagered even money on his horse.

Tifto, when he got into his bed, was altogether happy. He had added whisky-and-water to his champagne, and feared nothing. If Prime Minister should win the Derby he would be able to pay all that he owed, and to make a start with money in his pocket. And then there would be attached to him all the infinite glory of being the owner of a winner of the Derby. The horse was run in his name. Thoughts as to great successes crowded themselves upon his heated brain. The Jockey Club! The mastership of one of the crack shire packs! Might it not come to pass that he should some day become the great authority in England upon races, racehorses, and hunters?

Lord Silverbridge had bought a drag with all its appendages. There was a coach, the four bay horses, the harness, and the two regulation grooms. When making this purchase he had condescended to say a word to his father on the subject. 'Everybody belongs to the four-in-hand club now.'

'I never did,' said the Duke.

'Ah, if I could be like you.'

The Duke had said that he would think about it, and then had said that he would pay the bill for this new toy; and now they were put into requisition to take their triumphant owner and his party down to Epsom. Tifto, with a cigar in his mouth, with a white hat and a new light-coloured coat, was by no means the least happy of the party.

Both Prime Minister and Quousque were beaten by an outsider named Fishknife. Dolly Longstaff and Lord Silverbridge drove the coach back to London. The young fellows bore their failure well. Dolly Longstaff had lost a 'pot of money', Silverbridge would have to draw something over two thousand pounds.

But Tifto felt it more than anyone. The horse ought to have won. Fishknife had been favoured by such a series of accidents that the whole affair had been a miracle. Tifto had these circumstances at his fingers' ends, and in the course of the afternoon and evening explained them accurately to all who would listen to him.

'What the devil is the good of that?' said Dolly from the coach-box. 'Take your licking and don't squeal.'

Before he went to the House next day, Lord Silverbridge went to see Lady Mabel Grex. Marriage would steady him. Upon the whole he thought it would be good that he should marry. And, if so, who could be so nice as Lady Mabel? That his father would be contented with Lady Mab, he was inclined to believe. There was no better blood in England. And Lady Mabel was clever, beautiful, and very wise.

He was aware, however, of a certain drawback. Lady Mabel as his wife would be his superior, and in some degree his master. Though not older she was wiser than he, and more powerful. He was not quite sure but that she regarded him as a boy. He thought that she did love him, but that her love would be bestowed upon him as on an inferior creature.

'Not at the Oaks!' she said as soon as he was shown into the drawing-room.

He told the whole story, and of a painful interview with his father after his return from the race. 'Then he said,' continued Silverbridge, 'that his children between them would bring him to his grave. Of course what I did at Oxford made him unhappy; and now there is this affair of Mary's. Of course my father does not like it.'

'Do you approve of it?'

'No.'

'Why not? You like Tregear.'

'Certainly. He is the friend, among men, whom I like the best. I have only two real friends.'

'Who are they?' she asked, sinking her voice very low.

'He is one—and you are the other. You know that.'

'I hoped that I was one,' she said. 'But if you love Tregear so dearly, why do you not approve of him for your sister?'

'Mary ought to marry a man of higher standing.'

'Of higher rank you mean. The daughters of Dukes have married commoners before. The real reason is, I imagine, that Frank and I are almost beggars. I am obliged to hope that I may some day marry a man who has got an income.'

'I suppose so,' said he, blushing.

'You see I can be very frank with a real friend. But I am sure of myself in this—I will never marry a man I do not love.'

'But you do mean to fall in love?'

'That remains to be seen,. Lord Silverbridge. The man will have to fall in love with me first. If you know of anyone you need not tell him to be too sure because he has a good income.'

'I was thinking of—myself.'

'You are certainly one of the impossibles.'

'Why, Lady Mab?'

'You are too young, and you are to be wedded to Parliament, at any rate for the next ten years.'

'I suppose you don't like me well enough?'

'What a question to ask! No; my Lord, I do not. There; that's what you may call an answer. Don't you pretend to look offended, because if you do, I shall laugh at you. If you may have your joke surely I may have mine.'

'I don't see any joke in it.'

'But I do. Suppose I were to say the other thing. Oh, Lord Silverbridge, you do me so much honour! Would that suit you?'

'Exactly.'

'But it wouldn't suit me. There's Papa. Don't run away.'

'It's ever so much past five,' said the legislator, 'and I had intended to be in the House more than an hour ago. Good-bye.'

The Duke was in the gallery of the House of Commons which is devoted to the use of peers one evening soon after this, and Silverbridge had come up to him. The Duke was very anxious that his son should attend to his parliamentary duties, but he was too proud a man and too generous to come to the House as a spy. It was his present habit always to be in his own place when the Lords were sitting. He would never, however, come across into the other House without letting his son know.

'Where are you going to dine, sir?' asked Silverbridge. The Duke, with something of a sigh, said he supposed he should dine at home.

'You never were at the Beargarden, were you, sir?' asked Silverbridge suddenly.

'Never,' said the Duke.

'Come and dine with me.'

'I shall be glad to see the place where you pass many hours.'

They got into a cab and went to the club. The invitation had come on the spur of the moment, and Silverbridge did not quite know how the Duke would fare. 'The other fellows' would stare at a man whom they had all been taught to regard as the most un-Beargardenish of men. But he was especially anxious to make things pleasant for his father.

Nothing especial occurred during the dinner, which the Duke appeared to enjoy very much. He liked the feeling that he was dining with his son. A report that the Duke of Omnium was with Lord Silverbridge soon went round the room, and they who were justified by some previous acquaintance came up to greet him. To all who did so he was very gracious.

Then they went into the small library upstairs to have coffee, the son declining to go into the smoking-room, where he had glimpsed Major Tifto with his cigar and whisky.

'A club,' said the Duke, as he sipped his coffee, 'is a comfortable and economical residence. A man gets what he wants well-served, and gets it cheap. But it has its drawbacks.'

'You always see the same fellows,' said Silverbridge.

'A man who lives much at a club is apt to fall into a selfish

404

mode of life. He is taught to think that his own comfort should always be the first object. It is for that reason—among others —that marriage is so desirable.'

'A man should marry, I suppose.'

'Unless a man has on his shoulders the burden of a wife and children he should, I think, feel that he has shirked out of school.'

'I suppose I shall marry some day.'

'I should be glad to see you marry early. You are peculiarly situated. Though as yet you are only the heir to the property and honours of our family, still, were you married, almost everything would be at your disposal.'

Then the father looked round the room furtively, and seeing that the door was shut asked a straightforward question. 'You have never thought of anyone yet, I suppose?'

'But I have.' Lord Silverbridge blushed up to the eyes.

'Have you spoken to her?'

'Well, yes, in part. I suppose I may as well out with it. You know Lady Mabel Grex?'

'Is she not your senior?'

'No, sir; no; she is younger than I am.'

'She is very beautiful.'

'I think so, sir. Of course she has no money.'

'It is not needed. It is not needed. I have no objection to make. If you are sure of your own mind . . .'

'She has not accepted me.'

'But should she do so, you may.'

'She almost rejected me. But I am not sure she was in earnest, and I mean to try again.' Just at that moment the door was opened and Major Tifto walked into the room.

'I beg your pardon, Silverbridge,' said the Major, 'but I was looking for Longstaff.'

He was red in the face but was in other respects perhaps improved in appearance by his liquor. A second glass of whisky would always enable him to cock his tail and bark before the company with all the courage of my lady's pug.

'Your father, I believe?' said Tifto. 'My Lord Duke, I am Major Tifto.'

The Duke bowed graciously. 'My father and I were engaged about private matters,' said Silverbridge.

'I beg ten thousand pardons,' exclaimed the Major.

'I think we had done,' said the Duke. 'Pray sit down, Major Tifto.' The Major sat down. 'Though now I bethink myself, I have to beg your pardon—that I a stranger should ask you to sit down in your own club.'

'Don't mention it, my Lord Duke.'

'I am so unused to clubs, that I forgot where I was.'

'We didn't make a very good thing of our Derby nag the other day. Perhaps your Grace has heard all that?'

'I did hear that the horse in which you are both interested had failed to win the race.'

'Yes, he did. The Prime Minister, we call him, your Grace, out of compliment to a certain Ministry which I wish it was going on today instead of the seedy lot we've got in. I think, my Lord Duke, that anyone you may ask will tell you that I know what running is. Well; I can assure you—your Grace, that is—that since I've seen 'orses I've never seen a 'orse fitter than him. But I never saw a 'orse so bad ridden. I don't mean to say anything, my Lord Duke, against the man. But if that fellow hadn't been squared, or else wasn't drunk, or else wasn't off his head, that 'orse must have won—my Lord Duke.'

'Tifto, you are making an ass of yourself,' said Silverbridge.

'Making an ass of myself!' exclaimed the Major.

'Yes; considerably.'

'I think you are a little hard upon your friend,' said the Duke, with an attempt at a laugh. 'It is not to be supposed that he should know how utterly indifferent I am to everything connected with the turf.'

'I thought, my Lord Duke, you might care about learning how Silverbridge was going on.' This the poor little man said almost with a whine. His partner's roughness had knocked out of him nearly all the courage which Bacchus had given him.

'So I do; anything that interests him, interests me. But perhaps of all his pursuits racing is the one to which I am least able to lend an attentive ear. That every horse has a head, and that all did have tails till they were ill-used, is the extent of my stable knowledge.'

406

'Very good indeed, my Lord Duke; very good indeed! Ha, ha, ha!—all horses have heads, and all have tails! Heads and tails. Upon my word that is the best thing I have heard for a long time. I will do myself the honour of wishing your Grace good night. By-bye, Silverbridge.' Then he left the room, having been made supremely happy by what he considered to have been the Duke's joke. Nevertheless he would remember the snubbing and would be even with Silverbridge some day. Did Lord Silverbridge think that he was going to look after his Lordship's 'orses and then be snubbed for doing it?

'I am very sorry that he should have come in to trouble you,' said the son.

'If you are coming down to the House again I will walk with you.' They started together. 'That man did not trouble me, Silverbridge; but the question is whether such an acquaintance must not be troublesome to you.'

'He understands racing.'

'I thought that a gentleman on the turf would have a trainer for that purpose; not a companion. You mean to imply that you can save money by leaguing yourself with Major Tifto?'

'No, sir, indeed. I will get rid of him,' said Silverbridge. 'I cannot do so at once, but I will do it.'

'It will be better, I think. And so it is to be Mabel Grex?'

'I did not say so, sir. How can I answer for her? Only it was so pleasant for me to know that you would approve if it should come off.'

'When it is settled let me know at once.' Then in Palace Yard, turning to go, he said, 'I do not think that Mabel Grex and Major Tifto would do well together at all.'

'There shall be an end to that, sir.'

'God bless you, my boy!' said the Duke.

·　　·　　·　　·

It was known to all the world that Mrs Montacute Jones's great garden-party was to come off on Wednesday, 16th June, at Roehampton. Mrs Montacute Jones was an old lady who worked very hard to get round her all the rank and fashion of the day, and everybody liked to be asked to her garden-parties. Lord Silverbridge had been asked. He was well aware that Lady Mab would be there. What place could be better for putting the question he had to ask? Lady Mary, his sister, could not be asked, because her mother was hardly more than three months dead; but it is understood in the world that women mourn longer than men.

Entering through the house into the lawn he encountered Mrs Montacute Jones, surrounded by flowers. 'How very good of you to come, Lord Silverbridge. Have you met Miss Boncassen yet?'

'The American beauty?'

'Yes; and she particularly wants to be introduced to you. There they are, and I shall introduce you.' Mr Boncassen was an American who had lately arrived in England with the object of carrying out certain literary pursuits. He was a man of wealth and a man of letters. And he had a daughter who was said to be the prettiest young woman either in Europe or in America at the present time.

Isabel Boncassen was certainly a very pretty girl. Perhaps what struck the beholder first was the excessive brilliancy of her complexion. No pink was ever pinker, no alabaster whiteness was ever more like alabaster; but under and around and through it all there was a constantly changing hue which gave a vitality to her countenance which no fixed colours can produce. Her eyes were full of life and brilliancy, and even when she was silent her mouth would speak. It was the vitality of her countenance that made all acknowledge that she was beautiful.

'Lord Silverbridge,' said Mr Boncassen, 'I am proud to make your acquaintance, sir. Your father is a man for whom we in our country have a great respect. I think, sir, you must be proud of such a father.'

'Oh yes—no doubt,' said Silverbridge awkwardly. Then Mr Boncassen continued his discourse with the gentlemen around him. Upon this Silverbridge turned to the young lady. 'Have you been long in England, Miss Boncassen?'

'Long enough to have heard about you and your father.'

'I hope you have not heard any evil of me.'

'I know you didn't win the Derby.'

'You've been long enough to hear that?'

'Do you suppose we don't interest ourselves about the Derby in New York? Shall you have a horse at Ascot?'

'There will be something going, I suppose. Nothing that I care about.' He found himself walking alone with Miss Boncassen. It was thus that he had intended to walk with Mabel Grex. 'Oh yes,' said Miss Boncassen, when they had been together about twenty minutes; 'we shall be here all the summer, and all the fall, and all the winter. Indeed Father means to read every book in the British Museum before he goes back.'

'He'll have something to do.'

'He reads by steam, and he has two or three young men with him to take it all down.' He saw Mabel Grex walking with Tregear, and she bowed to him playfully. 'Is that lady a great friend of yours?' asked Miss Boncassen.

'A very great friend indeed.'

'She is very beautiful.'

'And clever as well.'

'Dear me! Do tell me who it is that owns all these qualities.'

'Lady Mabel Grex. That man with her is Frank Tregear, and they are cousins.'

'I am so glad they are cousins.'

'Why glad?'

'Because his being with her won't make you unhappy.'

'Supposing I was in love with her—which I am not—do you suppose it would make me jealous to see her with another man?'

'In our country it would not. Judging by English ways, I believe I am behaving very improperly in walking about with you so long. So I shan't walk about with you any more.'

'Oh yes, you will,' said Silverbridge, who began to think that he liked walking about with Miss Boncassen.

'Certainly not. Do you think I don't understand that everybody will be making remarks upon the American girl who won't leave the son of the Duke of Omnium alone?'

'May I come and call?'

'Certainly. Father will only be too proud—and I shall be prouder. Mother will be the proudest of all. Till we get a house we are at the Langham.'

Lord Silverbridge found himself close to Lady Mabel and Tregear, and also to Miss Cassewary, a friend of Lady Mabel. He had been much struck with the American beauty, but was not on that account the less anxious to carry out his great plan. 'Come and take a turn with me,' he said.

'What have you done with your American beauty? The truth is, Lord Silverbridge, you ask me for my company when she won't give you hers any longer.'

'I don't know that I ever saw a prettier girl,' said Tregear.

'I quite admit it,' said Lady Mabel. 'But that is no salve for my injured feelings. I have heard so much about Miss Boncassen's beauty for the last week, that I mean to get up a company of British females, limited, for the express purpose of putting her down.'

'That is so like an Englishwoman,' said Silverbridge. 'Because you cannot understand a manner of life a little different from your own you will impute evil.'

'I have imputed no evil, Lord Silverbridge. She is a beautiful girl, and very clever, and would make a charming Duchess. And then it would be such a delicious change to have an American Duchess.'

'She wouldn't be a Duchess.'

'Well, Countess, with Duchess-ship before her in the remote future.'

Lord Silverbridge went away in a very ill humour, which, however, had quite left him when in the course of an afternoon three weeks later he found himself up at Maidenhead with Miss Boncassen. During those weeks he had often been in her company. Miss Boncassen at any rate did not laugh at him. She was so pleasant, so full of common sense, and so completely intelligent. 'I like you,' she had said, 'because I feel you will not think you ought to make love to me. There is nothing I hate so much as the idea that a young man and a young woman can't be acquainted with each other without some such tomfoolery as that.'

But that night he did tell Isabel Boncassen that he loved her.

'Lord Silverbridge!'

'I do. I do. Can you say that you will love me in return?'

'I cannot,' she said slowly. 'I have never dreamed of such a thing.'

'I ask you to be my wife.'

'Then you must listen to me. I know a great deal about you. We Americans are an inquiring people, and I have found out pretty much everything. You among young men in England are about the foremost. You are, no doubt, supposed to be entitled to the best and sweetest of God's feminine creatures.'

'You are she.'

'I will tell you something of myself. My father's father came to New York as a labourer from Holland. Then he built houses, and became rich, with the good sense to educate his only son. What my father is you see, but he is not like your people. My dear mother is not at all like your ladies. For myself I am—well, meaning to speak honestly, I will call myself pretty and smart. I think I know how to be true. But what right have you to suppose I shall know how to be a Duchess?'

'I am sure you will.'

'Go to your friends and ask them. Ask that Lady Mabel; ask your father. And above all, ask yourself. And allow me to require you to take three months to do this. Do not come to see me for three months.'

'And then?'

'I want three months also to think of it myself. Till then, good-bye.' She gave him her hand and left it in his for a few seconds. He tried to draw her to him, but she resisted him, smiling.

CHAPTER THREE

IT was a custom with Mrs Phineas Finn almost every autumn to go off to Vienna, where she possessed considerable property. Sometimes her husband would accompany her. One morning in September they were together at an hotel at Ischl, whither they had come from Vienna, when as they went through the hall into the courtyard they came upon the Duke of Omnium and his daughter. The Duke and Lady Mary, having passed through the mountains, were about to take up their residence in the hotel for a few days. They had travelled very slowly, for Lady Mary had been ill, and the Duke had expressed his determination to see a doctor at Ischl.

'It is so nice to find you,' said Lady Mary. 'We are this moment come. Don't say that you are this moment going.'

'At this moment we are only going out as far as Hallstadt.'

'And are coming back to dinner? Of course they will dine with us. Will they not, Papa?' The Duke said that he hoped they would.

At dinner the conversation turned largely on British politics. Phineas was decidedly of opinion that the present Conservative administration could not live another Session. Later in the evening the Duke found himself sitting with Mrs Finn in the broad verandah over the hotel garden. 'How do you think she is looking?' asked the father.

'Of course I see that she has been ill.'

'Yes; indeed for three or four days she frightened me much. She suffered terribly from headaches.'

'Nervous headaches?'

'So they said.'

The next morning Lady Mary could not leave her bed, and the Duke applied to Mrs Finn. She found the girl in great pain. Shortly after that Mrs Finn was alone with the Duke.

'One cannot tell what it comes from,' said the Duke.

'It must come from something wrong.'

'She says that she is unhappy. You know all the misery about that young man,' he added. 'I cannot encourage a hope that she should be allowed to marry him. There are insurmountable discrepancies.'

'You would not have her——break her heart?'

'No,' he said; 'I would not have her break her heart—if I understand what such words mean. They are generally, I think, used fantastically.'

'I must be more plain in my language, Duke. Though such a marriage be distasteful to you, it might perhaps be preferable to seeing her sorrowing always.'

'Thank you,' he said, rising from his chair.

'I think I should take her to some place on the seashore in England,' said Mrs Finn.

'Custins is close to the sea,' he replied. 'It is Lord Cantrip's place in Dorsetshire. It was partly settled that she was to go there.'

'I suppose she likes Lady Cantrip.'

'Why should she not?'

'She has not said a word to me to the contrary. I only fear she would feel that she was being sent there as to a convent.'

In a day or two Lady Mary was better. 'It is terrible while it lasts,' she said, speaking to Mrs Finn of her headache.

'I dare say you will be happy at Custins.'

'No, I shall not. Have you heard anything about him, Mrs Finn?'

'Do you mean Mr Tregear?'

'Yes, Mr Tregear.'

'I think I heard that he was shooting with Lord Silverbridge.'

'I am very glad they should be together. While I know that I feel that we are not altogether separated. I will never give it up, Mrs Finn—never; never.'

.   .   .   .   .

The Leger was to be run on the 14th September, and the indefatigable Major was hard at work in the stables. On the

413

Friday before the race Silverbridge dined with Tifto at the Beargarden. On the next morning they went down to Newmarket to see Prime Minister gallop, and came back the same evening. During all this time Tifto was more than ordinarily pleasant to his patron. The certainty of the horse's success was the only subject mooted. Mr Pook, the trainer, assured his Lordship that for health and condition he had never seen any horse better. And then there were various evidences produced of his pace—how he had beaten that horse, giving him two pounds; how he had been beaten by that, but only on a mile course; the Leger distance was just the thing for Prime Minister; how Coalheaver was known to have had bad feet. In the course of the day, however, they met a gentleman who was of a different opinion. He said he looked on the Heaver as the best three-year-old in England. All this ended in a bet being accepted, and in this way Silverbridge added two thousand four hundred pounds to his responsibilities.

On the Sunday afternoon he went down to Doncaster in company with the Major. All the racing-men there were occupied with Prime Minister. The horse and Mr Pook had arrived that day from Newmarket. Tifto, Silverbridge and Mr Pook visited him together three times that afternoon and evening.

There was a club at which many of the racing-men dined, and there Lord Silverbridge spent his evening. He was the hero of the hour, and everybody flattered him. They dined at eight and much wine was drunk. Large sums were named, and before the night was over he stood to lose about seventy thousand pounds upon the race.

While this was going on Tifto sat not far from his patron, but completely silent. During the day and early in the evening a few sparks of the glory which scintillated from the favourite horse flew in his direction. But though the horse was to be run in his name he had very little to say in the matter. Not a boast came out of his mouth during dinner or after dinner. He was so moody that his partner, who was generally anxious to keep him quiet, more than once endeavoured to encourage him. But he was unable to rouse himself. It was still within his power to be on the square with Lord Silverbridge. As he heard all that was being done, his conscience troubled him sorely. If Prime Minister should lose he was to have three thousand pounds from a certain Captain Green, and then there would be the bets he himself had laid against the horse—by Green's assistance. It would be the making of him. At last he slunk away to bed.

On the following morning, the morning of the day on which the race was to be run, the Major tapped at his patron's door. 'What the devil does this mean?' said his Lordship angrily. Then Tifto told his story. He and the groom had taken the horse out of the stable for slight exercise, and while doing so a nail had been picked up. The iron had driven itself into the horse's frog and there was no possibility that the horse should run on that day.

The story was soon the one matter for discussion in all racing quarters. The intention had been to take the horse round a portion of the outside of the course near to which his stable stood. A boy rode him and the groom and Tifto went with him. At a certain spot on their return Tifto had exclaimed that the horse was going lame in his off fore-foot. As to this exclamation the boy and the two men were agreed. The boy was then made to dismount, and Tifto commenced to examine the horse's foot. The boy saw him raise the off fore-leg. He himself had not found the horse lame under him, but it was led into the stable as lame as a tree. Here Tifto found the nail inserted into the very cleft of the frog of the near fore-foot.

Silverbridge would not lend himself at all to those who suspected mischief. He was miserable enough, but in this great trouble he would not separate himself from Tifto. But before one o'clock, at which hour the races would commence, general opinion had formed itself; and general opinion had hit the truth—that the nail had been driven in wilfully, by Tifto himself, and that Tifto had been instigated by spite against his aristocratic partner. 'I have got my little money on, and what little I have I lose,' Tifto said in answer to inquiries. But everyone suspected that he had a great interest in the race. There was one man who asserted it as a fact that Tifto and one Gilbert Villiers were in partnership together. It was very well known that Gilbert Villiers would win two thousand five hundred pounds from Lord Silverbridge. It was said that one at least of the large bets made on that Tuesday evening could be traced to the same Villiers though not actually made by him. But there was no proof forthcoming as to the cause of the laming, nor of the extent to which Tifto himself had benefited from it.

Silverbridge carried himself well, taking, or affecting to take, great interest in the race, explaining that he would consult his father's agent and would then appear on settling-day. They were all full of sympathy and the blandest courtesies.

He went back to London and called upon his father's agent, Mr Moreton, with the news that he had incurred debts to the sum of seventy thousand pounds. Mr Moreton knew the Duke's mind. A very large discretion had been left in Mr Moreton's hands in regard to moneys which might be needed on behalf of that dangerous heir—so large that he was able to tell Lord Silverbridge that the money should all be forthcoming. It was for his son's character and standing in the world, for his future respectability and dignity that the Duke's fears were so keen, and not for his own money. By one so excitable, so fond of pleasure as Lord Silverbridge, some ravaging would probably be made. Let it be met by ready money, had been the Duke's instructions to his own trusted man of business.

The Duke and his daughter had just returned from their travels and were at Matching. Silverbridge presented himself there without delay.

'I am glad to see you, Silverbridge,' said the Duke, putting out his hand.

'I hope I see you well, sir.'

'Fairly well. Thank you. Travelling I think agrees with me. I miss, not my comforts, but a certain knowledge of how things are going on.' This was said with something even of banter in it, and the Duke was smiling. But in a moment the young man felt almost like a culprit. 'We might as well have it out about this racing,' continued the Duke. 'Something has to be said. You have lost an enormous sum of money. And worse than that, you have lost it in as bad company as you could have found had you picked all England through.'

'I will never own a horse again, or a part of a horse. I will have nothing more to do with races. You will believe me?'

'I will believe anything you tell me.'

Then the father came up to the son and put his arms round the young man's shoulders. 'Of course it made me unhappy. But if you are cured of this evil the money is nothing. Who owns the horse now?'

'The horses shall be sold.'

'For anything they may fetch so that we may get clear of this dirt. And the Major?'

'I know nothing of him. I have not seen him since that day'

'Has he claims on you?'

'Not a shilling. It is all the other way.'

'Let it go then. Be quit of him, however it may be. Mr Moreton might perhaps see him.'

That his father should forgive so readily affected the son's feelings so strongly that he could make no answer.

'There shall not be another word said about it,' said the Duke again. 'And now, do you remember what you were saying when you walked down to the House with me from your club that night?'

'Yes, sir.'

'Then is there nothing to be told? I hope you have not changed your mind.'

Just at present, after his folly in regard to those heavy debts, he could not at once risk his father's renewed anger by proposing to him an American daughter-in-law. That must stand over, at any rate till the girl had accepted him positively.

'I can't explain it all, sir—but I fear it won't come off with Lady Mabel Grex.'

Then the Duke made a final little speech. 'But you must not be surprised if I am anxious to see you settled in life, Silverbridge. No young man could be more bound by duty to marry early than you are. I could never bring myself to dictate to a son in regard to his choice of a wife, but I will own that when you told me that you had chosen I was much grati-

417

fied. Try and think again whether that be possible.' Silverbridge said that he would bear this in mind, and then escaped
from the room.

Miss Boncassen saw the Duke of Omnium for the first
time at Custins, where Lady Mary Palliser was now staying
with Lady Cantrip.

'I do not know whether you approve it,' Lady Cantrip
said to the Duke; 'but Mary has become very intimate with
our new American friend.'

'They seem to be sensible people,' said the Duke. 'I don't
know when I have met a man with higher ideas on politics
than Mr Boncassen.'

'His daughter is popular with everybody.'

'A nice ladylike giri,' said the Duke, 'and appears to have
been well educated.'

The park at Custins was spacious, and wanderers
might walk for miles. Here, Lady Mary and Miss Boncassen
found themselves one afternoon, and the latter told her story
to her lover's sister.

'Your brother has asked me to be his wife.'

'Silverbridge!'

Lady Mary was very much astonished. 'I thought there
was someone else.'

'I think not,' said Miss Boncassen slowly.

'Then you have accepted him?'

'Would you have me for a sister?'

Lady Mary could not answer all at once.

'Shall I tell you what I said to him? I told him that he must
ask his friends; that I would not be his wife to be rejected
by them. Nor will I. Though I love your brother down to
the ground he shall not marry me without his father's consent.'

'I at any rate will love you,' said Lady Mary, kissing her.

'I wish you would call me Isabel,' her friend said to her.
'May I call you Mary?'

'Of course you may.'

'Mary is the prettiest name under the sun. But Plantagenet
is so grand! Which of the kings did you branch off from?'

'From none of them, I should think. There is some story

418

about a Sir Guy who was a king's friend. I never trouble myself about it. I hate aristocracy.'

'Do you, dear?'

'Yes,' said Mary, full of her own grievances. 'It is an abominable bondage, and I do not see that it does any good at all.'

'What do you mean, Mary?'

'Suppose that Silverbridge loves you better than all the world, but cannot marry you, because of his—aristocracy?'

'But he can. Under certain circumstances I would not marry him. I think myself good enough for the best man God ever made. But if others think differently, and those others are so closely concerned with him, and would be so closely concerned with me, as to trouble our joint lives, then will I neither subject him to such sorrow nor will I encounter it myself.'

'It all comes from what you call aristocracy.' And yet Mary could not bring herself to tell her tale in return. She could not show the reverse picture.

On the last day of the Duke's sojourn at Custins, and the last also of the Boncassens' visit, the Duke and Mr Boncassen, with Lady Mary and Isabel, were walking in the woods together. Each of the girls was walking with the other girl's father. Isabel had calculated what she would say to the Duke should a time for speaking come to her. She could not tell him of his son's love. She could not ask his permission. She could not explain to him all her feelings. But there was something that she could tell. 'We are so different from you,' she said, speaking of her own country.

'And yet so like,' said the Duke smiling; 'your language, your laws, your habits.'

'But still there is such a difference! I do not think there is a man in the whole union more respected than Father.'

'I dare say not.'

'Many people think that if he would only allow himself to be put in nomination he might be the next president. And yet his father was a poor labourer who earned his bread among the shipping at New York. That kind of thing would be impossible here.'

'My dear young lady, there you wrong us. A Prime Minister with us might as easily come from the same class.'

'Here you think so much of rank.'

'The sons of merchants have with us been Prime Ministers more than once, and no Englishmen ever were more honoured among their countrymen. Our peerage is being continually recruited from the ranks of the people, and hence it gets its strength.'

'Is it so?'

'There is no greater mistake than to suppose that inferiority of birth is a barrier to success in this country.'

He in all this was quite unconscious of the working of her mind. Nor in discussing such matters generally did he ever mingle his own private feelings, his own pride of race and name, his own ideas of what was due to his ancient rank with the political creed by which his conduct in public life was governed. He would as soon sit in counsel with Mr Monk, whose father had risen from a mechanic to be a merchant, as with any nobleman. But there was an inner feeling in his bosom as to his own family, his own name, his own children, and his own personal self, which was kept altogether apart from his grand political theories. It was this which made the idea of a marriage between his daughter and Tregear intolerable to him.

The Duke before he left Custins had an interview with Lady Cantrip, at which that lady found herself called upon to speak her mind freely. 'Mary is a very peculiar girl, with great gifts—but . . .'

'But what?'

'She is obstinate. Perhaps it would be fairer to say that she has great firmness of character. She will do nothing without your permission. But she will remain unmarried unless she be allowed to marry Mr Tregear.'

'What do you advise then?'

'That you should yield. As regards money, you could give them what they want. Let him go into public life. You could manage that for him.'

'He is Conservative!'

'What does that matter when the question is one of your daughter's happiness? Everybody tells me that he is clever and well conducted.'

He betrayed nothing by his face as this was said to him. As he got into the carriage with Mary he was a miserable man, but he endeavoured to make himself pleasant to his daughter. 'I suppose we shall stay at Matching now till Christmas,' he said.

'I hope so.'

'Whom would you like to have there? You will be very sad without somebody. Would you like the Finns?'

'I like her. He never talks anything but politics.'

'I wonder whether Lady Mabel Grex would come.'

'What made you think of her, Papa?'

'Perhaps Silverbridge would come to us then. And perhaps we might get the Boncassens to come to us.' Mary was silent, feeling the complication of the difficulties.

'It is for your sake I wish them to be there. I think that Lady Mabel and Miss Boncassen are just such girls as you would like.'

'I do like them; only . . .'

'Only what?'

'Miss Boncassen is an American.'

'Is that an objection? It seems to me that Miss Boncassen is a young lady with whom any other young lady might be glad to form an acquaintance.'

'She is so beautiful,' she said.

'Very beautiful. But what has that to do with it?'

'Perhaps—Silverbridge might admire her.'

'Why should he not admire her?'

'I don't know,' said Lady Mary sheepishly.

To Mary's great horror all the invitations were accepted, and all the guests came rattling in at Matching one after another. Lord Silverbridge was the last. He only entered the house as his father was taking Mrs Boncassen into the dining-room. He dressed himself in ten minutes, and joined the party as they had finished their fish. 'I am awfully sorry,' he said, taking the seat left vacant for him next to Lady Mabel Grex. 'We've had a political caucus of the party, and I was bound to attend.'

'We've all heard of that,' said Phineas Finn.

Miss Boncassen was sitting on the other side of the table,

421

between Mr Monk and Phineas Finn, and throughout the dinner talked mock politics with the greatest liveliness.

After dinner there was music. Lord Silverbridge had hardly spoken to Miss Boncassen, till after the music he offered her sherry or soda-water.

'Come and play a game of billiards,' he said to her. She got up very slowly from her seat, and looked round as though expecting others to follow her. None of them did follow her. Silverbridge led the way quickly across the hall, and Isabel Boncassen followed him very slowly. When she entered the room he at once shut the door, and spoke one word. 'Well?'

'What does "well" mean?'

'The three months are over. You told me to wait for three months. I have waited, and here I am.'

'How very—very—downright you are.'

'Is not that the proper thing?'

'I thought I was downright, but you beat me hollow. Yes, the three months are over. And now what háve you got to say?' He stretched out his arms as though he were going to take her and hold her to his heart. 'No, no; not that,' she said laughing. 'But if you will speak, I will hear you.'

'You know what I said before. Will you love me, Isabel?'

'Do they know that you love me? Does your father know it?'

'Nobody knows it. But say that you love me, and everyone shall know it at once.'

'I have told Lady Mary. And then she told me something.'

'What did she tell you?'

'Has there never been reason to think that you intended to offer your hand to another?'

'Did she tell you so?'

'You should answer my question, Lord Silverbridge. I have a right to ask.'

'Yes, there has. To Lady Mabel Grex.'

'Has she a right to expect that she should be your wife?'

'No, certainly not. Why should you ask all this? Do you love me? Come, Isabel; say that you love me.'

'Love you! Oh, my darling!' But she retreated from him round the corner of the billiard-table, and stood guarding

422

herself from him with her little hands. 'From the sole of your foot to the crown of your head I love you as I think a man would wish to be loved by the girl he loves. You have come across my life, and have swallowed me up, and made me all your own. But I will not marry you to be rejected by your people. No; nor shall there be a kiss between us till I know that it will not be so.'

'May I speak to your father?'

'For what good? I have not spoken to Father or Mother because it must depend upon your father. Lord Silverbridge, if he will tell me that I shall be his daughter I will become your wife. If it can never be so, then let us be torn apart at once.' Then she made her way round to the door. But as she went she made a little prayer to him. 'Do not delay my fate. It is all in all to me.' And so he was left alone in the billiard-room.

On the following day the Boncassens went, and then there were none of the guests left but Mrs Finn and Lady Mabel Grex. The Duke had especially asked Lady Mabel to remain, in the hope that something might be settled. He had never spoken quite distinctly to Mabel; but he had so spoken as to make Lady Mabel quite aware of his wish. More than once she was half-minded to speak openly to the Duke, to tell him all that Silverbridge had said to her and all that he had not said, and to ask the father's help. But she could not find the words with which to begin.

That evening Silverbridge went hurrying to his father's study, and finding the Duke still there explained that the Member for Polpenno, in Cornwall, had died, and Frank Tregear had been invited to stand for the borough. He had written to his friend to ask him to come and assist in the struggle. The Duke, who was by no means the man to make light of the political obligations of friendship, raised no objection.

'I wish,' said he, 'that something could have been arranged between you and Mabel before you went. I have set my heart very much upon it.'

'There is no time for that kind of thing now,' the young man said weakly.

'I thought that when you were here together . . .'

'I must dress now, sir; but I will tell you all about it when I get back from Cornwall.'

On the following morning the Duke proposed to Lady Mabel that she should stay longer at Matching. Lady Mabel, whose father was still abroad, was not sorry to accept the invitation. After nine days Lord Silverbridge was able to write to his father, telling him that Frank Tregear had been returned as Conservative Member.

'It will be a good thing for Mr Tregear, I suppose,' said Lady Mabel to the Duke.

'I do not know,' said the Duke coldly. He did not wish to be made to talk about Tregear.

CHAPTER FOUR

LORD SILVERBRIDGE returned to Matching knowing that he must meet Mabel Grex. At dinner Lady Mabel sat next to his father, and he could watch the special courtesy with which the Duke treated the girl whom he was so desirous of introducing to his house.

It had been arranged that she should leave Matching on Saturday, the first day of the new year. Time hung heavily over Christmas. It had become a matter of course that Silverbridge and Mabel should walk together in the afternoon. He himself had felt that there was danger in this, but Mary, who watched it all, was sure that misery was being prepared for someone.

On the Thursday after lunch they were again out together. Though the sun was shining, the snow under their feet was hard with frost. Though water in the shade was freezing at this moment, there was no feeling of damp, no sense of bitter wind. It was a sweet and jocund air, such as would make young people prone to run and skip.

She spoke to him of the coming Session, and had managed to display to him the interest she took in his parliamentary career. In doing this she flattered him to the top of his bent. 'What a happy fellow you ought to be.'

She was standing very close to him, leaning upon his arm, with her left hand crossed upon her right. There was something in it of declared affection—of that kind of love which most have been happy enough to give and receive, without intending to show more than true friendship will allow at special moments.

'May I tell you something?' she asked.

'Don't tell me anything I shan't like to hear.'

'Ah—that is so hard to know. I wish you would like to hear it.'

'What can it be?'

'You do not know? Oh, Silverbridge, I think you know.' Then there came upon him a glimmering of the truth. 'Silverbridge, what did you say to me when you came to me that morning in the Square?'

'What did I say?'

'Was I not entitled to think that you—loved me?'

'You only laughed at me.'

'No! I never laughed at you. How could I laugh when you were all the world to me? Can any girl suppose that such words as these are to mean nothing when they have been spoken? You knew I loved you.'

'No.'

'You must have known it. Why should your father be so sure of it?'

'He never was sure of it.'

'Yes, Silverbridge; yes. There is not one in the house who does not see that he treats me as though he expected me to be his son's wife. Do you not know that he wishes it?'

'I think he does,' said Silverbridge; 'but it can never be so.'

'Oh, Silverbridge—oh, my loved one! Do not say that to me!' The tears were now streaming down her face, and they were not counterfeit tears.

425

'I have given all I have to give to another.'

'That American girl!'

'Yes—that American girl.'

Then she recovered herself immediately. 'You know that cannot be. What will your father say? You have not dared to tell him.'

'Look here, Mabel, I would sooner lose everything that fortune has done for me than lose her.'

Now at any rate he was a man. His strength reduced her to weakness. 'And I am nothing,' she said.

'You are Lady Mabel Grex, whom all women envy and whom all men honour.'

'The poorest wretch this day under the sun.'

'Do not say that.'

'I do say it. Do you not feel what you owe me? You must have taken me for some nursemaid on whom you had condescended to cast your eye! It cannot be that even you should have dared to treat Lady Mabel Grex after such a fashion as that! And now you have cast your eye on this other girl.'

She had now lost all the caution which she had taught herself for the prosecution of her scheme. 'You could not show yourself after it in your clubs, or in Parliament, or in the world. I will go back, and will tell your father everything. If my father were other than he is, if my brother were better to me, you would not have done this.'

'If you had a legion of brothers it would have been the same,' he said, turning sharp upon her.

They walked without a word till the house was in sight. Then she looked round at him, and stopped him on the path as she caught his eye. 'Silverbridge,' she said. 'I beg your pardon. Give me your hand, and say we are friends.'

'Certainly we are friends,' he said, as he gave her his hand.

'And never forget that I love you. No one can tell what may come to pass.'

Lady Mabel at once went up to her room. She had played her scene, but was well aware that she had played it altogether unsuccessfully.

'How is it now between you and her?' That was the question the Duke put to his son as soon as Lady Mabel had departed on her journey, and there could be no doubt as to the 'her' intended.

'I'm afraid that it is all over, sir,' he said.

'All over! Has she refused you?'

'Well, sir—it isn't quite that. Mabel did not seem to care for me much—in London. And then I saw someone—someone I liked better.' Then he stopped, but as the Duke did not ask any questions he plunged on. 'It was Miss Boncassen.'

'Miss Boncassen!'

'Yes, sir,' said Silverbridge, with a little access of decision.

'Do you know anything of her family?'

'I think I know all about her family. It is not much in the way of—family.'

'You have not spoken to her about it?'

'Yes, sir; I have settled it all with her, on condition . . .'

'Settled it with her that she is to be your wife!'

'Yes, sir—on condition that you will approve.'

'Did you go to her, Silverbridge, with such a stipulation as that?'

'She stipulated. She will marry me if you will consent.'

'I cannot give you my consent.'

'Then I am very unhappy.'

'How can I believe as to your unhappiness when you would have said the same about Lady Mabel Grex a few weeks ago?'

'Nearly eight months,' said Silverbridge.

'What is the difference? I cannot give you my consent. The young lady sees it in the right light, and that will make your escape easy.'

'I will not be separated from her,' said Silverbridge.

'I can only hope that you will think better of it, and that when next you speak to me on that or any other subject you will answer me with less arrogance.'

This rebuke was terrible to the son, whose mind was filled with two ideas, that of constancy to Isabel Boncassen, and of respect and affection for his father. 'Indeed, sir,' he said, 'if I have answered improperly I beg your pardon. But my

427

mind is made up about this, and I thought you had better know how it is.'

'I do not see that I can say anything else to you now.'

The Duke spent the rest of the day alone, and was not happy in his solitude. He had already been driven to acknowledge that these children of his—thoughtless, restless, though they seemed to be—still had a will of their own. In all which how like they were to their mother! With her, however, his word, though it might be resisted, had never lost its authority. When he had declared that a thing should not be done, she had never persisted in saying that she would do it. But with his children it was otherwise. What power had he over Silverbridge—or for the matter of that, even over his daughter? They had only to be firm and he knew that he must be conquered.

.   .   .   .   .

'Well, Silverbridge,' said the Duke, suddenly, one day shortly after their return to London; 'how are matters going with you?' There seemed to be something in his father's manner more than ordinarily jocund and good-humoured.

'With me, sir?'

'Yes, you. Mr Boncassen told me . . .'

'Have you seen Mr Boncassen?'

'I happened to meet him and he walked home with me. He was so intent upon what he was saying that I fear he allowed me to take him out of his way.'

'What was he talking about?' said Silverbridge.

'He was talking about you,' said the Duke. 'I suppose you can guess what he said. He wished to know what I thought of the offer you have made to his daughter.' The great subject had come up again so easily, so readily, that the young man was almost aghast when he found himself in the middle of it.

'I hope you raised no objection, sir,' he said.

'The objection came mainly from him; and I am bound to say that every word that fell from him was spoken with wisdom.'

428

'I am sure he did not say that we ought not to be married.'

'He did say that he thought you ought not to be married, if . . .'

'If what, sir?'

'If there were probability that his daughter would not be well received as your wife. Then he asked me what would be my reception of her.'

Silverbridge looked up into his father's face with beseeching imploring eyes, as though everything now depended on the next few words that he might utter. 'I shall think it an un-wise marriage,' continued the Duke.

Silverbridge when he heard this at once knew that he had gained his cause. His father had spoken of the marriage as a thing that was to happen. A joyous light dawned in his eyes, and the look of pain went from his brow, all which the Duke was not slow to perceive. 'I shall think it an unwise marriage,' he repeated; 'but I was bound to tell him that were Miss Boncassen to become your wife she would also become my daughter.'

'I am sure that everybody would like her,' said Silverbridge eagerly.

'I like her. I like her very much.'

'I am so glad.'

'She has a brightness and a grace all her own,' continued the Duke, 'which will ensure her acceptance in all societies.'

'Yes, yes; it is just that, sir.'

'You will be a nine days' wonder—the foolish young noble-man who chose to marry an American. But her place will I think be secure to her. That is what I told Mr Boncassen.'

'It is all right with him then?'

'If you call it all right. You will understand of course that you are acting in opposition to my advice—and my wishes. However, perhaps we had better let that pass,' said the Duke, with a long sigh. Then Silverbridge took his father's hand, and looked up in his face. 'I most sincerely hope that she may make you a good and loving wife,' said the Duke, 'and that she may do her duty by you in that not easy sphere of life to which she will be called.'

'I am quite sure she will,' said Silverbridge, whose ideas

as to Isabel's duties were confined at present to a feeling that she would now have to give him kisses without stint.

'A wife ought to feel the great responsibility of her position. I hope she will.'

'And the sooner she begins the better,' said Silverbridge stoutly.

'And now,' said the Duke, looking at his watch, 'we might as well have lunch and go down to the House. I will walk with you if you please.' Then the son was forced to go down and witness the somewhat faded ceremony of seeing Parliament opened, whereas he would have preferred to disregard his parliamentary duties and rushed at once up to Brook Street, where the Boncassens had taken a furnished house. He was at Brook Street at half-past seven, though.

'Lord Silverbridge, who ever dreamed of seeing you?' Mrs Boncassen greeted him. 'I thought all you Parliament gentlemen were going through your ceremonies.'

'Where is Isabel?'

'She's gone.'

'Gone! Where on earth has she gone to?' asked Silverbridge, as though fearing lest she had been carried off to the other side of the Atlantic. Then Mrs Boncassen explained. Within the last three minutes Mrs Montacute Jones had called and carried Isabel off to the play. 'I hope you did not want her very particularly,' said Mrs Boncassen.

'But I did—most particularly,' said Lord Silverbridge. The door was opened and Mr Boncassen entered the room. 'I beg your pardon for coming at such a time,' said the lover, 'but I did so want to see Isabel.'

'I rather think she wants to see you,' said the father.

'I shall go to the theatre after her.'

'That might be awkward—particularly as I doubt whether anybody knows what theatre they are gone to. Can I receive a message for her, my lord?' This was certainly not what Lord Silverbridge had intended. 'You know, perhaps, that I have seen the Duke.'

'Oh yes; and I have seen him. Everything is settled.'

'That is the only message she will want to hear when she comes home. She is a happy girl and I am proud to think that I should live to call such a grand young Briton as you my son-in-law.' Then the American took the young man's two hands and shook them cordially, while Mrs Boncassen bursting into tears insisted on kissing him.

'Indeed she is a happy girl,' said she; 'but I hope Isabel won't be carried away too high and mighty.'

Three days after this it was arranged that Isabel should be taken to Carlton Terrace to be accepted there into the full good graces of her future father-in-law, and to go through the pleasant ceremony of seeing the house in which it was to be her destiny to live as mistress. The visit was made not quite in the fashion in which Silverbridge himself had wished. 'Mother must go with me,' she had said. 'Don't be selfish,' she added, laughing, when he looked disappointed. 'Do you think that Mother will not want to have seen the house that I am to live in? Love me, love my mother.'

When they arrived Silverbridge led them first of all into the dining-room. 'My!' said Mrs Boncassen, 'I thought our Fifth Avenue parlours whipped everything in the way of city houses.'

'What a nice little room for Darby and Joan to sit down to eat a mutton-chop in,' said Isabel.

'It's a beastly great barrack,' said Silverbridge, 'but the best of it is that we never use it. We'll have a cosy little place for Darby and Joan, you'll see. Now come to the governor. I've got to leave you alone with him.'

'Oh me! I am in such a fright.'

'My belief is that he's almost as much in love with you as I am,' said Silverbridge, as he took her to the door of the Duke's room. 'Here we are, sir.'

'My dear,' said the Duke, rising up and coming to her, 'I am very glad to see you. It is good of you to come to me.' Then he took her in both his hands and kissed her forehead and her lips.

She, as she put her face up to him, stood quite still in his embrace, but her eyes were bright with pleasure.

'Shall I leave her?' said Silverbridge.

'A few minutes, and then I will bring her up to the drawing-room.' Upon this the door was closed, and Isabel was

431

alone with her new father. 'And so, my dear, you are to be my child.'

'If you will have me.'

'Come here and sit down by me. If you will love me you shall be very dear to me. You shall be my own child—as dear as my own.'

'I will love you,' she said, pressing his hand.

Then the Duke unlocked a little drawer that was close to his hand, and taking out a ring put it on her finger. It was a bar of diamonds, perhaps a dozen of them, fixed in a little circlet of gold. 'This must never leave you,' he said.

'It never shall, having come from you.'

'It was the first present that I gave to my wife, and it is the first that I give to you. You may imagine how sacred it is to me. On no other hand could it be worn without something which to me would be akin to sacrilege. Now I must not keep you longer or Silverbridge will be storming about the house. He of course will tell me when it is to be; but do not keep him long waiting.' Then he kissed her and led her up into the drawing-room.

Silverbridge dined at Brook Street that evening, but returned to Carlton Terrace quite early. As he opened the door with his latch-key, who should be coming out but Frank Tregear—with an unmistakable look of general satisfaction.

'And what are you doing here?' asked Silverbridge.

'Well; if you'll allow me I'll go back with you for a moment. What do you think I have been doing?'

'Have you seen my sister?'

'Yes, I have seen your sister. And I have done better than that. I have seen your father. Lord Silverbridge—behold your brother-in-law.'

'You don't mean to say that it is arranged?'

'I do.'

'What did he say?'

'He made me understand by most unanswerable arguments, that I had no business to think of such a thing. I did not fight the point with him, but simply stood there, as conclusive evidence of my business. He told me that we should have nothing to live on unless he gave us an income. I assured him that

I would never ask him for a shilling. "But I cannot allow her to marry a man without an income," he said.'

'I know his way so well.'

'I had just two facts to go upon—that I would not give her up, and that she would not give me up. When I pointed that out he tore his hair, in a mild way, and said that he did not understand that kind of thing at all.'

'How did he give way at last?'

'He asked me what were my ideas about life in general. I said that I thought Parliament was a good sort of thing, that I was lucky enough to have a seat, and that I should take lodgings somewhere in Westminster till . . . "Till what?" he asked. "Till something is settled," I replied. Then he turned away from me and remained silent. "May I see Lady Mary?" I asked. "Yes; you may see her," he replied, as he rang the bell. Then when the servant was gone he stopped me. "I love her too dearly to see her grieve," he said. "I hope you will show that you can be worthy of her." Then I made some sort of protestation and went upstairs. While I was with Mary there came a message to me, telling me to come to dinner tomorrow.'

'The Boncassens are all dining here.'

'Then we shall be a family party. So far I suppose I may say it is settled. When he will let us marry heaven only knows. It is all a matter of money.'

'Did he say what he meant to give her?'

'Oh dear no; nor even that he meant to give her anything. I should not dream of asking a question about it. My chief object is that he should not think that I have been looking for her money. Well; good-bye. I suppose we shall all meet at dinner?'

Silverbridge went to his father's room. He was anxious that they should understand each other as to Mary's engagement.

'I met Tregear at the door. He tells me you have accepted him for Mary.'

'I wish that he had never seen her. Do you think that a man can be thwarted in everything and not feel it?'

'I thought you had reconciled yourself—to Isabel.'

'If it were that alone I could do so the more easily, because personally she wins upon me. And this man, too; it is not that I find fault with himself.'

'He is in all respects a high-minded gentleman.'

'A gentleman should not look to live on means brought to him by a wife. A man should own his means or should earn them.'

'How many men, sir, do neither?'

'Yes; I know,' said the Duke. 'Nowadays, one must live as others live around one, I suppose. I could not see her suffer. It was too much for me. Gerald I suppose will bring me some kitchen-maid for his wife.'

'Oh, sir, you should not say that to me.'

'No, I should not have said it to you. I beg your pardon, Silverbridge. Perhaps, after all, it is well that a pride of which I am conscious should be rebuked. And it may be that the rebuke has come in such a form that I should be thankful. I know that I can love Isabel.'

'That to me will be everything'

'And this young man has nothing that should revolt me. He will dine with us tomorrow.'

Silverbridge then went up to see his sister. 'So you have settled your little business, Mary?'

'Oh, Silverbridge, you will wish me joy?'

'Certainly. Why not?'

'Papa is so stern with me. Of course he has given way, and of course I am grateful. But he looks at me as though I had done something to be forgiven.'

'Take the good the gods provide you, Mary. That will all come right.'

'Papa just told me that he would consent, and that I might write to him. So I did write, and he came. But Papa looks at me as though I had broken his heart.'

'I tell you what it is, Mary. You expect too much from him. He has not had his own way with either of us, and of course he feels it.'

.   .   .   .   .

Not very long after these events the Prime Minister made a statement in the House. The Chancellor of the Exchequer had very suddenly resigned and had thereby broken up the Ministry, so that he had found himself compelled to place his resignation in the hands of her Majesty. This happened on a Friday. During the Saturday it was considered probable that the Cabinet would come to terms with itself, and that internal wounds would be healed. But on the Tuesday the House met and Mr Monk announced, still from the Opposition benches, that he had that morning been with the Queen; and all the Liberals knew that the gates of Paradise were again about to be opened to them.

The Duke had consented to assist Mr Monk in forming a government, and to take office under Mr Monk's leadership. He had had many contests with himself before he could bring himself to this submission. He knew that if anything could once again make him contented it would be work; he knew that if he could serve his country it was his duty to serve it; and he knew also that it was only by the adhesion of such men as himself that the traditions of his party could be maintained. He had declared to himself that he would never more take office. He had much to do to overcome this promise to himself; but when he had brought himself to submit he was certainly a happier man. On the Wednesday morning his name appeared in the list of the new Cabinet as President of the Council.

There was only just time for the new elections before the Easter holidays. For the respective lovers this was convenient. The day for the marriage of Isabel and Silverbridge had been now fixed. That was to take place on the Wednesday after Easter, and was to be celebrated by special royal favour in the Crypt at Whitehall. All the Pallisers would be there, and all the relations of all the Pallisers, all the ambassadors, and of course all the Americans in London. It would be a 'wretched grind', as Silverbridge said, but it had to be done.

The wedding was declared by the newspapers to have been one of the most brilliant remembered in the metropolis. There were six bridesmaids, of whom of course Mary was one, and of whom poor Lady Mabel Grex was equally of course not

435

another. Lady Mabel was at this time with Miss Cassewary at Grex, paying what she believed would be a last visit to the old family home, her father having died. The breakfast was of course given by Mr Boncassen at his house in Brook Street. Poor Mrs Boncassen had not perhaps a happy time with her august guests on that morning; but when she retired to give Isabel her last kiss in privacy she did feel proud to think that her daughter would some day be an English Duchess.

It was not till November that Lady Mary Palliser became the wife of Frank Tregear. It was postponed a little in order that the Silverbridges, as they were now called, might be present. The Silverbridges had gone to the States when the Session had been brought to a close early in August, and had remained there nearly three months. Isabel had taken infinite pleasure in showing her English husband to her American friends, and the American friends had taken a pride in seeing so glorious a British husband in the hands of an American wife. Everything was new to Silverbridge, and he was happy in his new possession.

The marriage of Silverbridge had been august. But both the Duke and Mary were determined that this wedding should be different. It was to take place at Matching, and none would be present but they who were staying in the house, or who lived around. Four clergymen united their forces to tie Isabel to her husband, one of whom was a bishop, one a canon, and the two others royal chaplains; but there was only to be the vicar of the parish at Matching. And indeed there were no guests in the house except the two bridesmaids and Mr and Mrs Finn. As to Mrs Finn, Mary had made a request, and then the Duke had suggested that the husband should be asked to accompany his wife.

It was very pretty. The church itself is pretty, standing in the park, close to the old Priory, not above three hundred yards from the house. And they all walked, taking the broad path through the ruins. The Duke led the way with his girl upon his arm. The two bridesmaids followed. Then Silverbridge and his wife, with Phineas and his wife. Gerald and the bridegroom accompanied them. It was very rustic—almost improper! 'This is altogether wrong, you know,' said

436

Gerald to Frank. 'You should appear coming from some other part of the world, as if you were almost unexpected. You ought not to have been in the house at all, and certainly should have gone under disguise.'

But perhaps the matter most remarkable in the wedding was the hilarity of the Duke. One who did not know him well might have said that he was a man with very few cares, and who now took special joy in the happiness of his children —who was thoroughly contented to see them marry after their own hearts. And yet, as he stood there on the altar-steps giving his daughter to that new son and looking first at his girl, and then at his married son, he was reminding himself of all he had suffered.